T0312481

Praise for T. Orr Munro

'An impressive start in an exciting new series.'
The Sun

'A page turner that will appeal to fans of *Broadchurch*.'
Adele Parks, *Platinum*

'Packed with authenticity.'
Mail Online

'Fresh, vivid and totally engrossing: this is gold-standard crime
writing bearing the unmistakable hallmark
of authenticity.'
Erin Kinsley, *Sunday Times* bestselling author of *Found*

'This could turn into a gem of a series.'
Sunday Post

'I genuinely found it hard to put down. The writing is beautifully
paced and the double viewpoint creates great tension.'
**Alex Gray, *Sunday Times* bestselling author of the
DCI Lorimer Series**

'Brimming with suspense and filled with memorable and
brilliantly rendered characters – I can't get enough of
the Ally Dymond books!'
**Heather Darwent, *Sunday Times* bestselling author of
*The Things We Do To Our Friends***

'It's difficult to accept that *Breakneck Point* is a debut novel as
T. Orr Munro's writing is exciting, genuine and convincing.'
My Weekly

'CSI Ally Dymond is a gem, engaging, relatable, smart – everything
you want in a main character.'
Trevor Wood, author of *The Man on the Street*

'Compelling crime fiction with a beating heart of authenticity
and characters you really feel for.'
Hayley Scrivenor, author of *Dirt Town*

T. Orr Munro was born in Aldershot in Hampshire to an English mother and a Greek-Armenian father who moved to deepest Devon after recognising it would be a great place to raise their children. She has a degree in Economic and Social History from Liverpool University and a PGCE in History and English. After university she trained as a CSI, then later became a secondary school teacher. She changed career at thirty-three to become a police and crime journalist and is currently freelance. She has since returned with her family to live in North Devon, the setting for the Ally Dymond series, but heads to Greece as often as she can. Her time as a CSI provides much of the inspiration for her novels, shining a light on what happens behind the crime scene tape.

Also by T. Orr Munro

The CSI Ally Dymond series

Breakneck Point
Slaughterhouse Farm

LIARS ISLAND

T. ORR MUNRO

ONE PLACE. MANY STORIES

HQ
An imprint of HarperCollins*Publishers* Ltd
1 London Bridge Street
London SE1 9GF

www.harpercollins.co.uk

HarperCollins*Publishers*
Macken House, 39/40 Mayor Street Upper,
Dublin 1, D01 C9W8, Ireland

This edition 2024

1

First published in Great Britain by
HQ, an imprint of HarperCollins*Publishers* Ltd 2024

Copyright © T. Orr Munro 2024

Tina Orr Munro asserts the moral right to be
identified as the author of this work.
A catalogue record for this book is
available from the British Library.

ISBN: HB: 9780008644703

MIX
Paper | Supporting
responsible forestry
FSC™ C007454

This book contains FSC™ certified paper and other controlled sources to ensure responsible forest management.

For more information visit: www.harpercollins.co.uk/green

Printed and bound in the UK using 100% Renewable Electricity at CPI Group (UK) Ltd

For Richard. Thank you.

CRIME SCENE EXAMINATION REPORT RELATING TO THE MURDER OF KIERAN DEVENEY

<u>CSI</u>: Jim Dixon
<u>OIC</u>: DI Harriet Moore
<u>DIVISION</u>: North Devon, Devon County Police
<u>LOCATION</u>: Drogan Island (aka Liars Island), situated in the Bristol Channel, about 12 miles from the North Devon coast
<u>EXAMINATION COMMENCED</u>: 2.00pm, 25 May 2023

EXAMINATION NOTES

Suspicious death. Body – fully clothed – located just below the high tide mark in bay known as Devil's Cauldron, on the southern tip of Liars Island. Injuries to the head.

Scene filmed and photographed. Items recovered from beach for forensic examination.

EVIDENCE COLLECTED

Scene and forensic items photographed REF LR1–LR15
Items recovered include:

- A child's doll REF LR16
- A drinks can REF LR17
- Casio watch REF LR18
- Used syringes REF LR19
- Printer cartridge REF LR20
- Fishing net REF LR21

1

'She was a mother too, you know.' Dr Cassius from the South West Marine Stranding Scheme stares down at the huge carcass at her feet, a slick of bright red sinew pressing through the slashes, criss-crossing her back. 'And somewhere out there is her pup.'

'An orca, right?'

She looks at me with unexpected gratitude. 'Thank you for not calling Maisie a killer whale. That's a very unfair moniker for such a beautiful animal.'

'My dad would never have forgiven me for getting it wrong, but I've never seen an orca in North Devon before.'

'You're right. She's a long way from home. A couple have been sighted off the Cornish coast, but Maisie belongs to a pod in the Hebrides.'

'And I think I'm right in saying orcas aren't whales either, but a species of dolphin.'

'The largest. Impressive, Miss . . .'

'Dymond. And it's Ally. You called her Maisie so I take it you knew her.'

'We've been tracking her for decades, part of an ongoing

programme to try and understand more about these wonderful animals, and others.'

'Decades?'

'Orcas can live for up to fifty years, but not our Maisie here.' She shakes her head in genuine sorrow and I wonder if there's anyone in the human world that could provoke this level of grief in her.

'Did she beach herself? Dad used to tell me how sick or injured dolphins and whales would get themselves stranded on land.'

'He knows his stuff, your father, but no, Maisie didn't die on land. As you can tell, she's in the advanced stages of decomposition.' Dr Cassius looks out at the calm waters barely able to muster the effort to break on the shore. 'She died out there.'

'So she was harpooned?'

'God, no, nothing like that. Believe it or not, Maisie drowned.'

'Drowned?'

'Your father must have skipped that lesson.' She smiles. 'Maisie is a mammal. She has to surface to breathe although they can stay under for up to fifteen minutes. My guess is she got caught in fishing nets and couldn't escape. It happens a lot. Not on purpose, of course.'

'It's still a criminal offence which carries six months in prison. Not enough in my book.' PC Bryan Rogers appears at my side, nose wedged in the crook of his arm to ward off the stench. It's not the first time he's bemoaned light penalties for wildlife crime. As if on cue, he follows up with, 'You know what I always say, Ally, if they're hurting animals, they're hurting humans.'

'Not just her, but her baby too,' says Dr Cassius. 'Orcas make wonderful mothers. They nurse their pups until they're two. Never leave their side. Now the poor little thing has to fend for himself.'

'Will he survive?'

'No, not unless another matriarch steps in. Whether you're an orca or a human being, all children need a mother figure in their lives, don't you think? Let's hope Maisie has a bestie out there willing to raise her son.'

'Let's hope so.' I smile.

'Right, now Ally's here, I'll leave you to it. I'm going to get a coffee from the Coffee Shack before I chuck my guts up. Want one, Dymond?'

I glance at the Airstream café at the top of the slipway, catching sight of its owner, Liam, my friend. Or he was. I'm not sure what he is now.

'Please. Black, no sugar.'

'I'll get them then. Actually, I wasn't expecting you. Aren't you meant to be back on Major Investigations? I thought we'd be getting that lanky fella with red hair.'

'Jake? He's on a burglary in Wellacombe and I'm just waiting for the paperwork to go through. Till then, you're stuck with me, I'm afraid.'

'Their loss is our gain, but if you're sticking around Bidecombe for a bit longer then I've got some bad news for you.'

'Oh?'

'Cal Meeth is back in town.'

'Cal Meeth? The guy that sent Bidecombe's crime stats through the roof?' Church roofs to be precise, which he systematically relieved of their lead.

5

'The very same. He did a stretch and then went up country for a while, and now he's back. God knows why. Bidecombe's not exactly rich pickings, is it?' Maybe I should defend my hometown, but Bryan has a point. A rundown coastal town lying further along the North Devon coast, Bidecombe peaked when Queen Victoria was on the throne and the well-to-do would seek out its restorative air and waters. The harbour area still manages to put on its best for the summer visitors but, off-season, the town struggles to know what to do with itself.

'Maybe he's gone straight.'

'He was working on the quay when I saw him, but he said he'd just been taken on at The Albion so let's hope that's the case for all our sakes. He was a tricky little sod to catch. Always gloved up. Got rid of his shoes after every job. Got rid of the goods as soon as he nicked them. No one prepared to grass him up.'

'I remember. Cocky, too. He told the detectives interviewing him that they'd just got lucky. They'd never catch him again.'

'The way policing is today, he's probably right.'

'Thanks for the heads-up, Bryan, and the secret is to mouth-breathe.'

'What?'

'That's what I do when the smell is really bad. I breathe through my mouth.'

'Yeah, I think I prefer my method of getting as far away as possible before I gag. Your coffee'll be waiting for you at the Coffee Shack.'

I watch him leave and turn back to Dr Cassius.

'I'll finish photographing her and then she's all yours. Will you tow her out to sea?'

'No, she'll be taken to the landfill site where I'll do a full PM.'

'Landfill?'

'Yes, a sad end to a magnificent animal.'

But before I have time to commiserate, my phone rings. It's DI Harriet Moore, head of Major Investigations.

'Excuse me, I should take this.'

I walk clear of Maisie's corpse to answer the call.

'Hello, Harriet. Good to hear from you. I assume this is about my transfer?'

'No, I'm on Drogan Island.'

Instinctively, I look out at across the Channel at the small dark plateau of land moored on the horizon.

'You mean . . . Liars Island?'

Saying its name after all these years unsettles me in a way I hadn't expected. I removed it from my vocabulary a long time ago: an act of self-preservation.

'Of course.' A loud tut reaches me. 'I forgot this is Devon where everywhere has a bloody nickname. Why can't you just use the actual one on the map?' DI Moore is newly transferred from London. She's still got a lot to learn. 'Anyway, we got a lad washed up on the beach this morning so—'

'Sorry,' I cut her off, preempting what's coming next. I'm not going back there, for Harriet or for anyone. Liars Island needs to remain where I left it: in my past. 'I'm on a job. I don't know when I'll be done.'

'That's not why I'm calling. There's a team out there already. We've flown the body back to the mainland. The lad's at the mortuary at Barnston Hospital. I need you to get over there and photograph the PM for me.'

'A postmortem?' I check my watch. 'But it's only 2pm. I thought he was found this morning.'

'He was. We had to move him. The tide was coming in. Alex has done his bit and is ready for you whenever you can get down to the mortuary. DS Henry Whiteley will meet you there and take you through it.'

'Okay, I just have to finish up here and then I'm on my way. So what are we looking at? A drowning?' I stare down at the great black-and-white hulk that was once an orca called Maisie, and wonder what the chances are of attending two drownings in one day. A first. Even for me.

'We would be,' sighs Harriet, 'if there wasn't a bloody great big hole in his head.'

2

Top notes of formaldehyde, bottom notes of methane and ammonia; I know I'm in the mortuary at Barnston Hospital long before I'm shown into the postmortem room. It's a constant battle between preservation and decay. But decay always wins. I'd like to think I've grown used to the smell of death over the years, but that would be a lie. As I said to PC Rogers, I've just got good at mouth breathing.

Gary, the assistant mortician, greets me in the corridor, after buzzing me into the building. He's changed since I last saw him. His ponytail has been lopped off and his face is shaved smooth.

'Ally, it's been a while.' He stops short when he catches a whiff of me. 'Woah, no offence, but you reek.'

'Dead orca at Morte Sands.'

'That'll do it!' He grins. 'I once read decomposing blubber can be smelt from five miles away, but since we don't do animal postmortems, I take it you're here for the lad they found out on Liars Island.'

'That's right. How are you, Gary? How's the band?'

'Good, although I'm cutting down on the gigging since I found out I'm gonna be a dad.'

'A dad?'

'Yep. Trisha is four months gone.'

'Congratulations. Give her my best. You'll be great parents.'

'Thanks. She'll appreciate that. You know she's still upset about what happened last year to your daughter. She still can't believe she didn't spot the signs.'

I don't blame Trisha. Her colleague, Simon Pascoe, the seemingly mild-mannered paramedic, who killed at least two women and tried to kill my daughter Megan, had everyone fooled.

'Tell her not to worry. Megan is doing just great, living it up in North Wales with her dad as we speak.'

'Thanks, Ally. Alex is all ready for you. The tox report will be with you in the next week or two,' he says, handing me a gown, mask and paper slip-on shoes.

'Ally Dymond, as I live and breathe, and as you know, there aren't many of us down here who have that ability,' says Alex, the pathologist, when I walk into the examination room. 'I take it you and DC Whiteley here know each other.'

'DS,' the officer corrects him.

'Sorry, DS Whiteley.'

'Yes, we do.'

'Anyway, good to see you back on MI.'

'It's not official yet. I'm just waiting for it to be signed off,' I reply, setting my case down on the stainless steel bench running the length of the room. 'But how are you? How's Margery?'

'Still sending me out to work, as you can see.' But his eye roll is full of good humour.

'You love it, really. And the boys?'

'The bank of dad is still open for business, apparently. How's your girl?'

'She's well, Alex. It was touch and go for a while, but once she was out of the coma, she was on her way. She's bonding with her dad in North Wales at the moment. Thank you for the flowers, by the way.'

'Our pleasure. Margery and I were devastated to hear what happened to her. Then the cowardly bastard escapes justice by throwing himself off a cliff. I only hope you can get some kind of closure.'

'Yes, thank you, I think we have.' I smile. I have a feeling that if I told Alex the truth, I'd find a sympathetic ear, but now is not the time to admit to a Home Office pathologist that I killed Simon Pascoe.

DS Whiteley clears his throat, reminding Alex why we're all here.

'Right, yes, where was I?' says Alex, taking the hint. 'DS Whiteley was just filling me in on what they know so far which, I think it is safe to say, isn't a great deal.'

'That's right,' says Henry. 'His name is Kieran Deveney. His father, Hilton Deveney, formally identified his body a few hours ago.'

'*The* Hilton Deveney?' Hilton Deveney is a local hotshot property developer.

'The same.'

'This one will be all over the papers, and social media.'

'Well, considering his son had just died, he didn't seem that upset at the ID. Just angry, as if it was his lad's fault.' Henry pushes the memory to one side. 'Anyway, Kieran ran the Bara Watersports Centre on the southern tip of the island with his friend and business partner Ben Dawson.'

'Liars Island has a watersports centre? I thought the whole place was a conservation area.'

'It is, but Hilton is head of the board of trustees for the island so I guess he pulled some strings to get it built. Anyway, Kieran's body was found in a small bay, a little way from the centre, pretty place, but weird name. The Devil's Cauldron. Anyway, the DI just wants you to photograph his injuries and anything else Alex thinks is worth recording.' Henry turns his attention back to Alex. 'And, if we can ascertain an approximate time of death as well as cause, of course, that would be very helpful. In particular, we need to know if the injury to his skull could be accidental?'

'Accidental?' says Alex, raising an eyebrow.

'Yes, could Kieran have just slipped off a rock, banged his head and fallen into the water and drowned, that kind of thing?'

'Well, let's see, shall we?'

Alex treats me to a knowing smile. He already has the answer, of course, but he likes to hold off on the big reveal. Maybe it's the long hours spent alone in the company of corpses, but Alex is a pathologist who enjoys an audience, gently leading them through his findings towards the final dramatic climax.

Pulling back the sheet to reveal Kieran's naked torso, he stands back to allow me to take a couple of overall shots. My lens focuses on Kieran's face. His youth shocks me. It always does. Death has no place among the young. An unblemished, unlined complexion points to a life barely begun. His vital force has deserted him leaving behind an empty casing.

'First things first. As you can see' – Alex waves a hand over the Y-shaped track across Kieran's chest – 'we've already done the PM and I can tell you that Kieran didn't drown. In fact, even though he was found on the beach, at no time was he submerged in the water which leaves us with this rather nasty head wound.'

'And?' says Henry, leaning against a side counter, arms crossed.

'Well, you're not going to see anything from there, son. Come closer.' Tensing up at being called son, Henry hesitates before edging nearer. He wouldn't be the first cop to be squeamish around dead bodies.

'That's better,' Alex says. 'Now, this injury here' – his finger circles the wound in Kieran's head – 'is a blunt force injury which is consistent with a fall from height or a heavy blow to the top of the skull with a rock. Now, if Kieran had fallen, I'd have expected other evidence such as cuts, grazes, bruises, that sort of thing, but there's nothing. That doesn't mean it didn't happen. It just means there weren't any.'

'It's unlikely to be a fall. His body was too far from the rocks unless he died elsewhere and was washed up on the shore, but you already said he didn't spend any time in the water.'

'That's correct.'

'So it's more likely to have been caused by someone hitting him over the head?' Henry reenacts someone bringing a rock down hard.

'Yes, that's also very possible. You might want to go in closer too, Ally.'

I focus my camera lens on the top of Kieran's head and the mash of brain tissue visible where the bone has cracked and splintered under the force of the blow. I fire off several shots, shifting the angle each time.

'How do you know the weapon was a rock?' asks Henry.

'We picked some of it out of his skull. If you're interested, it's granite.'

'Granite? That's very specific.'

'Yes. Margery decided I needed a hobby some years back, said I was spending too much time with the dead, so she enrolled me in an evening class on geology. We go all over the country. It's great fun. You can take a look through the microscope, if you like.'

Henry stays put, not wanting to delay the proceedings, but curiosity gets the better of me. Through the eyepiece, I adjust the dial and am rewarded with the sight of a slither of black-and-white stone.

'Granite is igneous rock formed when magma cools slowly. You can just make out the tiny little crystals,' says Alex. 'What you're looking at, Ally, has taken millions of years to form, and started life deep within the Earth's crust.'

'So just to be clear,' says Henry, steering Alex back to the postmortem. 'Kieran was killed at the hand of another.'

'Yes. I would say so.'

'And what about the time of death?'

'What have your enquiries narrowed it down to so far?'

'Narrow isn't the word I'd use. Kieran was last seen around 11pm the day before yesterday when he left the pub. His body was found by his business partner at 11.30 this morning. All we know is that his death happened some time during that twelve-hour period.'

'Oh, I think we can do better than that. As you know it's not an exact science especially when there's so many variables at play, but my calculations would put his death somewhere between midnight and 5.13am, just before it got light.'

'5.13am?' Henry frowns.

'Yes, I mean it's possible that we could extend the window to later, say 7.30am, but I'm fairly certain he died before dawn which would have been at 5.13am.'

'Wow. How can you be so specific? That's incredible.'

'Not really.' Alex grins at me. He's been leading up to this moment since Henry arrived. 'Kieran had a broken torch in his pocket. It was still switched on. It was dark when Kieran died.'

3

Closing my eyes, I tilt my head upwards in thanks to the onshore wind embracing me like an old friend. My arms raised in the form of a cross, the stiff breeze cools my skin and sieves my clothes of the cloying effluvium of chemicals and decay accumulated in the course of my day.

Satisfied I no longer reek of tangy chemicals and rotting flesh, I step back from the cliff edge and sit down on the bench nestled at the lowest point of the narrow sheep path that leads down from the clifftop. This is Breakneck Point, a grassy headland jutting out of North Devon's towering coastline into the Bristol Channel. This is where I come to cleanse myself of the dead: animal and human.

Scanning the horizon, my eye is drawn to a hazy outline anchored midway between the coasts of North Devon and Wales – Liars Island, so called because only the foolish believe its beauty is benign. This is a land where impenetrable mists lure the lost into fathomless ravines, where riptides clamp themselves around unsuspecting swimmers, where gusting winds sweep the hapless over cliff edges. Death is its core business. I, of all people, know that. And now death has come once more to its shores. What of the island's inhabitants?

How must they be feeling about Kieran's death? I remember the islanders from long ago. Knitted together by adversity, they were hardy people who relied on one another to stay safe on an island constantly trying to evict them, but Kieran didn't drown or fall to his death. That poor young man lying in the mortuary was murdered. So what happens when the killer isn't a stormy sea or dense fog? What happens when the killer is one of your own?

'Sorry, Ally, I didn't see you there.'

Startled by the sudden intrusion, I look up to see Liam hovering in front of me. He seems equally surprised to see me and I suspect if he'd spotted me earlier he would have retreated back up the path. Now, all he can do is shift awkwardly, running a hand through his sun-streaked hair.

'So . . . how's things?'

'Good. You?'

'Good. Sorry, I couldn't chat this morning. It turns out dead orcas are good for business.'

When I'd finished photographing Maisie at Morte Sands, Bryan had a coffee waiting for me at the Coffee Shack. Even though the queue snaked back to the car park, I sensed Liam was avoiding me.

'That's okay.'

'I was surprised to see you. I thought you'd be out there,' he says, nodding towards Liars Island.

'You heard about the death then?'

'Ally, come on,' he teases. 'This is North Devon. Everyone's heard about it. Apparently, it's Hilton's son who runs the kayak centre out there.'

I doubt Liam knows Hilton Deveney personally, but

as a prominent local property developer who constantly graces the local press to remind us that his various nefarious plans for North Devon come from nowhere other than a place of pure benevolence, Hilton's surname is no longer necessary.

'Yes, it is and I'm impressed by your sources.'

'My sources also tell me it was murder.'

'I take it one of your old police buddies told you, or was it the gossip in the coffee queue?'

'That would be telling.' He grins. 'Actually, I knew the lad a little bit. He'd sometimes kayak to Morte Sands. Nice guy. Can't imagine he'd have too many enemies. So why aren't you out there?'

'My transfer papers aren't through yet.'

'They're taking their sweet time,' he says, frowning.

He's right. Even by police standards, my return to Major Investigations has been tortuously slow.

'You know what HR is like.'

But Liam isn't letting it go.

'You should talk to them, make sure someone isn't blocking you.'

'Blocking me?'

'You know the score, Ally. Upset the wrong person in policing and you're forever on the outside of the tent pissing in, and let's be honest,' he adds, 'you upset an entire unit.'

In a normal world, I'd be one of the good guys, exposing a senior officer, among others, trying to fix the evidence in a murder trial, but policing isn't a normal world. Instead of a commendation for rooting out corruption, I was unceremoniously dispatched to the outer reaches of the force area and it's taken over a year and a new SIO to even get close to getting back on the Major Investigations Unit.

'That was ages ago now. There's practically no one left. Not after the witch hunt by Professional Standards. It's all new faces now.'

'You're probably right. Ignore me.'

Our safe conversational go-tos exhausted, we lapse into silence, a silence that is entirely my fault. When Liam asked me out some months ago, I told him a relationship was off the cards while Megan was recovering from her injuries after her attack. That part wasn't the problem. The part that was, was that I then jumped into bed with someone else. I couldn't keep that from Liam. Telling him was the right thing to do because for us to stand a chance he needed to know everything. Besides, he already knows my biggest secret – one that only two people in the world know, one that could send me to prison for the rest of my life. If ever there was a deal breaker, knowing I killed a man would be it. Surely an ill-judged fling didn't come close. But I was wrong and despite my insistence it was a terrible mistake, that I hadn't been thinking straight, that it meant nothing to me, you know, the usual clichés, Liam couldn't see past it. Not that he said anything. Maybe it would have been better if he had. Instead, he just upped and left and I've barely seen him since.

'So how's Megan?' he says, pleased to have found something to say.

'On holiday with her dad. In Wales.'

'Really?'

I forget he doesn't know this, but why would he? He's no longer a fixture in my life, or Megan's.

'Yes. She's been through so much.' Christ, what an understatement. Megan recovered after Simon Pascoe attacked her, only to lose her best friend to arson at our home. Her visible injuries have healed, but it's the scars that can't be seen that trouble me. 'I thought it'd do her good to get out of Bidecombe for a while and it's a chance for her to get to know her dad and his family properly. He's got fifteen years to make up for.'

'Must be weird not having her around the place.'

'Yeah, it is, but Penny and I are having a catch-up with her later.'

'Well, give her my best.'

'I will.'

He points a thumb towards the hill behind us.

'I better be getting back.'

'Of course. See you around.'

He lingers a little longer.

'Actually, Ally, I'm glad I bumped into you. There's something I should tell you.'

'There you are.'

A female voice reaches us from halfway down the path. I look up to see a woman in heeled boots picking her way gingerly through the sheep shit sprinkled on the uneven track. Heels and sheep paths don't mix. I recognise her. Her name is Tanya and she runs Timeless Treasures, a gift shop on Bidecombe quay, selling shells with googly eyes, but what does she want with me? When she reaches us, to my surprise, she slides her arm around Liam and kisses him on the cheek. It isn't me she's come for. It's Liam and the thought of that causes something to shift in my chest.

It's then that I notice his hair has been trimmed and styled although a bout of self-consciousness ruffling appears to have unleashed it again and he's thrown a brown jumper over one of his normal exotic-bird themed shirts. I sense a woman's touch, but it's not mine. I guess this is what Liam was about to tell me.

'How did you know I was out here?' he asks and I wonder if I detect an edge in his voice that Tanya is an unwanted arrival before dismissing it as wishful thinking.

'One of the surfers at the café said you often walk out this way so I thought I'd come and say hello.'

'Great,' Liam replies, smiling. 'Tanya,' he says, then turns to me, 'this is Ally.'

'We've met before. I'm a CSI. I attended your gift shop on the quay when it got broken into a while back.'

'Oh. Right. Yes, of course.' She's being polite. She doesn't remember. Why would she? 'Actually, it's a gallery. Anyway, Liam, we should get going. The table is booked for seven.'

'Sure. Sure.' I sense he's waiting for her to go first, but she remains where she is, smiling, so he leads the way. 'See you around, Ally.'

Tanya slips her hand into his and the two of them stroll back up the path. That could have been me, should have been me, if I hadn't fucked it up. My disappointed sigh is lost on the breeze and I no longer want to be here on my own. I turn to take the path in the opposite direction when Liam calls down to me.

'I know what I meant to tell you.'

'What was that?'

'When I was in Bidecombe today, down by the harbour, I saw a boat come in.'

'That's pretty standard for a harbour.'

'Yes, but you'll never guess what it's called.'

'I've no idea.'

'*The Aloysia*. That's your full name, isn't it?'

'Yes, but are you sure?'

'Positive. It's such an unusual name.'

It can't be her. Not after all this time.

'What . . . what did she look like?'

Liam takes a moment to think while Tanya looks around impatiently.

'She had a blue hull, that's all I can remember about her, but a weird coincidence, hey?'

'Yes.' I smile, but it's not as weird as Liam thinks because the blue-hulled fishing boat that sailed into the Bidecombe Harbour this morning is named after me.

4

She wasn't always called *The Aloysia*. She was *The Perfidious* when we first got her. Dad hated the name. He told me it meant deceitful so I asked him what he was going to call her instead.

'*The Aloysia*, of course,' he said, surprised by my question. 'I can't think of a better name than one that means famous warrior.' Then he smoothed his beard like he always did when he was thinking. 'But renaming a boat isn't as simple as just scraping the letters from her hull. Boat names are recorded in the Ledger of the Deep kept by Poseidon, god of the sea. They must be completely removed before we rename her.' It was just one of dozens of sea tales he'd tell me and, of course, I lapped it up.

'How do we do that?'

'We hold a purging ceremony.'

And that's exactly what we did. Erasing *Perfidious* from the maintenance logs, the transom and even the engine, Dad then wrote it on a name tag and threw it into the harbour.

'The ink's soluble,' he explained. 'A few days in the water and it'll fade and finally disappear just like the *Perfidious*. If it doesn't, we're all in trouble.'

Next came the naming ceremony where Dad called on Poseidon to accept her new name – *The Aloysia* – and implored the four great winds – Boreas, Zephyrus, Eurus and Notus – to give us safe passage. And that was it. *The Aloysia* was official. Nothing bad would happen to her or those who sailed in her. But it did happen.

I grab a bottle of Sam's Cider from the fridge and, sinking down into the sofa, I flip open my laptop. The news article flashes up on my laptop screen: 'Popular Bidecombe Harbour Master Goes Missing Off Liars Island.' Still the headline shocks me as if there's still a tiny part of me that is learning of my Dad's death for the first time.

The Aloysia was found adrift in the Bristol Channel. There was no sign of her captain, Arthur 'Davy' Dymond. Arthur was my adoptive dad's real name, but everyone called him Davy, a nickname acquired after a friend ribbed him for his wild hair, likening it to some old picture they'd seen of the mythical pirate Davy Jones with octopus-tentacled locks.

The town reacted to Dad's disappearance with collective disbelief. How could it happen? Davy knew the sea better than anyone. People were mystified. They'd stop me in the street to share their condolences. 'Of all people . . .' 'He was the last person . . .' 'If it can happen to him, it can happen to anyone.'

I kept my fears to myself. Still young enough to believe in silly superstition, I was certain Dad made a mistake with the renaming ceremony and had incurred the wrath of the gods. If only he'd kept the name *Perfidious*.

A huge search was mounted for him. His fishermen friends went out in fleets determined to find him. Their search far outlived any faith the waters would give him up alive, but still they looked because those who fish the oceans know better than most that it is one thing to die at sea, but not having a body to bury is a double cruelty. It condemns you to a life of misplaced hope that they'll return in the face of overwhelming evidence that they never will. Even now, there are times I expect Dad to stroll through the front door of my cabin, whistling 'Blow the Man Down'. Only he doesn't know where I live, or that I work for the police, or even what I look like now. But that doesn't stop me holding on to the possibility of his return. That's the irrationality of incomplete grief.

I skip the article's reported facts, knowing I can still rattle them off without missing a beat: the seas were calm, the engine had been switched off, there were no signs of any damage to the boat, no other boats were in the vicinity, there were no signs of an altercation. In the cabin was a mug of warm tea and a half-eaten sandwich. *The Aloysia* became Bidecombe's very own *Mary Celeste* as people debated why Dad had abandoned her. A pullout box next to the article – entitled 'Whatever happened to Davy Dymond?' – mused over a Bermuda Triangle-type phenomenon, pirates and even an alien abduction. A fun puzzle for anyone, but my adoptive mother Bernadette and me.

My chest tightens at the sight of the two photos accompanying the article. The first is a head-and-shoulders shot taken for Dad's ID for his job as Bidecombe's harbourmaster, his dark hair smoothed back and his beard neatly trimmed, almost certainly at Bernadette's insistence, but I can still sense his discomfort at wearing a shirt so tight the collar looks like it's trying to take off. In the second photo, taken a year or so before Dad died for an article about winching the boats out of the harbour to spend the winter months in dry dock, he stands next to *The Aloysia's* gleaming hull. Dad and I would repaint her every spring whether she needed it or not. For a man who cared so little for his own appearance, he was fastidious when it came to *The Aloysia*. Look after her, he used to say, and she'll look after us. Only she didn't. And now she's back. The question is why.

5

When I walk into the reception at Seven Hills Lodges, Penny
Fields, the owner and my closest friend, looks up from her
computer and smiles, but it's a tired smile. It's May, and
there's still much to do to get the park ready in time for the
summer season.

'Everything okay?'

'Yes. Of course.' She leans back and eases out a knot in
her shoulder covered by her long hair, which is threaded with
coloured beads and a feather, offsetting the grey flecks. 'Bookings are looking good for the summer.'

'Great. I was just popping in to remind you we're Face-
Timing Megan in a few minutes.'

'Right, yes. About that. I'm going to have to give it a miss.
There's a problem with a shower curtain in one of the cabins.'

'Can't it wait? Megan would really love to see you.'

'And I'd love to see her.'

Years of minding Megan when I was on call or working
shifts mean Penny is close to Megan too. Sometimes I think
she's closer to my daughter than I am. Seven Hills Lodges has
been home ever since Penny found us shivering in the local
park having escaped my abusive drunk of an ex on Boxing

Day. It was only meant to be for a few days until we got ourselves sorted, but Penny had her own story. Maybe that's why
she took us in. She recognised herself in me, I don't know,
but our friendship blossomed and the days turned into weeks
turned into years. Eleven years later and I couldn't imagine
Megan and me living anywhere else.

'And it's been ages since we got together.'

Three weeks to be precise, but every time I've floated the
idea of getting together, Penny's batted me away.

'Sorry. Duty calls.'

'Can't Lottie do it? Isn't that why you took her on?'

'She's finished for the day. Besides, it's quicker if I do it
myself and then it's done properly.'

Over the years, I've grown used to sharing my day with
Penny. Adamant that running a holiday park was far too
dull, she'd insist I recount the crime scenes I'd visited. Her
questions would nudge me away from the facts towards the
emotional impact of being exposed to violent death. It eased
the burden and I often wondered if she did this on purpose.
Penny Fields, unofficial child minder and personal therapist,
is probably the only reason I'm still in the job. Today I want
to tell her Hilton Deveney's son Kieran is too young to die,
and that someone on Liars Island is responsible for the hole
in his skull and I want to tell her *The Aloysia* is back in Bidecombe, but I've no idea why.

'Okay, how about you come to the cabin later then? It
would be good to have a proper catch-up.'

'I can't. I need to get back to the farm. Will's expecting
me.'

'I'm sure he won't mind if you're a bit late.'

'But I mind,' she snaps. 'Can you tell Megan I'll call her tomorrow?'

She returns to her computer, but I haven't finished.

'Pen, what's going on? Have I said or done something to upset you?'

'No, why?'

'I get the feeling you're avoiding me.'

'Of course not.'

'You and Will are okay, aren't you?'

'Yes. We're fine. You know what it's like this time of year, Ally. I'm up to my eyes in it.' She laughs, raising a hand to her eyebrow to emphasise her workload.

'Okay, but if you need any help, you just have to ask.'

'Hey, did you hear about that orca that washed up at Morte Sands?' she says, changing the subject.

'Hear about it? I had the pleasure of smelling it at very close quarters.'

'So you saw Liam at the Coffee Shack then?'

Penny has an enduring fascination with my love life, or lack of. Since she got together with Will five months ago, she's convinced I also need to be in a relationship. The problem is it takes two and the person I want a relationship with isn't interested.

'Not really. He was really busy.'

'He'd have made time for you.'

'I got the impression he was giving me the cold shoulder.'

'Rubbish, it's just hurt pride is all. If you made a bit of effort, he'd come round.'

'I'm not so sure. I think he's seeing Tanya from the gift shop on the harbour.'

'Tanya? She's so not his type.'

'She looked like his type when I saw them hand in hand at Breakneck Point and please don't give me that *it's your own fault* look.'

'I told you not to tell him. Some things should remain a secret.'

Penny's attention returns to her computer screen and I leave her wrestling with spreadsheets. Strolling back up the path to my cabin, I can't help thinking I've experienced many season starts at Seven Hills with Penny and I don't recall any of them being like this before. Maybe Penny has some secrets of her own.

I lob my keys onto the small round table inside the cabin door just as my phone buzzes in my pocket. It's Megan. There are plenty of times when I craved a break from my teenage daughter's emotional unpredictability, but the truth is life is duller without her. She's only been gone a few days and already I miss her.

'How are you, love?'

'Okay,' she says, offering me a hint of a smile. She's fifteen. I'll take that as a win. 'Did you get to Jay's grave?'

'I did. First thing this morning before my shift.' It's been several months since Jay's death. It's one of the reasons I encouraged her to go on holiday with Julian, her biological father. She barely knows her dad, but it was a chance to escape Bidecombe and the physical reminders of what happened in the hope it would ease her grief, if only for a few days. 'I picked some violets. I thought they'd look nice. I'll send you a photo so you can see for yourself.'

'Thank you.' She nods and two parallel lines of pale red hair fall forward, the same colour as Julian's when he had some and nothing like my black curls, which I once loved for their accidental similarity to my dad's but now just irritate me because of their refusal to be tamed. Megan's hazel eyes and delicately light complexion belong to Julian too and I sometimes wonder if the only gene I can lay claim to in my daughter is her stubbornness.

'How's things with Julian, Cam and the boys?'

'Okay.'

'What have you been up to?'

'We went to a petting farm today.'

'A farm? You could do that here. For free.'

My efforts to humour her receive the usual disdain.

'They all live in the city so a hen's a big deal to them.'

'So, how are you getting on with Julian and Cam?'

'Fine.'

'And the boys?'

'Fine.'

'Is something up?'

'No, why should it be?'

'You seem a little low.'

'They're just a bit in my face, that's all. They keep making comments about me being on my phone. I let Noah play a game on it and Julian told me off as the boys are only allowed a half hour of screen time a day.'

'Give it time. You're all still adjusting to each other.'

'Where's Penny?'

'She couldn't make it. She'll call you tomorrow. She's still dealing with a problem in one of the other cabins.'

Megan smirks. 'Yeah. That'll be it.'

'What's that supposed to mean?'

'Nothing,' she says quickly.

'She would be here, if she could, Meg. She has got a holiday park to run.'

'I know, I was agreeing with you. There's no need to go on about it.'

'I wasn't, I was just—'

'Omg,' she bursts out. 'Did you hear about what happened on Liars Island? A guy got murdered.'

I know a deflection when I see one but I go with it.

'Who told you that?'

'Helena's dad knows the captain of the boat that takes supplies and stuff out there. Apparently, it's our kayak instructor from our school trip last month. Kieran. He was really funny, but a bit full of himself and a real flirt.'

'In what way?'

'He had his own personal kayak with his name on it which he gave to Helena because he said he only let special people borrow it and he kept asking if we had boyfriends.'

'Okay, could he have just been being friendly?'

'Probably, but he must be at least twenty-five. We're fifteen. I know some girls would love that, but me and Helena were *ew* about it.'

'I'm glad to hear it, but you should have told me at the time. I could have done something.'

'No way, you'd have just gone off on one like you normally do. Besides, we weren't the only ones to notice because he and the other kayaker had a massive row.'

'About Kieran's behaviour?'

'Dunno, but Helena forgot to give her life jacket back so she had to go back to the centre. Anyway, she found them having a right go at each other. Kieran was saying to the other guy that he should have told him.'

'Told him what?'

'Dunno, but when they saw Helena, they stopped rowing and Kieran just walked off. Do you think it has anything to do with his death? Do you think his friend did it?'

'I've no idea.'

'Imagine if I just solved a murder.' Her eyes widen with delight at the thought. 'How cool would that be?'

But I'm not listening. Maybe Kieran Deveney isn't so innocent after all.

6

Every senior investigating officer runs murder investigations differently. DI Harriet Moore takes the 'as many eyes on this as possible' approach which means the briefing room at police headquarters is full when I arrive this morning.

DS Henry Whiteley, Harriet's gopher, is already stationed at the front by the drop-down white screen talking with a female detective, DC Juliette Hollis. I remember her from the Slaughterhouse Farm murder inquiry. Dressed in a sombre black suit, her hair dragged into a ballerina's bun, her face devoid of make-up, she wants those around her to take her as seriously as she takes herself. I get that. In policing, appearances count, especially for those young in service. Henry is nodding in a way that suggests Juliette is telling him something he already knows and I sense a rivalry between them: Henry's already a DS and Juliette thinks she should be one. I watch them for a few moments before realising I am also under surveillance.

Instead of looking away when I catch his eye, Jim Dixon, MI's crime scene manager, holds me in his gaze as if I shouldn't be there. He's right. It's unusual for a lowly CSI to be in a murder briefing, but that's not the reason for his hostility.

After the dust settled on the corruption inquiry, he was one of many who stonewalled me until it became impossible for me to stay on MI. He must be clean otherwise he wouldn't have survived the inquisition by Professional Standards. I can only put his attitude down to that golden rule in policing; never rat on a colleague. No matter what they've done. Well, screw you, Jim Dixon. I'm not the one that needs to examine their conscience here.

'Morning everyone.' DI Harriet Moore sweeps into the briefing room, phone clamped to her ear. In her beige palazzo trouser suit and chunky necklace, she looks like a cop that never leaves her desk – a shiny arse, as we say in the job – but the truth is DI Moore likes to be in the thick of it. We met when she called me in to help with the murder of a farmer at Slaughterhouse Farm shortly after she transferred from London. With the stench of corruption still lingering over the unit, she was unsure who to trust so she turned to me: another outsider.

'Let's get started, shall we?' The room falls silent. This is Harriet's show and we're her players. 'I'm not gonna lie, a murder on an island is a first for me, and before you ask, we're not talking *Death in Paradise* here, more like death in the arctic. Anyway, I'm going to hand you over to DS Whiteley who'll bring us all, including me, up to speed on where we're at. Feel free to chip in.'

Juliette dims the lights unasked, earning her an appreciative smile from Harriet that she accepts with a quiet pride. Henry presses the remote and the photo of a fresh-faced young man appears. Hair dampened by the sea spray, he's sitting on a kayak in the ocean grinning into the camera. It's a normal photo, the kind we take millions of every day. Never could he or the person who took it have imagined it would be headlining a murder briefing. Henry allows us a moment to take it all in, to not lose sight that Kieran was once a vital, vibrant human being whose life has been snatched from him.

'Okay, so our victim is twenty-eight-year-old Kieran Deveney. He runs Bara Watersports on Liars Island with his friend, Ben Dawson. They've been mates since uni. Keiran's father, Hilton Deveney, is head of the board of trustees that run the island and helped set the two lads up in business. It's been open for just over two years. Doing well, by all accounts, until two days ago, when Kieran's body was found on a beach in the southern part of the island by his business partner. He was wearing jeans and a kayak jacket and he had sustained a fatal head injury.'

The screen flicks to another photo. This one is mine. A headshot from the postmortem, showing the top of Kieran's skull staved in. A couple of people recoil at the shocking contrast of the two images.

'So,' continues Henry, 'initially we thought Kieran had drowned, but the postmortem shows he died of blunt force trauma to the head.'

Juliette raises her hand. 'Couldn't he have just slipped and hit his head on the rocks?'

'No, the pathologist doesn't believe the injury was accidental. He believes Kieran received a single blow from behind with a lot of force too.'

'Was death instant?' asks an older detective in an ill-fitting brown jacket, his doughy features moulded by decades of shift work and late-night takeaways. I don't know him.

He must have joined MI after I left, transferring in from one of the divisions in the south of the county. He looks like he's nearing his 'thirty' so to move to somewhere as intense as MI for his last years of service is impressive, or he needs the overtime.

'Alex doesn't believe so,' continues Henry. 'The force wasn't great enough. He thinks if Kieran had been found in time he could have been saved.'

'Okay. Talk us through time of death,' says Harriet.

The screen goes blank.

'Based on Kieran's movements, we originally put it at between 11.30pm and 11.30am when he was found, but Alex has narrowed that down to somewhere between 11.30pm and 5.13am. Basically just before dawn.'

'Why before dawn?' Harriet presses Henry.

'A broken torch was found on Kieran's body, the batteries were waterlogged, but it was still in the on position suggesting it was still dark when he was killed.'

Harriet nods, impressed by Alex's powers of deduction.

'So what do we know about Kieran's movements the day before he died?' the older detective asks.

'Nothing unusual. He and his business partner, Ben Dawson, are getting the watersports centre ready for the new season. They ate at the only pub on the island which is just up the hill from the centre.'

'How did they seem?' asks Juliette.

'The landlady said normally they'd have spent the time with the others, chatting, playing darts, but that night they tucked themselves away in a corner. She described the conversation they were having as quite intense.'

'Were they arguing?' asks Harriet.

'No, she said it was more like they needed to talk something out. We asked Ben about it. He said they were just discussing their plans to extend the watersports centre. Anyway, they left together, returning to the centre where they each have a flat. They said goodnight and that was it.'

'So when did Ben notice his friend was missing?' continues Harriet.

'He didn't. Kieran often goes kayaking early in the morning but when Ben saw his kayak was still there he just assumed he'd changed his mind and gone for a hike instead.'

'Was that normal for him?' asks the older detective.

'Apparently, but it wasn't until Ben decided to do a beach clean of Devil's Cauldron around mid-morning that he came across Ben's body.'

'Devil's Cauldron?' Harriet pulls a face. 'Where do they get the names for these places?'

'It's a small sandy cove just beyond the watersports centre, but hidden by the rocks,' says Henry, oblivious that Harriet's question was rhetorical. 'So named because the water is warmer there, but also particularly treacherous which is why kayaks are launched in front of the watersports centre in Seal Bay, named because—'

'It has seals. Yes, I get it,' says Harriet, her patience thinning.

'It also has a jetty where the boat from the mainland docks.'

The jetty. I dismiss the image of the wooden structure built a little way out into the sea as quickly as it appears. I haven't thought about it in years and I don't intend to start now.

'So let's be clear,' says Harriet. 'No one else saw Kieran between the time he left the pub with his friend and business partner Ben Dawson after they were witnessed having a serious debate until the same Ben Dawson found Kieran dead on the beach the following morning.'

Harriet's statement attracts a few knowing exchanges. We're all thinking the same thing. It wouldn't be the first time a killer tried to deflect an investigation by pretending to be the innocent who found the body. If I'm not mistaken, Ben Dawson just became a person of interest.

'Okay, let's dial back a bit,' says Harriet. 'At some point between 11.30pm and 5.13am, Kieran walks to Devil's Cauldron where he's then killed. What was he doing there?'

'Maybe a noise woke him up and he went to investigate,' offers Juliette.

'I doubt it. I went to the centre,' says the middle-aged detective. 'You're not going to hear much over the sound of the waves and in any case why didn't Kieran wake Ben if he thought there was an intruder?'

'Or,' continues Juliette undeterred, 'he arranged to meet someone there and that person either intended to harm him or something went wrong.'

'Strange place to meet.'

'Maybe it was a secret meeting. Henry said Devil's Cauldron can't be seen from the centre.'

Harriet nods.

'Yeah, that has legs. Okay, what else? I hesitate to ask, given this place barely has electricity, but any digital forensics?'

A young girl dressed all in black and wearing Harry Potter glasses tentatively lifts a hand.

'Not yet, ma'am. Kieran's phone hasn't been recovered. We do have his laptop though, which we're working on.'

'Let me know as soon as you get anything from it. What about physical forensics?'

All eyes turn to Jim Dixon.

'Not much.' He shrugs.

'Really?'

'Really. It's a beach.'

'So?'

'So I'm a CSI, not King fucking Canute. We had to battle the incoming tide to recover what we did, but I wouldn't get too excited. It's just the normal flotsam and jetsam that gets washed up.'

'Let's have a look anyway. Henry.'

The screen comes to life once more, this time showing an assortment of plastic bottles, drinks cans, a broken watch, a doll with faded writing on her legs and arms, used syringes all tangled in blue netting; the detritus of human existence.

'All these items were a good twenty metres from the body,' says Jim. 'Obviously, we've photographed them all individually and bagged them up, but I'd bet money none are connected to Kieran's murder.'

Much as I hate to admit, he's almost certainly right. As CSIs we're taught not to discard anything. Overkill, not underkill, but cordons can only extend so far.

'What about the watch? Where's that from?' says Harriet, unwilling to give up just yet.

'Casio. Manufactured in Japan. Eight million were sold last year. Cheap as chips,' Henry pipes up, smiling at Juliette. Definitely rivals. 'I checked before I came here.'

'Which means the chances of finding its owner are next to zero,' says Harriet. 'And the doll?'

'Made by Chad Valley. A UK firm. Can only be bought from Argos. This model hasn't been in production for ten years.' Juliette glances at Henry. 'I also checked before I came here.'

'Okay, good, that narrows it down. Let's see if we can find its owner.'

'Is there any point? I mean it's a kid's toy. It probably came from a passing ship,' says the older detective.

'I know, Norm, but sometimes the point isn't always immediately obvious. We need belt and braces on this. I'm already getting flak from Kieran's dad. Apparently, he's some local bigwig who thinks we should have solved this yesterday,' says Harriet. 'Jim, any fingerprints from the cans recovered?'

'Too wet.'

His dismissiveness earns him a hard stare from Harriet. Not just me then. But even Jim wouldn't withhold evidence just because he didn't like his DI.

'Okay, let's look at where Kieran's body was found.'

A wide-angle image of a small sandy beach, semi-circled by rocks, appears on the screen: Devil's Cauldron. Close to the shoreline, if it weren't for the forensics tent shielding Kieran's corpse from view, it would look like something from a holiday brochure. Henry points to a dark smudge running the width of the beach.

'This is the high-tide mark. As you can see, Kieran's body was found below this line.'

'So why wasn't he washed out to sea?' asks Norm.

'The night he was killed, it was a neap tide which means the tide was much lower than usual.'

'So it didn't reach the normal high-tide mark?' asks Harriet.

'No. What's more, it's fairly common knowledge that bodies that go into the water in and around Liars Island are never found, something to do with the currents,' adds Henry.

Arthur 'Davy' Dymond – missing, declared dead. Once again, I push aside my past life. It has no place in a murder briefing.

'So we're looking at the killer making a mistake with the tides?' asks Harriet.

'Potentially.'

I don't realise I'm frowning until Harriet turns her attention to me.

'Ally, do you have something to say?'

'Um, not really, other than Henry's right. Bodies are rarely if ever found.' A thought drifts into my mind. 'Actually, I'd be surprised if it was a mistake. When you live on an island, you make it your business to know the tides. It could save your life one day.'

'I can see that if you're a fisherman or you run a watersports centre, but are you saying people know the tides just as a matter of course? How?'

'By looking up in the sky and seeing what the moon is doing. Neap tides happen when the moon is in its first and last quarter. Half-moon in other words.'

I don't add that Dad taught me this the first time he took me out. No one should be near the water unless they understand the tides, he used to say.

'So what you're saying is that the killer knew Kieran's body would be discovered?'

'Possibly.'

'That doesn't sound right to me,' says Harriet, shaking her head. 'You don't have to watch that many cop shows to know how difficult murder investigations are when there's no corpse.'

Unless, for some reason, the killer wanted Kieran's body to be found.

7

Harriet calls a short break and the room immediately fills with the urgent buzz of a dozen or more iPhones. Kieran's murder isn't the only crime on people's crime sheets, including mine. Stepping outside for some air, I find I have a missed call from PC Bryan Rogers so I call him back.

'What can I do for you, Bryan?'

'I'm at the Land Rover showroom at Heale Cross. They had a big break-in last night. Just wondering when you'd be able to get here.'

'Not sure. I'm at a murder briefing at HQ. The lad they found out on Liars Island.'

'The Deveney kid? I heard about that. Okay, no problem, I've got another shout, but I've told the manager here not to touch anything 'til you get here. Actually, can you give me a buzz when you're on the way and I'll come back and meet you here?'

'You want to see me?'

The conveyor belt of crime means police officers are usually long gone by the time I get to a crime scene, especially for a break-in. Often, it's just me, the victim and the locksmith or the joiner. 'What's up? Can't get enough of my scintillating company?'

'Something like that,' he says, laughing.

'Don't keep me hanging.'

'See you at the car showroom.'

He rings off before I can quiz him further. I'm making my way back into the building when I spot Jim Dixon on his phone. His hand is cupped around his mobile so he can't be overheard. That's not unusual. Crime Scene information is highly sensitive and police officers are the worst gossips. As I draw alongside him, he looks up at me. I force a smile. After all, when I return to MI, we'll be colleagues once again, but he immediately turns his back to me.

Shrugging off his rudeness, I return to the briefing room, but something about Jim's expression when he saw me lingers. It's as if I'd caught him out. But doing what? It's then that I remember Liam's concern over the length of time it was taking for me to return to MI, telling me I should chase up my transfer papers just in case someone was deliberately holding things up. Is Jim Dixon trying to stop me returning to MI?

'Right, let's talk about suspects,' says Harriet, calling the room to order. 'This should be a little easier, thank God. It's an island and from what I understand, the island's tourist season hasn't started so it's currently manned by a skeleton staff along with a handful of residents. I think we can safely say our killer is one of them.'

'Unless someone snuck onto the island.'

'Let's keep it simple in the first instance, shall we, Henry?

45

Right, let's start with who was on the island when Kieran was murdered.'

'There's a commune or something in the north,' says Juliette, keen to be in pole position in this conversation.

'Hippies?'

'Er . . . I don't think we call them that anymore, boss,' says Norm.

'Really? So, what are we meant to call them?'

'I think the correct term is New Age dwellers,' says Juliette.

'Noted.' Harriet sighs. 'So what do we know about these New Age dwellers?'

'They live at Grannus House,' says Henry. 'A large property leased from the Trust. They farm the land in return for board and lodging, selling the produce to the pub and the shop next door. Normally, there's around fifteen people living there at any one time. It's a pretty transient population but most of them left for a two-week retreat the day before Kieran's body was found.'

'A retreat?' Norm screws his face up. 'From what? They live on a pissing deserted island, for God's sake.'

Henry waits for the laughter to subside. People continue to grin at Norm, grateful for the lightness he brings to the proceedings. Every murder inquiry needs a Norm.

'Anyway, three of them stayed behind at Grannus House. The first is the woman who runs it, a Jocasta Marwell. Tricky lady, by all accounts.'

'I'll say,' says Norm. 'I interviewed her. She's one of these eco-warriors. You name it, she's glued herself to it. Been arrested numerous times. One of our frequent flyers. Hates the police, by default.'

'Naturally.' Harriet sighs. 'Until they need us, of course.'

'And for all her peace and love, she was not a fan of Kieran,' says Henry. 'Called him a poor little rich kid, reliant on hand-outs from daddy. Accused him of playing pranks on her.'

'Pranks?' asks Harriet.

'Silly stuff, like nicking her carrots. Not enough to kill him over.'

'You'd be surprised.'

'She got her revenge according to the landlady's husband,' says Juliette. 'Apparently, she scuttled several of their kayaks.'

'Do we know about this officially?' Harriet checks with Henry.

'Not reported.'

'Clearly what happens on the island, stays on the island,' says Norm.

'Anyway,' continues Henry. 'Things got worse after she found out Kieran and Ben were looking to build a bunkhouse next to the centre. They'd already got planning permission and Kieran had spoken to a builder on the mainland. Jocasta was threatening all sorts if it went ahead.'

'Will the bunkhouse still get built now that Kieran is dead?'

'Don't know, we'll get on to that.'

'Okay. Who else was in Grannus House?' asks Harriet.

Henry refers to his iPad.

'Dove Sunrise and Forrest Stream.'

'Not their real names, I'm guessing.'

'No, their real names are Stacy Pratt and Scott Budleigh-Smith.'

'Hang on.' Harriet trawls her memory. 'Budleigh-Smith? Is he the kid . . .'

'Who burnt a fifty-pound note in front of a homeless man a few years back when he was at uni? Yes, he is. His dad, Oliver Budleigh-Smith, is a government minister. Almost lost his job over it.'

'So how'd he end up on Liars Island?' asks Harriet.

Norm leans forward, signalling this is his call.

'The Budleigh-Smiths are family friends of the Deveneys. The mothers knew each other from their days at Cheltenham Ladies College. You know what toffs are like, they all stick together. Anyway, when it all kicked off and the Budleigh-Smiths needed to get shot of their embarrassment of a son, Mrs Budleigh-Smith happened to have a friend whose husband, Hilton, pretty much owns a remote island.'

'So Kieran Deveney and Scott Budleigh-Smith, aka Forrest Stream, knew each other?'

'Knew of each other would be more accurate,' says Norm. 'There are eight years between them. They never hung out, as my kids would say.'

'Okay, tell me about this Stacy Pratt, aka Dove Sunrise.'

'She and Forrest got handfasted last year.'

'What the hell is handfasting when it's at home?' Harriet lifts her hand to cut down any attempts to explain. 'Actually, I don't want to know. Carry on, Norm.'

'Okay, so Dove Sunrise has lived on the island for around four years. First at the pub as a live-in barmaid, then at Grannus House. Before that she drifted from town to town, never staying in a job for more than a few months. A bit of a sad backstory. She was in a car crash that killed her sister when she was a kid.'

'Who told you that?'

'The landlady. They're quite close. Anyway, Dove says she didn't know Kieran that well. And before you ask, none of them left Grannus House that night, which is about two and half miles from Devil's Cauldron.'

'Any proof of this?'

'No.'

'Thought not. So who else was on the island when Kieran was killed?'

Juliette's hand shoots into the air.

'Ash Griffiths, ma'am. He lives at The Barbary Inn on the island. He's married to the landlady.'

'Barbary?'

'As in pirates,' says Henry.

'Pirates. Of course,' says Harriet, rolling her eyes. 'How could I have not known that? So where was this Ash Griffiths when Kieran was getting his head bashed in? Walking someone off a plank?'

A chuckle ripples through the room. No one including Harriet finds murder remotely funny, but SIOs know the pressure to find a killer makes for a stressful environment. Jokes, even lame ones, release some of that tension even if people like Henry don't get them.

'Er no,' he says, frowning, 'he was kayaking to the mainland. He'd already set off from Seal Bay.'

'Apparently, it's something he does regularly,' Juliette cuts in. 'Sometimes Kieran goes with him although he hadn't been off the island for a good month or so, not since he met the builders. Anyway, CCTV in Bidecombe Harbour picked Ash Griffiths up at around 6.30. It takes around four hours to paddle from Liars Island to Bidecombe, and that's going some. He says he left at 2.30am.'

'That's very precise.'

'He wanted to make sure he caught the tide which is why he left in the early hours.'

'But he could have killed Kieran and then hopped on his kayak, given the proximity of Devil's Cauldron to the water-sports centre?' says Harriet.

'No, he'd have had to cover twelve miles of sea in just over an hour,' says Henry. 'Even with an outboard motor on his kayak, he couldn't have made it to Bidecombe in that time. Plus, there's no obvious motive. He seemed to get on well with Kieran.'

'Did he see anything suspicious?'

'No, the centre was in darkness so he helped himself to a kayak and set off.'

'What else do we know about this Ash Griffiths?'

'Not much. Dropped out of law school to crew yachts. Got a bit of form, low-level drugs offences when he was a teenager. Cannabis possession, that kind of thing.'

'In my experience, where there's low-level drugs, there's high-level drugs,' says Harriet.

'But he's got the best alibi of all. The CCTV shows he wasn't there.'

'Still, let's keep him on the list. Maybe he's just a very fast paddler. Who else have we got?'

'Ash Griffith's wife, Rose,' says Juliette before Henry has a chance to speak. 'She's the landlady of The Barbary Inn which she took over from her parents about two months ago.' Juliette checks her notes 'They've been together for three years but got married a couple of months ago. Ash is her second husband.'

Could this be my childhood friend Rose? She often said she'd never leave Liars Island, but we were young then and I assumed she was joking. How could three miles of granite and moor grass be enough for anyone?

'So where was she the night Kieran died?'

'She spent the evening working behind the bar at the pub, then went to bed as normal. Her husband kissed her goodbye when he left to go to the mainland.'

'Time?'

'Doesn't know. Says she barely came round and went straight back to sleep.'

'Okay, is that everyone?'

'Not quite. There's a vicar,' says Henry.

'A vicar? He wasn't in the library with the candlestick was he?' says Harriet.

Henry frowns.

'Er, no. He was in the vestry.'

'Cluedo, mate,' says Norm, appalled at Henry's lack of boardgame knowledge.

'Never played it. Anyway, his full name is Reverend Humphrey Bagshaw.' The name sounds familiar but I can't place it. 'He's only just arrived to take up a new position at the church.'

'Thoughts?' asks Harriet.

'He didn't have much to say. He'd only been there a couple of weeks, still finding his feet. He didn't socialise in the pub so he didn't know any of them well, if at all.'

'Had he met Kieran?'

'Briefly. Rose invited him for a meal in the pub and intro-duced him to everyone there, including Kieran. He stopped going to the pub after that,' says Juliette.

'It sounds like we can probably discount him,' says Har-riet. 'So that leaves us with Ben Dawson, Kieran's business partner.'

'Who interviewed him?'

Norman raises his hand. 'Me.'

'Thoughts?'

'He seemed genuinely shocked at Kieran's death.'

'Aren't they all?' says Harriet. 'What about when he answered your questions?'

'No obvious repetition. No shielding. If he's lying, he's very good at it.'

I have the impression not much gets past Norm.

'Okay, what do we know about him?'

'Not much,' says Norm. 'A good friend of Kieran's. They met at uni. He's not from a moneyed background though. It seemed to be a point of pride for him. He got a lucky break when Hilton Deveney agreed to back their idea for a water-sports centre. That opened last year.'

'Any financial problems?'

'No, the opposite. They had a great first season and were looking to expand.'

'With Hilton's money I take it?'

'No, this time they planned to get a business loan with Hilton acting as a guarantor.'

'And where was Ben when Kieran was murdered?'

'Asleep at the centre. Alone.'

'So no alibi to speak of then?'

'No.'

'Okay, so no obvious suspects and no obvious motives. Apart from irritating the local hip— er, New Age dwellers, it seems Kieran was an all-round nice guy.'

'Not quite,' says Juliette.

'Go on.'

'Kieran was arrested for sexual assault when he was a first-year uni student.'

'Was he now?' says Harriet, her interest piqued. 'So what happened?'

'It didn't go anywhere,' says Juliette. 'It turned out to be a false allegation.'

'Or maybe daddy bailed him out,' says Norman.

'How come he's working at a watersports centre then? He must have had a DBS check,' says Juliette.

'Arrests don't always show up and it was eight years ago. Are there any other reports of Kieran being involved in anything similar since?' asks Harriet.

There's a collective shrug and shaking of heads.

'In that case, it sounds like a malicious allegation.'

I raise my hand. 'I'm not sure it was.'

CRIME SCENE EXAMINATION REPORT RELATING TO SUSPECT KIERAN DEVENEY

<u>CSI</u>: Kate Ringwood
<u>OIC</u>: DS Marvin Parr
<u>DIVISION</u>: Central, Thames Valley Police
<u>LOCATION</u>: Reading Hospital (Sexual Offences Referral Suite)
<u>EXAMINATION COMMENCED</u>: 1.30am, 5 Sept 2016

EXAMINATION NOTES

Alleged sexual assault. Alleged location Littleham Park. (CSI Brad Mayhew attending scene)

Victim presented herself at the hospital. Injuries photographed. Sexual Offences Officer DC Julie Fenwick i/c of intimate samples for submission.

EVIDENCE COLLECTED

Photographs - REF: RH1–RH5
  • Light bruising on one arm

8

The spring sunlight pours through the floor-to-ceiling glass windows of the car showroom at Heale Cross, on the outskirts of Bidecombe, illuminating a row of gleaming white Land Rovers, perfect in every way other than the hollows gouged either side of the grilles.

'So, they only took the headlights?' I ask.

'Yep. All twelve of them,' says PC Bryan Rogers. 'Each worth around eight hundred pounds. That's if you can get them.'

'What do you mean?'

'There's a massive shortage at the moment. I'm in a Land Rover club. I own a 1976 Series 3 Soft Top,' he says, by way of explanation. 'So that's at least ten thousand pounds they just netted themselves. Not bad for a night's work. Who says crime doesn't pay? Take me months to earn that.'

'Why just the headlights?'

'Apparently, they're excellent for growing cannabis which makes it harder for us because it means they're passing straight into the hands of drug dealers.'

'So where did they get in?'

'Around the back. Crowbarred fire exit open.'

'And they didn't attempt to disconnect the alarm?'

'You serious?' he scoffs. 'The days when an alarm activation would bring the blues and twos racing to the scene are long gone, Dymond.'

'Is there any evidence that they went anywhere else in the building?'

'Not that I can see. They knew what they wanted and took it. Didn't even bother with the petty cash tin in the office.'

'That suggests they already have a buyer for them. Okay, I'll get started.'

'Great, meet me in the security office when you're done.'

I remove a pot of aluminium powder from my case and slide my brush from its plastic tube, its fine hairs splaying open, ready for action. I dip it into the fine powder and begin gently swirling it over the first of the Land Rovers. Immediately, a crop of silvery smudges appear and I go in close, searching for a fragment of fingerprint detailed enough for a match, but there's nothing and I move on to the next vehicle. Twenty minutes later, I find Bryan in the office enjoying a cup of tea with the security guard.

'Any joy?' he asks hopefully.

My mobile's ringtone answers him before I can.

'Hold on a sec.'

I get my phone out and immediately notice a text from Penny asking me to come back to the holiday park as soon as I can, although there's 'nothing to worry about' which is code for it's nothing to do with Megan. I've no idea what she wants, but Seven Hills is less than two miles away and I'm due a refs break. I'll deal with it then. I take the call.

'Ally, hi, it's Jake.' Jake is the other CSI who works out of

Barnston Station, covering mid-Devon. Our patches border each other and occasionally, we help each other out. Just a few years out of uni, he's not long in the job and he's still learning, but he's got the makings of a great CSI. 'I heard you were attending a theft at the Land Rover showroom out at Heale Cross.'

'Yes, that's right. I'm here now. Why?'

'I just wanted to let you know that I went to a vehicle that was broken into at a house in Wellacombe yesterday. Also a Land Rover. The owners have been away. They think it happened two weeks ago.'

I'm impressed. Criminals travel, but CSIs don't. We tend not to stray beyond our divisions which makes it hard to join the dots for roaming thieves.

'Did they try and steal the vehicle? Or anything else?'

'No, they just took the headlights.'

'Same as here then.'

'That's what I was ringing to ask.'

'Did you find any forensics at Wellacombe?'

'Only glove marks. You?'

'Same. We could be looking at a repeat offender so stay in touch. Let me know if you get any similar thefts.'

I ring off. 'That was Jake. He went to a vehicle theft at Wellacombe yesterday. Another Land Rover, but they only stole headlights.'

'Sounds like we might have a problem on our hands.'

'It does, but I wouldn't hold your breath on this one, Bryan. You probably heard Jake didn't find any dabs and neither did I, I'm afraid. I took some tool impressions from the door where they used a screwdriver to prise open the back door, but unless we recover it, this isn't going any-where. Sorry.'

'Don't sweat it. You tried.'

'I don't understand why you were so keen to meet me here.'

Bryan pats the shoulder of a man in a navy jumper with ND Security on it sitting at a desk in front of a row of screens.

'My friend Saeed here has got a bit of CCTV I'd like you to take a look at. Take it away, Saeed.'

'We caught him on all three cameras we have operating in the building. I've knitted the footage into one for you.' He turns his screen towards us and taps his keyboard with a triumphant flourish. 'This camera is mounted on the corner of the building. You can just see here is the top of his head as he passes under it.'

'Do you think he knew the camera was there?'

'Almost certainly. The second camera covers the corridor at the back of the building. As you can see, he's got his hood pulled right down. He knows he's being filmed. Then the final camera is behind the Land Rovers and you can see him duck-ing down in front of the bonnets where he then removes the lights out of sight. Then he goes out the same way he came in. Cool as you like.'

'Can you play it again?' says Bryan.

We study the slight figure in the baggy black tracksuit, his face is obscured by his hood, gym bag slung over his shoulder in silence as he strides through the building with the confi-dence of someone who already knows they've got away with it. Just as he leaves, he can't help himself. He turns back. Head still bowed, he gives the camera the finger.

'Freeze it there,' says Bryan.

He turns to me.

'I know it's not a church roof, but does he remind you of anyone, Dymond?'

9

Penny is standing in her kitchen, leaning against the sink, apology written all over her face.

'I didn't know what to do.'

'It's okay, I was only up at Heale Cross. The showroom got done over and I'm on a meal break now. Why are you whispering?'

'He wouldn't leave.'

'Who wouldn't?'

'I don't know. He wouldn't give his name. Just said he knew your dad and he wanted to see you. I told him you were working, but he said he'd wait. I didn't know how long you'd be so I put him in my living room.' She glances at the closed door. 'I felt a bit sorry for him so I made him a cup of tea.'

Opening the door silently, I peer into the room and glimpse the profile of a man I haven't seen in twenty years. I quickly close the door again.

'It's Howard.'

'Who?'

'A friend of my dad's. They owned a boat called *The Aloysia* together. I guess he still owns her.'

'How do you know that?'

'Liam saw her in the harbour yesterday. Can you tell him I've been called to a job in Exeter and I won't be back tonight? I don't want to see him.'

'Why not?'

'Because just after dad went missing, he took *The Aloysia* without telling us.'

'And now he's brought it back.'

'It's more complicated than that.'

'What do you mean?'

I hesitate. It's been so long since I thought of her, of dad, of us, but Penny isn't going to let up and finally I relent.

'It was on *The Aloysia* that I finally became a daughter. She brought Dad and I together. I wasn't much interested in the sea at first, but in calmer waters Dad would cut the engine and school me and I became fascinated by how the earth and moon pushed and pulled at the oceans. Nothing was ever said, but when he asked me to recount the wind conditions or the size of the swell, I could see it in his eyes. I was his little girl. It was the best feeling in the world and it was all down to *The Aloysia*. So when Howard Trevelyan raised her anchor and sailed her out of Bidecombe after the inquest, he stole much more than a boat from me.'

'I get it, Al,' says Penny softly. 'But maybe he had good reason to leave. At least hear him out.'

'No.'

'Why do you always have to be so difficult?' she says, shaking her head.

'I wasn't aware that I was. Howard was like an uncle to me but he left without saying a word. He abandoned Bernadette and me when we needed him most. I didn't ask him to come here and I don't owe him anything.'

'I get that too, but maybe he wants to say sorry.'

'I'm not interested.'

'Christ, you're stubborn. He's obviously made the effort to find out where you live and to come and see you, why don't you at least listen to what he has to say?'

'Why the hell should I?'

'Because he's an old man and it probably took a lot of guts to come here after all this time. Honestly, Ally, sometimes you can be so unforgiving.'

'What? Where's that come from?' I have the strangest impression we're not just talking about Howard.

'Just speak to him. He won't go until you do and I'd like my living room back.'

'Okay, okay, I will, but only to please you.'

'Good.' She opens the back door. 'I'll leave you to it then.'

'Penny, wait a moment.'

'What is it?'

'Are you sure nothing's up?'

'What? No, why should it be?'

'You just seem a little off with me.'

She pauses as if she's going to say something before breaking into an apologetic smile.

'Do I? Sorry. I'm just really busy that's all.'

'That's okay. As long as you're all right. I take it you sorted out that pesky shower curtain then?'

She frowns. 'What shower curtain?'

'The one you couldn't fix in time to join the call with Megan.'

'Oh yes, that one, yes, thanks, all sorted now. I've really got to get on.' She jerks her head towards the living-room door. 'Now go in there and play nice.'

I let her leave. Now is not the time to ask Penny why she needs to make up lies about shower curtains.

'Hello, Howard.'

The man I used to call uncle twists round in his seat and presses his cracked lips into a smile that says he has no idea the pain he has caused Bernadette and me.

'Look at you, Squid.'

Squid. His pet name for me because I was Davy's kid and my hair was just as wild as his. I want to tell him he forfeited the right to use it the moment he sailed out of Bidecombe Harbour without telling anyone, but I don't. I just want this over and done with and, anyway, I promised Penny I'd be nice.

Howard shuffles to the edge of the sofa and uses his hands to push himself into a standing position. Unable to fully straighten himself, he remains hunched. He's grown old. Lucky him.

'All grown up now, but I'd have recognised you anywhere. That hair. Those eyes.'

I ignore his outstretched arms. I'm in no mood for a hug. A hug suggests forgiveness where there isn't any.

'What do you want, Howard?'

His arms drop to his side. 'Can we talk?'

I sense he won't leave until he's said what he's come to say. 'I don't have long. I'm on a break.'

'Oh? What do you do?' Lowering himself back down, his knees give way at the last moment and he rolls back into the sofa. He pats the space next to him, but I opt for the armchair opposite. There's a flash of disappointment in his eyes, a sense that this is going to be harder than he thought. Too right it is. 'Don't tell me you're Bidecombe's harbourmaster?'

'No. I'm not.'

'You wanted to be once upon a time,' he says, ignoring my curtness. 'Just like your old dad. I remember how you'd follow him around on the quay, hanging on his every word. Davy's little shadow. Wherever he was, you weren't far away. I'd come back down and find the two of you crabbing off the quay wall. He'd be telling you all about the sea and you'd lap it all up. You couldn't get enough of it. You were like a walking encyclopaedia.'

The memory prompts a reluctant smile. I can also see Dad sitting next to me on the harbour wall, our legs dangling over the edge, raw bacon attached to a fishing line to draw the crabs as he shared some nautical nugget about how the Channel has the second highest tidal range in the world or how tide tables repeat themselves every eighteen years or so. I remember it all. But after he disappeared, Bernadette never spoke about him and every time I brought him up, she found a reason to talk about something else, her pain too great. It meant my memories of Dad went unvoiced, shunted to the back of my mind until I could barely recall them at all, but that doesn't mean I want to hear them from Howard.

'Fat lot of good it did me.' I shrug. 'I became a police crime scene investigator.'

'Really? That sounds impressive,' he says. 'I imagine the criminals of Bidecombe must quake in their boots when they see you coming.'

'Not really.'

'The lovely lady at reception said you had a daughter too.'

For Christ's sake, what the hell is Penny doing telling him that? The less this man knows about my life, the less chance he has to wheedle his way back in, if that's the game he's playing.

'Er . . . yes. I do.'

'I reckon your old dad would have loved that. A grand-child.'

He would have done, but he never lived to see Megan and I stopped having those 'what could have been' thoughts years ago.

'Why are you even here, Howard?'

'I just wanted to see how you were getting on, Squid, that's all.'

'Why now? It's been over twenty years.'

'I know, but I've thought about you a lot. I've missed you.'

'Well, you could have come and seen us anytime. We haven't gone anywhere. You abandoned us, remember?'

'Us?'

'Yes.'

'Bernadette is still around then.' His smile wavers a fraction long enough for me to pick up that Bernadette's continued existence isn't necessarily the news he was hoping for. 'And abandoned? I-I didn't realise my leaving had such an impact on you. I was just another mate of your dad's.'

'You were more than that and you know it. You were like an uncle to me. I lost two people that day. Dad and then you. And you took *The Aloysia*. You knew how much she meant to me.' I let that sit for a few moments. He doesn't say anything. What is there to say? 'Anyway, now you've seen how I'm getting on, I'll say goodbye.'

I go to get up, but Howard lifts a hand to stop me.

'Wait, Squid, please. Don't leave. Not like this.'

'That's a bit rich, coming from you.'

'I know and you've every right to be angry with me. I did a terrible thing, taking *The Aloysia* and leaving you and your mum like that. I'm sorry. I should have told you I was going, said goodbye properly, instead of just taking off like I did.' He looks down at his calloused hands. 'If I could change things I would.'

Something inside me gives. He's right. I am angry, but now in the presence of an old man's regret, my anger ebbs away.

'Look, Howard, I don't know what you want me to say. It was all so long ago. Bernadette and I have moved on. If you want forgiveness, then . . . then I forgive you.'

'Thank you,' he replies, genuinely moved. 'That means a lot. I just wanted to try and make things right. Your dad was my best mate.'

'I know, but honestly it doesn't matter anymore.'

He looks up at me. 'It does to me and I know I'm decades too late, but at least let me try and make things up to you.'

'But how?'

He leans over and it's then that I notice a white plastic bag at his feet. He picks it up and hands it to me. It's so light that at first I think it's full of scrunched-up paper until I open it and a huge ball of crumpled twenty-pound notes spills out.

10

It's forty-eight hours since Kieran's body was discovered at Devil's Cauldron and when I walk into the briefing room, I'm met by a wall of excited chatter, the kind that tells me there's been a breakthrough – a big one. Either someone has been arrested or is about to be.

I was surprised to receive Harriet's text early this morning, asking me to come to HQ. There's no official reason for me to attend the latest briefing on Kieran but since the Slaughterhouse Farm murder Harriet's increasingly taken me into her confidence. I guess she still feels like an outsider. Join the club.

Among those gathered are DS Henry Whiteley and DC Juliette Hollis and who I now know is DC Norm Grundig, who is just the kind of straight-talking, experienced detective MI needs. MI's Crime Scene Manager Jim Dixon is also there. If he's seen me, he's chosen to ignore me which suits me just fine.

Everyone assembled, Harriet makes her entrance, sweeping into the room, nodding into the mobile attached to her ear, reminding us that she also has people she must answer to.

'Yes, yes, of course, I'll let you know, sir.' She rings off, switching her attention to those gathered. 'Thank you, everyone, for coming in at such short notice. I know some of you have had to drop everything to be here, but we've had a rather dramatic, and potentially very positive, development in the Kieran Deveney murder. In fact, spoiler alert. We may even have our killer.' She pauses while several people trade their surprise. 'I know right, but I'll let DS Whiteley fill you in.'

Henry steps forward as Harriet begins furiously texting on her phone.

'Put us out of our misery then, Henry,' says Norm. 'Who is it?'

'So,' Henry pauses for effect. Taking a leaf out of Alex the pathologist's playbook, he'd obviously planned to work up to some kind of big reveal, but hadn't counted on Harriet's impatience.

'Get on with it, Henry. We haven't got all day,' she says without looking up from her phone.

'Okay,' he reluctantly concedes. 'It's Dove Sunrise.'

'What? The New Age dweller?' Norm holds his fingers up in an inverted V sign. 'So much for peace and love, man. Can't wait to hear this one.'

'It's early days,' says Henry over the snickers, 'but we got a call from one of the detectives from Liars Island this morning. There's a small team still out there doing some follow-up interviews after yesterday's briefing about Kieran's behaviour towards women. One of them was interviewing Dove, formerly known as Stacy Pratt, and—'

'She's the one whose sister died in a car crash, right?' interjects Harriet, still texting.

'Correct. Anyway, halfway through the interview, Dove breaks down in tears and says she killed Kieran.'

'She actually confessed to murder?' Norm is right to be astonished. In our world, offenders never cough to a crime even when they're caught red-handed.

Harriet puts her phone down on the table she is leaning against.

'Obviously, that's good news. Even better if she's telling the truth.'

'You think she's lying?'

'Not necessarily, but we still need to approach with caution. What I'd like to know is a, why confess to killing Kieran when you're not even a suspect? And b, why confess now, three days after you supposedly killed him?'

'Guilt. Maybe she couldn't take it any longer, knowing what she'd done,' says Juliette.

'Silly girl' says Norm. 'She should have done what everyone else does. Lawyer up and keep her gob shut. She'd probably have got away with it.'

'Well, lucky for us she didn't,' says Harriet. 'But let's start at the beginning. Henry, take us through Dove's version of events.'

'About three weeks ago, when her um . . . partner Forrest went to the mainland, Dove decided to go to the pub with a few of the others from Grannus House. Ben Dawson, Kieran, Ash and Rose Griffiths, of course, were also there. The other commune members left early, but Dove stayed on until closing just before 11pm. Then she and Kieran left together, both the worse for wear for drink. Kieran offered to walk Dove home. About midway, they stopped. After chatting for a bit, they started kissing and ended up having sex.'

'What? Out in the open?'

'Yes.'

Harriet shudders. '*Ew*, as my kids would say. Is that a thing in the countryside? I can't think of anything worse. All that dirt. Was it consensual?'

'So she says.'

'Would Dove be able to show us exactly where on the island it happened?'

'No. She says she isn't sure. It was dark.'

'Convenient.'

'Anyway, afterwards Kieran took this as a green light that she was interested in him and started pestering her.'

'Clearly no respect for the handfasted,' says Harriet.

'Dove, for her part, insisted it was a drunken mistake and that she was happy with Forrest. Anyway, Kieran continued to harass her and threatened to tell Forrest so she decided to go and see him to ask him to leave her alone once and for all.'

'In the middle of the night?' says Harriet.

'Yes, so she wouldn't be seen. Anyway he made another play for her so she grabbed the nearest thing to hand, a rock, and hit him over the head with it. He went down and she ran home. She thought she'd just knocked him out. She'd no idea she'd killed him until his body was found later that morning.'

'She specifically said she hit him with a rock?'

'Yes, and it was just the once.'

'Right,' says Harriet. 'Apart from the fact she knows how Kieran died which I admit suggests some level of involvement, we need to prove she had physical contact with Kieran. DNA, in other words?'

Harriet looks at Jim.

'We've already sent the clothes she says she was wearing to the lab. Apparently, they were stuffed at the bottom of her wardrobe at Grannus House. It looks like they have blood on them. We won't know whose until we get the results back.'

'Thanks, Jim. Let Henry know as soon as they're in. Did anyone see Dove making her way towards the watersports centre in the early hours of Kieran's murder?'

'No,' continues Henry. 'The electricity generator goes off at 11pm. The whole island is in darkness. Plus, Dove says she didn't take the main track to the centre which would have taken her past The Barbary Inn and the church. Instead, she took a deer path that runs through some woods along the lower east side of the island.'

'What time did she leave Grannus House?'

'She doesn't remember. All she knows is that it was dark.'

'So why didn't Ben hear anything?'

'She says when she got to the watersports centre she threw stones up at Kieran's window so as not to disturb him. She didn't want anyone to know she was there. Kieran came downstairs and opened the door to her. She suggested they go for a walk.'

'And they went straight to Devil's Cauldron?'

'Yes.'

'Can anyone else corroborate her story that she and Kieran had had sex three weeks before his murder and that he was harassing her?'

'Not so far. Rose Griffiths wasn't there that night in the pub, but Ash Griffiths remembers Dove and Kieran leaving together. They seemed quite merry. Kieran said he'd walk Dove back to Grannus House which wasn't unusual. It's a good two miles and it was dark.'

'Ben was Kieran's closest friend. Did Kieran tell him he had sex with Dove?'

'No, he seemed shocked. He'd never even seen Kieran show any interest in Dove.'

'Did he know about these sexual assault allegations against his pal when they were at uni?'

'Yes, he said the girl only accused Kieran of assaulting her because her boyfriend found out she had sex with him.'

'What about this argument Ally's daughter's friend saw them having?'

'He couldn't recall it, but was adamant that Kieran would never act inappropriately with customers.'

'He sounds like a loyal friend,' says Harriet. 'Okay, so . . . we've currently only got Dove's word that she killed Kieran. Thoughts, people.'

The room becomes still, each of us fingertip-searching our minds for inroads into Dove's confession.

'Why keep her clothing?' Juliette throws the question out for the room to respond.

'She didn't intend to kill him,' says Henry. 'She thought she'd just knocked him unconscious and he'd come round.'

'Not many people survive a bloody great big hole in their head and why wasn't she concerned about the incoming tide?' says Harriet.

'She says she really wasn't thinking straight. She was upset and just wanted to get away. When she heard he'd died, she panicked and shoved her clothing in the bottom of her wardrobe.'

'Well, that explains why the body was found where it was, I suppose. Not a mistake after all.' Harriet glances at me. 'Nor was it deliberate.' She turns to Juliette. 'You interviewed Forrest Stream, the husband or partner or whatever, didn't you? What did you make of him?'

'He seemed genuinely horrified by Kieran's death. He didn't know him particularly well. What he'd seen of him, he liked. He described him as a friendly guy. Not his type but no real issues.'

'So Forrest had no idea Kieran had got off with his missus then?'

'If he did, he kept it to himself.'

'He also told the detectives that interviewed him again today that he didn't notice anything unusual about Dove's behaviour,' says Henry. 'They went to bed at 11pm just before the lights were turned off and he woke up the next morning at around 7.30 to find Dove sleeping next to him, her usual cheery self.'

'Okay, so let's see what we've got so far,' says Harriet. 'Number one: Dove appears to have a clear motive for killing Kieran. He was threatening to tell Forrest that she'd been unfaithful after they had drunken sex in a field. Two, we know that Kieran might have had form for sexual assault,' she looks at me again, 'along with more recent reports of an overtly flirtatious nature. Three: Dove knows exactly how Kieran was killed, right down to the number of blows to the head, even though this information hasn't been publicly released. Four: clothing belonging to Dove was found stashed at Grannus House with blood on it which potentially belongs to Kieran.'

Norm leans back in his chair, hands behind his head. 'Sounds like a stonebonker to me, boss.'

Henry frowns. 'A what?'

Norm sighs.

'A dead cert.'

CRIME SCENE EXAMINATION REPORT INVOLVING DOVE FROM THE FATAL CRASH

<u>CSI</u>: Matt Birch
<u>OIC</u>: Traffic Officer Ava Best
<u>DIVISION</u>: Solihull South, West Midlands Police
<u>LOCATION</u>: A566 three miles from town centre
<u>EXAMINATION COMMENCED</u>: 4.00am, 7 Nov 2013

EXAMINATION NOTES

Fatal collision on bend on the A566. Head-on collision between a Golf GTI and a Ford Escort. Two fatalities. Both drivers of the vehicles pronounced dead at the scene. Female survivor – sister of the driver of the Golf GTI – conveyed to hospital.

Examination, as directed by TO Best

EVIDENCE COLLECTED

Video footage of the scene: REF SR1
Photographs of:

- deceased persons in situ REF 2–16
- Vehicle wreckage. Exterior/interior where possible REF 17–25
- View of bend from both directions REF 26–35

Forensic evidence gathered:

- Glass REF 36–40
- Interior tapings REF 41–45

11

My phone buzzes just as I'm leaving the briefing room. It's HR returning my call. After seeing Jim on the phone at yesterday's briefing, I took Liam's advice and called them for an update on my transfer. I've waited long enough.

'Hey, Al. It's Lou Reed, from HR here. Not that Lou Reed, obvs.' She giggles, her cheerful familiarity bordering on abnormal because I'm pretty sure I've never met any version of Lou Reed. 'Got ya message about your transfer back to MI.'

'Any news?'

'Hey, listen, right, for some reason, it's all a bit weird, we don't seem to be able to find your file at the moment.'

'What do you mean you can't find it?'

'Mad right? Anyways, my lovely, we're not too sure where it is right now. Obviously, we can't give you a date until we can be certain everything is signed off and without the file we don't know.'

'Okay. So where is it?'

Lou blows down the receiver like I've asked her to explain the theory of relativity.

'That's what we'd like to know. We *think* Mel was dealing

with it, but she went off sick last Friday. Shingles. I thought only your granny could catch that. Anyway, it's not good. She's likely to be off a while, but I'll speak to her when she gets back.'

'What am I meant to do until then?'

'Mmm. Not sure. Good question. We could have another look for it. It must be somewhere. I bet it's in her to-do pile, you know how it is.'

'Not really.'

Lou laughs although I'm not aware I've said anything funny.

'Anyhoo, I'll be in touch, my lovely, just as soon as we track it down.'

She rings off. Mel only went off sick a few days ago, that doesn't account for the last eight weeks. Harriet has made it clear she wants me back as soon as possible. This should have gone through on the nod. There's only one reason I can think of why it hasn't.

Jim Dixon is halfway down the stairs when I catch up with him.

'Jim, can I have a word?'

He looks up at me. 'Can it wait? I'm busy.'

'No, it can't. Who were you on the phone to yesterday during the break in the briefing?'

'What's that got to do with anything?'

'I'm fairly certain you were talking about me.'

'Why would I be talking about you?'

'Have you said something to HR?'

'About what?'

'About why you don't want me back on MI.'

A couple of uniformed officers pass Jim on the stairs. Sensing a row brewing, they linger to relish the drama until a glare from Jim sends them on their way.

'I've no idea what you're talking about.'

'My transfer papers appear to have gone missing.'

'And you think it's me?' He laughs. 'You're paranoid.'

'I don't know what to think, but you've never hidden the fact you don't want me around, and Stride was a mate of yours.'

'Stride was bent. He overstepped the mark and he paid for it. I've no more time for corrupt cops than you have.'

'That doesn't answer my question, Jim. Have you had something to do with my file going missing?'

'I don't have that kind of clout,' he says, looking me directly in the eye.

'Then who is it?'

'I don't know, but it sounds like someone is having second thoughts about you. I mean you're already on a final warning over what happened to your daughter last year and rumour has it that you slept with a suspect. You might have Harriet fooled, but let's be honest, Ally, you're a total liability.'

'A liability that has pretty much solved two fucking murders in the last year.'

He shrugs.

'Then I've no idea, but it isn't just about pieces of paper, is it?'

'What's that supposed to mean?'

'You really need me to spell it out?' He takes several steps towards me and leans in, his eyes hard with loathing. 'You're not a team player. You never were. Everyone knows it. I need people I can trust and I don't trust you. No one does. Go back to your shed break-ins, Ally. You don't belong on MI.'

Is that how everyone feels about me? That I'm some kind of loose cannon, that I'm unreliable, that people can't depend on me? But by the time I recover myself, Jim Dixon has walked away.

12

Outside Bernadette's house, I take my usual few seconds to brace myself before talking to my mother. She isn't going to like what I'm about to tell her. She never had any time for Howard before Dad died and is likely to have even less now. Lazy, feckless and untrustworthy were the words that would pepper her conversations about him with Dad. His flaws never bothered me. It meant he bailed on our potting trips, often at the last minute and often because of some lady he was pursuing, leaving Dad and me on our own which suited us both.

'He doesn't get the sea like you and I do, Ally. Besides, it's more fun when it's just the two of us,' Dad would say, alongside a conspiratorial wink.

I ring her doorbell and wait. She always takes her time to answer, but several minutes pass and she still hasn't come to the door. As I step back to check for signs she's in, a high-pitched screech reaches me from the back garden. Hurtling through the side gate, I find Bernadette at the bottom of the lawn trying to batter a huge ginger tom with a broom.

'Shoo. You horrible creature. Get away from my lawn.'

Arched up against the fence, the cat appears to momentarily fancy its chances against my mother before wisely deciding to call it quits. Leaping effortlessly to the top of the fence, it disappears over the other side.

'Everything all right?' I ask.

'It would be if that vile beast learnt to do its business elsewhere. Look at all those horrible yellow patches.' She points to several spots of faded turf in despair.

'Is there anything you can do to stop it?' I ask, fully aware that cats urinating in gardens is outside my sphere of knowledge and, if I'm honest, my interest.

'Pray it gets run over.' Yep, that's the Bernadette I've come to know and mostly love. 'Anyway, what are you doing here?'

'Sorry to turn up unannounced, but I need to talk to you.'

She rests the broom against a garden chair.

'What is it? Is it Megan?'

'No. She's fine. She's with Julian. Can we go inside? You probably need to be sitting down to hear this.'

She leads me through her French windows into her house where there's little evidence of the owner's timeline. Were there ever photos of Dad on her mantelpiece? I can't remember but there are none now. There's none of me either. No surprises there. The disgrace of a teenage pregnancy saw to that although the result of that pregnancy, Megan, has pride of place above her fireplace and in her heart. I'll settle for that.

'So, what's this about?'

Bernadette doesn't sit down and neither do I. Bernadette and I have never been close. I don't know what she was expecting when she decided to adopt a child, but it turns out it wasn't me. Dad was our buffer. Ever the peacemaker, he'd re-frame her criticism as her way of expressing love for me. 'She only wants the best for you, Ally,' he'd say. But after he died, there was no one to soften her words or build me back up and Bernadette and I grew even further apart.

'Uncle Howard is back in Bidecombe.'

'Howard?' She frowns, taking a moment to reacquaint herself with a name she hasn't heard in over twenty years. 'He's here?' The idea that Howard is less than a mile from where she's standing appals her.

'Yes.'

Her hand reaches out for the mantelpiece to steady herself. 'Are you sure?'

'He came to Seven Hills yesterday. He wouldn't leave until I spoke to him.'

'So you've seen him? Well, I hope you called the police,' she says, restoring herself. 'He stole your dad's boat.'

'Yes, I know. That's why he's back. He wants to give you Dad's share of *The Aloysia*.'

I open the bag of money in my hand. Bernadette peers in before turning her head away as if it's just released a terrible stench.

'What makes you think I'd be interested in accepting anything from Howard Trevelyan?'

'I know, but I promised him I'd try.'

'You're wasting your time. I don't want anything from that man.'

A silence fills the room as I search for another way in. It's her money after all.

'He's changed, Bernadette. He's genuinely sorry. Maybe it would be a good thing for the two of you to meet. It's been a long time and . . . it might be a nice opportunity for the two of you to share your memories about Dad.'

She looks at me in utter horror. 'What on earth are you talking about?'

'It's just that we never really . . . reminisce about Dad.' She looks at me, ready to pounce the moment I stray into unacceptable territory. I take my time, finding the right words. 'You know, there were lots of good times before . . . it happened, probably even more before I came along. This might be a chance for you to talk to someone who was there, who knew him since he was a boy and loved him like you did.'

'Loved him?' She scoffs. 'Don't be so ridiculous. If Howard had loved your dad, he wouldn't have done the things he did.'

'I know he was unreliable, but can't we just move on from that? After all, it's not Howard's fault Dad died. It was an accident.'

She looks at me with a face full of scorn. 'Well, that just goes to show how much you know, doesn't it?'

'What?'

'Nothing.'

But it's too late. In her determination to win our latest bout of conversational sparring, she has let something slip.

'It's clearly not nothing. What is it?'

'You've upset me with all your talk about that horrible man,' she says, shifting the blame to me. 'Forget I ever said anything.'

'No, I won't. Are you saying Dad's death wasn't an accident and Howard had something to do with it? He wasn't even there that day. What's going on, Bernadette?'

She presses her lips together and fixes me with a defiant stare, but I'm not giving up.

'I'm not leaving until you tell me.'

Given that I rarely spend more than a few minutes at her house, the idea that I could be there indefinitely is enough to trigger action. Just not the kind I was expecting. She turns and exits the room. This has never happened before. Bernadette always has the last word. Maybe I should go after her and apologise for suggesting she meet Howard, however mundane a transgression that feels like. Or maybe I should just leave. Let her cool off. Pretend the conversation never took place. Bernadette and I are good at that. I'm still deliberating what to do when she returns and thrusts a piece of paper, yellowed with age, at me with an unmistakable air of triumph.

'Read it.'

It's from the Harbour Authority, Dad's employer, and addressed to him. It's dated a month before he disappeared and my life changed forever.

I scan the words, briefing myself on what it's about before tackling the detail, but I can't believe what I'm reading. I go through it again, this time word by word, trying to comprehend its contents, but still unable to marry them with the man I knew as my dad.

'Oh my God.' I look up at Bernadette. 'Dad was smuggling.'

Bernadette snatches the letter back.

'Of course he wasn't. Howard was.'

'Howard?'

'He had an arrangement with someone from France. They'd leave cigarettes in one of the lobster pots at sea for him. He'd then sell them in the pubs around North Devon.'

'Did Dad know about this?'

'No, Howard would take the boat out on his own, but someone tipped the Harbour Authority off and they searched *The Aloysia* and found the cigarettes.'

'Didn't Dad tell him it was nothing to do with him?'

'It wasn't as simple as that. Your dad owned half *The Aloysia*, he was liable for her so the authority hauled him in. He was devastated that Howard could do this to him.'

'Did the Harbour Authority go to the police with this?'

'No. They had a lot of time for your dad. I think deep down they knew he was innocent, but they couldn't ignore what they found so they decided to sort it out in-house, quietly, through a disciplinary. Your dad was due to go up in front of the disciplinary board the day after he died.'

'What would have happened to him?'

'He was certain he would lose his job, even though he hadn't done anything wrong. He couldn't face that. His job was his life. It meant everything to him. He couldn't imagine himself doing anything else. Howard and his greed took that away from him. He . . . he just couldn't handle it.' She looks out of the French windows. 'He . . . he couldn't see any way out of it, I suppose.'

'What do you mean? What are you saying?'

Bernadette gives me a look I've never seen before and it takes me a moment to work it out. Pity. She feels pity for me.

'I think you know what I'm saying, Aloysia.'

'No, no.' I shake my head to emphasise the impossibility of what she's implying. 'That can't be right.'

For once I want her to argue with me, to tell me I'm wrong, to call me a fool, but she doesn't say a word.

'No, please no.'

Bernadette looks at me. For a moment, I think she's going to do what she always does, move the topic to something mundane, something trite: the weather, the potholes, the tourists, anything but the truth because truth means pain, but she doesn't.

'Aloysia, your dad's death wasn't an accident. It was suicide.'

13

Dad took his own life. Those five words play on repeat in my mind as I drive back to Seven Hills. All these years I thought it was an accident. Something he couldn't help. Hell, if I believed in fate and predetermination, I could even tell myself, it was always going to happen. A tragic destiny he had no control over. Nothing could have prevented it. It was written in the stars. Fuck that. It wasn't written anywhere. Dad decided his own fate. He chose to leave me. So much for being a super dad.

It was our own little private joke. One day on *The Aloysia*, we hauled up a pot and in it was a seahorse, visibly pregnant. When I referred to her as a *she*, Dad corrected me and told me it's the male seahorse who rear their young, which is why they are known as the super dads of the sea to which I replied he was my super dad. He loved it. He'd joked that he drew the line at physically carrying me, his belly reserved for pasties and pints, but he would stay by my side for as long as I needed him, but he didn't. He left me. By choice.

My car comes to a halt outside my cabin where the low roar of an aging engine is replaced by the sound of my mobile: someone is trying to call me. I ignore it, my bandwidth too full of the revelation that twenty years of grief over my father have been shaped by lies and betrayal. But what good will it do to wallow in self-pity, to trawl back over Dad's every word, his every look, every interaction in search of answers? Now I know why Bernadette never wanted to talk about him. Maybe I should erase him from my thoughts too because he doesn't deserve to be there. My phone goes again. Whoever it is is keen to get hold of me which means it's probably work. I fish my phone out of my jacket pocket. It's Harriet.

'What's going on?'

'What do you mean?' For a moment I think she's referring to Dad before realising that isn't possible.

'The last thing I need on my team is my CSIs at each other's throats.'

'Oh, right. That.'

'Yes. That. The whole force has heard about it.'

'I rang HR. They've lost my transfer papers. I thought Jim might have had something to do with it. I thought maybe he'd put in a call to someone in HR, someone who owes him a favour.'

'Okay, but you do know it's entirely possible they've genuinely lost your file? This is HR we're talking about.'

'Yes, but Jim's never made any secret of the fact he doesn't want me on MI and the other day I got the feeling he was talking about me to someone on the phone.'

'Feeling? I thought you CSIs were only interested in evidence. It's not Jim's call to make, besides I doubt he has the influence to block your transfer. Favour or no favour. This would have to be at least DI level, maybe Superintendent, and it's not the Super because I cleared it with her and the other DIs are perfectly happy at the prospect of your return.'

'Maybe I'm imagining it then.' I lean back in the car seat. Movement in my rear-view mirror catches my eye. A young man in a blue suit is strolling up the path towards me, an iPad in his hand.

'I'll tell you what,' says Harriet. 'I'll give HR a call. They probably just need a rocket up their arse. We're going through another restructuring and I want you back on MI, working with me. You know what policing is like. Everyone has their own agenda. I need someone I can trust, someone who knows what they're doing. I want you back, Ally.'

'Okay. Thanks.' But I'm still distracted by the man who is holding his iPad up to take a photo of my cabin.

'Can I also suggest you stay out of Jim Dixon's way until then?'

'Will do.'

'By the way, we've had the results back from the lab. Kieran's blood is all over Dove's clothing.'

'That's pretty conclusive,' I say absently. The man is still taking photos.

'Yes, it is.'

'So you're backing her story that she went to the watersports centre to tell Kieran to back off after she'd had sex with him and ended up accidentally killing him?'

'It wouldn't be the first time.'

'So, what now?'

'The DNA, along with a full confession, means it's pretty much a full house. Just waiting for the go ahead from CPS to charge her and then it's on to the next case. No peace for us DIs. Nice when they land in your lap though. Thanks for your input, by the way.'

'Any time. I better go. There's someone wandering around the holiday park.'

By the time I get out of the car, the young man is already striding off into the distance. I jog down to the entrance, but I'm too late as he passes me in a white BMW. Through the reception window, Lottie, Penny's new assistant, is reading a book. I poke my head around the door.

'Penny around?'

She looks up and removes one of her earphones.

'No, she's gone out. Hospital appointment. She'll be back later.'

'Okay. Do you know who that guy in the suit was?'

'Which one?'

'The one with the iPad.'

'You mean Ethan?'

'You know him?'

'Yeah, Ethan Hyde, I was at school with his little sister.'

'Oh, okay, so do you know why he was here?'

Lottie shrugs. 'Dunno, Penny said he'd be dropping by some time.'

'But she didn't say why.'

'No, but he's an estate agent if that helps.'

'An estate agent? Is she putting Seven Hills on the market then?'

'Dunno. Guess so,' she says, plugging her earphone back in.

What the fuck? Penny is selling my home.

14

The soft dark sludge closes around my boot as if deliberately trying to prevent me reaching *The Aloysia* marooned at low tide near the mouth of Bidecombe Harbour. I ease my foot out with a satisfying squelch. It'll take more than a bit of silt to stop me. Howard and I have unfinished business.

It's dusk, but even in the gloom, *The Aloysia* is a sorry sight; her hull is chipped and her propeller dented. I begin to think how heartbroken Dad would be to see her now before reining myself in. He doesn't deserve my head space and in any case the boat's paintwork isn't my concern.

Howard must have spotted me coming because when I get within touching distance of the boat, he leans over her side, a beer in each hand.

'Want one?' He calls down to me.

'I'm not staying. I'm just here to return your money.' I hold the bag up for him to take. 'Bernadette wasn't interested.'

'I get it. She's still angry with me for taking *The Aloysia* and leaving you both. Thanks for trying. What about you?'

'I don't want it either.' I point towards the stern. 'Maybe you should use it to fix her propeller.'

He takes the bag from me.

'It's been like that forever, since your dad's time. You sure you don't want this? It's yours, by rights.'

'No. Bernadette called it blood money.'

Howard recoils at that accusation.

'That's a bit over the top, isn't it? But then she always was one for the drama, was Bernadette.'

'She's not far wrong though, is she?'

'What?'

'You heard me.'

I want him to admit it. I want him to tell me in his own words what he did to Dad.

'I've no idea what you're talking about, Squid,' he says, lobbing his beer bottle into an unseen bucket at his feet. Bernadette can add cowardice to the list of Howard's failings.

'It's Ally, and you know full well what I'm talking about, but let me jog your memory for you. You were using *The Aloysia* to smuggle fags.'

'What?' His face drops. He's been caught out. 'But how—?'

'Bernadette told me everything.'

'She knew?'

'Yes, she knew. Dad told her that someone tipped off the Harbour Authority and they searched the boat and found them stashed away.'

Howard dips out of sight, returning with another beer bottle in his hand.

'It was just a little sideline I had going.' He takes a swig and releases a loud gasp. 'Nothing serious.'

'Did Dad know what you were up to?' Bernadette has

already told me that he didn't, but she also told me Dad's death was an accident so I don't know what to believe.

'No,' he says adamantly. 'If I'd told Davy, he'd have put a stop to it.'

'But you must have known the Authority had raided *The Aloysia* and that Dad was facing disciplinary action?'

'Yes, I told him he'd just get a rap on the knuckles and be told not to do it again.'

'Dad didn't seem to think so. He was certain he was going to be sacked.'

'What? Over a few fags?'

'Why didn't you just tell the Authority Dad was innocent and that it was you who was smuggling cigarettes? Then maybe Dad wouldn't have done what he did.'

Howard looks away.

'It was complicated. I already had a criminal record, petty thieving when I was a lad. If I'd have said something, the police would have got involved and I could have been looking at a stretch. Davy knew that.'

'So you said nothing.'

Howard grips the side of the boat.

'Yes, I thought it'd go away. Wait . . . what do you mean do what he did?'

'I think you know exactly what I mean.'

'But . . . but the coroner said it was an accident.'

'Yes, they do that from time to time, or they did. It lessens the pain for some families, especially those who believe it to be sin.'

'So . . . so it wasn't an accident then?'

'No, Howard. It wasn't an accident. Dad took his own life . . .'

The harbour lights flicker on, illuminating his face. I don't need to finish the sentence because the ending is written in Howard's eyes. *Because of me.*

15

Cal Meeth, aka PC Bryan Rogers's numero uno suspect in the theft of Land Rover headlights at Wellacombe and the Heale Cross Land Rover Showroom, is standing behind the bar in The Albion, pretending to polish glasses. He's the last person I want to see, but The Albion is next to Bidecombe Harbour and by the time I'd left Howard and waded through the mud back to the slipway, Christ, I needed a drink.

Bryan's right. Cal hasn't changed a bit. He's still a skinny streak of piss, topped by a pasty complexion de rigueur among small-time criminals. A life of petty crime sure doesn't do much for your looks.

'Well, if it isn't Ally Dymond herself. I wondered how long it would be before I enjoyed the pleasure of your company.'

Although I never faced Meeth in court, we're well acquainted. Criminals make it their business to know the local plod including the CSIs. Meeth took it a step further by regularly taunting me for my failure to catch him whenever I had the misfortune to bump into him in town.

'Does Bill know you've got a criminal record as long as a chimpanzee's arm?' I reply, referring to the landlord.

'He knows, but some people believe in second chances. I'm straight now.'

'Is that a fact?'

'Actually, it is,' he says, looking me straight in the eye as if that proves he's telling the truth, but he can stick his pseu-do-psychology where plants don't grow.

'Anyway, what can I get you?'

'I'll have a Sam's Cider please.'

He fetches a bottle from the cooler behind him. Prising the top off, he tilts a glass and pours the cider in.

'You off duty then?'

'Looks like it.'

Jesus, this is what my life has become, making small talk with a local toerag.

'There you go.' He slides my drink across the bar. 'You guys busy at the moment?'

His question is as loaded as he intends it to be. We both know he's involved in the break-in at the Land Rover show-room and on Jake's patch at Wellacombe. Just like we both know I've got no proof. Otherwise we'd have arrested him by now.

'Not especially,' I say, taking a sip of cider.

'That's good. Great to hear crime is still very low around here. Makes us all sleep better at night.'

Fuck you, Cal Meeth. Once a gloating bastard, always a gloating bastard, but I refuse to rise to it. Just.

'Well, we wouldn't want anything to disturb your beauty sleep, would we? You need as much as you can get.'

'Meow,' he says. 'And I hear you have to rely on signed confessions these days to up your detection rates.'

'Well, you heard wrong then, didn't you?'

'So what's the story about that hippy chick and the lad out on Liars Island? Good bloke too. I heard she led him on.'

'Who the hell told you that?'

'Common knowledge.' Sadly, he's probably right. Twelve miles of water between Liars Island and Bidecombe isn't enough to dampen the local rumour mill, but Cal hasn't finished. 'See the problem with you women is you give off mixed signals.' Great, this is all I need: Cal Meeth explaining my own sex to me. 'We never know where we are with you. First you want it, then you don't want it. We guys are simple beasts. How are we meant to know the difference?'

I tell myself his time will come, but until then I've had enough of this idiot.

'Cal?'

'Yeah.'

'Shut the fuck up.'

Collecting my glass, I seek out an empty table in a darkened corner where several glugs of cider eventually soothe my irritation with the odious Cal Meeth, removing him from my thoughts and replacing him with Howard.

I left him on *The Aloysia* contemplating his role in my father's death. In the shimmering harbour lights, I thought I detected tears, but I had no comfort to offer him. He was complicit in my dad's suicide. He let Dad take the entire blame for his smuggling activities. Not that that excuses Dad. He could have stayed. He should have stayed. Christ, he had a fifteen-year-old daughter who adored him. Wasn't that enough?

I finish my drink, but wait until Cal has nipped out the back, before returning my empty glass to the bar. There's only so much misogyny I can handle in one evening, especially from a lowlife like him. As I turn to leave, my phone goes. It's Harriet again.

'Is this about my transfer?'

'No. Where are you?'

'The Albion in Bidecombe.'

'Great. Stay where you are. We'll be there in ten. There's been a development.'

16

Harriet looks approvingly at the corner of the pub I've tucked myself away in. 'Good, we won't be overheard here.'

She throws her coat over the back of the chair and sits down.

'You all right? You look like someone's pissed on your parade.'

'Long story. So, what brings you to the wilds of North Devon?'

After she'd rung off, I remembered that Harriet lives in Exeter which is a good seventy miles from Bidecombe, which means she must already have been in the area when she called me. The question is why.

'Let's wait for Henry,' she says, making herself comfortable.

DS Whiteley is at the bar ordering drinks but Cal can smell cops a mile off and has come over all coy. He pours the drinks at the other end of the bar, his back to the detective. Henry pays for his drinks and joins us.

'Sorry,' he says, looking at my empty glass. 'Did you want one?'

'No, thanks. So what's this all about?'

Harriet plants her drink on her beermat and waits for Henry to sit down.

'Okay. I can't believe I'm saying this but . . . someone else has confessed to killing Kieran Deveney.'

'You mean Dove had an accomplice?'

'No, I don't mean that. I wish I did. No, I mean someone else says they did it. Not Dove.'

'What? But how's that even possible? Dove gave you a full confession, including motive, means, opportunity. The full set. Plus you have Kieran's DNA on her clothing. Even the CPS wouldn't quibble over this one.'

'Tell me about it.'

'So who is it then?'

Harriet looks at me as if she can't quite believe what she's about to say.

'Only the fucking vicar of all people.'

'The vicar? What's he got to do with any of it? He's not been on the island five minutes.'

Harriet knocks back half of the wine in one go. She is one pissed-off DI. Unable to bring herself to carry on, she nudges Henry with her elbow.

'You fill her in, Henry.'

'Okay. So, around 4pm this afternoon, the Reverend Humphrey Bagshaw, who is the new vicar at St Nicholas Church on Liars Island caught the boat to the mainland, walked into Barnston Police Station and told the desk sergeant that he and he alone is responsible for the murder of Kieran Deveney.'

'You're kidding.'

'Wish we were. Turns out he's not so fucking reverend after all,' says Harriet grimly.

'Are you taking it seriously?'

I sense Henry is about to give me the party line about how all lines of inquiry need to be followed up but Harriet cuts him off.

'It's a load of crap, but the problem with shit is that you can't ignore it.'

'Why not? People confess to stuff they haven't done all the time.'

'Not ones who also know the murder weapon and how it was used.'

'He knows Kieran was killed with one blow to the head with a stone?'

'Yep.'

'Could someone have told him?' I glance over at Cal, who seemed to know more about Kieran's murder than he should. 'You know what people are like around here.'

'Well, if I find out someone from the team has leaked Kieran's cause of death, there'll be hell to pay, but I don't think so. Norm interviewed him the first time round and I've seen him in action. He's Tupperware, Norm. Totally leakproof.'

'So what's this guy – Bagshaw's – story?'

'The chair of the board of trustees, Hilton Deveney, is looking to start offering weddings at the church and Bagshaw got the job. He moved to Liars Island a few weeks ago after years of missionary work overseas.'

'So how did he go from arriving on the island to killing Kieran?'

Harriet leans back in her seat, arms folded. 'Tell her, Henry. You'll love this one.'

'A few days ago, he started hearing voices.'

Harriet gives me a knowing look. It wouldn't be the first time the 'voices in my head' defence has been used to reduce a murder charge to manslaughter on the grounds of diminished responsibility. The issue is whether Bagshaw would know that.

'He says it's something he's experienced before. Obviously, we're trying to check his medical records. Anyway, he tried to ignore them, but they wouldn't go away.'

'And what were these voices saying to him?'

'They told him Satan had followed him to the island and was waiting for him at Devil's Cauldron so he takes himself off down there, spots Kieran on the beach, assumes he's the dark lord and whacks him over the head with a stone,' says Harriet. 'Kieran hits the deck and Bagshaw believes he's saved humanity and goes home or some such bollocks.'

'I don't understand. Why would Kieran be randomly strolling around Devil's Cauldron in the early hours of the morning?'

'I'm not buying it either. Bagshaw is talking crap.'

'Apart from the fact he knows how Kieran died.'

'Apart from that.'

'But you said he'd heard voices before.'

'According to him, it started when he was a missionary in Africa. He went there after his divorce. Apparently, he had a nervous breakdown.'

'A breakdown is a long way from thinking the lad that runs a watersports centre is the Prince of Darkness.'

'Exactly.'

'So what happened after he killed Kieran?'

'It seems he just went home and carried on as if nothing had happened. He lives in the vestry attached to the back of the church,' says Henry.

As a CSI, my role in the case is officially over, but that doesn't stop my mind flagging the vestry is now a crime scene.

'Did anyone see him?'

'No.'

'So why give himself up now?'

'Good question. He says he woke up the next day with no memory of the night before. Even when Kieran's body was found, it didn't trigger anything. Then he started having flashbacks and that's when he realised what he'd done.'

'Perhaps he and Dove are in on it together. Dove killed Kieran and maybe Bagshaw is trying to get her off. Or the other way around.'

'Yes, that's pretty much the only thing that makes sense. We're trying to find a link between them to prove they're in cahoots. I'm sending Norm and Juliette back to the island tomorrow to try to get to the bottom of this, but my gut feeling is Bagshaw's a nutter.'

Henry winces. 'Not sure you can use that word anymore, ma'am.'

'Well, I just have. I'm telling you this Bagshaw bloke is a complete time waster.'

'What happens if you can't find a link between Dove and Bagshaw?'

Harriet looks at me. 'They both walk. Kieran's killer goes free.'

'If Bagshaw is lying, surely, he'll crack eventually.'

'Probably. They usually do, but he's standing firm at the moment. He keeps telling us that God told him to confess so he can be absolved of his sins.'

'God's a lot more forgiving than the criminal justice system. Does he realise he's looking at fifteen years inside?'

'We've told him that, but it doesn't faze him. So, in answer to your question, no, he isn't going to crack anytime soon.'

'So where does this leave the investigation into Dove?'

'Put this way, we were about to charge her until this idiot Bagshaw popped up.'

'So she's still the prime suspect.'

'Yes, but you know the deal, we have to dot the t's and cross the i's.'

'It's the other way around, ma'am.'

Harriet gives Henry a withering look. 'I know. Anyway, Ally, the reason I'm here . . .'

'Hang on a minute, did you say Bagshaw was a vicar at the Bidecombe church?'

'Yes. Why?'

'I know him.'

'Never had you down as a god-squader.' Harriet glances at Henry. 'Yes, I know I'm not allowed to say that either.'

'It was only in a CSI capacity. His church got turned over. About eight years ago. A lot of expensive artefacts nicked, along with the lead from his roof.'

'Did they ever get anyone for it?'

'They did.'

'What's so funny? Why are you smiling?'

'The guy who burgled the Bidecombe church is called Cal Meeth.'

'So?' asks Henry.

I nod towards the wiry figure pulling on a beer pump. 'He just served you at the bar.'

Harriet twists around. 'Him? You're kidding.'

'No.'

'Maybe you should try a pub with fewer criminals.'

'If I did that, I'd never go out in Bidecombe.'

'So what did our friend here do?'

'He was caught red-handed removing lead from another church in Barnston and asked for five other offences to be taken into consideration, including Bidecombe church. He got two years. He disappeared after he came out and now he's back and, we think, up to his old tricks and stealing Land Rover headlights, only we can't get near him . . .'

'Sounds like we need a little chat with Cal. Thanks, Ally. Kills me how everyone knows everyone in Devon, but as far as I'm concerned, Bagshaw is still full of it but if, and it's a massive if, if Bagshaw killed Kieran, Alex reckons he would have had a fair amount of blood on him so he must have cleaned himself up somewhere, probably at the vestry.'

'What's Bagshaw's line on all this?'

'He says he was wearing a brown jacket, but he can't remember what he did with it.'

'I take it the voices in his head couldn't help him out?'

'Apparently not, so we need to find it asap. We need to get it examined, so we can prove Bagshaw's confession is weapons-grade bullshit once and for all. Then we can charge him with wasting police time and charge Dove Sunrise with Kieran's murder.'

'Makes sense,' I say. 'But why are you telling me all this?'

'Isn't it obvious? I need a CSI to examine the vestry and find Bagshaw's clothing. I want you to go to Liars Island.'

CRIME SCENE EXAMINATION REPORT RELATING TO REVEREND HUMPHREY BAGSHAW

<u>CSI</u>: Ally Dymond
<u>OIC</u>: PC Bryan Rogers
<u>DIVISION</u>: North Devon, Devon County Police
<u>LOCATION</u>: Bidecombe Methodist Church, Bidecombe
<u>EXAMINATION COMMENCED</u>: 10.00am, 5 June 2016

<u>EXAMINATION NOTES</u>
Point of entry via secured window in the vestry. Glass pane smashed to unlock window from inside. Religious artefacts removed from an unsecured cupboard in the vestry. Point of exit is the same as the point of entry. No other rooms entered.

Evidence of a quantity of lead removed from the roof. See diagram. Scuff marks on drainpipe. Partial footmark recovered.

<u>EVIDENCE COLLECTED</u>
- Glass REF 1 (collected from inside the church – see diagram)
- Footmark impression, below drainpipe, photographed and cast REF 2 (Submitted)

17

Penny looks up at the sound of the bell against the doorframe as I walk into the reception at Seven Hills. She tenses, her eyes widening at the sight of me. She thought I was on earlies.

I've been trying to get hold of her ever since I discovered the suited young man strolling around Seven Hills was an estate agent, but she wasn't picking up which means I still have no idea why she's selling up, or why she neglected to tell her closest friend.

She turns the music down and the Beatles' insistent 'all you need is love' fades to nothing.

'I was going to tell you,' she says.

'Were you? Or were you just going to wait until I came home and found a For Sale sign up?'

'I'm sorry. I just didn't get round to it. I've just had so much going on lately.'

'A text would have done it. Instead, I have to bump into some fourteen-year-old estate agent taking photos of my home.'

'What else can I say other than I messed up?'

'Why are you selling Seven Hills anyway?'

'Because my future lies with Will and the farm. I'm practically living there now anyway.'

'But you've only been seeing each other for five months.'

'It's long enough to know I want to be with him.'

Is this why she's been so distant towards me? After years of swearing off men, she didn't want to admit she'd fallen head of heels for a guy, but Penny knows I'm happy for her and Will. There must be more to it than that.

'He's not pushing you into this, is he, Penny? The farm's not in trouble, is it?'

'No, of course not. It's not about the money.'

'Then I don't get it. This place saved you. And me. Why would you give that up?'

'Because we all have to move on.'

'Well, then, I wouldn't be your friend, if I didn't tell you the truth. You're making a huge mistake.'

'See. This is why no one tells you anything,' she says, exasperated. 'If someone does something that doesn't fit your view of the world, you just go off on one.'

'I'm not going off on one at all. I'm just being honest. Seven Hills has been your refuge, and mine, I just think you're being hasty, that's all. I mean what's the rush?'

'There's no rush,' she says quickly, 'but I'm not getting any younger and Will is the one for me so why hang around? Some of us know when we're on to a good thing, you know?'

'Don't make this about Liam. He's with someone else now. It's over. Not that it ever started.'

'Why can't you just be happy for me? Megan is.'

'You told Megan? But not me.'

'Yes, I told you I was going to call her. She's having a miserable time with Julian.'

'I'm not sure I'd go that far. He's made a few comments about being on her iPhone all the time, that's all.'

'I think it's more than that.'

I shift uncomfortably at the thought of Megan sharing confidences with Penny rather than me.

'So why didn't she call me?'

'Maybe she felt she couldn't tell you.'

'What does that mean?'

'Well, you were so keen for her to go. She doesn't want to let you down.'

'She wanted to go too.'

'To please you. Maybe you should fetch her home before it gets any worse.'

'She's overreacting. It's kind of a default setting for teenagers. She needs to give it time. She can't keep running away as soon as something gets a bit difficult.'

'She's so unhappy, Ally. If you're busy I could go get her.'

'I thought you were snowed under here. Hold on. You didn't tell her she could come home, did you?'

Penny looks away.

'I might have mentioned it.'

'For God's sake, Penny. This parenting malarky is hard enough without you undermining me.'

'I'm not undermining you. I've known Megan almost all her life. I can tell when she's unhappy.'

'But she's my problem, not yours.'

'Really? What about all those times you were on night shift, all those emergency call-outs? It was okay for her to be my problem then. And . . .'

'And what?'

Penny looks at me levelly. 'And last year when she was attacked and lying in a coma. Where were you then?'

'That's not fair. I had to find him, Penny. He'd have come back for her sooner or later.'

'Fair or not, I was the one by her bedside, night and day.'

As always, I convert my hurt into defensiveness – the best form of attack.

'What are you saying? You're a better mother than I am. Okay. Fine. Yes, you are. You were there for her and I wasn't. Happy now?'

'No, of course not.' She pulls back. 'What I'm saying is that I care about Megan. I care about both of you.'

'Well, you don't care that much. You're selling up and leaving her.'

'That doesn't mean I don't want to be in her life.'

'Being in Megan's life doesn't give you the right to overrule me. I'm her mother. Believe it or not, I know what's best for her.'

'I don't know why you're making such a big deal out of it. I've only ever tried to support you, be a mum to Megan when you weren't around and now you're giving me a hard time about it.'

'You know what, Pen? I'm grateful for your help when Megan was little, but she's nearly sixteen now. I think I can take it from here. We don't need you anymore. Good luck with the sale.'

18

Under a dull grey sky, the cries of the seagulls chase me down the gorse-lined sheep track to Breakneck Point where they're swallowed up by the roar of the waves far below the cliffs.

It's only when I reach the bottom of the path that I see the bench is already occupied. He came. He said he would, but I wasn't sure. I've no right to ask anything of him, but reeling from my run-in with Penny, and desperate for a friendly voice, I called him. Surprised he even picked up, I realised I needed a reason so I told him I was having problems at work. It was his suggestion that we meet at Breakneck Point. I try not to read too much into this. He's with Tanya now. He's just being polite.

'You okay?' asks Liam.

I look across the dark waters of the Bristol Channel.

'Not really.'

'Is this about your transfer to MI?'

'Among other things.'

'Oh?'

I want to tell him about all of it: Dad's death, Penny selling Seven Hills, Megan hating her holiday with Julian, Cam and the boys, Harriet asking me to go to Liars Island. He'd know what to do, but I can't because he isn't in my life anymore. Not like he was. Not like he'll ever be again.

'You were right about someone trying to block my return to MI.'

'Really?'

'I thought it was Jim Dixon. He denies it, but something's going on, I'm sure of it and even if it isn't, do I really want to work with people who don't want me around?'

'I take it Jim said something to you.'

Jim's words stayed with me long after he'd uttered them. I've always seen myself as someone who has my colleagues' backs. Maybe I was wrong.

'He said I wasn't a team player and that I can't be trusted which is why no one wants me on MI. You know what it's like in the police, Liam, we all have to pull together, and if we don't then that's when the shit happens. Perhaps he's right. Perhaps I should stay on division.'

'Bullshit, Ally. You've only got Jim's word on this and, in any case, Harriet wants you back and she's the DI.'

'I'm not sure she does anymore.'

'Why? What happened?'

'She asked me to go out and do a crime scene examination on Liars Island.'

'I thought they had someone for Kieran's murder.'

'They do, a young girl called Dove, but now someone else has confessed to it and they're saying they did it alone.'

'Shit.'

'Exactly and all of it has hit the fan.'

'So who is this second person?'

'A vicar who hasn't been on the island two minutes. He heard voices telling him to do it, apparently.'

'That old chestnut.'

'Yeah, Harriet thinks it's rubbish too, but she's got to prove it. Until then the case is wide open.'

'So she wants you to go out there to prove he's a time waster? That's good, isn't it? It means you're back on MI as far as she's concerned.'

'I turned her down.'

'What? Why?'

'I gave her a load of bullshit reasons about having too much work on. She wasn't happy and she knew I was lying, but I couldn't tell her the truth.'

'Which is?'

'I can't go back, Liam.'

'Why not?'

'It's complicated. It's to do with my dad and stuff.'

'He drowned, didn't he? On a fishing trip.'

Of course Liam knows. A well-loved harbourmaster who went missing at sea is the kind of story that becomes folklore in a place like Bidecombe.

'Yes, he did although his body was never found.'

'So what's that got to do with Liars Island?'

'When I look out into the Channel, Liam, all I see is a gravesite. Why would I want to go back there?'

'But he didn't die on the island.'

'No, he didn't.'

'So what's the deal?'

I turn to look at him. I can't say it. I've never said it. The rare moments I've spoken about Dad, I absented myself from the story, unable to bear the pitying looks I knew it'd attract. But that was before I found out Dad's death wasn't an accident.

'Liars Island was the last place I saw my dad alive.'

'What?'

'I was there the day Dad went missing, waiting on the jetty for him to come back to collect me.'

There it is in Liam's eyes. The horror and then the pity.

'You were there? Why?'

'We were potting. Catching lobsters. Dad used to sell our catch to the local restaurants, including The Barbary Inn on the island.'

'So what happened that day? Why were you there alone?'

'We were out in *The Aloysia*, chatting about tides and currents like we often did, when Dad told me he was dropping me off on the island because there was a storm coming. I couldn't understand it. There wasn't a cloud in the sky. The water was like glass that day, but the weather can change in an instant so I didn't argue. He set me down on the jetty, told me he'd be back for me soon. I never saw him again. *The Aloysia* was found drifting, her engine cut. Dad's life jacket was on the deck, but there was no sign of him.'

'I can see why you don't want to go back.'

'I know it sounds crazy, but I've always blamed the island for his death. Nothing good happens on Liars Island.'

An image of Kieran's body lying in the mortuary, his head caved in, drifts to the front of my mind.

'It doesn't sound crazy at all,' says Liam. 'It sounds like a terrible accident. If you'd been on board, maybe you wouldn't be here either.'

'It wasn't an accident, Liam. Dad took his own life.'

'Suicide?'

'Yes.'

'I'm sorry. Do you . . . ?'

'. . . Know why?'

'You don't have to tell me if you don't want to.'

'It's okay. To be honest, I only found out a few days ago when Dad's friend Howard sailed back in on *The Aloysia*.'

'The boat I saw in the harbour?'

'Yes, Howard co-owned it with Dad. He tried to pay Bernadette Dad's share of the boat, but she refused. She called it blood money.'

'That's a bit strong.'

'Maybe, but she told me Howard was using *The Aloysia* to smuggle cigarettes without Dad's knowledge. Hardly the crime of the century, but Dad was harbourmaster so when the authorities found out, he was facing the sack.'

'How can Bernadette be so sure it was suicide if he was never found?'

'She told me that he took his life jacket off. It was found on the deck. Dad was a stickler for safety. He'd never have taken his off.'

'Surely, the coroner would have picked up on that.'

'Bernadette played the Catholic card. Taking your own life is a sin. I think the coroner decided she'd been through enough without the stigma of suicide hanging over her so he glossed over the life jacket and ruled misadventure.'

'And Bernadette kept this to herself all these years.'

'Yep. To protect herself. I don't think she could bear the shame of people knowing, that was more important to her than telling her daughter the truth.'

Which is exactly what I said to Bernadette when she finally told me what happened. Slamming the door behind me before she had time to respond.

Liam nods. 'But if it wasn't an accident then the island had nothing to do with your dad's death. You could go back. It might even be good for you.'

'Yes, I suppose so. I hadn't really thought of it like that, but it's too late now. I already turned Harriet down and she'll have found someone else by now. Let's hope she forgives me by the time my transfer papers come through,' I joke. 'Anyway, enough about me. What about you and Tanya?'

Liam smiles sheepishly. 'Still early days.'

'Well, I'm really pleased for you. I hope it works out for you. I really do. She seems nice and you deserve to be happy,' I say, drawing on all my reserves of sincerity. 'Anyway, I should go. I'm expecting a call from Megan,' I lie. 'Thanks for listening.'

'Anytime.'

I take the narrow path back up the hill towards Seven Hills.

'Ally?' Liam calls after me. 'I don't know what to say about your dad, but I do have some advice for you.'

'What's that?'

'You belong on MI so fuck Jim Dixon . . .' He grins and jerks his head in the direction of Liars Island. 'Go do your job.'

19

My stomach lurches as the police helicopter rises from the helipad and tips forward before banking sharply towards the Bristol Channel. Opposite me, headphones clamped over a clump of bright red hair, Jake grins and gives me the thumbs-up. We could have taken the boat, but time isn't on Harriet's side and she insisted we fly.

I called her as soon as I'd spoken to Liam at Breakneck Point expecting her to tell me she'd already found a replacement, but she told me she hadn't even bothered looking.

'I knew you wouldn't be able to resist it.' She laughed. She knows me better than I thought and she's right. If it had been anywhere else but Liars Island, I'd have said yes before she'd even asked the question. There's an undeniable buzz about being involved in a murder inquiry. Everyone has a role to play but it could be you that swings it from a cold case to a conviction. 'And I suppose you want to take someone with you?'

'I was thinking of Jake Harris. It'd be good experience for him.'

'Consider it done.'

A few minutes after take-off, Liars Island sharpens into view. A carpet of purple moor grass hemmed by fraying cliffs, it's difficult not to be beguiled by its beauty, but just as I'm succumbing to the island's charms, the sun dips behind a cloud, plunging the plateau into shadow, reminding me once more of its unpredictability. As I said to Liam, nothing good happens here. It may not be to blame for my dad's death, but the sooner I'm out of here the better.

I shake the thought as we reach the island's southern tip where the helicopter swoops down low past St Nicholas Church, our rotor blades level with the top of its square tower. Nestled on a hill of heather, its spire is the highest point on the island. St Nicholas: the patron saint of sailors, merchants and repentant thieves, apparently. Not sure how he feels about killers.

Below the church, at the bottom of the slope, lies a handful of greystone buildings huddled around the largest: The Barbary Inn. It doesn't look like it's changed. I can still picture Rose and me on the patch of grass in front of the pub; she playing Ring a Ring o' Roses with the tourists' children – she loved little kids – and me with my head in a tattered copy of *The Observer's Book of Sea and Seashore* I'd borrowed from the island's 'library', a large bookshelf that inhabited the corner of the pub. Happy times. Times when I was still young enough to believe life would stay the same forever.

As the helicopter descends, I glimpse the uneven track leading past the pub. It disappears abruptly, as if axed by an unseen hand, but I know where it goes. It goes down to the jetty where I last saw Dad alive, but I can't think about that now. I'm here to do my job. The past has no relevance to my present.

The helicopter settles on the island's makeshift helipad,

a grassy field contained by a drystone wall, fifty metres or so from the main buildings. The downdraft from the rotor blades batters the two people in dark suits, standing by the edge, DC Juliette Hollis and DC Norm Grundig, waiting for their ride out of here. I remember Harriet saying they'd return to re-interview the islanders following Bagshaw's confession. Judging by their grim expressions, it's not gone well.

The co-pilot jumps out amid the deafening 'chuff' of the blades. He opens the door for us and invites us to disembark. Keeping our heads bowed, we're guided to the edge of the field, assisted by the downdraft just as Juliette and Norm are ushered towards the helicopter.

'Talk about a tough crowd,' shouts Norm. 'Nobody saw anyone do anything.'

'So no one was able to shine any light on Bagshaw's confession then?' I shout back.

'Nope,' says Juliette. 'So far, we can't corroborate his story and we can't contradict it.'

'There's something weird going on here though,' says Norm. 'Can't put my finger on it, but we can't do anything more now. We'll be back tomorrow. 'Til then, it's down to you two. No pressure.' He grins. 'Bit of advice though.'

'What's that?' asks Jake.

'Don't trust any of them.'

'But they're witnesses, aren't they? Not suspects,' says Jake, alarmed by Norm's observations.

Norm leans into him, but Jake has a good foot on the detective so it looks like he's talking to his jacket pocket.

'Everyone's a suspect in my book, son. You'd do well to remember that.'

I smile – Norm is my kind of detective – and watch the two of them board the helicopter. Our cases unloaded, seconds later they take off, and everything falls silent, the sudden stillness an unsettling contrast to the deafening noise of a moment ago. A shiver rattles through me. Despite the sun, there's a chill in the air.

'So, what do you think Norm meant by everyone being a suspect?' asks Jake.

'No idea, but let's get this over and done with, shall we?'

We collect our cases and amble through the open gate and down a short incline towards the tiny hamlet of buildings. The season hasn't started, the only shop on the island is closed, but the pub remains open year round. Despite this, there's no sign of life.

I decline Jake's offer of an energy bar.

'Sure? I've got loads. My girlfriend Sophie packed them for me. If I don't eat regularly I get hangxiety.' He rips the top off and starts munching. 'So where is everyone?'

'At the moment, there's only five people on the island.'

'Creepy place,' he says, looking around. 'Soph says it's haunted.'

'Here and practically anywhere else in North Devon wanting to attract tourists.'

'The whole place looks abandoned. It reminds me of that film where the guy wakes up and everywhere is deserted and he can't work out where everyone's gone because they've all been killed by a virus. Wait, did you see that?'

'What?'

Jake fixes his eyes on the corner of a barn. 'Over there.'

'It'll be a sheep.'

'They have sheep here?'

'And cows.'

'You're probably right,' he says, dragging his gaze away. 'Anyway, we'll be gone soon enough. Soph and I have a table booked at the Sea Grill in Bidecombe this evening.'

'Special occasion?'

'It's our fifth anniversary from when we started going out.'

'Five years. That's impressive.'

'Yeah, I think she'd like me to pop the question, but I don't know. I mean she's the one and all that, but well, marriage sounds so grown up, doesn't it? Anyway, is it okay if I let her know I got here in one piece?'

'Sure,' I say, ignoring the pang of regret that there's no one at home awaiting a call from me. I'm still not talking to Penny and I couldn't get hold of Megan. I thought about calling Liam but I'm not sure of the rules of our friendship anymore.

Jake takes his phone out. 'No reception.'

'That's right. Harriet said something about the church being one of the few places you can get a signal. You go on up and give her a call. I'll go to the pub and see if I can find someone to open the vestry for us.'

'Cool. Thanks.'

Jake ambles up the hill towards the church. He's spooked enough as it is, which is why I didn't tell him that I saw something too, or that it had two legs, not four, or that they appeared to be wearing a red coat.

'Hello? Anyone here?'

I'm standing in the bar of The Barbary Inn, which has barely changed since I last saw it twenty years ago. Its walls and wooden ceiling a bubonic rash of red-and-white-striped life buoy rings, another reminder of the island's dark past. Most of these rings floated ashore empty, having never saved a soul.

As I wait for someone to appear, my attention wanders to the photos hanging on a pillar separating the bar from the darts area. There's one of Rose and me star-jumping off the end of the jetty. In another a group of pipe-smoking fishermen in chunky sweaters are gathered around the carcass of a basking shark. For a moment, I think of poor Maisie who died at sea. Another photo catches my eye. Its bleached road suggests it wasn't taken on Liars Island. A tattooed young man in cargo shorts grins into the camera. His arm is draped around a woman in a long skirt, glasses propped on her forehead fixing her long dark hair in place. Despite her smile, there's a sadness about her. I wonder what relevance the photo has to Liars Island when my eye reaches a young woman, glancing shyly up at the camera, reminding me of someone I once knew: Rose. So she left the island after all. And her purple scrubs tell me she became a nurse.

'Anyone around?' I shout again, but the high-vaulted ceiling sends my voice back unaccompanied so, lifting the bar top, I let myself into the narrow passageway in the back where, as children, Rose and I would sit on the beer crates stacked against the staircase, drinking industrial quantities of Coke and munching crisps while Dad chatted to Rose's parents out front.

I take the stairs leading to the private accommodation above the pub, pausing midway to listen out for signs of life.

I think I hear the sound of someone moving around in one of the rooms so I call out.

'Rose? Is that you?'

There's no reply, and I hesitate, wondering what to do, when there's a loud creak on the stairs behind me and I pivot round to be confronted by a roughly shaved man, the many rings in his ears competing with the tattoos on his neck for my attention. I've seen him before. He's a few years older, but he's definitely the man in the photo in the bar. Hand on the balustrade, he bounds up the stairs, inserting himself between me and the first-floor landing.

'What the hell do you think you're doing? This is private property.'

'There was no one downstairs in the pub. I did call out.'

'That doesn't give you the right to go snooping around our home without asking.'

'That really wasn't my intention,' I say, trying to defuse what feels like an overreaction. 'I was looking for Rose and I thought I heard someone.'

'Well, you heard wrong. Rose is out. Who are you anyway?'

'Police.'

'I thought you'd left and, anyway, aren't you meant to have a search warrant or something?'

His rudeness is beginning to rile me, but I haven't come here to make enemies.

'I'm not here to search the pub. I'm a CSI. I'm here with my colleague to examine the vestry at the church. I'm Ally Dymond, by the way.'

He ignores my outstretched hand.

'Like I told the detectives, the Reverend Bagshaw isn't here. He's on the mainland somewhere. He got the boat yesterday morning so you'll have to wait until he gets back and I don't know when that will be.'

He doesn't know Bagshaw has confessed to killing Kieran.

'We've already got permission to examine the church which is why we're here.'

'Okay, but what's the vestry got to do with anything? Kieran died on the beach and Dove lives at Grannus House. What's this got to do with Humphrey?'

'Just routine.' I smile.

He doesn't fall for it. From his demeanour I'd guess he's had his fair share of run-ins with the police.

'Really? So what do you want with Rose?'

'I was after the key to the vestry. I take it you must be her husband. Ash, is it?'

'That's right,' he says, unsettled at the thought that I know who he is. I have a sense he's wondering what else I know about him.

'Rose and I are childhood friends.'

'She never mentioned you.'

'It was a long time ago. So . . . could I have the key?'

'You don't need one. The church and the vestry aren't locked.'

'Sorry to have bothered you then. I'll get going. My colleague is waiting for me.'

I take the stairs back down to the bar. When I reach the bottom, I hear the noise again. It sounds like someone treading on a loose floorboard. Instinctively, I glance up to find

Ash hasn't moved. His eyes are firmly on me, but he must have heard it too. I wonder if I should say something before remembering I'm not a cop. I'm only here to examine the vestry, but that doesn't stop me wondering what the hell Ash Griffiths has got to hide.

20

Jake and I are not parishioners, we're CSIs, so when the door to the vestry, Reverend Bagshaw's converted living quarters, swings open neither of us moves.

Before us is a room, just large enough to hold a worn yellow two-seater sofa. On it, three cushions form a row of blue diamonds. On the coffee table is a stack of magazines, their edges flush. I'm not the only one to notice the place is immaculate.

'Wasn't the guy meant to have staggered back here covered in Kieran's blood?' says Jake after a few minutes.

'Apparently.'

'Maybe he spent the next day clearing up.'

'If he did, you'd think he'd ask himself a few searching questions like, oh I don't know, why is my home covered in blood, for instance. Let's take a closer look.'

I take out the UV light from its case and sweep it over the room.

'Blood doesn't fluoresce, right?'

'Yes. It doesn't reflect light so it just shows up as a black mark.' I try again.

'Nothing. Not a drop,' says Jake when I've finished.

'Smell the room.'

He looks at me like I'm joking. 'What?'

'Go on. Take a sniff.'

He leans into the room and inhales deeply. 'I can't smell anything. It's a bit musty maybe.'

'Exactly. No cleaning agents.'

He takes another deep breath and then looks at me as if I've just performed magic. 'Oh my God, you're right.'

'That's your first lesson over. Remember you need all your senses to be a CSI.'

'If there's no evidence of any blood, doesn't that mean Bagshaw's confession is complete crap?'

'That's what we're here to find out, young Jedi. At least the place is small. I'm guessing those doors lead to the kitchen and bathroom and he sleeps up there.' I point to a railed mezzanine overhanging the living room.

Already suited and booted, we start laying metal footplates on the ground floor so we don't contaminate the scene, placing numbered markers next to items of interest. We don't get beyond two.

'Is that normal?' says Jake. 'When I was training we did a mock-up murder scene and placed a dozen markers and the instructor said we still missed five.'

'There is no normal in crime scene examination. It's more a case of trying to explain what you have. Nothing can be as significant as something.'

Removing my camera from its case, I pass it to Jake.

'You sure?'

'No time like the present. Normally, major crime scenes are crawling with the great and the good of policing, most of whom just like to be in the thick of action. Here, it's just you and me in an empty vestry. We may as well make the most of it. As my old mentor Harry used to say to me, "The only way to learn this job, is to do this job".'

'Thanks,' says Jake, taking the camera. 'So what happened to Harry?'

'He retired to Portugal. He was a great mentor, as well as an all-round good bloke. Anyway, start with the living room and then move on to the kitchen and bathroom. We'll leave the mezzanine to last. Take your time with the filming. This isn't a Tarantino movie. I know we've already gone through the place with the markers, but sometimes you see things through a lens that you don't notice with the naked eye, so pop a marker next to it and zoom in on it. Obviously, we're most interested in blood spatters. Basically, if in doubt, film it. Overkill, not underkill.'

I spend a few moments watching Jake pan the camera slowly and deliberately around the living room, lingering over areas that catch his attention. He won't be winning Oscars any time soon, but he won't have missed anything either.

When he finishes, he moves into the bathroom which is my cue to take the stills. It doesn't take me long to photograph the markers and I'm beginning to agree with Harriet. The Reverend's confession is bullshit. Who knows why a vicar would confess to a crime he didn't commit but let's hope the good lord forgives him because the criminal justice system sure as hell won't if Harriet has her way.

I'm scanning the room for the umpteenth time when Jake's echoey voice reaches me from the bathroom.

'Ally? Can you come in here?'

Following the footplates to the small bathroom I find Jake kneeling in front of the sink, the doors of the cabinet beneath it wide open.

'What is it?'

He sits back on his haunches and points to a large black bin bag stuffed inside the cupboard. 'What do you think?'

'I think we should take a closer look. You videoed it, right?'

'Yeah.'

'Let me do some shots of the bag in situ and then we'll go in for a closer look.'

Jake stands back while I photograph the bag from all angles.

'Okay, I'm done. I want you to ease it out of its position.'

'Me?'

'You found it.' I smile. 'This is your shout. I know you've got gloves on, but try not to keep repositioning your hands on the plastic. Pinch it once between the tips of your fingers, if you can, and pull it gently towards you. I'll film it.'

Jake tugs the bag out until it slides onto the floor. The top is twisted, but not sealed. He looks at me and I nod back at him. He knows what to do. Carefully, he unfurls the black plastic and teases it apart, releasing a damp, earthy smell. Switching the camera off, I kneel beside him and we both peer inside.

'It looks like clothing,' he says. 'It could be his dirty washing.'

'Could be. Let me photograph the contents before we take them out. Then I'll film you taking them out, one at a time.'

The camera flash illuminates the inside of the bag, briefly exposing a pair of denim jeans and a dark brown jacket that have been shoved inside. I switch to the video camera.

'Okay. Let's see what we've got.'

Jake tentatively removes the jeans, rotating them for the benefit of the camera. He then lays them out on the tiled floor where my lens scours the fabric.

'Can you see anything?' asks Jake.

'Nothing obvious. Let's carry on.'

Next he removes a dark brown jacket, holding it up while my camera tracks over the back and then the sleeves.

'Okay. I'll do the front now.'

Jake turns the jacket around. A sea of brown corduroy fills my viewfinder as the camera makes its way from the shoulder to the elbow until it reaches the cuffs where the material appears to darken.

'Wait. Hold still a moment.'

'What is it?' asks Jake.

I put the camera down to inspect the sleeve more closely.

'I'm not sure. It could be ingrained dirt.'

I fetch the UV light and switch it on. Immediately, the sleeve glows purple with a couple of black dots on the edges.

'I think we're about to ruin Harriet's day.'

THE REVEREND

IPhone recording, 3 March 2023, between Archdeacon Quentin Brown and Reverend Humphrey Bagshaw

Archdeacon Brown: _You're a very fortunate man, Humphrey. God is smiling on you._

Reverend Bagshaw: _How so?_

Brown: _The bishop happened to speak to Hilton Deveney who is the head of the Trust on Liars Island. Apparently, they're looking to appoint a vicar, the first one in over thirty years, to take over the parish of St Nicholas._

Bagshaw: _And the bishop thought of me?'_

Brown: _Yes. It's not to bring spiritual light to the flock, of course. The church sits on the highest point on the island. It's a beautiful setting and Hilton Deveney knows a business opportunity when he sees one. He wants to promote it as a wedding venue and he needs a vicar to conduct the services. Anyway, the bishop immediately thought of you. The place has terrible 4G, apparently._

Bagshaw: _But it's a tiny island, and so remote._

Brown: _Beggars can't be choosers, Humphrey. Bishop Courtenay is of the mind that you're very fortunate to_ be offered a parish at all, given what has gone on. He took a lot of persuading. Will it be a problem?

Bagshaw: No, not at all. Please pass on my grateful thanks to the bishop. However, for the record, I would like to stress that it was just a mild indiscretion, Quentin. A momentary lapse of judgement. That's all. Nothing more. It won't happen again.

Brown: We all have our mad moments, Humphrey. To err is human and all that. Essentially, you're a good man, but if this problem . . . reoccurs, I won't be able to protect you.

Bagshaw: I understand and I won't let you down. Like I said, it's all in the past. I'm better now. Much better.

Brown: That is good to hear. I know this is hard, but it will get better. This could turn out to be the best thing that ever happened to you.

Bagshaw: I'm just grateful that I still have a job. The church is my life.

Brown: Then make the most of the opportunity you've been given. The bishop was all for getting rid of you. I had to argue your case most forcibly. I have put my own reputation on the line for you. This really is your last chance. Go to Liars Island, live your life quietly and the church will leave you in peace.

Bagshaw: I won't let you down, Quentin. I promise.

He hadn't expected that. In fact, he was so convinced he was going to be dismissed over his misdemeanours that he'd recorded the conversation in case Quentin said something inappropriate that would give him grounds to appeal. Instead, his old friend had offered him a reprieve: Liars Island.

At first, it felt like exile. A wild and tiny island in the middle of the Bristol Channel, barely any inhabitants, but the more he thought about it, the more he warmed to the idea. Very few residents and even less of them churchgoers and he could easily manage the odd wedding. No one would expect anything from him. With any luck, the church would forget he was even there. It was perfect. Best of all. Poor wi-fi meant no temptation.

That's why he'd chosen such a remote missionary in Gambia after his marriage to Celia collapsed. There was no internet there either and no chance of messing things up again, but progress waited for no man and eventually it was installed. After that, it was only a matter of time. He couldn't help himself. God knows he'd tried, but the temptation was just too great. Liars Island was his chance to heal once and for all. After all, it was a habit and habits could be broken. It just took a little time and effort. Then he would be cured of this unfortunate . . . affliction. For good.

Then, irony of ironies, he discovered the church was one of the few places on the island that could pick up a signal. Granted it was only 3G, but that was enough. Within days, his demons had returned. He was feeble-minded, a pathetic excuse for a man and he loathed himself for his relapse. He *fought the urges with all his might, praying nightly for forgiveness, hoping the Good Lord was listening to him. He pleaded with Him to help him find the right path, to help him turn away from this evilness that had corrupted him.*

His prayers were heard all right. Not by the Creator, but by that lad Kieran Deveney, Hilton's son, who ran the Bara Watersports Centre. Kieran had been standing in the doorway as he had knelt in the pews, berating himself for his sins and appealing to the Lord for forgiveness. He didn't know how much Kieran had heard, but the boy didn't seem to care. He seemed to be there for another reason. A far worse reason. If that was possible.

Somehow Kieran knew about his past, but how could he? He denied it, of course, but it didn't matter. Surely, he wouldn't be able to prove any of it, not after all this time, but that didn't mean he was safe. Accusations had a habit of sticking regardless of whether there was any foundation in them. And what if the lad told his father, Hilton? He'd be ruined. Quentin couldn't have made himself clearer on that score. No second chances. He'd promised to stay out of trouble and he'd failed.

But he belonged here now. This is his home. He couldn't leave Liars Island. Not now . . . Not ever.

21

Popping the lid off the small plastic container, I tease out a single strip, its tip coated with a reagent, and lay it across the top of the pot as Jake watches. Next I upend a clear plastic tube, letting the swab slide out onto my palm before moistening it under the tap.

'So are the marks on his jacket blood or not?'

'I think so, but it's a wool jacket. Like blood, animal fibres don't fluoresce either, that's why we need to do another test.'

Jake holds the sleeve of Bagshaw's jacket out for me as I rub the swab over it until the cotton wool discolours. Next I dab the end of the strip with it. Immediately, it reacts with the reagent and turns green, denoting the presence of haemoglobin. Blood in other words.

'Honestly, I wasn't expecting that,' he says. 'I mean, he's a vicar.'

'Welcome to the world of murder investigation. It's only a presumptive test to prove the presence of blood. It might not be Kieran's. We won't know that until we get the jacket to a lab and even if it is his blood there could be another explanation for why it's on Bagshaw's jacket.'

'So you still think he's lying about killing Kieran?'

'I don't know what to think, but we're done here. Let's finish up and get home. Then it's Harriet's problem.'

Jake checks his watch.

'We've still got three hours until the police chopper gets here. What do we do 'til then?'

Before I can answer, there's a knock on the vestry door causing us both to start.

'You finish up here. I'll see who it is.'

The footplates lead me back to the front door. As soon as I open it, two arms fling themselves around my neck.

'Oh my God, Ally, it really is you.'

'Rose.' Surprised by this display of affection, I let the hug play out before stepping back to look at the woman in front of me. Like the island, my childhood friend doesn't appear to have changed much. Jeans still tucked into wellingtons, an Alice band still holding back her elbow-length chestnut hair and a smile beaming as it always was. Rose was the kind of child adults would describe as having a sunny disposition. I'd forgotten how much I enjoyed spending time with her. 'How are you?'

'Great, thanks. I couldn't believe it when Ash told me your name and then when he described you. I thought to myself that's definitely my Ally Dymond. Sorry I missed you earlier. I was upstairs taking a nap.'

Is that why Ash was so guarded? He didn't want to wake his wife. Why didn't he just say so?

'How long are you here for?'

'Just a couple of hours.'

'Ash said you're a CSI.'

'That's right.'

Her eyes light up with interest, a familiar response when I tell people my job. If only they saw the countless forms I spend my life filling in.

'Ooo, that sounds very exciting but what are you doing in Humphrey's flat?'

As she peers over my shoulder, I shift to one side, shielding her view.

'Just following up on a few things.'

'Has this got something to do with Dove?'

'How do you mean?'

'She left the island two days ago with a couple of detectives and we've not heard from her since. Ash saw them getting into the helicopter. Apparently, she was in bits. He couldn't be sure but he thought she might be in handcuffs. Do you know what's going on?'

Rose doesn't know Dove has confessed to killing Kieran.

'I'm sorry. I've no idea,' I lie. 'I'm just the CSI.'

'Then some other detectives started asking us questions about Dove's relationship with Kieran. They don't think she had anything to do with his death, do they? That would be crazy.'

'Honestly, you're asking the wrong person.'

'Okay, but I'm pretty sure Dove never set foot in the Reverend's vestry though.'

'Oh, this? This is just routine, belt and braces stuff.' I shrug, but she isn't letting it go.

'You know the Reverend Bagshaw isn't here at the moment either, don't you? He's gone to the mainland. He didn't say when he'd be back.'

'Right, well, we're almost finished here. Actually, Rose,

do you have a secure cupboard I could use, just for a few hours?'

'Er . . . yes, probably. There's a large cupboard at the back of the church that's kept padlocked.'

'Great, I'll send my colleague down to the inn to pick up the key.'

'Sure.' She lingers, waiting for an explanation I have no intention of providing. She may be a former friend, but until Dove and Bagshaw confessed, Rose was on the suspect list.

'Do you . . . need anything else?'

'No, that's it. We're expecting the chopper later and then we'll be out of your hair.'

'That soon? That's a shame,' she says, genuinely disappointed. There was a time when we were thick as thieves, as they say, although we always had different ambitions. She never wanted to travel when it was the only future I saw for myself until I got pregnant. 'I was hoping we could catch up properly. It's been a long time.'

'It has, but we've got to get back.'

'I understand, but you must come again, Ally.' She claps her hands at the thought. 'I can't believe we lost contact.'

'That's on me. After Dad, I kind of didn't want anything to do with Liars Island. We were connected on social media but I ditched it all when I joined the police.'

'Me too. Obviously, I didn't join the police. I was on it for a while but then I deleted it all after my divorce.'

'Divorce? You were married before?'

'Yeah, Rob Lullcott.'

'As in Lullcott Construction?'

The Lullcotts are a very wealthy and well-known local family, the kind Bernadette wishes I'd married into.

'Yeah, we met when the cottages were refurbished. I moved to the mainland for him. Biggest mistake of my life. We were too young.'

'Sounds like a difficult divorce if you had to get rid of your social media.'

'You know what it's like in North Devon, everyone takes sides. I left in the end, couldn't stand it. I've got a good 'un now.' She holds her left hand up for me to inspect her wedding ring. 'Together for four years. Married two months ago.'

'Congratulations.'

'Thank you. Now, I'll get that key for you. So what time did you say you'd be off?'

'We're just waiting for the police helicopter, so soonish, assuming they don't get called out on another shout.'

'Great.'

I watch Rose stroll back down the path towards the pub. Jake joins me.

'Who was that?'

'Rose. She runs the pub.'

'So how do you know her?'

'She grew up here. I used to visit the island when I was a kid.'

'Cool. I'm almost finished here.'

He returns inside. When Rose reaches the bottom of the slope, she pauses to look back. Surprised to see me standing in the doorway of the vestry, she smiles and waves, but she's too late. I already caught her expression. Rose Griffiths doesn't want me here.

CRIME SCENE EXAMINATION REPORT RELATING TO ROSE POWELL

<u>CSI</u>: Bob Greene
<u>OIC</u>: PC Paul Howden
<u>DIVISION</u>: North Devon, Devon County Police
<u>LOCATION</u>: Lullcott Construction, Upper Fairleigh
<u>EXAMINATION COMMENCED</u>: 16 February 2010, 9.00am
<u>EXAMINATION NOTES</u>
Extensive damage to the bodywork of a black Range Rover SV. Vehicle believed to belong to MD Robert Lullcott. Victim believed to have threatened to kill the suspect with a cricket bat. Bat not recovered.

<u>EVIDENCE COLLECTED</u>
Photographs REF LF1–12:
- Smashed headlights
- Smashed back window
- Smashed driver's window
- Dented bonnet
- Dented driver's door
- Scratch (key?) running the length of the vehicle (offside)

Forensic samples recovered
- Glass
- Damage to a front door to garage where victim hid from assailant

22

'I'll catch you up.' Jake drops to one knee to tie his shoelace.

Knowing what's around the corner, I hesitate to go on without him, already grateful for the distraction of his conversation about the best places to eat in Bidecombe as we ambled down the track to the Bara Watersports Centre.

With three hours to kill until the police helicopter returns, I suggested we take a look around Devil's Cauldron where Kieran was killed. I'm not expecting to find anything, but it's a learning opportunity for Jake, as they call it, to examine a murder scene away from judgemental eyes. There's just one problem. Devil's Cauldron lies just beyond the jetty where I last saw my dad alive.

As I round the final corner, I wonder how my heart will react to the sight of the jetty, but it turns out it doesn't much care about the warped boardwalk and rusting struts. Maybe it's because I now know the island isn't to blame for Dad's death. He died by his own hand. Or maybe it's because the jetty I remember was different. It was smaller, the wooden slats neater, the struts freshly painted black. While I wait for Jake, I allow my mind a once-in-a-lifetime opportunity to take me back to the day I last saw my dad.

I'd been hanging out with Rose at the pub, playing darts badly, but as time marched on we'd grown tired of each other's company and I wanted to go home so I took myself off to the jetty in the hope my presence would hasten Dad's return.

I don't know how long I sat there, legs dangling over the side, scanning the horizon for *The Aloysia*. I don't recall being worried. If anything I felt mildly resentful. It was a warm, clear day. Whatever bad weather Dad had feared never materialised. I could have accompanied him after all.

Eventually, I spotted a boat in the distance. Assuming it was *The Aloysia*, I got to my feet in readiness to hop onto her deck. But as it drew nearer, I saw that her hull was red, not blue. It wasn't *The Aloysia*. It was the coastguard, chugging slowly towards me. Again, I wasn't unduly perturbed. Not at first, not even when I saw she was towing a smaller boat. *The Aloysia*. I figured it had broken down and Dad had called for help. How embarrassed he would be that the coastguard had to come out and rescue him. We would rib him over it for years to come.

I started waving, big sweeps of my arms so Dad would see me the moment I came into view. It was then that I heard someone shouting behind me. It was Rose. She was running down the hill towards me. Her parents followed behind her. I must have forgotten something, or perhaps they planned to buy some of Dad's catch. As she drew nearer, I saw Rose's face. She was crying but so was her mother while her father just looked at me with a mix of horror and pity. Still, I didn't make the connection. Not until the coastguard came alongside the jetty.

I knew them all. Fishermen by day, lifesavers when called upon, but not one of them returned my smiles. Some couldn't even face me while others couldn't look away. No one spoke. I knew then that Dad was gone, but it didn't stop me jumping down onto the deck of *The Aloysia*. I was certain they'd made a mistake. Dad was pranking us all. I called out for him, but there was no reply because he wasn't there and I realised he never would be again.

My phone buzzes. I frown, not expecting service and fish it out of my pocket to discover a text from Howard.

I've been thinking, Squid. I knew your dad. There's no way he'd have done what he did. No way at all. He wouldn't leave you. Or Bernie. No matter how bad things were. But I know you police people are all about the evidence so I'm going to prove it to you.

Poor Howard, still in denial. I feel sorry for him. He can't accept the fact that Dad took his own life or the part he played in that decision. I've seen this before, people in denial, scrabbling around for what they believe is incontrovertible evidence that proves their personal hypothesis, but is really nothing more than a random glance or comment. That isn't evidence. Not in my world. But that's for Howard, not me. His absolution isn't mine to give.

'So why's it called Liars Island?' asks Jake.

'There's a few theories,' I say, relieved to be thinking about something else. 'One is because lots of people have died here. Before the lighthouse, ships constantly ran aground here, but it was no safer on land where people had a tendency to fall down ravines.'

'Makes sense.'

'The official reason is because of a guy who owned the island and who won the contract to transport convicts to the Americas. Instead, he sailed up and down the Bristol Channel before dropping them off on the island and forcing them to build him a mansion. It's still there.'

'You're kidding. Why didn't they try to escape?'

'Even if you could swim the twelve miles to home, the currents in the Bristol Channel are treacherous. The island is surrounded by sheer cliffs. The only place you can land a boat is Seal Bay and even then the beach is stony and drops away quickly.'

'Not like the sandy beaches on the south coast where the migrant boats land then?'

'No, not at all. There's nowhere to land here. Liars Island is a fortress.'

'So what happened to these convicts?'

'Most of them died and are buried on the island. Those that survived were eventually taken home, the long way. They had no idea they'd been a few miles from shore all along.'

'Didn't anyone ever notice when they visited?'

'No, whenever a ship came to port, he hid them in the caves. The island is riddled with them.'

'So what happened to the house?'

'It's still there, but he got a bit complacent and got found out in the end.'

'And that's when it became Liars Island.'

'Yes.'

'From what Norm was saying about the interviews, it doesn't sound like much has changed.'

Before I can answer, Jake points to a low building squatting at the base of the cliff.

'That must be the Bara Watersports Centre, Kieran's place. Weird name.'

'It's Norse. It means wave.'

'How do you know all this stuff?'

'My dad. He was full of pointless facts about this place.'

'You should go on that quiz programme, *Mastermind*: CSI Ally Dymond, specialist subject, Liars Island.'

'Maybe I should.' I laugh. 'But I'm amazed they got permission to build a watersports centre. This is meant to be a conservation area.'

'My dad says that you can get anything built if you know the right people. Who do you reckon that is?'

Jake points to the two men standing next to an upturned kayak. The younger one, dressed in sports gear, is listening intently to an older man in a flat cap and Barbour jacket. We're too far away to hear their conversation, but the older man is doing all the talking. When he finishes, the young man's face breaks into a broad smile. He holds out his hand, but the older man pulls him in for a hug instead. He gets back into a sleek black Defender and roars up the track towards us, his wheels spitting grit. When he reaches us, he comes to an abrupt halt and lowers the window.

'And you are?' he says in a way that suggests he's entitled to an answer. He isn't, so he gets the shortest one possible.

'Police.'

'What are you still doing here? I thought you'd finished.'

'Not yet.'

My sharpness earns me a side glance from Jake.

144

'But that little gold digger has already confessed, and you have her in custody. What else is there to do?'

'Gold digger?' I feel myself bristle.

'I met her a couple of times, you know, but I didn't fall for that hippy crap. I knew her type immediately.'

'Her type?'

'Yes, I've been targeted myself many times. All flirty glances and butter wouldn't melt, but they know exactly what they're doing. As soon as things don't go their way, they cry blue murder. She's no different to that little bitch who tried to stitch Kieran up at university. Just another false allegation. But she's got you lot fooled, of course, making it out to be his fault.' It is then that I realise this is Hilton Deveney, head of the board of trustees that runs the island. 'Anyway, you still haven't answered my question. What are you doing here?'

'Follow-up work.'

'Like?'

'Like follow-up work.' I shrug. Something tells me Hilton and I are not destined to be pals.

My petulance earns me a hard glare from Hilton, but I learnt from the best. I have a fifteen-year-old daughter.

'So, you're not going to tell me what's going on? Kieran was my son.'

'No, sir. I'm afraid that's classified, but the FLO assigned to you will be able to answer any questions you may have.'

He studies me a little longer and I wonder if he's going to pull the old 'I know your chief constable' line, but he doesn't. Instead, he grunts, raises his window and drives away.

Jake grins at me. 'Classified? I didn't know we worked for MI5.'

'First thing I thought of.'

'He doesn't think very highly of Dove, does he? Or look like a dad devastated by the loss of his son.'

I remember Henry describing Hilton's behaviour when he identified his son's body at the mortuary, as if it was his fault that he was murdered. For people like Hilton, when life doesn't go their way someone else is always to blame. Even their own children.

'I guess grief affects people differently.'

I watch Hilton's car round the corner up ahead, but as I turn away I catch a flash of red on the clifftop. Jake and I are definitely being watched.

23

The crunch of the gravel beneath our feet alerts the young man waxing the upturned hull of a kayak to our arrival. He looks up and offers us an easy smile. His sunglasses are light enough for me to see his eyes and I realise he's wearing prescription reactolights.

'Hi. How's it going?' He stands up to greet us.

'Good thanks,' says Jake.

'I take it you're more police?' he says, still smiling.

'Sort of,' I say.

Dressed in a bright orange kayak jacket, a grey beanie pressed over a mass of brown curls, he has that 'life lived by the sea' glow about him that momentarily reminds me of Liam.

'I've already been questioned several times but I'm happy to answer more questions if it helps to find Kieran's killer.'

'We're not detectives. We're police crime scene investigators. I'm Ally. This is my colleague, Jake. We've come to take a look around Devil's Cauldron.'

The three of us look towards two tall rock formations, about fifty metres from where we're standing. From here, it looks like there's no access, but there's a narrow passageway that takes you through to the bay on the other side. They're known as Hell's Gates because too many have passed through them never to return.

'I thought you guys were done down there. I'm Ben, by the way, Ben Dawson.' Jake and I shake his hand in turn. 'I run, sorry, ran, the watersports centre with Kieran.'

'Nice to meet you, Ben, sorry to interrupt you again.'

'Again?' He frowns. 'Oh, you mean Hilton. That's fine. That's Kieran's dad. He just wanted to talk through a few things about the business.'

'Business?' says Jake.

'Yeah, he just wanted to check our end-of-year accounts.'

'You must have had a good year.'

'Why do you say that?' he asks.

'He hugged you.' I smile.

'Oh right, yes. That.'

'His son has only been gone a few days and he's more interested in money,' says an incredulous Jake.

'If you know anything about Hilton Deveney you'll know cash comes first.' He laughs. 'But Kieran was more than a business partner to me. He was my best mate. We met during freshers' week at uni.' He looks at the building behind him. 'I was doing Law and Accounting and he was doing Maths, but we were both mad about water sports.'

'So how did you end up here?'

'After uni we worked at Outward Bound centres. My family couldn't have cared less what I did after uni, but Kieran's dad wanted him to get a job in the city, but Kieran wasn't interested. Then he told me about this island and how his dad practically owned it. We came here a few summers back and as soon as I saw Seal Bay I knew it'd be perfect for a watersports centre so I came up with a business plan. Hilton loved it. He could tell I'm an entrepreneur like him. We just kind of hit it off straight away. I felt for Kieran a bit. He never seemed to be able to do anything right in his dad's eyes. Anyway, Hilton gave it the thumbs-up and here we are.'

'What will happen to the centre now?' I ask.

'That's the weirdest thing. I assumed Hilton would withdraw his investment, close the place down, but he's just told me to push ahead with our expansion plans to build a bunkhouse. Kieran had already sourced the building materials anyway.'

'That's great news. Good for the island too.'

'Yes, it is, although not everyone agrees, but I'm determined to see it through. I owe it to Hilton, but mostly I owe it to Kieran. It's what he would have wanted.'

'You must still be in shock.'

Ben nods, appreciating the acknowledgement of his loss.

'Yes, I don't think it's really sunk in. I keep thinking I hear him at night, walking around outside. He was the brother I never had, you know? I can't believe I'm never going to see him again.' His mind drifts somewhere else before he snaps himself out of it. 'Anyway, if you give me a couple of minutes to finish up here, I'll show you to Devil's Cauldron.'

'That won't be necessary,' I say, raising my hand. 'I know the way.'

'Seriously, I'm more than happy to take you. The rocks can be a bit tricky.'

'We're fine. Honestly.'

'Oh. Okay then. Let me know if you need anything.'

'We will.' I smile.

Jake and I make our way to Devil's Cauldron.

'What did you make of him then?' Jake asks.

'He seemed very disappointed not to be coming with us.'

'Why would anyone want to return to the place where they found their best friend murdered?' he replies, reminding me Ben discovered Kieran's body. He was also the last person to see Kieran alive.

'You didn't take to him then?'

'Bit too pally with Hilton for my liking and what was all that hugging about?'

'That's what I'd like to know.'

CRIME SCENE EXAMINATION REPORT RELATING TO BEN DAWSON

<u>CSI</u>: Louise Grant
<u>OIC</u>: PC Olly Stewart
<u>DIVISION</u>: Exeter Central
<u>LOCATION</u>: Lloyds Bank, High Street
<u>EXAMINATION COMMENCED</u>: 2.00pm, 2013

EXAMINATION NOTES

Collected cheques (suspected to be signed fraudulently by a young male, relative of cheque book owner, who had attempted to cash them in) from cashier.

EVIDENCE COLLECTED

- Three separate cheques to be submitted for forensic examination (Ninhydrin) REF LB1–3. Cheques removed from latter part of cheque book. Cheque numbers: 100012–100014

24

Jake nods approvingly at the aquamarine waters lapping the white sloping shore. 'Not sure why they call it Devil's Cauldron. On a hot day, you'd think you were in the Med. I might bring Soph here.'

But he doesn't see what I see.

'Don't be fooled. See those out there.' I point to two prongs of rocks guarding either side of the entrance to the bay. 'You can just make out the whirlpools. You get caught in one of those, you've got no chance. They can pull you under in seconds and the rips are treacherous.'

Jake shudders at the thought. 'Maybe I won't then. So what do we do now?'

'I thought we could do our own crime scene examination.'

'Do you think Jim and the team missed something?'

'No.' Much as I dislike Jim Dixon, he's a good CSI. He wouldn't have missed anything.

'It'll be good for your CPD, Continuous Professional Development, and there's no harm going over a scene again. As they say, slack sank the ship.'

'Do they?' says Jake, frowning.

'Sorry. It's an old sea saying of my dad's. Basically, you

should always double check everything or it could cost you your life.' But my explanation fails to unknit Jake's brow. 'To be honest, it's probably more relevant at sea than on land. Anyway, let's suppose you're the first CSI on the scene. What would you do first?'

'I'd head for the rendezvous point where I'd expect to be briefed on what we know so far.'

'Where would the RVP be?'

'On the outer cordon, far enough away from the body to preserve any potential evidence.'

'Let's say the outer cordon was placed on the corner where the shed storing the gas cylinders is. Why's that a potential problem?'

Jake thinks for a moment.

'Because there's only one road out from Devil's Cauldron so the killer must have come up the track.'

'Exactly. We're treading in the footsteps of the killer so what do you do to mitigate that?'

'I'd either search the outer cordon first for evidence, but that would take time and, given the body is on the beach and the tide is coming in, I'd probably opt for laying down the stepping plates to the inner cordon and searching the wider area later.'

'Good. Let's talk about that inner cordon. Obviously, we don't know what evidence we're going to gather until we examine the scene, but what could you expect to find here?'

Jake looks around for inspiration and smiles. 'Shoeprints. If Kieran's body was found below the tideline, the killer must have walked across the sand to Hell's Gates.'

'And what would be your biggest concern about those shoeprints?'

'Um . . . degradation?'

'Yes, especially if it's windy. They could just get blown away. One thing you could do to get around this is cover them with a bucket. What else would you be on the lookout for?'

'Blood. Kieran died of a head wound. That produces a lot of blood so I'd check for blood on the rocks to confirm the route the killer took.' Jake bends down and picks up a small rock. 'The rocks here are dark which would make it difficult to identify blood stains,' he says, bouncing the stone in his hand, 'but near the watersports centre I noticed they're paler grey. That would show up spatters.'

'Impressive. You've come a long way since Bidecombe Quay,' I say, referring to the first time I met Jake.

'Thanks.' He turns the stone over in his hand. 'What is this stuff anyway?'

'Um, it's probably slate. The entire southern section of the island is just one big slate quarry. It's everywhere, along with flint flakes and arrowheads.'

'Arrowheads?'

'Yes, there were loads of them on the main track down here. The island was first inhabited during the Middle Stone Age, apparently.'

'Blimey, is there anything you don't know about this place?'

'Sadly, probably not.'

Jake inspects the rock more closely. 'It's quite ugly, isn't it? But it's got lots of sharp edges, good for killing someone as well, I guess.'

He's about to toss it into the sea when I catch his arm. 'Hang on. Can I have a look at that?'

'Sure.'

He hands me the rock. I flip it over a couple of times to confirm it's slate.

'You're a genius, Jake.'

'I am?' he says surprised. 'How come?'

I press the stone between my thumb and forefinger, and hold it up against the greying sky. 'Because this, young Jedi, is what we in the trade call a mistake.'

25

The gnarly stone digs into the small of my back as I pin my body against the church wall to shield the phone from the wind that has whipped up since Jake and I returned from Devil's Cauldron.

I've dropped him off at The Barbary Inn for a well-earned pint while I carry on up to the church to call Harriet. She picks up immediately and I sense she's been waiting for my call.

'If you tell me another islander has confessed, I'm putting the phone down,' she says.

'No.' I laugh. 'You're safe on that score.'

'I hear a *but*.'

'Sorry to be the bearer of bad news. We found a jacket under the sink in the vestry and it had blood on the cuff.'

'Blood? You tested it to make sure, right?'

'Yes, we swabbed it. It's blood.'

'Shit. That's all I need. I was so sure Bagshaw was lying, we released him under investigation.'

'Obviously, we don't know who it belongs to, it could be Bagshaw's. If it is Kieran's I'd have expected there to be much more than a few splashes, given how much blood he lost, but Jake and I checked the place with a UV light. The only blood is on the jacket.'

'That's something, I suppose. Let's hope my theory that Bagshaw is full of bullshit holds up when we get the sample to the lab because at the moment he's sticking to his story.'

'Is it possible he's telling the truth?'

'If he is then he and Dove must be in this together, there's no other explanation, but we're no further on that score either.'

'Anything else from the scene?'

'No, in fact, the vestry was spotless, but there's another problem. It wasn't locked so everyone on the island had access to it. Anyone could have put that jacket there.'

'That would mean a third person is involved which makes no sense at all,' says Harriet, sighing. 'I'm just flagging it, although . . .'

'Although what?'

'I think Jake and I are being watched.'

'By who?'

'No idea. Like I said I can't be certain. I haven't told Jake. He's a bit spooked by the place as it is and it could just be curiosity getting the better of one of the islanders.'

'Okay, well, keep me in the loop on that one. We spoke to Cal Meeth, by the way, about the break-in at Bagshaw's church.'

'That's thorough.'

'You know me, I'd dig up your pet hamster from two decades ago if I thought it'd help me crack a case.'

'So how was Cal?'

'About the level of a dead hamster, as it happens. We went in with low expectations and he didn't disappoint. Not that we thought it'd result in anything. You know the game, it's always a process of whittling it down and then seeing what we're left with. Anyway, he couldn't even remember the church let alone meeting Bagshaw. He said he didn't tend to make a habit of bonding with those he nicked off. Cheeky shit. Then he gave us some spiel about police harassment.'

'That sounds like the lovely Cal. So where does all of this leave you?'

'We've got two suspects, both insisting they killed Kieran Deveney, completely independently of each other. Both with a motive, a means and an opportunity, and both potentially with his blood on their clothing. I'd say that leaves us with front-row seats for an utter shitshow. Anyway, thanks for your input, even if it wasn't the news I was hoping for. I'll see you when you get back.'

'Hold on, Harriet. I haven't finished.'

Clues are really just an investigator's word for mistakes. Smart killers, and there are less than you'd imagine, know it's their mistakes that will catch them out, which is why they go to extreme lengths to mitigate them, often very successfully. But, over the years, I've come to understand that the best clues are often the mistakes the killer doesn't even know they've committed. Just like the one Jake discovered at Devil's Cauldron.

'You know I did the postmortem photos on Kieran. Alex found shards of the rock used to kill Kieran embedded in his skull.'

'Go on,' says Harriet, sensing her investigation is about to be dismantled. Bad news is always kept to the end.

'As well as being a brilliant pathologist, Alex is also a bit of an amateur geologist. He was certain the fragments he found in Kieran's skull were granite. In fact, he showed them to me under the microscope. I didn't mention it in the briefing because I didn't think it was particularly significant.'

'But now you do.'

'Yes. Kieran was killed at Devil's Cauldron right?'

'Right.'

'Devil's Cauldron lies at the southernmost tip of the island. However, granite is only found in the middle and northern sections of Liars Island. The southern section, which is the area around The Barbary Inn and below, is slate.'

'Really?'

'If you look at a geology map, there's actually an invisible line that bisects the island. Everything above it is granite, below it is slate.'

'How do you know this?'

'Someone told me about it years ago,' I say, declining to share the memory of me asking Dad why the rocks on the southern tip of the island were always in shadow when there was no cloud.

'So what you're saying is the rock that killed Kieran didn't come from Devil's Cauldron?'

'Precisely. The nearest granite is at least a kilometre away. The line is somewhere above The Barbary Inn.'

'If you're right that means Bagshaw or Dove must have picked up the rock on the way down to Devil's Cauldron which makes Kieran's death premeditated. If they intended to kill him that puts a whole different complexion on things. Are you sure about this slate, granite thing?'

'As sure as I can be.'

'But why carry a heavy rock all the way to Devil's Cauldron when there's plenty of nice jaggedy slate ones waiting for you on the beach?'

'I don't know. Just like I don't know why they left his body above the tideline.'

'I thought we'd decided, they got it wrong. Neither of them knew it was a neap tide.'

'But what if they did know? What if they deliberately left Kieran's body there? To divert our attention.'

'From what?'

'Blood continues to flow for around ten minutes after death and head wounds produce a lot of blood. As you know, one way we work out where a person was murdered is the amount of blood at a scene. It's usually a straightforward process, but sand is highly porous. There's no way we'd be able to measure the quantity of blood Kieran had lost, regardless of whether the tide had come in or not, which means it's almost scientifically impossible to prove Kieran was killed at Devil's Cauldron.'

There's silence at the end of the phone and for a moment I think I've been cut off. I check the screen. The seconds are ticking by; Harriet is still there. Finally she speaks.

'So you're telling me Kieran was murdered somewhere else and his body dumped at Devil's Cauldron?'

'Yes.'

'But neither of them could have moved the body on their own.'

'You said you thought they were working together.'

'That's true although we haven't been able to find a link between them yet. They both deny ever having met each other. If your theory is correct, that means it isn't just Bagshaw who's lying. Dove is too. And if they're both lying, that takes us right back to square one.'

26

Jake is sitting at the bar in The Barbary Inn knocking back a well-earned pint. When he sees me, his leg nudges the stool out next to him for me to take. It takes me a few moments to clamber on to it much to his amusement.

'Careful,' I say, waggling a teasing finger at him, 'I'm pretty sure I could argue being a short-arse is a protected characteristic.'

Jake raises his hands in surrender and laughs.

'I didn't say anything.' He takes a sip of his beer. 'So how did it go with Harriet? Did she buy your granite theory?'

'She heard me out, but she didn't like it.'

'But it would help prove that Dove and Bagshaw are working together.'

'Yes, but she reckons if they wanted his body to be found, they could have dumped him anywhere. Why bother lugging him all the way down to Devil's Cauldron?'

'Well, I thought it was cool that you knew the rock was in the wrong part of the island. Maybe all that knowledge your dad taught you wasn't so useless after all.'

'Maybe, but it wasn't enough to convince Harriet. I don't blame her. It's pretty tenuous.'

'So what now?'

I smile at Jake.

'Now, we get you back in time for your anniversary meal with Sophie, and I, well, I get to go home too.'

'No one waiting for you then?'

'No.'

'Not even that barista guy, the ex-cop?'

'What? No, definitely not him.'

'Oh, I thought—'

I wave him away. 'Your intel is way off there.'

'Shame, he's a nice guy.'

'You met him?'

'Yeah, a load of cars got broken in to at Morte Sands car park a few days ago. You must have been on a rest day because I got the call. He seemed very disappointed that he got me, not you.'

'We're friends.'

Jake looks at me doubtfully. 'Well, he definitely gave me the impression you were more than that.'

Rose appears from the back of the pub with a crate.

'Ally, you're here at last,' she says, placing the crate on the floor. Whatever was bothering her before seems to have been forgotten as she's all smiles. 'I know you don't have much time before the helicopter gets here, so what can I get you? On the house, obviously.'

'Well, seeing as our shift has just ended.' I survey the tantalising-named beer pumps. 'A pint of Rockstar will do nicely, thank you.'

Rose pulls the lever steadily, watching the golden liquid fill the tilted glass before easing it into the upright position to produce the perfect frothy head.

'So, what were you two doing down at Devil's Cauldron?'

Her directness takes me aback.

'How—?'

'You can't do anything here without everyone knowing about it.' She laughs, sliding my pint across the bar. Except first-degree murder, it would seem. 'Hilton dropped in earlier. He's definitely not your biggest fan.'

'We met him on the way down to the watersports centre. He seems to have a very good relationship with Ben?'

'Yes, the two get along like a house of fire. It's a terrible thing to say, but I think Hilton preferred Ben to his own son. Ben's got a great business head, the success the centre has had is all down to him. Kieran was a nice guy, but never seemed to take anything seriously, and Hilton is all about the profit.'

'So where's Hilton now? I didn't see a boat come in.'

'No, he's too posh to take the boat, unless it's his own, of course. He's got his own private helipad over at his place.' She frowns. 'Although I usually hear his helicopter come over. I must have missed it. Remember the old doctor's house?'

'The old Georgian mansion?'

'Is that the one the convicts built?' asks Jake.

'The very same. Hilton reserves it for his own use. He stays there when he visits the island. Perks of being head of the board of trustees. It's the only property that's kept locked.'

'He doesn't think that highly of Dove, does he?'

'I don't know why. I'm not sure he's even met her.'

'That didn't stop him calling her a gold digger.'

Rose's head jerks back in surprise.

'Dove? A gold digger? No way. Why would he say that?'

'I was hoping you could tell me.'

'No way. Dove isn't interested in money or in Kieran, if that's what he's getting at.'

'So Hilton's wrong then?'

'Completely. Dove only has eyes for Forrest.'

DOVE

Facebook Messenger, 6 April 2021

Stacy: Mum, I've screwed up again.

Irene: Why? I thought you loved him.

Stacy: I cheated on him, Mum. Just like before. I don't know why I do it. I hate myself for it, but I can't help it. It's like as soon as I get something good in my life, I go all out to destroy it.

Irene: You've got to move on with your life, Stace. Messing guys around, hurting those you love isn't moving on. It isn't going to make you happy. And you deserve to be happy.

Stacy: Do I? I think I deserve to be dead. Then at least I'd be with Freya and all this would be over.

Irene: Don't talk like that. You know what happened to your sister wasn't your fault. I'm just thankful at least one of my daughters survived that crash.

Stacy: But if she hadn't come to get me . . .

Irene: Don't do this to yourself, Stace. For my sake. What you need is a fresh start. Look, I've seen an ad in the paper for a bar help. Board and lodging is free. It's on a tiny island, off North Devon. We used to holiday in Bidecombe when you and Freya were little, and I always wanted to take you to this island but we never made it. You could start again. Live your life differently. Leave this all behind you once and for all.

She had a reputation before she even met Tom. His friends tried to warn him off, telling him she'd cheat on him like she cheated on all the rest. For a time, she thought it would be different with him. Then one night she was out with her mates. They'd started on the shots before moving on to some Charlie. She couldn't quite remember how it happened, but before she knew it she was in a toilet cubicle shagging one of the barmen. Someone Tom knew saw them. She thought about saying he'd forced himself on her, but what was the point? Tom would never believe her with the reputation she had.

She didn't want to come to this crappy little island, freezing her arse off working and living in an old fart's pub: all real ale and pork scratchings. At least Rose and Ash were nice to her. She made a complete idiot of herself, of course, making a play for Ash. They'd get high together after she found him doing drugs behind Lookout Cottage one afternoon.

He kept telling her she was a great girl with so much going for her and she took this as a come-on so she grabbed his crotch and began kissing him. He pushed her off, telling her he was flattered but he was in love with someone else. She was so embarrassed. She didn't even know he and Rose were together, but the truth is it wouldn't have mattered if she did. Fuck the girl code. That was her motto. Which is all well and good on the mainland where you can get away from people, but not on an island not much bigger than a golf course.

Jocasta, the lady that ran Grannus House, found her, crying in the woods one day. She couldn't hold back and it all came spilling out. She'd heard Jocasta was a bit of a dragon but she put her arm around her and told her it'd all be all right. Shortly after that, she moved to Grannus House and that's where she met Forrest. One of the few guys that suited a beard. She nearly blew it with him too. Getting plastered on his homemade wine, she made a play for him. Forrest rejected her, just like Ash, making her feel like shit once again, but this time it was different. This time, the next day, he found her and told her that he turned her down not because he didn't like her, but precisely because he did.

'But you need to learn to love yourself before you can love someone else.'

From that moment on they were inseparable, bonding over their shared shame of being unable to change their past but determined to create a better future.

Changing their names was Jocasta's idea. Dove, a symbol of the peace she had finally found, and Forrest, the representation of growth and renewal. They even waited until after their handfasting to spend their first night together. It was as perfect as she imagined it would be. An affirmation of their love. Forrest was her everything. She didn't need anything else. Or anyone else. Then Kieran arrived on the island.

Confident, funny, flirty: the old Stacy would have made a beeline for him, but she was done with all that although that didn't mean she didn't find Kieran attractive.

He must have sensed it too because he seemed to seek her out. She'd be out walking and he'd suddenly appear as if he'd been waiting for her. It would have been rude to ignore him. In any case their conversations never strayed into the personal and she found herself looking forward to their exchanges.

Then one day, in the woods on the east side of the island Kieran stepped out from behind a tree. He began telling her about his plans for the centre when suddenly he leant over and kissed her. She pulled back, but a beat too late which was enough for him to know she had feelings for him. Flustered, she told him nothing would ever happen between them. She loved Forrest. But he just smiled and said: 'We'll see.'

She couldn't tell Forrest. He disliked Kieran as it was because he reminded him too much of his old life, and besides, the thoughts she'd had about Kieran made her feel she'd already been unfaithful. She resolved to never be alone with Kieran again.

But what if Kieran told Forrest what happened between them? If Forrest found out, it would be the end of their relationship. Jocasta wouldn't tolerate it either. She'd be kicked out of Grannus House and off the island.

But she belonged here now. This is her home. She couldn't leave Liars Island. Not now . . . Not ever.

27

A very different Ash Griffiths from the one I met a few hours earlier saunters into the bar. This Ash Griffiths greets us with a smile as he slides an arm around Rose and gives her a squeeze.

'Miss me, gorgeous?' he whispers loudly into her ear.

'Always,' says Rose, planting a kiss on his cheek. I never had her down as one for PDA, or maybe I'm just envious of what she has. She catches me looking at her.

'Don't worry. It'll wear off.' She laughs. 'Especially if he doesn't get the electrics fixed in the cottages.'

'No rest for the wicked.' He grins.

'Absolutely not. Anyway, you two must be starving. Ash can make you a sandwich or something before you leave?'

'Sure. Not like I have the electrics to fix in the cottages,' he teases.

'That's really kind of you but I don't think we have time,' I say, checking my watch. 'Jake and I should collect the exhibits from the church and make our way to the helipad.'

'Whatever you say.'

There's a loud ringing coming from the hallway behind the

bar. It's the landline. Rose looks to Ash to answer it, but he appears oblivious.

'I'll get it then.' She sighs, disappearing into the back, leaving myself and Jake with her husband.

'Ally.' Ash immediately turns his smile towards me. He was waiting for Rose to leave. 'I want to apologise to you for what happened earlier.'

'Forget it. I shouldn't have been in your private quarters.'

'No, no, I totally overreacted. I want you to know that's not me. I guess I'm a bit jumpy after what happened to Kieran.'

'That's understandable. You must all still be reeling from his death. Was he a close friend of yours?'

'Not really. He was a nice enough guy, but he and Ben spent most of their time at the centre. We kayaked to the mainland together a couple of times, but that was about it. I couldn't believe it when I got back from Bidecombe. All hell had let loose. Cops everywhere. For a horrible moment, I thought something had happened to Rose then I found out it was Kieran. Not that that makes it any better,' he adds hastily. 'I keep going over things, trying to see if I can remember anything from that night.'

'You left in the early hours, didn't you?' says Jake.

'Yeah, but we always launch the kayaks from Seal Bay, you know, in front of the watersports centre. It's much safer. You have to know what you're doing if you're going to take on Devil's Cauldron in a kayak and at that time of day I'm still half asleep. When I got down there, it was still dark, of course, but everything looked the same as it always did, you know.'

'You didn't see or hear anything?'

'Nah. Anyways, you can't see Devil's Cauldron from the centre.'

'But, wouldn't you have headed south if you were going to the mainland, taking you past the Cauldron?'

My familiarity with the island's geography takes him by surprise.

'Er . . . yeah, you're right. I did, but if there were lights there, I'm not sure I'd have seen them anyway. I was too busy concentrating on what was ahead, you know.'

'Were the conditions not good?'

'No, no, they were perfect, but you always need your wits about you. I wish I had taken a bit more notice though. I might have been more help to you guys.'

'I wouldn't be too hard on yourself. Witness accounts are full of *would've, should've, could'ves*, but the truth is no one expects something like this to happen on their doorstep.'

Ash looks at me as if I've said something profound.

'Thanks for that, I really appreciate it. I've never had much time for the police, but Rose is right. You're okay.'

I return his backhanded compliment with a smile, but in my experience being complimented for not being typical of the police isn't always a good thing. There's something about Ash Griffiths I can't quite get to the bottom of.

Rose returns to the bar, her face solemn.

'Everything okay?' asks Ash.

'That was your boss, Ally.'

'Harriet? Does she want to speak to me?'

'No, she just needed to pass a message on. Bad news, I'm afraid. Apparently, she's been trying to call your mobile.

Anyway, she said to tell you the helicopter's been delayed. It's been called away to another job.'

'Did she say how long it would be?'

'No, but she thinks it's unlikely they'll be able to pick you up today.' Now I understand why Harriet didn't want to speak to me directly. Jake and I are stranded here. 'The earliest they'll be able to get to you is 2pm tomorrow.'

'So we're stuck here?' says Jake, alarmed by the thought.

'I've got a double kayak,' says Ash, chuckling.

Rose scowls at him. 'Not funny, Ash.' She turns to me. 'Do you want me to call the lifeboat and the coastguard? You never know they might be prepared to come out and get you.'

'Honestly, they've probably got better things to do.'

'It's no bother.' She smiles, but it's not enough to dispel the pensive air hanging over her.

'It's okay, Rose. One night isn't going to kill us.' I wave her concern away. 'But it does mean we'll need somewhere to stay for the night.'

'Stay?'

'Yes. Will that be a problem? Didn't your mum and dad used to rent out the spare rooms upstairs?'

'No . . . I mean, yes, they did, but they stopped doing that a few years back.' She pauses. 'Um, I'm just trying to think what's best.'

'They can have Jenny's Cottage,' says Ash, breaking the awkward silence. 'It's just along from the pub before you get to the church. Still needs some attention, but at least the heating works.'

'I'm not sure, Ash. The electrics are still a bit dodgy.'

'No dodgier than anywhere else. They'll be fine.'

'Jenny's Cottage sounds perfect,' I say.

'That's assuming you don't mind ghosts, of course,' he adds.

'It's haunted?' Jake gives me a 'told you so' look.

'Yep, by the lovely Jenny Nancekevill. She drowned. She was returning from the Americas when her dad, a wrecker, lured her boat onto the rocks. Her body was washed up the next day. He went mad with grief. Threw himself off a cliff in the end.'

'And people have seen the ghost of this . . . Jenny Nance-kevill?' asks Jake.

'All the time.' Ash winks at me.

'He's having you on, Jake. It's just an old island legend. Do you have the keys to the cottage?'

'It's open. None of the properties are locked out of season just in case someone gets caught in bad weather and needs to take refuge.'

'I'd feel happier with a key,' says Jake.

'It won't keep Jenny out,' jokes Ash. 'Seriously, there's no need to lock yourself away on Liars Island. Nothing's going to happen to you here.'

28

Ash opens the back door to Jenny's Cottage and ushers us in. Our cases clatter against the tiled kitchen floor.

'There's tea and coffee in here,' he says, opening a cupboard above a chipped Formica counter that has already seen decades of service. 'And, something stronger, if you need it. I'll drop off some milk and a loaf of bread later so you can make yourselves some toast in the morning. You can cook although, like Rose said, the electricity isn't completely reliable at the moment so I'd suggest you eat in the pub tonight. This way to the bedrooms.'

I follow Ash up the narrow stairs. Behind me is Jake, his eyes sweeping the place for apparitions.

'So, how did you meet Rose?' I say, making conversation.

'It was years ago. In Greece.'

'Was Rose working there then?'

He stops outside a door. 'What makes you say that?'

'The photo on the wall in the bar. She's in a nurse's uniform.'

'Ah yes. She worked in one of the camps.'

'Did you work there too?'

'God no, hellish place. I don't know how Rose put up with

it for as long as she did. In fact that photo is the only time I ever went there. No, I crewed yachts for my sins. We'd moor up in the marina from time to time. I met her in a bar, on one of her nights off.'

'Crewing yachts. Sounds exciting.'

'This is the bathroom,' he says, finally opening a door. 'Yeah, it was for a while. I ditched the bar to go travelling all over the world. Great life, great money, but you start to miss having a place to call your own so I rented a small flat in Mytilene, the main town on Lesvos. Best ten years of my life. Lovely people. Beautiful country.'

'Sounds like paradise.'

'Yeah, it was for a time. I love the sea.'

'So what brought you back here?'

'Brexit,' he says without missing a beat.

'Brexit?'

'Yeah, I needed to apply for a residence permit to stay more than ninety days, but I . . . er, left it too late. My fault. Paperwork never was my strong point.' He turns the handle and the door swings open by itself.

'This was Jenny's bedroom.'

CRIME SCENE EXAMINATION REPORT RELATING TO
ASH GRIFFITHS (translated from the original)

CSI: M. Vasikakis
OIC: Insp. Papapoulous
DIVISION: Lesvos, Greece
LOCATION: *The Niki*, Mytilene port, Lesvos
EXAMINATION COMMENCED: 9.00pm, 15 December 2020
EXAMINATION NOTES
Boat raided and searched for drugs following a tip-off. Male – Belgian national – arrested. Second male fled the scene. Thought to be UK national. Ash Griffiths

EVIDENCE COLLECTED
- Bag containing unidentified substance photographed in situ REF HB1–5
- Contents submitted to the lab for analysis.
- Plastic bag submitted for fingerprinting.
- REF HB15–20: Fingerprints recovered from the scene.

29

Running my hand along the dusty shelf crammed with ancient maps and walking guides, I'm just about to select one when a cold draft blasts the back of my neck and Jake ambles into the living room, smoothing his red hair back into place.

'Wow, the winds are really beginning to pick up out there.'

'Everything okay with Sophie?'

'Just about. It took a while to get a signal. She wasn't exactly over the moon when I told her I wouldn't be coming home tonight, but she gets that it comes with the job.'

'She sounds very understanding.'

'Yeah, I guess she is. Thanks for taking Jenny's bedroom, by the way. I wouldn't have slept a wink.'

'Ash is having you on. He no more knows which room Jenny slept in than I do.'

But Jake isn't listening.

'This place reminds me of that Agatha Christie movie they showed last Christmas,' he says, eyeing the decor. 'You know, the one where a group of people are stranded on an island.'

'*And Then There Were None*,' I say, easing out a tattered map.

'What?'

'The film was called *And Then There Were None*,' I say, opening the map for closer inspection.

'Oh yeah. Hadn't they all committed a crime, or something? Although I can't remember what happened in the end.'

'I think they were all murdered.'

He looks at me as if it were my fault. 'Wish I hadn't asked now.'

Jake continues his tour of the living room while I smooth out the black-and-white line drawing of Liars Island on the mahogany dining table in the corner.

'Don't you find old photos really creepy?'

I glance up from the map to see him studying a faded black-and-white of a group of men staring out from a field in front of the cottage, their bowler hats and waistcoats strangely at odds with the pitchforks they're leaning against, as if it was normal to wear your Sunday best to work the fields. He's right, they're as creepy as fuck, but Jake's nervous enough as it is so I don't respond.

'They're never smiling and their eyes just seem to follow you around the room.' He shudders and points to a young woman in a long black dress and apron, wearing a glum expression. 'Do you think that's Jenny?'

'I doubt it. She died long before cameras were invented. You do know that's just another ghost story to amuse the tourists. My dad had a million of them. When Rose and I were young, this cottage was a ruin so we came up here with a ouija board we'd made. Believe me, Jenny isn't roaming the corridors, wailing at night, it's all nonsense.'

'You held a seance?' he asks, horrified.

'Yes, of course. Didn't you when you were a kid?'

'No.' He spies the map on the table and ambles over. 'It looks like one of those old-fashioned treasure maps.'

'Only in our case x marks the spot of a murder. Hopefully.'

'What do you mean?'

'Well, if we're not getting picked up until tomorrow afternoon, we may as well make ourselves useful and see if we can work out if Kieran was killed elsewhere.'

'I thought you said Harriet didn't go for your slate and granite theory.'

'She didn't, but that doesn't mean I can't. I understand her misgivings. Why would Dove and Bagshaw risk carrying Kieran's body to Devil's Cauldron so he could be found when there's a dozen other places just as public where they could have dumped him? Still, it all feels . . . staged.'

'Okay, but apart from the rock I found, how are you going to prove it?' I'm sensing Jake is Team Harriet on this one.

'I don't know yet, but see this line here?' My finger traces a solid black line that bisects the island about two-thirds of the way down. 'Everything above it is granite, everything below is slate.'

'So that means most of the properties on the island are in the slate area including The Barbary Inn and the church.'

'Yes.'

'So if Bagshaw killed Kieran he would have had to walk from a slate area to a granite area to pick up a granite stone before doubling back towards the south of the island and Devil's Cauldron.'

'Yes, but Dove already lives in the granite area.' I tap the map. 'See this small oblong shape here on the far north of the island? That's Grannus House.'

'So she already had a choice of rocks, any one of which she could have picked up on her way from Grannus House to Devil's Cauldron.'

'Right again, Sherlock, although that's assuming Kieran was killed on the beach, what if we consider the possibility that he was killed somewhere above this line in the granite area. Then no one was lugging granite rocks anywhere.'

'Okay, but where do we even start? I mean it was night-time. The electricity went off at 11pm and the whole island was in darkness. It's not as if people are roaming about the place at all hours, although I wouldn't put it past some of them, but it means Dove or Bagshaw or both could have killed Kieran literally anywhere on the island.'

'That's true, but, as you said, no one goes out walking on the island in the middle of the night which means they didn't just bump into Kieran on the off chance. That night he left the pub with Ben and returned to the centre. He had no reason to be wandering randomly around the north of the island at all hours, unless . . .'

'Unless he arranged to meet Dove or Bagshaw somewhere. But where?'

'Precisely.' I wave a hand over the map. 'The island is basically a plateau. It's very open and exposed to the elements. There's very little natural shelter and very few landmarks that you could identify as a good place to meet. But we know the properties aren't locked so maybe they decided to meet in one of those.'

'That's true.' Jake nods, his enthusiasm for my theory building. 'So what buildings are in the granite part of the island?'

'Grannus House, the retreat, but that's already been searched.'

Jake points to an oblong halfway up the island. 'What's this place?'

'That's the mansion built by convicts. The one Hilton stays in when he's here.'

'Okay.' Jake squints at the map. 'So that leaves . . . these two,' he says, circling two small squares about midway up the island.

'That's the lighthouse and Lookout Cottage. We've got the whole morning to ourselves tomorrow so I'm proposing we go take a look.'

Jake shudders. 'I'm in. The less time I spend in this place, the better.'

'Great, it's probably best if we don't mention it to anyone but if we find out that one of these places is where Kieran was murdered, then I'd like to see Dove or Bagshaw wriggle out of that one. Right, I'm going up to the church to call my daughter and let her know what's happening.'

'You're not leaving me on my own here, are you?'

I shake my head in mock disappointment at his jumpiness. 'Tell you what, why don't you go on over to the pub and wait for me there?'

'Good idea,' he says, making for the door so he's first to leave, but as he passes the living-room window, he glances out into the darkness and suddenly stops. 'What the—?'

'Don't tell me you've seen a ghost.'

He moves closer to the window.

'It's nothing,' he says with some relief. 'It's only Ash.'

I join him at the window in time to see Ash pause outside

a locked barn a little way down from the cottage. He checks the surrounding area and Jake and I step back into the room to avoid detection, giving it a few seconds before resuming our surveillance.

'What do you think he's up to?' says Jake as Ash unlocks the padlock and slips it into his pocket. He gives a final cursory glance over his shoulder before pulling the door open just wide enough for him to slip inside and close it behind him.

'I've no idea, but whatever it is, he doesn't want anyone to know about it.'

30

Ten minutes of stomping around the church finally results in a 3G signal on my screen and I dial Megan's number.

'Hi, Mum.' A glum voice reaches me over the stiff breeze quietly escorting slate-grey clouds across the evening sky.

'Hi, Megan. Want to tell me what's going on?'

I've been trying to get hold of her ever since Penny told me she was having a miserable time with Julian and wanted to come home.

'I thought Penny told you.'

'She did, but I want to hear it from you.'

'They hate me.'

'They don't hate you, Megan.'

'Then why do they keep making me do chores and making digs about being on my phone?'

'They just do things differently, that's all.'

'And I have to babysit Noah and Josh. They wear me out.'

'They are your brothers.'

'Half-brothers.'

'They're just very young and very excited to have a big sister. This holiday is a chance for you all to get to know each other.'

'I know, but I just feel really alone. I'm missing home. I'm missing Jay. Can you come and pick me up?'

'Did Penny put you up to this?'

'No. Why?'

'Nothing.'

'Please come and get me.'

I cast around the buildings clustered at the bottom of the hill, searching for words to reason with her, which is when I notice a figure moving between the buildings. At first I think it's Ash returning to the barn Jake and I saw him slip into earlier. We watched the building until he left as furtively as he'd arrived. God knows what he's up to, but this person is too small to be Ash.

'Mum, are you going to come?'

'I couldn't even if I wanted to. I'm stuck on Liars Island until tomorrow at the earliest.'

'What about Penny?'

'I can't ask her.'

'Is this because you've fallen out? You were pretty mean to her.'

So Penny has told Megan about our row. Doubtless Megan has taken her side.

'It's got nothing to do with that. It's because I'm not at home and you're my responsibility, not hers.'

'She won't mind. She's looked after me loads of times.'

The figure walks up the path towards the church before disappearing from sight. Perhaps they've gone inside.

'Are you even listening?' says Megan impatiently.

'I'm listening and I think you need to stick it out. You can't just go running home to Penny or me when things get difficult.'

'God, you're so unreasonable.'

There's a rustling sound behind me. I swing around to see Rose, her face illuminated by her iPhone torch. When she sees me on the phone, she raises her hands in an apology, but history has taught me there's no coming back from being called unreasonable and my conversation with Megan will just deteriorate further.

'We'll talk about this tomorrow when I get back,' I say to her. 'Until then, please try and make the effort. Love you.'

'K.'

The line goes silent.

'I'm sorry, Ally, I didn't mean to interrupt,' says Rose. 'I brought some supplies over for you and Jake. The poor lad looked quite terrified when I knocked on the door. I'm not sure who he expected. Anyway, he said you were up at the church so I thought I'd make sure you're okay.'

'Everything's fine. Ash's ghost story has given him the hee-bie-jeebies. Thank you.'

'Who was that you were on the phone to, if you don't mind me asking?'

'My daughter, Megan, I was just letting her know that I'm spending the night here.'

Rose's eyes light up. 'You have a daughter?'

'Yes.'

'Wow, that's wonderful, Ally.'

'Can't say it feels wonderful right now.' I laugh. 'She's fifteen,' I add as if that explains everything, but it barely raises a smile from Rose.

'You're so lucky.'

'I guess so, even if she does drive me to distraction.' I look at Rose, but she isn't listening. There's something else going on here. Her eyes are full of pain. 'What is it, Rose?'

She takes a breath. 'I-I can't have kids.'

'Oh God, Rose, I'm so sorry. I had no idea,' I say, embarrassed by my glibness.

'Why would you?' she says suddenly brightening. She pauses and in that space slides in the memory of the two of us sitting outside the inn one afternoon and she told me with an unshakeable conviction she was destined to have two children, a girl and a boy. 'But I never had you down as the maternal type.'

'Thanks.' I laugh.

'You know what I mean.'

'You're right,' I concede. Rose was always the one scooping up the little kids that came over on the boat. I was the one with my head in a book. I never factored in having kids, while Rose thought of little else. 'Megan wasn't planned, but I'm truly sorry, Rose. I know how much you wanted children.'

'It's okay. Life has a way of sorting itself out.'

'Does it? Seems to me that life fucks us over most of the time.'

'Things not great with your daughter then?'

'It's complicated.' I allow myself a weary sigh. 'She's with her dad at the moment. We're not together, and he wasn't in her life until a few months ago but it's not working out between them. She wants to come home, but I'm here so there's no one at home.'

'Isn't there someone else who can help?'

'My friend, Penny. She's known Megan almost all her life.' I refrain from calling her Megan's second mum. 'But things are a bit strained between us right now.'

'Oh?'

'She has a tendency to forget Megan is my daughter, not hers.'

Rose frowns.

'It's nothing. She told Megan she could come home without talking to me first.'

Rose nods. 'I guess she was just trying to help. What do they say, it takes a village to raise a child.' She smiles sadly. 'But what would I know?'

Rose and I return to The Barbary Inn together. Jake is there, launching darts in the approximate direction of a dartboard ringed by a lifebuoy with the word *Absolution* written around it. Next to him, propped against the bar and enjoying the spectacle is Ash. Taking a glass from the shelf above the bar, Rose pours me a pint of beer as I pull up a barstool. It's only then that I notice Ben Dawson sitting alone in the corner of the pub, staring morosely into an untouched pint. In a bout of uncharitableness, I wonder if this public wearing of his grief is deliberate. Leaning across the bar at Rose, I nod in Ben's direction.

'Is he okay?'

'He doesn't like being at the centre on his own at the moment,' she says, her pity putting my cynicism to shame. 'I can't blame him. He and Kieran were like brothers. He doesn't have a lot to do with his own family.'

'Why not?'

'I'm not sure. He never talks about them. Kieran and Hilton were his family.'

'He must be devastated to lose his friend like that.'

'Yes, we all are,' she says with genuine sadness.

'I'm sorry that Jake and I are intruding like this. It's obvious you've got enough on without having to put up with a couple of homeless CSIs.'

'It's fine. I was just a bit embarrassed, that's all. We're still getting the cottages ready for the new season. There's dust all over the place. Ash and I are responsible for maintaining all the properties.'

'Oh?'

'Yes, they're only cleaned once a month out of season.' She collects her drink and joins me on my side of the bar. 'We then do a final clean the week before visitors start arriving.'

'So when were they last cleaned?'

'A good three weeks ago. Same as all of them.'

'Jake and I thought we might take a look at the other properties tomorrow, if that's okay.'

'Sure, but why would you be interested in them?'

'Jake's not been a CSI long. It's an opportunity for him to learn a few tricks of the trade.'

'Okay. Do you want me or Ash to come too?'

'No, as long as you're happy for us to go into the properties, we'll be fine on our own.'

'Sure, help yourself. You know your way around. Nothing's changed. You know you're always welcome here, Ally.' She holds her glass up. 'Here's to old friends. I know the circumstances aren't ideal, but it's great to see you. How long has it been?'

'Old friends.' Our glasses clink and I take a sip. 'Over twenty years. Since Dad died.'

'It must be strange coming back here after what happened.'

'Not as strange as I thought, as it happens, but how about you? I'm sure you said you'd never leave the place.'

'We say a lot of things when we're young, don't we?' She smiles. 'But I left when I met my first husband. After we divorced, I went travelling for a bit and then ended up working in a camp in Greece.'

'Where you met Ash, right?'

'Sort of, as friends, but how did you know?'

'He told me when he was showing us around Jenny's Cottage. I was asking him about that photo.'

I nod at the picture, hanging on the wall partitioning the bar from the dining area.

'Ah yes, I'd forgotten that it was there. My parents put it up.' She studies it for a moment. 'Ash was going out with Hana then, of course. I worked there as a children's nurse, but around five years ago I decided I'd had enough and besides I always knew I wanted to come back. This place will always be home.'

'And Ash followed you.'

'A few years later, yes. He messed up his visa so had to leave Greece. He got a job on the island. That's when we got together and then when Mum and Dad said they were retiring we decided to take over the licence.'

'God, they don't still have that stupid rule that only married couples can run the pub, do they?'

'They do.' She laughs. 'And I definitely didn't think I'd ever marry again, but it's just a piece of paper, isn't it? So we just snuck off to Vegas and did the deed. Turned out to be the best thing I ever did.'

'You seem really happy together.'

'We are. I know the two of you got off to a bad start, but he's one of the good guys. Believe me, I had to work through some right muppets to get to him.'

'Your ex?'

'Don't remind me.'

'Sorry.'

'It's okay. I'm joking. It's no big deal. We all make mistakes.'

'We certainly do. I've made more than my fair share,' I say, Liam drifting momentarily into my mind. 'But what happened to you?'

'It was great at first. I thought Rob was the perfect guy. He was a Lullcott so you can imagine how big the wedding was. Anyway, as soon as we hit a rough patch, he jumped ship.'

'I'm sorry, Rose, that sounds rough.'

'Yeah, I lost it for a while. I couldn't stay in North Devon. You know what it's like around here so I got my shit together, as they say, and left and now I'm home where I belong with a man I love and trust with all my heart. Honestly, I don't think I'll ever leave here again. Why would I when I have everything I could possibly want? Well, nearly.'

'What do you mean?'

'Can't say. Don't want to jinx it.' She runs her pinched thumb and forefinger along her lips.

'Okay. Fair enough.' I look around the bar. 'So what have you got lined up for this place? Please tell me you're getting rid of those lifebuoys.'

'Don't worry, they're on their way. Ash and I are completely renovating the pub.'

'That sounds great. And expensive.'

'Yeah, but it needs it. Ash, very reluctantly I might add, did one last yacht delivery last month to cover the costs. He hated doing it. He did it for me, love him. Anyway, what about you? You say you're not with your daughter's dad anymore?'

Before I have time to answer her, the pub door bursts open, crashing against the wall. There's a rush of cold air. A large, bearded man stumbles out of the darkness, into the pub and crashes into the table.

31

Rose and I leap to our feet just as Ash appears from around the bar, closely followed by Jake. The man rights himself, but continues to sway unsteadily on his feet.

'Fuck you.' He throws a pointed finger across the room. 'Fuck the lot of you.'

'Steady on, Forrest.' Ash grabs him by the lapels as he's about to keel over and lowers him onto a chair.

'He's plastered,' says Rose. 'Ash, go make a strong black coffee for him.'

Ash disappears into the back while Rose rubs Forrest's back.

'Forrest, love. What do you think you're doing?'

He lifts his head. 'Dove should be here.'

'I know,' says Rose.

'No, you don't know.' He turns his glare on all of us. 'None of you have any idea. They think she did it.'

'Did what?'

'She . . . she told them she killed Kieran.'

Jake and I exchange glances. Forrest knows Dove has confessed to killing Kieran, but how?

'Confessed. What are you talking about?' asks Rose.

Forrest's eyes swell with tears. 'He got her drunk and they ended up having sex. Then he threatened to tell me. She didn't know what to do so she went to see him to beg him not to say anything. Instead, he tried it on again and so she hit him. She didn't mean to kill him.'

Rose's hand flies to her mouth. 'Oh my God. No.'

Ash appears and hands a steaming mug of black coffee to Rose who closes Forrest's hands around it. 'What's going on?' asks Ash.

'Dove killed Kieran.'

'What?' says Ash, as incredulous as Rose.

'I know. I can't believe it myself, but Forrest says he got her drunk and then got off with her. She was scared Forrest would find out.'

'Dove and Kieran?' says Ash. 'But when?'

'About three weeks ago. On the way back to Grannus House.'

'I don't remember,' says Rose.

'That's because you'd gone to the mainland, but now you mention it I remember them leaving the pub together.' Ash frowns. 'She seemed quite happy, a bit tipsy maybe, but I wasn't paying much attention. When Kieran said he'd walk Dove home, I didn't think anything of it.'

'Did you tell the investigation team this?'

'Yes, but they didn't say why they were asking.'

Forrest grabs Rose's hand. 'I don't understand it, why didn't she tell me what was going on?'

'I . . . I don't know, Forrest.'

'We tell each other everything. Everything. We don't have any secrets.'

'Maybe . . . maybe she didn't want to hurt you,' says Rose, still trying to make sense of it all.

'But I'd have understood. We all make mistakes. We'd have worked through it. I love her. It's tearing me apart, man. I can't live without her. And no one's doing anything to help her. She's completely on her own. She's terrified.'

'There isn't anything we can do. We know it's hard. She's our friend too. Drink the coffee. It'll make you feel better.'

Forrest smashes the mug on the floor. 'I don't want any fucking coffee.' He points in the vague direction of the mainland. 'We should be over there trying to get her out.'

He appeals to the room and it's then that he notices Ben in the far corner.

'You,' he roars. 'I'm going to fucking kill you.'

Ben leaps to his feet but Rose steps between them, placing her hand on Forrest's chest.

'That's enough, Forrest.'

He's twice her size, but he does as he's told, confining himself to jabbing a finger at Ben over Rose's shoulder.

'You knew what he was like, but you never said anything because the only thing you care about is your fucking watersports centre.'

'I've got no idea what you're talking about,' Ben says.

'Well, you're not going to get away with this because I know you,' Forrest slurs. 'Kieran told me everything and if my Dove doesn't come home, you can kiss your precious business goodbye.'

'Okay, I think it's time you went home, Forrest,' says Ash, grabbing Forrest's huge arm and throwing it around his shoulders. Forrest leans against him, but his weight threatens to topple both of them.

'You can't manage him on your own,' says Rose.

'Of course, I can.'

'No, it's safer if two of you go.' She nods at Jake. Ash goes to protest but thinks better of it.

'Sure,' says Jake. 'Let's go, mate.'

Jake levers Forrest's free arm around his shoulder. Forrest looks up at Ash.

'They're gonna charge her, man.'

Jake and I exchange glances. With Bagshaw in the frame for Kieran's murder now, no one is getting charged with anything.

'I know, mate,' says Ash.

'The thing is, man, she didn't do it.'

Ash gives him a helpless look. 'Mate, she confessed.'

'I don't care what she's told them, and I don't care what happened between her and Kieran. She didn't kill him.'

He continues to protest Dove's innocence as Ash and Jake escort him from the pub until the darkness swallows his voice.

Rose turns to Ben. 'Are you okay? You didn't deserve any of that. You haven't done anything wrong.'

'He's upset,' he says, slipping his coat on. 'But I think I'll get going too.'

'Poor guy,' says Rose, watching Ben leave before turning to me, her face full of hurt. 'I take it you knew all along.'

'Yes.'

'I can't believe it. Dove would never have cheated on Forrest.'

'It sounds like she'd been drinking.'

'So he took advantage of her?'

'No, what I mean is it sounds like they got carried away.'

Rose shakes her head, still trying to make sense of it all.

'But I thought she'd given up drinking. Maybe Kieran spiked her drink?'

'Do you really think that's possible? I mean, I'm guessing there isn't a ready supply of Rohypnol on the island.'

'I don't know, but it would explain it and it might help Forrest understand why she slept with Kieran.' She looks towards the door. 'Poor Forrest. He adores Dove. Why didn't she just tell him? He'd have forgiven her. He'd go to the ends of the earth for her. He's just about the nicest bloke you could wish to meet. A real gentle giant.'

Some things don't change. Rose still always sees the best in people, but I'm guessing she doesn't know Forrest Stream was once called Scott Budleigh-Smith, the son of a minister who burnt a £50 note in front of a homeless man for kicks. But I have other things on my mind. When Forrest fell through the pub door, it wasn't his brick shithouse dimensions that I noticed first. It was his red jacket. Forrest Stream has been following Jake and I ever since we arrived.

CRIME SCENE EXAMINATION REPORT RELATING TO FORREST

CSI: Sophie Garcia
OIC: PC Vine
DIVISION: West Surrey, Surrey Police
LOCATION: Hamwell House, Cobham, Surrey
EXAMINATION COMMENCED: 8 January 2020
EXAMINATION NOTES
- Faecal matter (possibly human?) posted through the letterbox of the family home.
- Possible revenge attack for incident relating to Scott Budleigh-Smith (son of the Minister Sir Oliver Budleigh-Smith)

EVIDENCE COLLECTED
- Faecal sample
- Fingerprints from letterbox (Elimination prints taken)
- Glove mark recovered

32

I stir at the sound of voices outside the back door below my bedroom window. I reach for the bedside light, but nothing happens. Checking my watch, I realise it's after midnight and the electricity was switched off an hour ago. My hand gropes the bedside cabinet until it finds my iPhone. Pressing torch mode, I follow the pale glow of light onto the landing and downstairs.

Through the kitchen window, I spy two shadowy figures. The height of one of them tells me it's Jake. I'm assuming the other is Ash who has steered him safely back to the cottage after escorting Forrest to Grannus House. Liars Island at night is no place for the uninitiated.

Jake thanks Ash before bidding him goodnight. He opens the back door, immediately jumping when he sees me.

'What the f—?'

'Sorry, I didn't mean to scare you. I heard voices.'

'That's okay,' he says, still clutching his heart.

'Did you get Forrest back okay?'

'Yeah. Took a while. He cried a lot.' Jake grimaces at the memory. 'He reckons Ben definitely knew about Kieran and Dove, but kept it to himself. He's adamant that if Ben had told him then Kieran would still be alive.'

'Maybe, but what bothers me is that he knew she'd confessed. She must have called him, which means she's broken any bail conditions that have been set.'

'What will happen to her?'

'Technically she could be re-arrested, but it means the whole island now knows which doesn't help the investigation. So what did you make of Jocasta Marwell when you got to Grannus House?'

'She flipped out when she found out I was with the police.'

'What? You're kidding.'

'Totally lost her shit. Told me to get out of her house.'

'But you were helping Forrest home.'

'That's what I said, but she said I was just trying to trick her into letting us into Grannus House without a search warrant.'

'Paranoid much?'

'I know. Anyway, I left.'

'What about Forrest?'

'He was still going on about Dove being innocent. Not sure what part of confession he doesn't understand, but he's having none of it.'

'He doesn't want to think of his life-partner being a murderer. Plus he was hammered. That lad is going to have a stinking hangover tomorrow.'

'More like a comedown.' Jake grins.

'What do you mean?'

'It wasn't until we helped him back to Grannus House that I realised I couldn't smell any alcohol on him. Forrest wasn't drunk. He was high.'

* * *

Unable to sleep, I wrap the duvet around me and move to the window seat where I'm hoping for a spectacular night sky, only to discover a bank of cloud has extinguished the stars and the only visible lights are the ones twinkling in the distance on the South Wales coast.

Jake and I came here today to answer just one question: is Bagshaw telling the truth? But now, as I stare out into the empty night, a dozen others tumble through my mind and I can't help thinking there's a hell of a lot more going on here that we don't know about. If Forrest was high, as Jake said, where did he get the drugs from? And why was he watching us? Ash has got form for low-level drug dealing. Is that what he's hiding in the barn he keeps padlocked? Drugs? And why was Ben so eager to join Jake and me at Devil's Cauldron? Then there's Rose, my old friend. One minute, she wants us to stay, the next she can't wait to see the back of us. And what of Hilton Deveney who prefers Ben to his own son? Rose didn't hear his helicopter. Does that mean he's still on the island? But the biggest question of all is, what, if anything, does any of this have to do with Kieran's murder? That's anyone's guess, and I'm not in the business of guessing. Tomorrow, Jake and I will search for evidence that Kieran wasn't killed at Devil's Cauldron.

I'm about to return to my bed when a light comes on in the upstairs room of The Barbary Inn. The generator was turned off hours ago so it's likely to be a torch or an oil lamp of some kind. A figure passes in front of the window. I'm sure it's Rose and I wonder what she's still doing up, long after lights out. A second light comes on. This time from another of the upstairs rooms. Years ago, it was a guest room. It could be anything now. A few seconds later, the silhouette of a man appears at the window. It's Ash. He seems to be staring in my direction, but I'm certain I can't be seen so I stay where I am. I wait for one of the lights to go out, but they both remain on and I have a sense that Rose and Ash are sleeping in separate rooms. But they've only been married a few months.

33

It's late morning. Jake and I are standing in front of a large white Georgian mansion sitting at the end of a short gravel driveway, fringed by the palms quietly flourishing on the more sheltered eastern side of an island that sits squarely in the path of the Gulf Stream.

We've already examined Lookout Cottage and the lighthouse. My hopes were raised when Rose told me last night it hadn't been cleaned for three weeks and I immediately pictured a layer of dust – a cleaner's enemy, but a CSI's best friend. When we arrived at the properties, the first thing we noticed was that it had been disturbed in places and I felt a familiar frisson that we might be onto something, but several sweeps of a blood-detecting UV torch failed to elicit the telltale black spots. Wherever Kieran was killed, it wasn't there.

'So this is Hilton Deveney's place then?' says Jake, surveying the building's impressive edifice in front of him.

'Not officially, no. It's owned by the Trust. He just stays here when he's on the island.'

'Cool. So what's the plan of attack?'

'Rose said she didn't hear Hilton's helicopter leave yesterday so I'm thinking he might still be here.'

'So Hilton's at home?'

'He could be, although he usually lets her know if he's staying on the island.'

'If he is in, what are you going to say? I mean you hardly hit it off yesterday.'

'I'm going to appeal to his better nature. Let's just hope he has one,' I say, stepping forward to ring the doorbell. 'His son has just been murdered. We're here to try to work out if the killer is Dove or Bagshaw or both.'

The chimes echo behind the door.

'No one in. I guess he left the island, after all,' says Jake after a few seconds. 'What now?'

I reach for the doorknob.

He grabs my arm. 'What are you doing?'

'Rose said it was okay for us to go into the buildings. Hilton doesn't own this place.' I turn the handle, but the door doesn't budge. 'It's locked anyway. Perhaps they didn't hear the bell. You wait here, I'll try the back.'

I slip down the side of the house to find a large conservatory attached to the rear of the building. I knock loudly on the glass and wait, but no one comes to the door. The door is also locked, but the key is lying on the sill next to it. Mulling my next move, I notice one of the window catches is raised. It would take seconds to prise it open and unlock the conservatory from the inside. Jake wouldn't be any the wiser. I could just pretend I found it like that, but I'm already on a final warning. It would only take Hilton to insist he'd secured the property and I'd be out for good.

Jake's concerned face appears around the corner.

'Ally,' he says in a loud whisper. 'There's someone inside.'

'What?'

'I think someone's moving around upstairs.'

'Are you sure? Was it Hilton?'

'I don't think so. I think it might be Forrest.'

'What?'

'I caught a glimpse of his red coat, but what the hell is he doing here? And why didn't he open the door to us?' says Jake, leading me back to the front of the house.

'The properties are meant to be left open out of season so the residents can take shelter if the weather turns. He must have locked himself in. Perhaps he's come here to sleep his hangover off in peace. Which window was it?'

'Top left.'

'Forrest, it's Ally Dymond from Devon Police,' I call up to the window. 'Looks like he doesn't want to open the door to us. There's nothing we can do about it. Let's go.'

We pick up our cases and start walking back down the driveway.

'What a waste of time.' Jake huffs. 'Nothing at the lighthouse or Lookout Cottage and Forrest refusing to open the door to us.'

'Yeah, but seventy per cent of the crime scenes we attend probably fall into that category.'

'True. God, I can't wait to get home.' He looks skywards at the darkening clouds overhead. 'It looks like rain too.'

'So what are you going to do when you get back?'

'Have a nice hot bath followed by a fat sleep in my non-haunted house.'

'What about Sophie? Isn't she still expecting a romantic meal for two?'

'I'd forgotten about that. Maybe she'll settle for a kebab.'

'And they say romance is dead.'

We stroll past Hilton's black Defender parked on the gravel driveway, a little way from the house. The light catches the bonnet. I didn't notice it yesterday when Hilton drove up to the track towards us, but now I see both headlights are clouded in smudges that have dulled the gleaming paintwork where they have been recently installed. I grab Jake's arm.

'Hang on a minute.'

'What is it?'

'Maybe it hasn't been a wasted journey after all,' I say, nodding at the Defender.

Jake frowns and bends down to take a closer look. 'Another mistake?' He grins up at me.

'I think I'd call this one serendipity.' I smile.

Jake and I join the main track that runs down the spine of the island, towards the inn, grateful for the strong tailwind ushering us on our way.

'So do you reckon this Cal Meeth has been nicking these Land Rover headlights and supplying Hilton, among others?'

'PC Bryan Rogers thinks so. The figure in the CCTV at the Land Rover dealership at Heale Cross looked suspiciously like Cal, but it's not clear enough to identify him, which is a shame because nothing would give me greater pleasure than to wipe the smirk off that little shit's face.'

'Not a fan then?'

'You could say that.'

'Why doesn't Hilton just buy himself new headlights?'

'According to Bryan, they're hard to get hold of at the moment. Problems with the supply chain.'

'But I'm guessing this Cal and Hilton don't move in the same circles so how would he know Hilton needed a new headlight? And how did they get out here?'

'Christ, it's breezy.' I brush aside the strands of hair the wind has whipped across my face. 'He's probably using a fence. He wouldn't be stupid enough to bring stolen headlights out to the island himself. We got some decent dabs from Hilton's Land Rover so let's hope his go-between is in the system.'

'Funny how things pan out.'

We continue in silence before Jake stops suddenly and looks around.

'Do you hear that?'

'Hear what?'

'Voices.'

'No.'

'I think they're coming from in there,' he says, pointing to woodland some distance from the track.

'Let's take a look.'

The grassy field softens our footsteps as we make our way towards the trees.

'Over there,' says Jake. I follow his gaze to a bespectacled woman standing in a clearing, wearing a Barbour jacket and purple harem pants tucked into a pair of green Hunter boots, her greying hair swept up into a messy bun. And she's alone.

Jake mouths 'Jocasta Marwell' at me. The two have already met. I'm about to step forward and make my introductions when Jocasta starts talking.

'Don't you think I'd change things if I could?' she says in a clear, well-spoken voice. She pauses as if waiting for a response.

'Who's she talking to?' Jake whispers.

'No idea. There's no one else here.'

'I know, but it's too late now,' Jocasta continues. 'What's done is done. There's no point going over it.' She pauses again. 'That's all right,' she says. 'I understand you're still angry. It was my fault. Yes, I know what they're planning to do. I've told him the island doesn't need a bunkhouse. It's environmental rape, but he won't listen. None of them will. They just see the money. Maybe I should burn it all to the ground. Direct action is the only thing that makes a difference.'

'Do you think she's all right?' whispers Jake.

'I think we should find out.'

As we step out from behind a tree, a twig cracks beneath my boot announcing our arrival.

Jocasta twists round. 'Who are you?' she snaps.

'It's okay,' I say, raising my hand. 'We didn't mean to startle you. We're police crime scene investigators.'

'What is this? Police surveillance?'

'No, like I said, we're CSIs and, even if this was police surveillance, then we're not very good at it, are we?' My joke fails to raise a smile. 'Anyway, I believe you already know my colleague, Jake Harris. He brought Forrest back last night with Ash. How is he this morning? He seemed very upset last night.'

'Can you blame him?' she says, squinting at Jake. 'How would you feel if your partner was wrongly accused of murder.'

'Wrongly accused? You do know she confessed?'

I suspect I'm not telling Jocasta anything she doesn't already know. Forrest would have told her about Dove's call.

'Coerced by your lot, no doubt.'

I sigh inwardly. The days of forced confessions are long gone and I'm not going to let Jocasta get away with thinking otherwise.

'If you're suggesting Dove has been pressured into confessing by the police, that is a very serious allegation and I'd be happy to pass on details of the Independent Office for Police Conduct. My colleague and I are no fans of police officers who abuse their position.'

'It's just a gut feeling,' she says defensively. She isn't used to being called out for her accusations, but she doesn't get off that lightly.

'Well, last time I checked, gut feelings weren't admissible in court.' My facetiousness earns me a glare.

'I'm well aware of court proceedings. My point is Dove Sunrise is innocent and if she's convicted of killing Kieran Deveney, it'll be the biggest miscarriage of justice this country has ever seen and God knows there's a few contenders. Even you can't deny that.'

She has a point. Just when I think the police is regaining some of the respect it seems to have lost in recent years, some idiot thinks it's a good idea to sprinkle WhatsApp with offensive messages. And don't get me started on taking pictures at crime scenes, for fuck's sake.

'I get that you don't like the police, Jocasta. Sometimes I don't like them either, but we have a job to do.'

'And what exactly is your job here?'

'We're following up a number of leads from the investigation.'

'Is that what you call it? Well, just make sure to stay away from my property. We're still clearing up after your last visit.'

She turns to leave. Without warning her legs give way. She grabs a branch to steady herself as Jake rushes forward to catch her. For a moment, it looks like she's about to crumple in his arms, but she manages to gather herself.

'Get off me,' she says, brushing Jake off.

'Are you sure you're all right? You've gone very pale,' I say.

'I'm fine. Maybe,' she says, brushing the hair from her eyes, 'I just don't like being harassed by the police.'

'It's hardly harassment, Jocasta, we're just concerned about you.'

'Well, take it elsewhere,' she says tersely, but before we can respond, she stalks off through the woods.

'She's no fan of the police, is she?' says Jake, watching her stomp through the undergrowth as if trying to prove she's in rude health.

'Apparently, she's been arrested more times than Pete Doherty.'

'Pete Doherty? Is he the drunk guy that keeps shouting his mouth off in Barnston Square?'

I eye Jake with some level of disappointment. 'Seriously?'

'What?'

'Never mind. Let's wait a little longer, make sure she's okay.'

We watch until the trees finally close behind her.

'Who do you think she was talking to just then?' asks Jake.

'I've no idea,' I shrug 'You definitely spoke to her last night, right?'

'Definitely. Unless she has a twin.'

'And she was wearing glasses then too?'

'Yes.'

'Then how come she didn't recognise you?'

CRIME SCENE EXAMINATION REPORT REGARDING JOCASTA MARWELL

<u>CSI</u>: Joe Horne
<u>OIC</u>: DC Don Isaac
<u>DIVISION</u>: Norfolk South, Norfolk Police
<u>LOCATION</u>: Respire Medical Laboratory, two miles from Melkshaw village
<u>EXAMINATION COMMENCED</u>: 3.00am, 5 July 2016
<u>EXAMINATION NOTES</u>
Break-in. Perimeter fence cut. Access to the building gained via fire exit which was prised open. Suspects arrested.

<u>EVIDENCE COLLECTED</u>
Photographs

- Point of entry and exit
- Extensive damage to the laboratory
- Empty cages

Forensic samples sent

- Tool impressions from point of entry
- Glove marks from point of entry

34

Warm air greets me as I open the pub door and an unexpected shudder shakes the remnants of an icy wind trying to follow me.

'That wind has got up,' I say to Rose, reading a magazine laid out on the bar.

'Yeah, it comes from nowhere.' She reaches for a glass. 'Rockstar?'

'Thanks.'

'On your own?'

'Yes, Jake has gone to book a restaurant for him and his girlfriend for tonight to make up for last night.' I managed to talk him out of his plans for a kebab and a night in. 'We'll be off in an hour. Thank you again for putting up with us.'

'Anytime. It was good to see you.' She looks at me. 'So . . . how were things at Lookout Cottage this morning?'

'You saw us?'

'Not me.' She smiles. 'But you can't do anything on this island without someone noticing.'

So who was it? Ash? Forrest? Jocasta? Ben? Christ, it could be any of them. I want to pursue it, but something holds me back. Our friendship is no longer unconditional like when we were kids. I'm a CSI investigating a murder and, until Dove and Bagshaw confessed, Rose was a potential suspect. Come to think of it, they all were.

'We were just killing time,' I say. Careless talk costs cases. 'I thought I'd show Jake around the place.'

'I hope he liked what he saw,' she says, going along with the lie.

'Actually, we met Jocasta. Is she okay?'

'What do you mean?'

'We bumped into her on our way back here. We stopped to chat to her but just as she was leaving she seemed to have a dizzy spell.'

'I don't know about any dizzy spells.' Rose frowns.

'She didn't recognise Jake either even though he met her last night when he brought Forrest back to Grannus House.'

'Maybe she just forgot.'

'And she seemed to be talking to someone, but there was no one there.'

'I think that might be her daughter, Amber. She died a long time ago but I think Jocasta sees her, or thinks she does. She died on the island.'

'Liars Island?'

'Yes, it must have been over ten years ago now. Jocasta thinks no one remembers, but of course my parents ran the pub at the time. Mum told me she recognised Jocasta as soon as she arrived to take over Grannus House.'

'But your mum never said anything to her.'

'No, she didn't want to remind her.'

'How did Amber die?'

'I'm not sure. I'd left the island by then. Mum thought it was a fit or something, but obviously there's no hospital here. By the time they got her to the mainland, she'd gone. From what Mum said there's nothing they could have done for her anyway.'

'That's terrible. Why would you come back to the place where you lost a loved one? I mean, after what happened to Dad, I never wanted to come back.'

'I don't know. Maybe she wanted to try and turn something terrible into something good.'

'How do you mean?'

'Most of the people that go to Grannus House are young. They'd be the same age as Amber if she lived. A lot of them, like Dove, are hurting in some way.'

'The car accident that killed her sister?'

'You know about that? Yes. It was years ago but she's never got over it. She arrived here in a bit of a state, to be honest. Jocasta spent a lot of time with her, teaching her to forgive herself.'

'Forgive herself?'

'For surviving. Jocasta helped her understand the best tribute to her sister would be for her to live her life, her best life. That's when she gave up drinking, supposedly. Next thing I know she's moved to Grannus House. She adores Jocasta.'

'Really?'

It's hard to marry the woman I just met in the woods with some Mother Earth-type figure.

'She hates the police,' says Rose. 'Sorry.'

'Not your fault.'

'The thing is she's like a mother to Dove, Forrest and anyone else who finds their way to Grannus House. I kind of respect her for that. She taught me that mothers can come in all kinds.'

I ignore the guilt gathering in the pit of my stomach. Penny has been like a mother to Megan, but that was before she crossed the line.

'I guess they do.'

'It doesn't make up for her behaviour, of course. I mean she's been horrible to Ben and Kieran about the watersports centre.'

'She seemed very wound up about their plans to expand.'

'Tell me about it. She only just found out. She and Ben had a big blow-up here this morning. It's not the first time. She was always having a go at Kieran, telling him they were destroying the island.'

'Who told her about the plans?'

'Hilton, probably. They got planning permission last week, although Kieran had already met the building suppliers. The two lads wouldn't have told Jocasta themselves. It wasn't worth the grief.'

'So what happens now to their plans?'

'Well, that's just it. I think Jocasta was expecting Hilton to close the centre now Kieran's gone, but the opposite has happened. Yesterday, he told Ben he can take it on himself. He's transferring directorship to Ben.'

'That explains the smiles and handshakes Jake and I saw between them yesterday afternoon. So what will Jocasta do now? She was talking about burning it down.'

Rose laughs. 'She won't do that.'

'But she already vandalised the kayaks.'

'How do you know about that?' Rose says sharply.

'It came up in a briefing and Jocasta doesn't strike me as very stable. She's been arrested numerous times for criminal damage.'

'She knows that if she touches the centre, Hilton will have her lease terminated. She's all talk.'

Ash wanders into the bar. 'Who's all talk?'

'Jocasta is threatening all sorts as usual.'

'Some things never change,' he says, rolling his eyes before turning to me. 'You're off in a bit, aren't you?'

'Yes, we are, but before we go, there's something I'd like to ask you.'

'Fire away.'

'I was showing Jake around the island this morning and we went by Hilton's place.'

'It's not Hilton's, much as he'd like people to think it is,' says Ash, correcting me. 'What were you doing up there?'

'Filling time, but we noticed Hilton's Land Rover has a new headlight.'

'Er . . . that's right,' he says, confused by the turn the conversation has taken. 'He cracked it on the corner of a dry-stone wall. Why?'

'Do you know where the replacement light came from?'

'No idea. Some guy brought them over from the mainland, I guess.' He shrugs.

'So you didn't fit them for Hilton then?'

'No, I would do normally, but I noticed it'd been sorted the other day so I'm assuming either Kieran or Ben fitted them. They were up at the house a lot.'

My attention is grabbed by the map on the wall at the Bara Watersports Centre, showing the water depths, shorelines, tide predictions and even the rocks and shipwrecks around Liars Island, reminding me of my childhood obsession with the sea.

'Do you sail?' asks Ben, looking up from the spreadsheets covering the counter.

'Not anymore.'

'I thought you guys had left.'

'Soon. There's something I wanted to check with you first.'

'Sure.' He smiles, pushing the spreadsheets away. 'It'll be more interesting than trying to make these figures add up for the new building.'

'I hear congratulations are in order. Hilton is putting you in sole charge of the business.'

'Nothing's signed,' he says, balking slightly. 'And not everyone sees it as a cause for celebration.'

'I gather we're talking about Jocasta Marwell? I heard the two of you had a run-in this morning. We bumped into her as well. We overheard her threatening all sorts to stop your building plans going ahead. We're aware that she vandalised several of your kayaks a little while ago.'

'You know about that? Kieran was furious. Almost destroyed the business before we even got started. She thought Kieran had nicked her carrots for a joke, or something. Anyway, she's lucky Kieran didn't tell his dad. He'd have thrown her off the island.'

'Why didn't Kieran say anything?'

'He thought his dad would blame him for not locking the kayaks away so he didn't bother. Hilton was really hard on Kieran like that. I felt sorry for him, but thanks for the heads-up and I'm not Kieran. If she tries anything, I'll be straight on the phone to Hilton. Is that what you wanted to check with me?' That smile again.

'No, it's not. Ash said that you or Kieran fitted Hilton's new Land Rover headlight a few weeks back.'

'Er, yes, that's right,' he says. 'Hilton clipped it on a stone wall. A guy brought it over on the boat. I remember it because it was the same day Reverend Bagshaw arrived.'

'Was the light in a box?'

He frowns, trying to recall the memory. 'Er, no, now you mention it, it was loose, in a carrier bag.'

'Do you remember anything about the person who brought it?'

'Not really. He was a pretty average-looking kind of a guy, a bit pasty like he didn't see much sunlight and he had a lot to say for himself. Expert on everything. Tried to tell me I was using the wrong kind of kayak and he could get better ones for me. I'm sure you've met the type.'

'Did you catch his name?'

'No, sorry. Actually, wait, yes I did. He was dropping some supplies off at the pub as well and the ship's captain called out to him not to be long as he didn't want to miss the tide.' He pauses for a few moments. 'His name was Kev, Cam, no, no, that's wrong. It was Cal. That's it,' he says triumphantly. 'He was called Cal.'

'Cal?'

'Yes, definitely.'

So Cal brought the stolen headlight to the island personally. I overestimated him. He is an idiot, after all.

'Why?' asks Ben.

'Just another crime Jake and I are following up.'

'Was the headlight stolen then? Because if I'd known that, I'd have told him to sling his hook. Sorry.'

'That's okay. You've been a great help. Thank you, and I hope you sort things out with Forrest. He was pretty upset with you last night.'

'The guy's lost his head. I can't blame him. I'd probably feel the same if my girlfriend was arrested for murder. I can't believe she confessed, but that explains why those detectives were so interested in how well Dove knew Kieran.'

'Forrest seemed to think you knew there was something going on between the two of them.'

'Well, he's wrong. I had absolutely no idea. Kieran never said anything to me. If he had I'd have told him to back off. Something like that can rip a small island like this apart and it's not just about Kieran. The centre is my home too.'

'What about the stuff Forrest said he knew about you?'

'Again, I haven't got a clue.' He shrugs. 'The guy was drunk and he's hurting. I suspect he was just shouting his mouth off.'

'So you and Forrest aren't friends then?'

'What is this?' Ben laughs. 'An interrogation?'

'God no, I'm not a detective.' My laugh is as insincere as his. 'I'm just curious.'

'Okay, well, for the record no, we're not friends especially. Forrest's a nice enough guy, but he's from a completely different background to me. He's a posh boy.'

'Wasn't Kieran a posh boy too? His father is the wealthiest property developer in North Devon.'

'Kieran comes from money, but he was a grafter. I did the books but it was Kieran that took people out, kept the place maintained. He did his fair share. Forrest pretends he's living off the land with his chickens and vegetable patch but we all know it's his parents' trust fund that keeps him here. They call it a donation, but Forrest's parents pay Jocasta to keep him here.'

'So you know Forrest's real identity then?'

'Yeah, Kieran told me a while back. Did you know when he was a student, he burnt a fifty quid note in the face of a homeless man.' Ben shakes his head in disgust. 'What kind of a human being does that? No, believe me, Forrest and I are nothing like each other. I've earned every penny I've ever been given.'

But behind the pride, there's a bitterness in his voice that doesn't escape me.

The door to the watersports centre flies open and Ash sails in on a gust of wind, taking Ben and me by surprise.

'Great, I found you both,' he says, trying to catch his breath.

BEN

You're not welcome at Nana's funeral, Ben. It might have been
two years ago now, but as far as the family are concerned,
your wickedness killed your grandmother. She never recovered. You broke her heart. She was making excuses for you
right up until the time she passed, but now she's gone you
need to know that we want nothing more to do with you. Do
not contact any of us, ever again.

*He had to do it. He had no choice. It wasn't as if he hadn't
asked her first, but she'd said no. He had to learn to stand
on his own two feet, she'd told him, but she didn't understand. That's exactly what he was doing and he'd pay her
back just as soon as he was straight. That's how business works. He just needed some money upfront to pay
off his supplier, that was all. All small businesses struggle
at first. It was just a cash flow problem. Once that was
sorted he'd be fine. But it wasn't fine. Cashing a couple
of Nana's cheques wasn't enough to keep him afloat. He
didn't know which was worse, his business going under or
his family finding out and calling the police. It was only
because of his nana that the charges were dropped. Then
they cut him off.*

*It was tough at first. Sofa-surfing at his mates' house kept
him off the streets, but uni saved him. Estranged from his
parents, he got the maximum support supplemented by his
job in a casino bar. It was enough to get by, but it wasn't
enough for him. He wasn't born to be poor like his parents.
He was destined for better, but everyone knows you don't get*

rich working for someone else. That's why he started his first business at sixteen.

He and Kieran were on the same uni course. Kieran wanted to do Sports Science but his dad wouldn't let him. Deveneys didn't become sports coaches. He didn't know why Kieran took to him instantly, but it wasn't reciprocated. Kieran was just another rich kid living off daddy's cash. He loathed his confidence, built on nothing but family wealth and connections. He had that relaxed attitude towards money that is only granted to the children of the well off, but it meant he was happy to pay for him to keep him in his circle, including travelling after uni. It was then that he began to see Kieran as his route to fulfilling his own potential and that's when he came up with a business model for their own Outward Bound centre. The first in a national chain, although he didn't tell Kieran that part. Kieran leapt at the idea. He could do what he loved: sport, and leave all the boring business stuff to him.

He'd never heard of Liars Island, but Kieran had spent family holidays there and knew of a disused boathouse near the beach that could be converted. He couldn't see how this was possible in a marine conservation area, but Kieran assured him his dad, Hilton, headed the island's board of trustees and could pull enough strings to get it through. That's the thing with strings, they're only available to the rich.

Hilton refused, doubting his son's competence entirely based on the fact that Kieran wasn't a clone of his father, but he was and Hilton liked him. He told him he reminded him of himself when he was starting out. He had that same hunger for success and a good business head. Kieran would joke that

Ben was the son Hilton never had. In the end, Hilton relented and pushed the planning application through.

And they smashed it. Customers flocked to them. That first season they had more bookings than they could cope with. There was no reason not to expect it to go on forever. Kieran loved being the front man, enjoying the banter with the clients, while he focused on business development. There was no end to what they could achieve together.

Then Kieran discovered the truth about him. The grand-daughter of his nana's friend read an article about the watersports centre. She recognised Ben from the accompanying photo and messaged Kieran. He lost his shit, accusing Ben of treating him like an idiot, telling him how he'd bigged him up to his dad only to discover he'd screwed over his own grandma. He tried to tell Kieran it was no big deal, that no one needed to know, that if he told Hilton, his father would likely blame Kieran for his poor judgement in friends. That seemed to placate Kieran, but for how long? Since he found out, Kieran had become more distant. Did that mean he was planning to tell Hilton? If he did, it would all be over. But he was so close to having everything he'd ever wanted. Here he was Ben the entrepreneur. People treated him with respect, admired him for his business acumen. All that would be gone. He'd have to leave the island.

But he belonged here now. This is his home. He couldn't leave Liars Island. Not now . . . Not ever.

35

'What is it? Are you all right?' Ben frowns.

'There's a storm on its way. A big one.'

'How long is it expected to last?'

'Long enough for us all to be in for a rocky ride. You need to make sure the centre is secure. I'll stick around to give you a hand. When you're done, come up to the pub for the storm briefing. We should have a better idea then just how bad it's going to be by then.'

'Okay. Thanks, Ash,' he says, already tidying his paperwork away.

'In that case, Jake and I better get back to the helipad.' I make towards the door, but Ash raises an arm to stop me.

'You're too late. The police helicopter isn't coming. You and Jake won't be able to get off the island until the storm passes. God knows when that will be.'

'Are you serious?' I've spent twenty years avoiding this place, only to be marooned here.

'I never joke when it's about the weather. You're stuck here whether you like it or not, I'm afraid. It's likely it will affect the phone lines and signal so if you need to let anyone know, I'd make that call now.'

The charcoal sky presses down on me as I trudge up the hill to the church. It won't be long until the storm is upon us. Searching out a stony corner to conceal myself from the icy wind, I take my phone out.

I hesitate to call Megan in case I just receive another barrage of complaints about her father's unreasonable attitude towards her phone usage, but I've no idea how long I'm going to be here and the fact she hasn't spammed me with calls and texts gives me some hope that things have improved between them.

She answers immediately.

'Hi, love. Just ringing to say hello.'

'It's not Megan. It's Julian.'

I check I've dialled my daughter's number. 'What are you doing with Megan's phone?'

'We've confiscated it.'

'You did what?'

'She's constantly glued to it and so we decided a little digital detox would do her good so I took it off her.'

'I'm not okay with that. It means I've no way of contacting her. You're going to have to give it back.'

'You can speak to her through me.'

'No, I can't. Give the phone back to her.'

'I can't.'

'Why not?'

'Because then I'll have lost the argument.' He sighs. 'It'll make me look weak. She'll never respect me or anything I say again.'

'I need to be able to speak to her, Julian. I want to let her know that there's a storm coming and I'm stuck on Liars Island at least for another night.'

'I'll tell her.'

'That's not good enough. Please go and get her.'

'She didn't take it well, if I'm honest. She's in her room and refusing to come out. Quite frankly, she's being completely unreasonable.'

'She's fifteen. They're all unreasonable. It's when they're nice to you that you have to worry. You have to find a way around it. Maybe not confiscate her phone, for a start.'

'Then we'd be setting a bad example to Josh and Noah. They look up to her. The thing is, Wish, we're beginning to think this holiday wasn't such a good idea after all.'

'Don't call me Wish,' I say, tensing at his use of the nickname he gave me at uni. 'Megan just needs to calm down. Returning her phone would be a good start. It's about compromise.'

'I think we're past compromises. We've tried our best. Cam is frazzled. We were thinking of cutting our holiday short and bringing Megan home tonight.'

'There's no one to look after her at Seven Hills and you can't leave her at the cabin on her own.'

'We wouldn't do that.' He lets out a long sigh. 'I don't know, Ally. It's just so much harder than I thought. Teenagers are so . . . tricky.'

'Welcome to my world.'

'There's no need to take that tone.'

'There's every need. You're her dad. She's your responsibility. You asked for this, now own it.'

'What about Bernadette?'

'What about her?'

'Would she take Megan?'

'I am not calling my mother. She can just about manage the odd teatime, but she's too old to be running around after a fifteen-year-old with an attitude problem.'

'What about your friend Penny? She's helped out before, hasn't—?'

'Absolutely not,' I say, cutting him off. 'She's your daughter. You can't just palm her off to the nearest person who'll have her when things get a bit tough.'

'But she doesn't want to be here either. We're all having a hellish time of it.'

'This is what parenting a teen looks like. You can't do this to her again.'

'What do you mean *again*?'

'You left her once before, remember?'

'That's not fair, Ally. She wasn't even born. Look, I'm trying to find a solution before things get really bad between us. I don't want my relationship with Megan to be ruined before it's even got off the ground.'

'Just fucking sort it out, Julian.'

36

I don't know if it's my run-in with Julian or the plummeting air pressure but when I ring off a pain shoots across my forehead. I slump back against the church walls and pinch the top of my nose to ease the throbbing. Nothing happens and I'm about to launch myself back into the crosshairs of the gale gusting violently around me when my phone buzzes again. I answer it without checking the caller, hoping Julian has seen sense and it's Megan calling.

'Just heard the news. How long are you stuck there for?' says Harriet, not concerning herself with pleasantries.

'I don't know. At least until the storm's over, I guess.'

'Which means we won't be able to get Bagshaw's jacket to the lab for a few more days.' Harriet sighs.

I'd almost forgotten the brown exhibit bag locked safely away in a cupboard in the church.

'Sounds like it's urgent.'

'It is.' She pauses before delivering the bad news. 'Bagshaw's mental health problems all checked out.'

'Really?'

'I wasn't expecting it either,' she says, noting the surprise in my voice. 'But his ex-wife, Celia, confirmed that Bagshaw had a breakdown when their marriage ended.'

'Why did they split up?'

'Lots of reasons. On duty 24/7, I can relate to that one,' she says ruefully. 'Plus she couldn't compete with God and the collection plates weren't paying enough, usual strains of being married to a man of the cloth, I guess. The Deacon also confirmed he had mental health issues while he was in Africa.'

'So it's entirely possible Bagshaw has been telling the truth all along. He did hear voices telling him to kill Kieran?'

'Yes. We're still waiting for the official psyche report, but the shrink said that he could have had some kind of psychotic episode.'

'Wouldn't the attack have been more frenzied in that case? My understanding of psychosis is that the person loses all control. Kieran was hit once and was still alive when he was left.'

'That's what I said, but apparently that's not always the case, which means so far both Dove and Bagshaw's stories stack up.'

'So where do you go from here?'

'We're still working on the theory they're in it together, but by taking individual responsibility for killing Kieran and insisting they acted alone, they're hoping to both get off.'

'So have you found anything?'

'Not so much as a sodding like on social media so far and they swear blind they've never set eyes on each other, but it's early days. I don't suppose anyone has said anything that could help us, have they?'

'No, Dove is either a gold digger or Mother Teresa

depending on who you talk to and no one's even mentioned Bagshaw. I guess that's because he wasn't here five minutes before Kieran was killed. But . . . ?'

'But what?'

'There's something weird going on here. I've no idea if it's relevant or not. It's such a small community and living in close proximity they're bound to clash. Tempers are always going to flare from time to time.'

'Coming from South London, I'm not sure what you mean. I'm intrigued though.'

'Firstly, Dove told Forrest she killed Kieran so they all know.'

'Shit. Okay, I'll get on to that right away.'

'What will you do?'

'I'll send Norm around to read the riot act to her. We could have done without this, to be honest.'

'Well, it sent Forrest into a bit of a spiral. He was off his face last night. Jake thinks it was drugs and, anyway, he had a go at Ben for not telling him about Dove and Kieran.'

'Ben told us he didn't know.'

'He said the same to me, but more interestingly Forrest then threatened him.'

'In what way?'

'He seemed to imply that he knew something about him, something damaging. I asked Ben about it today, but he didn't know anything about that either. He put it down to Forrest being smashed.'

'And what do you reckon?'

'I think Ben's hiding something, but he isn't the only one. I'm pretty certain it's Forrest who's been watching Jake and

231

me. We saw Ash acting suspiciously around one of the barns last night and today we came across Jocasta talking to herself about how she was going to destroy the watersports centre.'

'Well, at least your friend Rose seems relatively normal.'

'She can't get rid of us fast enough.'

'Okay. We'll look into all of this. In the meantime, try and find out why Forrest is so interested in you. Like you say, it could be something and nothing, and let me know if anything else comes up, and Ally?'

'Yes.'

'You're CSIs, not detectives, so no going full-on Colombo, okay? Keep it on the lowdown.'

'Will do, but at least it will give Jake and me something to do.'

'Ah yes. Actually, that's why I called. I have some home-work for you both.'

37

An ominous rumble of thunder escorts me down the hill from the church to The Barbary Inn for Ash's storm briefing. Somewhere in the distance, a door bangs in protest at the wind furiously chasing itself around the buildings.

I pass Jake on his way to tell Sophie he won't be coming home for a second night. I can't deny a twinge of envy and I briefly find myself imagining another world: the one where I didn't randomly sleep with someone else and I'd just had a call with Liam. The truth is the only significant other in my life is a stroppy fifteen-year-old who's just had her phone confiscated.

The Barbary Inn is empty. Everyone is out, making sure that anything that doesn't have foundations is tied down. Dipping behind the bar, I leave money by the till and help myself to a bottle of cider while I wait for the others to arrive. As I return to the customer side, I glance down the hallway leading to the back door. Sticking out of a cardboard box at the end is what looks like the barrel of a rifle. I tug it free only to shake my head that I was fooled by a toy nerf gun.

'What are you doing behind the bar?' Rose snaps at me like I'm an errant customer.

'Sorry, there was no one around so I thought I'd help myself to a drink. I've put the money by the till.'

She lingers on the stairs in a way that reminds me of the first time I met Ash.

'I was only in my room. You could have waited.'

'Sorry. Why have you got a toy gun?'

Still irritated by my presence, she casts around for the reason before deciding to tell the truth.

'Look, it's meant to be a secret but I guess it's okay to tell you. You're used to keeping secrets. Ash and I are hoping to foster a teenage boy.'

'Rose, that's incredible.'

My enthusiastic response prompts a shy smile.

'Thank you. I didn't say anything before because I didn't want to jinx it. It's down to us and another family.' She holds up crossed fingers. 'It's been really stressful so sorry if I've been a bit distant. I've had so much on my mind.'

'I hadn't noticed,' I lie, but I'm comforted by the thought that Rose isn't trying to get rid of us. 'Is this what you meant when you said life has a way of working itself out.'

'Yes. I can't wait,' she says, her eyes glassy with joyful tears. 'A mum, at last. I already know I'll love him as much as if he was my own. Jocasta has taught me that.'

'I hope it works out for you. Liars Island is a great place to grow up.'

'We should find out in the next few months. Everything takes ages. It's killing me. I couldn't help myself, buying all these things. I want him to feel right at home when he arrives.'

'I'm sure he will.'

She rummages in the box and produces several football shirts.

'Apparently, he supports Manchester United, but I wasn't sure which was which so I got them both.' She laughs.

'Any child would be lucky to have you as a parent and, yes, of course, I won't say anything.'

She gives me a gentle nudge. 'I'll be coming to you for parenting tips.'

'I'm not sure about that. It's all kicked off. Julian, Megan's dad, wants to bring her home, but there's no one there.'

Rose closes the lid once more. 'Can't your friend help?'

'No.'

'That's a shame. Parenting strikes me as hard enough, but when you're on your own, it must feel impossible.' She stops herself. 'Sorry, because you're not with Julian I assumed you were single.'

'You assumed right. I am, but you don't have to worry about that. You've got Ash.'

'He'll be brilliant, but having another woman around can't be a bad thing. Jocasta's already offered to help out.'

'I'm sure the two of you are more than capable of bringing him up.'

'Thanks.' The air between us shifts.

'Rose, is something wrong?'

'I think you should know that Dove called here today on the landline.'

'She shouldn't be talking to anyone on the island.'

'That's what I thought. That's why I'm telling you. I wasn't sure if I should speak to her, but I didn't want to cut her off. After what Forrest said last night, I didn't want her to feel that we didn't care about her.'

'How is she?'

'She sounded absolutely terrified. I asked if it was true that she killed Kieran. I needed to hear it from her.'

'What did she say?'

'She did it.'

'I'm sorry. I know she was a friend of yours.'

'If only she'd told me about her and Kieran. I could have helped.' Rose looks at me. 'She said the police keep asking her about Reverend Bagshaw.'

I reply with a noncommittal shrug. 'Murder investigations have dozens of lines of inquiry, some more significant than others. Most are dead ends, but they still have to be checked.'

'But the Reverend's only been on the island for a few weeks. What does he have to do with anything?'

'Like I said, they just want to make sure.'

I must be losing the art of fobbing off unwelcome questions because Rose isn't satisfied.

'Now I come to think of it, they asked us as well. The day you and Jake arrived, two detectives were here. They wanted to know if Dove and the Reverend knew each other before he arrived on the island.'

'It's just routine.'

Even I know how lame that sounds. Rose doesn't fall for it. 'Then I find you and Jake going through the Reverend's home. The police think Reverend Bagshaw was involved in Kieran's death in some way, don't they?'

'I don't know. I'm just a CSI. I'm not privy to the ins and outs of the investigation.'

She doesn't believe me. 'What's going on, Ally?'

'I can't tell you.'

'Why not? Oh my God . . . you don't trust me, do you?'

'It's not about trust.'

'So why won't you tell me?'

'It's police business. I don't talk about it with anyone. It's nothing personal.'

But it is for Rose. 'I thought we were friends.'

'We are.' An awkward silence fills the passageway. It's a risk, but maybe I can play the situation to my advantage. 'Okay, please don't tell anyone, but Bagshaw has also confessed to Kieran's murder.'

Rose's hands fly up to her mouth in horror. 'The Reverend killed Kieran?'

'I didn't say that. I said he confessed to killing him.'

'I don't understand.'

'It's complicated, but basically Reverend Bagshaw walked into a police station and told them he murdered Kieran.'

'But why?'

'We're not sure yet. There's no obvious motive,' I reply, not wanting to divulge any more than I have to.

'Oh my God.' Rose's eyes widen further. 'He's a psycho.'

'I wouldn't go that far.'

'I knew all along it couldn't have been Dove,' she says with satisfaction. 'So does that mean she's going to be released? Forrest will be so relieved.'

'Hang on a minute. It's not as easy as all that. Dove is sticking to her story.'

'What? I don't understand.'

'Join the club. Rose, I'll keep your secret about fostering a child, if you keep mine. Please don't tell anyone I told you, including Ash.'

She nods rapidly. 'Yeah, of course, but why would Dove confess to killing Kieran if she didn't do it? And how can two people confess to the same crime? That's not possible, is it?'

'It is, if they're in on it together.'

'Together?'

'I know. Unlikely right? I mean they've never even met, have they?'

Rose frowns at me. 'What are you talking about? Have you seen the size of Liars Island? Of course Dove and Humphrey have met.'

'Okay, everyone, thank you for coming.'

Outside, the wind shrieks at being barred from the storm briefing as Ash takes centre stage. Jake and I are perched on the bar stools while Jocasta and Forrest occupy a table. A fierce hangover has distilled Forrest's anger into a hard stare at Ben, who is propped against a table on the other side of the pub, apparently oblivious. Standing next to Ash is Rose, adoring eyes fixed on her husband.

'We don't have long before it'll become too dangerous to be outside so I'll keep this short. Those of you who live on the island already know the golden rule during a storm which is, stay in your homes. If you do that, you'll be perfectly safe.' We all nod at the wisdom of Ash's advice. 'Ben, it's a spring tide and with the rain we're expecting, a very high tide is on the cards. The centre should be safe, but you never know with these things. If you are worried, you're welcome to stay here tonight.'

'Thanks, Ash. Appreciate it, but I'll stay put.'

Ash turns to Jocasta and Forrest.

'Grannus House is the most solid property on the island so you should be fine as long as you stay put, same with you guys in Jenny's Cottage,' he says, pointing to Jake and me. 'I can't impress upon you how important it is that you don't leave your accommodation, under any circumstances.'

'No chance of that.' Jake grimaces.

'You'd be surprised, which is why it needs to be said,' says Ash. 'You don't stand a chance in gale force winds. We've had numerous sheep and even the odd cow go over a cliff. Rose or I will call you all tonight before the electricity goes off and tomorrow morning at 10am. If the internal comms system gets knocked out overnight, and the weather is calm enough, make your way to the pub by midday, just so we know you're safe. Any questions?'

We shake our heads.

'Great, I reckon we've time for a quick last drink, on the house.'

Forrest grabs his jacket from the back of his chair. 'Not for me, thanks. I'm going to get back to Grannus House. I want to call Dove before the storm hits.'

As the others crowd around the bar, I slip off my stool and follow Forrest out of the pub.

'Forrest, can I have a quick word?' I call after him as the wind blusters around us.

He turns, the single light above the pub illuminating the confusion on his face. This is the first time we've spoken.

'You're the CSI right?'

Considering he's had Jake and me under surveillance since we got here, I'm surprised he has to ask.

'Yes. You shouldn't be talking to Dove. She's on bail. She could be re-arrested if she breaks her conditions.'

'Have you people no heart? Have you any idea what she's going through?'

'I'm just warning you of the consequences of speaking to her, that's all.'

'Yeah, and Jocasta warned me about you.'

'I know she has no time for us, but we're here to help.'

'Is that what you call it?'

'When you confronted Ben in the pub last night, you told him you knew something about him? Something that could damage him.'

'You were there?' He frowns.

'Yes.'

'It was nothing.'

'It didn't look like nothing to me.'

Forrest pulls his jacket tighter around himself. 'I was upset about Dove. She'd just told me she'd killed Kieran, and I'd had too much to drink. Forget it.'

'I get the impression something's really bothering you. You've been following us since we arrived yesterday. If you have information for us that you think will be helpful to the investigation, you can speak to me. I'll make sure it gets back to the team.'

'What? No, I'm fine. I'm just a bit of a mess, you know? My wife is looking at a life sentence because some guy couldn't keep his hands to himself.'

He doesn't get rid of me that easily.

'Does Ben have something to do with this? Have the police got the wrong people in custody?'

'From what I know of the police, they're not bothered if they get the right person or not. In any case, I don't want to get involved.'

'Please, Forrest. You must know that Dove is in real trouble. Right now, she needs all the help she can get.'

'But it's got nothing to do with Dove.'

'Maybe, but let the investigation team be the judge of that. It might help Dove's cause.' I wait. There it is, a tiny nod that tells me he's softened enough for me to swoop. 'So . . . what do you know about Ben that could finish him?'

'Only that he . . .'

A shrill voice cuts across through the wind.

'Don't say another word, Forrest. You can't trust them.'

Shit. It's Jocasta.

38

The wind and rain take it in turns to thrash the living-room windows as Jake deposits a mug of steaming hot tea in front of me and sits down at the table next to me.

'That was close,' he says, referring to our near miss with the deluge the clouds unleashed just as we made it back to the cottage. 'So we still don't know why Forrest is watching us or what he has on Ben?'

'No, as soon as Jocasta turned up, Forrest shut down on me.'

'What's going on there then?'

'That's what I'd like to know. I told him he needed to stop talking to Dove, but I doubt he's going to listen.'

'So what do we do other than just sit here and watch the rain?'

I turn my laptop screen towards him, and tap it back to life.

'As it happens, Harriet has a little job for us.'

Jake scans the screen for a few moments. 'What's any of this got to do with Kieran's murder?'

'Nothing as far as I can tell. Harriet's just crossing the t's.'

'Or scraping the bottom of the barrel.'

'She's getting a lot of flak from the top floor. Kieran's death is all over the local papers and Hilton's been very vocal about the lack of progress in the investigation. I guess she needs to demonstrate to the powers that be that she's doing everything she can.'

'Fairs.' Jake's done the job long enough to feel the constant pressure to get results. He checks the screen again. 'Don't you think it's weird that every single person on Liars Island has a CSI examination report?'

It's my turn to squint at the screen.

'You're right. I hadn't noticed that before although I'm guessing they're not all perpetrators otherwise they'd have criminal records too. They could be a victim or a witness, which isn't that unusual when you think about it. Most people have had their lives touched by crime one way or another.'

'So where do you want to start?'

'We already know Dove and Bagshaw's backstories so let's start with someone else.'

I open a document marked 'Crime Scene Examination Report Relating to Ben Dawson' and a familiar form flashes up on my screen.

'Looks like some kind of fraud,' says Jake, after we ponder it in silence for a few minutes. 'He tried to cash some cheques that he stole from his gran's cheque book. I knew he was too good to be true.'

'Maybe that's what Forrest had on him. If Hilton found out that he'd ripped off his granny, he'd kick him off the island. That would be the end of the watersports centre.'

'Stealing from your nan is a pretty shitty thing to do.'

243

'He was very young. Looking at the date, he couldn't have been more than nineteen.'

'Don't care. If you can do that, you're capable of just about anything.'

'Well, I can't see anything unusual about this. It's just a list of reference numbers relating to the cheques sent off for fingerprinting. Let's try Jocasta's.'

Before I can open her file, the phone in the hallway rings, making us both jump.

'Even the ring tone sounds creepy,' says Jake.

'It'll be Rose checking in on us. She said she'd call.'

I go into the hall and lift the huge old-fashioned receiver from its cradle.

'Hi, Rose.'

'Not Rose, I'm afraid. Ash. I'm finishing the safety calls. Rose is down in the cellar trying to stop the water from getting in. Everything okay?'

'Everything's fine, thanks.'

'Good, well, I'm not sure how much sleep you're going to get, it's blowing a hooley out there, but we'll see you both tomorrow morning, and remember don't leave the cottage.'

'Not even if Jake meets the ghost of Jenny Nancekevill on the landing?'

Jake scowls at me through the open door.

'Not even that.' Ash laughs. 'Either me or Rose will call again in the morning, but come to the inn as soon as it's safe. Rose'll make you one of her famous fry-ups.'

'See you there.' I put the phone down and rejoin Jake in the living room. 'We're invited for breakfast if the winds die down tomorrow morning.'

There's a sudden crack overheard. The lights flicker before staging a comeback.

'That's if we make it,' says Jake.

'Come on. We've got work to do.'

He opens another file, whistling at its contents. 'Wow, Jocasta's been busy.'

'She was an activist, although she seems to have given it up years ago.'

'The last time she was arrested,' says Jake, 'she broke into a medical lab that specialised in medicine for respiratory diseases and released the dogs. I'm not condoning her behaviour, but I kind of get that. Sophie loves animals, but if it weren't for her inhaler which has definitely been tested on animals, she wouldn't be alive. But I can't see anything relevant here, can you?'

'No. Try another one.'

We read Forrest's report in silence.

'I'm sorry,' Jake says, laughing. 'But I can't say I blame someone for shoving shit through his letterbox after what he did to the homeless guy. I'm surprised Jocasta let him into Grannus House.'

'Forrest's parents pay for him to live at Grannus House, I'm not sure Jocasta knows about his past. Rose certainly didn't. In fact, the only one who definitely knows is Ben because Kieran recognised Forrest and he told Ben who he really was. Their families know each other from way back.'

'What a shock that would be for them all, to discover Forrest isn't all peace and love, after all, just some poor little rich boy who taunts the vulnerable for kicks?'

A loud crash shakes the house and lights go out. This time the house is plunged into darkness.

'Fucking hell. What was that? It sounds like a jumbo jet has flown into the roof. I can't see a thing,' says Jake.

'The lightning must have knocked out the electrics. There'll be some torches in the kitchen drawer. Shit, I've left my iPhone in the kitchen. Wait here.'

There's just enough light from my laptop to guide me along the back of the sofa towards the hallway. Jake is right behind me.

'I'm not staying in the living room on my own.'

'Okay.'

We inch our way into the hall.

'Ow,' says Jake.

'You okay?'

'I think I walked into a table.'

A distant flash of lightning briefly illuminates the room enabling us to reach the kitchen without further injury where I'm able to trace the kitchen counter towards the sink and pull open a drawer. As I rummage inside, the rain hammers the kitchen window under the wind's instruction. Somewhere overhead there's another crash.

'Shit,' says Jake. 'That one sounded like it was somewhere in the house.'

'It's probably just a window or something. We'll sort it out tomorrow. Remember Ash told us not to leave the cottage. And before you say anything, it is definitely not a ghost.'

'Never crossed my mind,' he lies.

My hand closes around a cold metal cylinder. I pull the torch out and pass it to Jake before resuming my search for a second. Jake turns it and sweeps the kitchen as if to make sure we're still alone. I finally locate a second torch, but it takes a couple of thumps against my palm to bring it to life. It flickers a couple of times before going off for good.

'Batteries are probably flat,' says Jake, blinding me with his torchlight.

'Yeah. Probably.'

But as I go to return the torch to the drawer, I stop myself. Kieran's torch was also broken, but still in the on position which allowed Alex to conclude he'd died during the hours of darkness, but what if . . . ? Oh God, how could I have not seen it before?

39

Jake peers out of the kitchen window into the early morning light. The rain has eased, but the wind, albeit downgraded to a squall, is still sending upturned plastic chairs skidding across the small courtyard garden.

'Are you sure about this?' he asks.

Jake and I have barely slept, kept awake by what sounded like a thousand arrowheads attacking the roof, accompanied by the occasional crack of lightning.

'About the weather or my torch theory?'

'Both,' says Jake. 'It still looks blowy out there and, well, it's a bit left field, isn't it?'

'Yeah, but it's worth a try and I think Harriet will take left field right now. You fire up the laptop so we can finish these reports and I'll be back in a jiffy.'

Zipping my coat up and ramming a bobble hat over my head, I step outside where the wind immediately tries to launch me against a stone wall. Head bowed, as if in deference to its power, I make my way up the hill to the church. Amazingly, there's phone reception.

'Good, you're alive,' laughs Harriet. 'How was it?'

'Noisy.'

'Okay. You might have to put up with it a bit longer. We were hoping to get you guys and Bagshaw's jacket off the island today, but it's not looking good. It's too rough for the helicopter and the coastguard and RNLI say as your lives aren't in imminent danger, you'll have to wait. How are the CSI reports going?'

'We haven't finished looking at them, but I do have something that might help you. Didn't you say that Dove and Bagshaw both denied meeting each other?'

'Yes, that's right.'

'Rose told me last night that Dove and Bagshaw had definitely met. They had some kind of welcome for Bagshaw in the pub and Dove was there.'

'I knew it. Was it just the one time?'

'As far as she knows.'

'Okay, well it's a start.'

'Not only that, but I think we potentially might have Kieran's time of death wrong.'

'Go on.'

'Alex originally estimated Kieran's time of death as somewhere between 11.30pm and 7.30am, but because Kieran's torch was still in the on position when it was broken, Alex assumed it was dark when Kieran died, hence he narrowed time of death down to sometime before sunrise which was at 5.13am.'

'That's right.'

'What if the reason Kieran's torch was on had nothing to do with it still being nighttime? What if Kieran's torch was on because he was meeting someone in a dark place? That would change the window of death.'

'Considerably, but what do you mean *a dark place*?'

'Kieran dropped his torch. It broke but was then stuffed back in his pocket before his body was found at Devil's Cauldron.'

'I don't follow.'

'Kieran wasn't killed at Devil's Cauldron. He was killed in a cave.'

Jake looks up from the laptop containing the CSI reports when I return from talking to Harriet. I shake my head in response to the one question he wanted me to ask Harriet.

'So no one's coming to get us then?'

'Not yet, no. Still too dangerous and we're not a high priority.'

He glances anxiously out of the window. 'I'll have to let Sophie know at some point. So what did Harriet have to say about your theory?'

'She agreed it was possible, but like everything she wants evidence not ideas. As she said, we'd need to find the cave where they met and examine it to prove anything, but we've no chance, there's dozens of caves all over the island.' I sit down next to Jake. 'Let's crack on and finish these CSI reports.'

I click open a file. The crime scene examination report includes a shaky diagram of the window where the perpetrator gained access with arrows pointing to glove marks on the frame and the glass fragments found outside the church. 'This one's mine. It's the break-in at the Bidecombe church. As you can see, art isn't my strong point.'

'It must be weird looking back at your own work years later,' says Jake.

'It was one of the first jobs that I did on my own as a CSI. My mentor had gone off sick. It was probably too soon, but you just get on with it, don't you? Besides, it was a standard break-in. They nicked the lead and then broke into the vestry and took the silverware.'

'And Cal Meeth, the guy who works at The Albion, took the rap for it?'

'Yes, it was a TIC.'

'Taken into consideration, right?' queries Jake, still learning police lingo.

'Yes. Sorry. He was convicted of another crime and a couple of detectives trying to improve clear-up rates interviewed him in prison where he coughed to a few burglaries including the one at the Bidecombe church. Apparently, he didn't even remember doing it.'

'So Bagshaw wasn't even the perpetrator?'

'No, he was the victim. If I remember rightly he was quite upset by it all.' I do a final check of the examination report. 'But I don't see anything here. Let's try another one.'

Jake scans Rose's CSI report and lets out a low whistle.

'This looks more like it. That is one angry lady,' he says, running his finger down the extensive list of criminal damage done to a vehicle belonging to Robert Lullcott, including a threat to kill him with a cricket bat. 'She doesn't look like she has it in her. She's a friend of yours, isn't she?'

'Yes. She told me she'd done some stuff she wasn't proud of, but I had no idea it was this bad.'

'What did her husband do?'

'Had an affair with her best friend.'

'Still, I'm not sure he deserved that.'

'That's not the end of it. Rose can't have children. Not only did her husband run off with her best friend, he got her pregnant too.'

'I guess that would do it.'

'Especially if having kids has been your main goal in life.'

'Sophie wants kids eventually, and to be honest, you just assume it's going to happen.'

'Until it doesn't. But there is a happy ending. She and Ash are adopting a child, hopefully by the end of the year although it's not confirmed. Rose'll make a brilliant mum.'

Jake looks at me. 'How can she, though? She's got a criminal record.'

'I didn't think that stopped you from adopting.'

'It doesn't unless it's a serious offence. According to this report, Rose threatened to kill her husband.'

'How do you know this?'

'Soph works in the children's courts. She sees this stuff all the time.'

There's a rap on the back kitchen door but before Jake and I can move from our seats, we hear it open and a voice call out.

'Speak of the devil,' says Jake.

'In here,' I shout back.

Rose appears in the doorway, her face ashen.

'It's Forrest. He's gone missing.'

FORREST

Minister's Home Attacked Following TV Star Son's Shame

The family home of Minister for Culture Oliver Budleigh-Smith has been targeted by vandals after a video appeared on TikTok showing their eldest son Scott burning what appeared to be a £50 note in front of a homeless man.

Scott Budleigh-Smith is at Cambridge University studying English Literature. He is also a popular member of reality TV show Birthright.

A video showing him offering a man sitting in a shop doorway a £50 note before snatching it away and setting fire to it appeared online three days ago.

Budleigh-Smith was expelled from his college. He has apologised for any offence caused, adding that he was under the influence of drugs and alcohol at the time, a claim disputed by at least one source.

Budleigh-Smith added that his life has since been made a misery with constant online trolling and abuse in the streets.

The Minister has distanced himself from his son's actions, saying he had let himself and his family down and they are not the values or standards to which he had raised his children. He said his son would receive the help he needed.

He never denied what he did. It was a horrible and cruel thing to do, but he was young and stupid. Only you can't be young and stupid in this world anymore. Everything is recorded, snapped, Facebooked, TikTok-ed and replayed for eternity. He would forever be the kid that burnt fifty quid in the face of a homeless man, but by God he'd paid dearly for it. Disowned by his father, hounded by the paps, shit shoved through his letterbox, death threats, he'd endured the lot. There were times he wanted to end it all.

The statement his dad made to the press was bullshit. He never got the help. All his dad cared about was distancing himself from his son's behaviour in case it damaged his career. He even got him to sign a non-disclosure agreement and told him to leave.

It was an old school friend who contacted his mother and told her about Grannus House on Liars Island. Her husband ran the island's trust. She'd seen the news reports and got in touch. The island, she said, was the perfect place for him to disappear. No one would ever find him there.

He refused to go at first. He thought he could ride it out. Eventually, the trolls would tire of the story and move on, but they didn't. Months after it happened, he still couldn't go out without someone hurling abuse at him. None of his so-called friends would have anything to do with him. In the end, he had no choice. He either went to the island, or irony of ironies, he'd be homeless.

He intended to give it a few months, until things had properly died down before quietly returning home, but, as soon as he set foot on the island, a crushing weight he didn't know he carried seemed to lift. The expectations, the disappointment, the blame: all of it disappeared. No one followed the news here. No one cared.

Then he met Dove, the sweetest, gentlest person he'd ever known. She was interested in him, not his connections. She told him the witty putdowns he was famous for weren't funny, just nasty. A sign of a person in pain, wanting to cause those around them pain. But she had her own pain. She helped him to understand he didn't need to destroy others to make himself feel good and he taught her to accept herself.

Then Kieran arrived on the island. He knew he was Hilton's son. Apparently, they'd met as small children, but he didn't remember. Still, he avoided him. Only Dove knew his past and the last thing he needed was to be recognised even though three years had passed and his hair and beard were past his shoulders.

Inevitably, he came across Kieran on the track one day. It would have been odd to pass without comment so they stopped and chatted, but Kieran wasn't listening, too intent on studying his face.

'Mate, I'm sure I know you from somewhere.'

They weren't mates. They never would be. Kieran was a reminder of what he'd left behind, a reminder of who he once was. The memory of that person still filled him with shame.

'No, I don't think so,' he replied, making his excuses to leave.

Then one night, he was walking home from the pub and Kieran came chasing after him.

'I've got it,' he said breathlessly. 'I knew I knew you. You're that twat who burnt fifty quid in front of the tramp. The politician's son. Bet the paps would love to know you ended up here. A minister's son living like a hermit on an island. You'd be splashed all over the front pages all over again.' He laughed.

After that Kieran would seek him out. Treat him like a

friend. One of their own. Tell him things he wasn't interested in. About Ben. He listened, pretending to care, hoping all the while that if Kieran thought they were friends then he wouldn't tell the papers about him, but sooner or later he was sure Kieran wouldn't be able to help himself. He'd blab. He couldn't bear it if that happened. He'd found peace when he didn't really deserve it. He'd found Dove.

And he belonged here now. This is his home. He couldn't leave Liars Island. Not now . . . Not ever.

40

Disappointment flashes across the faces of those gathered when Jake and I walk into The Barbary Inn. We're not who they were hoping for.

'Forrest isn't with you then?' asks Ash.

'No, sorry, we haven't seen him. Jake and I didn't leave the cottage the whole night.'

'I don't understand it,' says Jocasta. 'I was certain some-one would have seen him.'

'Are you sure he isn't at Grannus House?' asks Ash, lean-ing against the bar. 'It's a big place, lots of outbuildings.'

'No, I checked everywhere before I came here.'

'Okay, let's rewind for a moment,' says Ash. 'When did you last see Forrest, Jocasta?'

'Last night. When I went to bed. That was about 9pm.' She pauses, retracing the previous evening in her mind. 'Forrest said he wanted to do one last check on the animals before the storm got really bad. I wasn't concerned. We've had worse than this.'

'What about this morning?' asks Rose.

'He's normally up and out before me so I didn't think anything of it when he wasn't at breakfast. It wasn't until mid-morning that I began to worry so I checked his bedroom and that's when I saw that . . .' She frowns at the memory. '. . . his bed hadn't been slept in. It was then that I thought maybe he'd come here.'

'Why would you think that?' asks Rose. 'The storm was already on us by 9pm.'

'I don't know.' Jocasta stares down at her brandy glass. 'Oh my God.' She looks up at Rose. 'What if he's gone into the water? We'll never find him.'

The pub door crashes open.

'Sorry, I'm late, guys,' says Ben, shaking the rain out of his beanie. 'There was a landslip on the track down to the watersports centre. I've spent the morning trying to clear it.' When no one replies, he registers the sombre mood. 'What is it? What's happened?'

'It's Forrest. He went out last night and hasn't been seen since.'

The news of Forrest's disappearance doesn't unduly worry Ben.

'He probably lost bearings and decided to take shelter in one of the properties.'

'He'd have been here by now. He knows I worry about him. He'd have either returned to Grannus House or come here,' Jocasta says.

'She's right,' says Ash. 'Forrest should have shown up by now. We can't discount the possibility he's got into difficulty and is out there somewhere.'

'Oh God,' groans Jocasta. 'I knew it.'

'He'll turn up,' says Rose, rubbing Jocasta's back. 'It's not that unusual for people to wander off and get lost, but we always find them.'

'Look, I've been involved in a few search and rescues, it's inevitable when you work in outward pursuits and one thing I know is that most people are found, safe and well,' says Ben. 'I guarantee you, Forrest is holed up somewhere waiting for us to come and get him.'

'Thank you, Ben.' Jocasta holds out her hand for him to take. 'I'm so sorry about the things I said to you. It wasn't fair of me.'

'Forget it. I understand. Liars Island is my home too you know. I belong here as well and I wouldn't do anything to jeopardise that.' He takes her hand and she draws him in for a hug.

'Okay, everyone, let's focus on finding Forrest,' says Ash. 'Ben, it's probably best if you take charge of things.'

'Right. I need the most up-to-date and most detailed map you have of the island.' Ash nods and disappears out the back. 'So, what do we know about Forrest's last movements?'

'Jocasta last saw Forrest at around 9pm when she went to bed. At ten, he took the safety call and that's the last time anyone saw or spoke to him,' says Rose.

'So we know he was still at Grannus House then. He was intending to do a final check on the animals so, given the weather, I think we should work on the premise that he somehow got disorientated in the storm and wandered off.'

'Makes sense,' says Rose.

Ash returns with a map and spreads it out on the table while the rest of us gather round. Ben studies it for a few moments.

'Right, we've only got a few hours before the weather

closes in again, but what I suggest is that Jocasta and Rose check the lighthouse and Lookout Cottage. They're the properties nearest the main track. Ash, you take the north of the island. Be careful, there's a lot of grykes and crevices around that area, not to mention the caves and hidden tunnels. Ally and Jake, you take the east side, focusing on the woods. There's plenty of fallen trees he could be sheltering under. Hilton's place is out that way so check that too.'

'It's locked, isn't it?' says Jake.

'There's a key under a stone beneath one of the palms. Hilton refused to leave it completely unlocked,' explains Rose. 'But he agreed to leave a key nearby.'

'Stay away from the cliff edges,' continues Ben. 'The wind is still strong. Take your time, and check everywhere. It's better to take it slowly and know you haven't missed anything than to have to go back over the same ground.'

'What about you?' asks Ash.

'I'll take the west side. I'll also check out the known caves and tunnels.'

'Isn't that a bit dangerous on your own?' asks Rose.

'I'll work quicker alone. Don't worry. I've done enough caving to know what's safe and what's not.'

'What about the area around Devil's Cauldron?' asks Ash.

'I don't think we need to bother with the south of the island,' says Ben. 'I've already checked the area for storm damage. If Forrest was there, I'd have found him.'

'Should we let the coastguard or the police know?' asks Jocasta.

'Let's hold off until we've searched the island,' says Rose.

'They're likely flat out and the last thing they need is a false alarm.'

'Okay, the sooner we start, the sooner we'll find him,' says Ben.

All of us make a move apart from Jocasta.

'I don't understand it,' she says, shaking her head. 'Why would Forrest wander off in the middle of the night, knowing a storm was coming? It's suicide.'

41

The ground squelches beneath our boots as Jake and I emerge from the dense tangle of ancient woodland that we've spent the last couple of hours scouring for signs of Forrest.

'That just leaves Hilton's house,' says Jake.

'Let's hope Forrest made it there, or one of the other properties.'

'Maybe he's in a cave or a tunnel. Didn't you say the island is riddled with them?'

'Yes, that's possible.'

'I still don't get why he would just wander off like that.'

'Like Ben said, he could have got disorientated in the storm.'

Jake digs around his coat pocket and produces a couple of energy bars and hands me one.

'Lunch? We'll have to eat them standing up,' says Jake, casting around the sodden ground for somewhere to sit.

'It's okay, we're in waterproofs.'

'It's not the wet grass that bothers me.'

I look down where the grass is scattered with thousands of tiny dark pellets.

'Ah, that'll be the famous Liars Island rabbits. Apparently, they've been here since medieval times.'

'There must be thousands of them,' says Jake, unwrapping his bar and tearing the top off it.

'Yep, they don't have any natural predators on the island so I guess they're all breeding like, well, rabbits.'

'At least someone's having fun,' he says through his munching. 'I've never seen so much shit. It's everywhere.'

'What about there?' I say, pointing to a pale patch of grass a few metres away that appears to have escaped the rabbit's attention. I've seen this somewhere before.

'That's odd.'

'What is?' asks Jake.

'I'm not sure.'

'Well, I'm not risking it,' says Jake, interrupting my thoughts. 'Let's carry on.'

We carry on walking, finishing the energy bars in silence, until we find ourselves back on the gravel drive leading to the white mansion so beloved of Hilton. To our left, despite last night's downpour, silvery powder clings stubbornly to the bonnet of Hilton's Land Rover, remnants of yesterday's examination. God, it feels like a lifetime ago.

'It feels empty,' says Jake.

'No face at the window this time then.'

'I'm not sure there ever was. It was probably just a trick of the light.'

'Now we've got permission to enter the house, we'll check it for blood spatters.'

Jake retrieves the key from underneath a stone next to a palm tree and slides it into the lock. There's a loud click and the door opens onto a large black-and-white tiled hall-way. Leading from it is a broad wooden balustrade stairway wrapped in the musty smell of a home rarely used. We set our cases down. Jake takes out the UV lamp and the two of us spend the next half hour inching our way from room to room until we've checked the entire premises and returned to the kitchen.

'That answers that question then,' says Jake, returning the UV light to its case. 'Kieran wasn't killed at Hilton's house.'

'Forrest isn't here either. All the rooms looked immaculate and, judging by the undisturbed dust, I don't think anyone has been here for a while.'

'So I did imagine someone at the window.'

'It sounds like it.'

Jake shivers.

'You okay?' I ask.

'Yeah. It's just that this place is freaking me out a bit and before you ask, it's nothing to do with any ghosts.' Jake takes out another energy bar. 'Do you want another one? There's one left.'

'No, thanks. So if it isn't ghosts, what is it?'

'Don't you think everyone is acting really weird?' he says between chews. 'You must have seen it.'

'Seen what?'

'Did you notice how Ash didn't want me to help him take Forrest back to Grannus House the other night? Then Jocasta pretends she's never met me before and stops Forrest from telling you what he's got on Ben. Even your friend Rose is acting strange. One minute she loves you, the next she's trying to get you off the island as quickly as possible. It's like they're all hiding something. All of them apart from Forrest. He's the only normal one.'

'What do you mean?'

'He got smashed and was raging about Dove which is exactly what I'd do if Soph told me she'd got drunk and cheated and then killed him.'

'So what are you saying?'

'I don't know other than I get the feeling we don't know half of what's really going on here.'

So it isn't just me, but I keep my misgivings to myself. As Jake said he's already freaked out by the islanders' behaviour, there's no point making it worse.

'Maybe they just don't like outsiders. It's a very close-knit community.'

'Maybe.'

Jake screws up the wrapper and flips up the bin lid. He's about to drop his rubbish when he stops himself.

'What is it?'

Jake removes a pen from his jacket and hooks something in the bin. He eases it out slowly for me to see.

'Does Hilton strike you as a pink Fanta kind of a guy?'

42

Ben and Ash are poring over maps laid out across several tables pushed together when Jake and I return to the inn. Jocasta has squirrelled herself away in the corner by the window under the watchful eye of Rose who is sitting on a bar stool. There's an unmistakable air of gloom over the place. Forrest is still missing.

'Anything?' asks Ben, the sudden rush of cold air alerting him of our return.'We're not sure.' My reply gets everyone's attention.

'Really?' says Jocasta.

'It could be nothing, but have any of you been in Hilton's house recently? Ben, you and Kieran were there fixing Hilton's headlight recently, weren't you?'

'Yes, but we didn't go into the house,' he says.

'Rose and I cleaned the place about a month ago. We were due back next week to get it shipshape for the season,' says Ash.

'Would you have emptied the bins then?'

'Of course.'

'Obviously Hilton was here the day before yesterday. It's possible he popped into the house before he got the helicopter back to the mainland.'

'Does Hilton drink Fanta?'

There's an exchange of frowns.

'I've no idea. We sell Fanta in the shop,' says Rose. 'I've never seen him drink it, but he's been known to go into the shop and just help himself to anything.'

'What about Forrest? Does he drink Fanta?'

'What's this all about?' asks Ben.

Jake produces a clear plastic bag containing the drinks can. 'We found this in the bin in the kitchen at Hilton's house.'

'How did that get there?' says Rose.

'If Forrest put it there, then it narrows down the search,' says Jake.

'Well, it definitely doesn't belong to Forrest,' says Jocasta. 'He doesn't touch that toxic muck. I won't allow it at Grannus House.'

Rose looks at her. 'Sorry, Jocasta, but Forrest has bought the odd can or two.'

'What?' she says, briefly thrown before recovering herself. 'All right then, if the can belongs to Forrest, where is he now?'

'I don't know,' says Rose helplessly.

'This isn't getting us anywhere and time isn't on our side,' says Ben. 'I suggest we grab some food and go back out. Ash, you and Rose focus on the area immediately around Grannus House. Ally and Jake can carry on working their way down the east side of the island. I'll finish up around the west side and if I don't find anything, I'll join you both. Jocasta, I think it might be better if you stay put, just in case Forrest finds his way here.'

It's hard to tell if Ben just wants to get on with the search or he doesn't want us dwelling on the Fanta can. Jake is having the same thoughts.

'So what about the can?' he asks.

Ben turns to us both. 'Thanks for trying but we've no way of knowing if the can belongs to Forrest so we're just going to have to park that one.'

People start to move, but I hold a hand up to stop them.

'Wait a moment. There's a very easy way to find out if the drinks can belongs to Forrest.'

'How?' Ben frowns.

'We're CSIs.' I smile. 'We'll fingerprint it. Jocasta, if you could find something smooth like a glass that you know Forrest has touched, we'll be able to compare the fingerprints. I'm no expert, but I know the basics, and I'm willing to give it a try. Then we'd know for certain if Forrest has been at Hilton's house.'

'Absolutely not,' snaps Jocasta.

'But it might help us find Forrest more quickly, stop us looking in the wrong place.'

'I don't care. I know what you people are like. Once Forrest is on your databases, he's there for good.'

I look to the others, assuming they'll step in to help me persuade Jocasta, but I'm met with a wall of silence.

43

My mobile goes quiet. I check the screen. I have one bar. That should be enough but maybe I've been cut off.

'You still there, Harriet?'

'A misper?' she says, her voice barely audible above the wind rushing around the church. 'For a tiny island, a hell of a lot seems to happen there. Who is it?'

I turn my back to the view to shield my phone.

'Forrest. Dove's partner. He left Grannus House last night and didn't return. We've just spent the entire morning looking for him.'

'Surely the island isn't that big.'

'No, but there's no sign of him anywhere. Although there's evidence that someone has been in Hilton's house recently. Jake found a drinks can in the bin. It could belong to Hilton. He uses the place when he's on the island. It could also be Forrest's. He could have taken shelter there, but we can't confirm that because Jocasta won't give us any items with his prints on to compare it to.'

'We have everyone's dabs on file. I'll send them over.'

'Including Hilton Deveney's?'

'I'm not sure, but we'll get them too. It just might take a

little while that's all. Hilton isn't being very cooperative. He's apparently unhappy at the lack of progress. He's refused an FLO,' sighs Harriet. 'Anyway, this Forrest guy, could it be foul play?'

'More like foul weather. It's more likely he got lost and fell down a ravine and is lying injured somewhere. That's the best-case scenario.'

'The worst case being he's dead, I take it?'

'It isn't unheard of for cattle to get blown off ridges and cliffs during high winds. Maybe Forrest suffered the same fate. There's no warning signs anywhere on the island. It's an environmental thing. The whole island is a conservation area. It ruins the aesthetics.'

'Sounds like Forrest might have had more than his aesthetics ruined.'

'Jake thinks there's something weird going on here.'

'Based on what?'

'Based on everyone on the island is as suspicious as fuck.'

'And what do you think?'

'Jake's got a point, but Ben's the only one Forrest seemed to have beef with. Jocasta treated him like a son, although less so since she found out he might be polluting his body with Fanta, and Rose and Ash don't have much to do with him.'

'Could his disappearance have anything to do with Kieran's murder?'

'It can't be ruled out. He's Dove's husband, but at the moment I don't see how.'

'Do you want me to let the local plod know he's missing?'

'Not yet. It's too soon. We could still find him alive and

well. I wouldn't want to worry his family unnecessarily. We're going to resume the search this afternoon before the weather closes in again. If we don't find him by nightfall, Rose will call it in. I just thought you should know.'

'Keep me in the loop and let's hope he's okay. I don't need another body on my hands, quite honestly. Speaking of Kieran, we've had something of a breakthrough, but I need your help.'

'Fire away.'

'Digital forensics finally came back with something. They managed to get into Kieran's Garmin data.'

'I didn't know he was wearing a Garmin.'

'He wasn't and Jim didn't find one at his digs at the watersports centre either. We don't know what happened to it, but the data is on his laptop.'

'And what does it say?'

'Kieran took his kayak out the morning he was killed.'

'Where did he go?'

'It looks like he kayaked north around the island and stopped off at a place a little farther up the coast called Hidden Cove. He spent about ten minutes there before paddling back to the watersports centre.'

'What time was this?'

'Around 5.30am.'

'So Kieran was still alive after sunrise.'

'Possibly.'

'What do you mean?'

'According to the Garmin data, and this is the really interesting bit, Kieran took twice as long to kayak back to the beach as he did to get to Hidden Cove.'

'That's strange. The return journey should have been a lot quicker than the outward journey. The current runs north to south around the island.' Another fact I have Dad to thank for. 'I take it you don't think Kieran was just taking his sweet time, enjoying the scenery.'

'No. At first, we thought maybe he was hit over the head at Hidden Cove and, injured, he tried to kayak back to the centre which we estimate is about half a mile down the coast.'

'Wouldn't he have gone back to Seal Bay where the centre is?'

'Exactly.'

'What does the heart monitor data say?'

'Nothing. He switched it off. In any case, Alex said Kieran's wound was too severe. He wouldn't have made it and he certainly couldn't have put his kayak back on the rack so then we started to think what else could have slowed him down.'

I can think of only one thing.

'Additional weight.'

'Yes,' says Harriet. 'We think it took longer because either Dove or Bagshaw was carrying Kieran's body back to Devil's Cauldron so Kieran wouldn't be found for a while before placing his kayak back on the rack.'

'But you need to know what you're doing to navigate Devil's Cauldron. I wouldn't risk it.'

'It turns out Reverend Humphrey Bagshaw was in the rowing club at university.'

'That is interesting. What's he got to say about that?'

'Nothing.' Harriet sighs. 'They both insist they killed Kieran on the beach.'

'Which is still possible. Kieran's Garmin data doesn't prove he was killed at Hidden Cove. It just proves he was wearing a Garmin.'

'It doesn't even prove that. Someone else could have taken Kieran's Garmin and worn it to Hidden Cove. By the way, I spoke to Alex about the granite found in Kieran's skull. You're absolutely right. There's a clear line between the granite and slate areas of the island, but it's not conclusive either.'

'I take it you want us to examine Kieran's kayak for fingerprints.'

'You read my mind. I need to know if Dove or Bagshaw touched that kayak.'

'Do you want us to go to Hidden Cove? See if we can find any evidence that Kieran was attacked there?'

'Is it safe?'

'Yes. I used to go there all the time when I was a kid.'

'Okay, we've got the same issue we had at Devil's Cauldron. The tide's been in and out dozens of times and there's been a huge storm, but if we can prove Kieran was hit over the head at the Cove that will be the first decent break we've had in the entire investigation.'

'No pressure then,' I joke.

'Sadly, there's a shedload of pressure on you and Jake,' says Harriet. 'As things stand, we've got nothing on these two.'

Detectives will tell you that murder investigations take time, but the truth is most don't. Most are solved within days and then it becomes about shoring up the evidence. If no one is charged, they can turn cold quickly and I'm sensing the temperature on Kieran's murder is rapidly plummeting.

'Leave it with us. If there's something to find, we'll find it.'

'Thanks, Ally. I could really do with some good news.'

Our call ends, but it's only then that I realise Harriet doesn't know that there's a cave at Hidden Cove.

44

It's only been two days since I last spoke to Megan, but when Harriet rings off, I feel a sudden urge to hear her voice. Maybe Julian is still holding on to her phone or maybe she's just mad at me, but she doesn't pick up so I put my phone away. Pulling my collar around my neck to ward off the wind, I glance skywards at the slate-grey clouds. Another storm is on its way and if I wait around any longer, I'll get caught in the downpour.

Passing in front of the church, I notice its door is ajar. Concern ripples through me. The exhibits are stored in a cupboard by the altar. I step inside and as my eyes adjust to the gloom, I detect the padlock firmly in place. I'm about to leave when a murmuring sound reaches me and I spy Jocasta sitting in the front pew, her shoulders heave with silent sobs between her mutterings, but she's the only one here.

'I know, I know you're right. I can see that now. Forgive me. I wasn't thinking clearly. These days, my thoughts are not my own. So much going on. Things are hard, and getting harder, but I know that's no excuse.'

I remember what Rose said about how Jocasta often talked to her daughter, Amber, and I consider leaving her in peace, before stopping myself. I know what it feels like to want to be a better mother.

A side glance tells me Jocasta has registered my presence when I slide in next to her and I think she's going to object, but she doesn't.

'You think I'm an old fool, don't you?' she says, twisting the corner of the handkerchief on her lap.

'No. I don't.'

She closes her eyes and takes a deep breath before releasing it.

'Sorry. When you've spent your whole life fighting, you don't know anything else. Everyone becomes the enemy.'

'I understand. I've had a few fights of my own.'

'I bet you have,' she says, eyeing me. 'Maybe we're more alike than either of us would care to admit.'

'Maybe. We're both mothers.'

'Thank you for using the present tense. Boy or girl?'

'A daughter. She's with her dad at the moment. It's the first time they've been away together. I miss her, more than I thought I would.'

'How old is she?'

'Fifteen.'

'Amber never made it to her teenage years. Asthma, of all things.'

'I'm so sorry. I almost lost Megan a year ago and the pain of that was bad enough.'

'It never goes away. It's always there. A great big unpluggable hole. I tried to fill it, of course, with the retreat. Some time after Amber died, I realised that I wasn't done with being a mother. It's not for everyone, but if that's your desired role in life, that feeling never leaves you whether you have children or not. It's just in you.'

'I've never really thought about it. I got pregnant when I was nineteen. It wasn't planned. In fact, I never saw myself as a mother at all and there are times when I think I've been terrible at it, but . . . I've never regretted it. Not for a moment. Megan matters to me more than anything.'

'Then you understand me. The youngsters come to the centre quite lost. They're my children now. Often they don't have parents or their parents have abandoned them. They're always so weighed down by their pasts. I never ask what brought them to the island. It's not important what they did, only what they do next.' I take this to mean Jocasta doesn't know about Forrest's behaviour towards the homeless man. 'I try to heal them in a way that I wasn't able to heal Amber. Or so I tell myself.'

'I hear you've made quite a difference to a lot of the young lives.'

'Yes, and hopefully I'll be able to help Rose.' She stops herself, aware she's said too much.

'It's okay. She told me she and Ash are fostering.'

'Raising a child is a big job for one person or even a couple, don't you think? If the help is there, I believe you should take it.'

I think about Penny and all that she's done for Megan and for me, only for me to dismiss her. How could I have been such an idiot? Penny was, is and will always be Megan's second mum.

'Yes, I think you might be right.'

'But I'm not their real mother though, am I?'

'I don't think that matters. I'm adopted. I never knew my

biological parents and although me and Bernadette don't always see eye to eye, she's my mum as far as I'm concerned.'

'And your father?'

'The same. When he left me, it hurt like hell.'

She looks at me quizzically.

'Left you?'

'It turned out I wasn't enough for him.'

Jocasta waits for more, but I shrug her off. 'It doesn't matter now.'

She nods, like she's read my thoughts. 'Maybe he had his reasons.'

'Maybe.'

'I've let Forrest down.'

'Don't give up just yet. He might still be out there, waiting for us to rescue him.'

'Yes, yes, he might.' She reaches down to the bag at her feet and takes out a brown paper bag. 'I made a mistake once. I don't intend to repeat it. You and I are on different sides of the fence, but that doesn't mean Forrest should suffer.'

I unroll the opening of the paper bag to take a peek inside. 'What changed your mind?'

'I've already lost one child. I don't want to lose another. And Amber can be very persuasive.'

JOCASTA

Dear Ms Marwell,

Further to our previous correspondence, we recommend that you begin medical treatment as soon as possible in order to slow the progression of the tumour...

When they booked a holiday on Drogan Island they believed the pure island air would act like a balm on Amber's asthmatic lungs, but attacks can happen anywhere and Amber's happened in the worst place possible on a tiny island with no hospital.

Jocasta had found the inhaler several weeks before their trip. She and Marcus had a huge row about it. How could he go against her wishes? How could he put those horrific chemicals into their daughter? Chemicals that had been tested on poor defenceless animals. Hadn't she spent most of her adult life fighting against animal cruelty? Fighting against all the world's injustices. There wasn't a cause she wasn't passionate about.

She threw it away but came across another one when packing. Marcus had ignored her again. Not wanting to ruin their holiday, she removed it and said nothing.

Marcus left her six months after Amber died. Maybe he knew what she'd done, she didn't know, but a year later he remarried, a year after that, the first of his three children arrived. It's so easy for men, isn't it? They just seem to have this capacity to forget pain, to put it to one side and move on. Nothing to be served from dwelling on the past.

He started another family while she still mourned the loss of hers.

Motherhood never figured in her life plan and when she discovered she was pregnant with Amber she feared she'd be no good at it, having been raised by nannies and shunted off to boarding school at six, but Amber brought out a mothering instinct she never knew she had.

Activism was her purpose in life, or so she has assumed, but she's assumed wrong. It had been Amber and now that she was gone, she became a recluse, drifting through life.

She ignored the headaches and dizzy spells at first until she couldn't bear them. A specialist told her the cancer was slow growing but terminal. Her time was coming to an end and that was when she knew she needed to be close to Amber, close to where her little girl had drawn her last breath.

Not knowing if it was months or years she had left, she leased Grannus House offering it as a retreat to others while she waited for her cancer to take its course. She didn't think anyone would come, but they did. The lost and the damaged. She was there for them all. In time she realised she'd become a mother once more.

She declined treatment, of course. She didn't want any of that poison in her system, preferring her own alternative remedies which seemed to be working until recently when things had begun to change. She was certain she'd seen Amber several times, from a distance. She wasn't surprised. Wasn't Drogan, the proper name for the island, derived from the old Norse word for spirits? There were plenty of recorded incidents of people seeing apparitions on these shores. Deep down, she knew the cancer had spread to her brain and she was hallucinating, but she didn't care. It meant her time was coming near and she was at peace with that. She was ready to be with her little girl.

Then one day she was out walking and she took a funny turn, blacking out completely. When she came to, she was lying on the ground, a pillow of moss underneath her head as if Amber herself had laid her head there.

A figure bent over her, but her vision was too blurred to make out who it was at first.

'Jocasta?'

It was Kieran. The shock focused her eyes. His face was full of concern, but she didn't trust him. She loathed what he was doing to the island and that he treated her as a bit of a joke. She knew he called her the wacky witch behind her back. She couldn't prove it, but she was sure he'd stolen carrots from her vegetable plot for a prank. He denied it, of course. In retaliation, she had vandalised his kayaks. It was a foolish thing to do. After all, his father was Hilton Deveney, head of the island's Trust, but the boy needed to be taught a lesson. Since then, they'd given each other a wide berth.

'Are you all right?' he asked. As if he cared.

'Of course, I'm all right,' she'd snapped back, ignoring his outstretched hand, but as she tried to get up, she felt a rush to the head and stumbled backwards. This time Kieran caught her.

'You don't seem all right. Maybe Rose should take a look at you or I could call my dad and get a doctor flown out here.'

She pulled away from him, brushing the moss and dirt from her robe.

'No, don't do that,' she said, trying to sound calm while all the time her head swam.

'It's no bother. One of the perks of your dad running the place, you can get things done quickly.'

'I don't want a doctor.'

'Honestly, better to be safe than sorry. We can have one here in ten minutes. Just check it's nothing serious.'

'I said I didn't want a doctor.'

She was almost shouting now, but Kieran wouldn't let it go.

'Okay, but what if I hadn't found you? You could have died. I think you should have a quick check-up. I'll go to The Barbary Inn now and phone Dad. I'll let Rose know too. She might be able to give you something, make you feel better.'

'Nothing's going to make me feel better, you stupid boy, I'm dying.'

She regretted the words as soon as they left her mouth, but Kieran just looked at her in bewilderment.

'What?'

'You heard what I said. Now, just leave me alone.'

She shook the moss threads from her coat and stalked off. Her head still pounding, her pride was the only thing keeping her upright even though the trees around her resembled an impressionist painting. When she reached the edge of the woods, she glanced back. Kieran was still there, watching her. She knew what he was thinking. If he told his dad she was dying, he'd revoke the lease on Grannus House. This was Kieran's chance to get rid of her for good.

But she belonged here now. This is her home. She couldn't leave Liars Island. Not now . . . Not ever.

45

Jake retrieves a magnifying glass from his case – archaic as it looks, it's still a vital part of a CSI's kit – and holds it a few centimetres from the glass.

As his unofficial mentor, I decided it would be good practice for Jake to examine the glass Jocasta gave me in the church, and compare his findings with the prints from the Fanta can. I sat back and observed him dipping his brush into the aluminium powder, tapping the excess off, and swirling it across the surface of the glass and then the Fanta can. We exchanged smiles at the sight of the silvery smudges responding to Jake's brush. I waited while he carefully lifted them and transferred them to acetate sheets for comparison.

He trains the magnifying glass on each sheet containing a fingerprint, before handing it to me to repeat the process. Analysis, comparison, evaluation, verification: ACE-V – that's how the process works, though I'm no expert and neither is Jake. Fortunately, we don't have to be. I put the magnifying glass down.

'What are your thoughts?' I ask him, not wanting to sway his findings.

'Both sets were pretty good and enough to show that the

person held the can and the glass with their right hand which means . . .' He slides out two acetate sheets from the rest. '. . . I'm pretty certain, these are right thumb prints.'

'I agree. It really helps when you have similar items and the surface is non-porous. So . . .' I look at Jake. 'The question is do these thumbprints belong to the same person?'

He checks them again with his magnifying glass. Check, check, check again. *Slack sank the ship.*

When he's ready, he sets the glass to one side.

'To be honest, they couldn't be more different. One has a whorl pattern, the other an arch. The thumbprint on the can doesn't belong to Forrest so one of them is lying about going into the house.'

'Yes, but we won't know which one until Harriet gets those elimination prints.'

'But why would any of them lie about being in Hilton's house? It's not even his. I know it's locked but I get the impression they're all allowed to come and go as they please.'

Unless the fingerprints on the can belong to Hilton Deveney who supposedly left the island two days ago.

A rack of kayaks, four-deep, sits by the front door of the Bara Watersports Centre. Next to it is a large plastic barrel containing the paddles. Ben is searching for Forrest elsewhere on the island, but I still check to make sure we're alone. The less the islanders know about what Jake and I are up to, the better.

On our way here, I delivered the news to them in the pub that although there were fingerprints on the Fanta can we were as sure as we could be they weren't Forrest's. Only

Rose seemed interested in knowing who they belonged to. The best answer I could give was that they belonged to Hilton or a shop customer who picked it up and put it back on the shelf.

'I'm a bit of a kayaker myself,' Jake says, setting his case down on the gravel.

'I thought surfing was more your thing.'

'I'm up for anything that gets me out onto the water. Sophie and I got ourselves one of those double kayaks last year. We take it out all the time. Anyway,' he says, shrugging the memory off, 'what are we looking for?'

'Well, according to Kieran's Garmin data he paddled his kayak back from Hidden Cove to Seal Bay just after dawn but if he was killed at Hidden Cove and someone else kayaked his body back here then fingerprints that don't belong to Kieran would be a very useful starting point.'

'Cool.' Jake peruses the four kayaks stacked on top of each other. 'So how do we know which one is Kieran's?'

I study them in turn, before pointing to the top one.

'It's definitely this one.'

'How do you do that? Seriously,' he says, screwing his face up. 'What clever CSI shit are you using now?'

'None.' I grin. 'It's got Kieran's name on the back.'

Jake rolls his eyes and shakes his head at his gullibility.

Putting fresh gloves on, we each take an end of the kayak and lower it onto the ground. A sheen of rainwater covers its iridescent hull.

'It's drenched. We've got no chance of any forensics.' He looks at the barrel full of kayak paddles next to the rack. 'And they're not going to be any good either.' says Jake.

'Okay, perhaps we'll find something at Hidden Cove. We could really do with a break on this.'

We heave the kayak back into its place when a thought occurs to me. 'Hang on. You said that you kayak, right?'

'A bit.'

'Talk me through how you'd get this kayak from the water to the rack?'

'Sure. I'd paddle as close to the shoreline as possible. Then I'd get out and drag it the rest of the way onto dry land. I might pick it up and balance it on my shoulders, if it's light enough, and then I'd just bring it here and slide it onto the rack.'

'Without touching Kieran's kayak, can you show me exactly how you'd remove it from the water?'

Jake motions towards the kayak and stops.

'I'll get the kit out.' He smiles.

46

Jake takes a few steps down the hillside, craning his neck over the boulders littering the route to the bottom of the ravine. 'I don't see any beach. It just looks like some kind of inlet.'

'You can't see the bay from here. That's why the island's a smugglers' paradise. It's peppered with coves that are impossible to find unless you know they're there.'

'So how do you know about it?'

'Rose showed me. When we were kids. There's nowhere on the island that she doesn't know about. We used to come here on a hot day when the tide was out. We had the place to ourselves. It was idyllic.'

Jake looks at me doubtfully. 'I'll take your word for it.'

Leaning back to slow our descent, our boots occasionally slipping on the wet grass, Jake and I tentatively make our way down the hillside, slaloming rocky outcrops until we reach the edge and can drop down onto the stony beach. To our right, white-tipped waves grab at the shoreline, reminding us the tide is on its way in and we don't have long.

'Wow, I wasn't expecting that,' says Jake, staring at a rupture that has torn apart the lower part of the cliff face. 'How big is it?'

'Big enough to hide barrels of rum from the militia. It's probably best if I go in alone. One of us should stay outside, just in case.'

'Just in case what?'

'I'll check to see if Forrest is there too,' I say, ignoring his question.

Inching my way in, I let my torchlight scour the cave floor for footprints. The grey pebbles cramming the bay like fossilised spheres have disintegrated into grit, but there's nothing resembling a shoe impression. The sea has swept in and out a dozen times since Kieran was killed.

Despite its fierce entrance, the chamber narrows quickly and before long even I have to bow my head to clear the jagged ceiling. The cave tapers and I can go no further. Forrest isn't here. And neither is anything else.

It's too tight to turn around so I shuffle backwards until I judge there's enough headroom to straighten myself, but I'm wrong and crack my forehead against a protruding rock.

'Shit.'

Brushing my hair to one side, my fingers search out the wound, but the skin isn't broken. I give the offending rock a scowl before swinging my torch over the walls to ensure there's nothing else lying in wait for me. Halfway down the cave wall, the stone pales where the rock has sheared off. Nothing unusual about that, on an island where landslides and rockfalls happen all the time. What is unusual are the stains blooming on the stone. They remind me of lichen, only lichen isn't red.

'Have you found something?'

Jake recoils as my flashlight hits his pupils.

'Christ, you almost gave me a heart attack. I thought I told you to stay outside.'

'Sorry, didn't mean to make you jump. I was worried.'

'Check this out.'

Jake squints at the splash marks, illuminated by my torch. 'Blood?'

He fishes the UV torch out of his case and switches it on, drenching the cavern in pink glow, apart from the marks on the cave wall which remain resolutely black.

'Bingo,' says Jake.

'Let's hope so. This could be the breakthrough we're looking for. If this blood belongs to Kieran, we can prove he wasn't killed at Devil's Cauldron.'

'And prove both Dove and Bagshaw are lying through their arses.'

'Exactly, but let's not get ahead of ourselves. Who else could it belong to?'

'We can rule out animals,' says Jake. 'It's too high up and there'd be other evidence like fur or bones.'

'What about Forrest? Maybe he fell down the hillside.'

'In that case, he'd still be here,' says Jake.

'Unless . . . he was swept out to sea.' Could Forrest have found sanctuary here only to be claimed by the sea? 'Let's keep it simple for now,' I say. 'Let's work on the theory that Dove and Bagshaw attacked Kieran here in the cave and the blood belongs to Kieran.'

Jake swings his torch around the cave. 'Then why didn't they just leave his body here?'

'I don't know. It doesn't make any sense to me either, especially as they risked being seen paddling Kieran's body back to Devil's Cauldron.'

'It looks like it's sheer cliffs from here to the watersports centre. If you hugged the coastline closely enough, you wouldn't be visible from the land but you'd have to be a pretty confident kayaker to be able to do that.'

'Bagshaw was a university rower.'

'That'll do it,' says Jake.

'Let's do the necessaries and get out of here before the tide cuts us off.'

Jake takes out a paper ruler and holds it next to the blood spatters while I fix a lens on my camera and photograph it and the surrounding cave. When we're finished, I swab the stains.

'I'll test these later, but I think we're done here.'

We put our kit away. Jake takes charge of the torch and leads the way out of the cave, but as it widens, he stops.

'I trod on something.' He hands me the torch and lifts his foot to reveal a black plastic rod protruding from the gritty sand.

'What is it?'

'I don't know. I missed it on the way in. Let's not take any chances, shall we?'

I take my camera out once more to photograph the item as Jake holds a paper ruler alongside it to give a sense of its size. Next I take a brush out of my case and gently sweep the gritty sand away from the object until it reveals itself.

'It's a pair of glasses,' says Jake. 'What are they doing here?'

47

'It's only a presumptive test. Just like the blood we found on Bagshaw's jacket in the vestry, we can't confirm it's even human, let alone Kieran's, until we get the samples to the lab.'

I'm leaning back on the church wall, talking to Harriet who responded to our discovery of blood at Hidden Cove with relief more than anything.

'Could it belong to Forrest?'

'We can't rule him out although there was no sign he'd been to the cave.'

'So he's still missing?'

'Yes.'

She doesn't linger on this. Kieran is her priority.

'How much blood was there?'

'Not a huge amount, and maybe not enough to prove conclusively that a violent assault took place there, but it was more than a paper cut, that's for sure.'

'Okay, well, it's a start. And you say that you got fingerprints and tapings from the kayak?'

'Yes. Jake found some marks under the lip of the cockpit. Their position suggests they were made by someone dragging the kayak along the ground, but again we can't do anything with them until we get back to the mainland. It's not like the marks on the Fanta can.'

'That reminds me, did you get the elim prints? I told Jim to send them over to you. We managed to persuade Hilton although obviously he doesn't know it's in connection with Forrest's disappearance.'

'Thanks. They came through just now. I didn't need them in the end. Jocasta gave me a glass with Forrest's prints on.'

'And?'

'And they didn't belong to Forrest. I'll check them against Hilton's, when I have a moment but it looks like they probably belong to one of the others who live at Grannus House. Maybe they dropped it in the bin and Ash and Rose missed it when they were cleaning.'

'We don't have their prints. They weren't on the island when Kieran was killed.'

'It doesn't matter. They could just as easily belong to the person who packed the can in the factory. It's impossible to date prints.'

'So what about the ones on the kayak? Who do they belong to?'

'Unfortunately, they're fragments, you need a trained eye for this one, and I'm not good enough.'

'Fair enough. So where are these kayaks stored?'

'Outside the watersports centre.'

'But the positioning of the prints is unusual. If they belong to Dove or Bagshaw, it would be hard for either of them to explain what their dabs are doing there.'

'Hard but not impossible. That rack is in a public place right?'

'Yes.'

'Great,' she says sarcastically. 'So where are all these exhibits now?'

'Under lock and key in a cupboard in the church along with the other exhibits we took from the vestry.'

'And you didn't find any footmarks in the cave?'

'No, the ground was very churned, probably the tide. We did find something else though just inside the entrance.'

'Oh?'

'A pair of glasses.'

'Glasses?' she says, her mood lifting.

'I'll send photos of them over. They look like standard glasses to me. Quite a strong prescription. Jake thinks they're women's glasses, but I'm not sure. They look quite old to me. They could have been washed up of course, although there's no evidence of erosion so . . .'

'They could have been dropped by someone recently.'

'Yes.'

'Okay,' says Harriet, trying not to get ahead of herself. 'We know Bagshaw wears glasses, but you say they belong to a female?'

'Jake thinks so but they could be unisex.'

'All right. Dove doesn't wear glasses.'

'Jocasta does.'

'Are you sure?'

'When we met her the other day in the woods, she was wearing a pair. Gold frames. Very different to the black-framed glasses we found. They could be Ben's too.'

'Ben's?'

'Yes, the first day we met, he was wearing sunglasses.

I thought it was a bit odd as it was quite cloudy which is why I noticed he was wearing reactolights.'

'Right, well, we'll check all three of them out, along with the rest of the residents at Grannus House, and if the glasses have got a serial number on them we might be able to locate where they were bought. Thanks, Ally. With the blood at Hidden Cove and the forensics from the kayak, this could be enough for Dove or Bagshaw to crack. Once that happens, we've got this in the bag. One of them did it and I'm going to bloody well nail them for it.'

48

Most investigations have their fill of wild theories especially in the absence of facts. It's the what-ifs of a crime. The trick is knowing what's worth pursuing and what isn't, which is why I didn't bother Harriet with a thought that found its way into my mind when we were discussing the glasses Jake found at Hidden Cove. She doesn't need to know, but it still needs to be ticked off the list of suppositions and I know just the person to do it.

His phone rings for an age. Maybe he doesn't want to talk to me. Why would he? His new girlfriend Tanya occupies his mind now and who can blame him? She'll give him more than I ever could. Then just when I think he isn't going to answer it, he picks up.

'Ally. Hi. Sorry about that. Just got out of the shower,' he says, sounding his usual breezy self.

'I'm sorry to bother you,' I reply, embarrassed that I'd read so much into his failure to respond to my call immediately.

'No you're not.' He laughs, his voice underscored with that gently teasing humour of his.

God, I miss him. I want to ask him about Tanya. I want

him to tell me it's off between them and for him to ask me out again, only this time I don't hesitate to say yes. But I had my chance and I blew it. It's too late for us.

'You're right. I'm not,' I say.

'Where are you?'

'Liars Island.'

'You went? That's good.'

'Not that good. Jake and I are stuck here.'

'Ah, it was a pretty big storm, a lot of flotsam and jetsam washed up at Morte Sands. So when are you likely to get home?'

'I've no idea. The weather's expected to take another turn for the worse tonight.'

'Well, I'm sure you and Jake are keeping yourselves amused.'

'That's kind of why I called. I'm after a little favour.'

'So this is a business call, not pleasure then?'

Did I detect disappointment in his voice? Is he waiting for me to say something? But he's with Tanya now.

'Yes,' I say, apologetically.

'Okay,' he replies, businesslike. 'What can I do for you?'

'It's nothing major. I need help to eliminate something, just for peace of mind more than anything.'

'Sounds cryptic.'

'Yeah, sorry. I'm not even sure it's doable.'

'Try me.'

Liam is one of those ex-cops that rarely refers to his police service. I know he spent time in CID and the hi-tech crime unit, but he's also one of those former officers who just seems to know everyone.

'Thank you. I'll send over what I have. I need a little time to get it together and one of the images isn't great.'

'Send me what you have. I'll see if I can find someone to help you. Is there anything else I need to know?'

My heart spikes at his question. Does he mean the case? Or us? Maybe I should say something. Maybe the situation is recoverable. I'm deliberating how to respond when I notice Jake striding up the hillside towards me, his long legs quickly covering the ground. Something's up.

'Sorry, Liam, I've got to go.'

I ring off just as Jake reaches me.

'It's Forrest,' he says breathlessly. 'They've found him.'

49

'He's dead, Ally.' Rose is waiting for me outside The Barbary Inn, her face ashen, her eyes raw from trying to rub out her tears. She steps forward and hugs me. 'I can't believe this has happened. It's horrible. Just horrible. I don't understand it. I was so certain he was just waiting for us to find him.'

'I'm so sorry, Rose.' I gently ease her away from me. I can't be the support my grieving friend needs. Jake and I have work to do. In police parlance, the discovery of Forrest is classed as an unexpected death. The question is whether it's natural causes, an accident, suicide or homicide.

'Where was he found?' I say as sensitively as I can muster.

'I found him at the bottom of a ravine.'

'Can you take me to him?'

'He's not there now,' she says. 'Ben and Ash carried him to Lookout Cottage.'

'You moved him?'

'Yes. I said we should ask you first, but Jocasta insisted.'

A haughty voice slices through the cold air and I turn to see Jocasta marching towards us.

'Of course I insisted. It would have been inhumane to leave him there.'

'You should have waited for me.'

'Don't be so ridiculous.' She dismisses me with a wave of hand. 'No crime has been committed. The poor boy was blown off a ridge. Anyone can see that.'

'Well, I can't, can I? Because you've moved him.'

She glares at me. 'We weren't going to leave him there.'

'That wasn't your call to make, Jocasta. You know you should have left Forrest exactly where you found him.'

She moves in closer to me. With a good half a foot on me, she uses her height to try to intimidate me.

'People like you don't have a shred of decency.'

I understand then that what passed between us in the church this morning was nothing more than a temporary truce and whatever restraint I have deserts me.

'You know what, Jocasta? I've had enough of this bullshit. Now get out of my way and let me do my job.'

'I knew I'd be the one to find him,' says Rose, staring down into the deep-sided gully where Forrest met his death. 'There isn't an inch of this island I don't know. Not that that makes it any better. Poor Forrest. I can't believe it.'

Ash slips his arm around his wife's shoulders.

'At least he's been found, Rose. That'll help give his family closure.'

Surveying the landscape, I estimate we're about halfway between Grannus House and The Barbary Inn. The middle of nowhere in other words.

'Weren't you meant to be searching the properties and the north of the island?' says Jake.

'Er . . .' Rose frowns, unsettled Jake appears to be challenging her behaviour. 'Yes, I finished so I thought I'd help Ash. I was looking for him when I came across the ridge. I didn't see Forrest at first, but I know it drops suddenly at the bottom so I decided to take a closer look.'

'Can you remember exactly how you found him?' I ask.

Rose closes her eyes.

'Can't this wait?' says Ash.

'No, it's okay, Ash. Ally and Jake have a job to do. I didn't see him at first and I was about to turn back. It's then that I noticed Forrest's red coat by a gorse bush. I remember thinking, why would he take his coat off?' She shakes her head at her foolishness. 'I went to pick it up and that's when I saw he . . . he was still wearing it.'

'What did you do then?'

'My medical training kicked in. I took his pulse but he was frozen and I knew then he was gone.'

'Did you have any sense as to how long he'd been dead?'

'I'm a nurse, Ally, not a pathologist,' she says curtly.

'Yes, of course. Sorry.'

'Anyway, I went to find Ash and Ben.'

'And the three of you came here?'

'With Jocasta. She was absolutely distraught.'

'And you say he was behind a bush?'

'Yes. I guess he slipped or got blown into the gully. Maybe he was hurt and he couldn't get back up so decided to take refuge behind a bush and wait for help.'

'So he could have died of exposure?'

'Hypothermia? Yes, he's been out long enough. Or the fall. Then Jocasta said we had to move him so Ben and Ash went back to the centre to get the stretcher while we waited with

Forrest.' She looks at Ash. 'I couldn't stay with him down in the gully which I know was terrible of me.'

Ash rubs her arms. 'Don't do this to yourself, Rose. You're in shock. We all are.'

'But I should have stayed, Ash. Instead, I just left Jocasta all on her own with him.'

'Who lifted Forrest's body onto the stretcher?' says Jake, bringing Rose back to the present.

'Ash and Ben.'

'Did Jocasta touch him?' I ask.

'No. I mean yes. She cradled his body while we waited for Ben and Ash to return with the stretcher.'

'She held his hand all the way back to the inn,' added Ash.

Jake and I trade looks and I wonder if he's also resisting a sigh. Every contact leaves a trace.

'Okay, so am I right in thinking that at some point all four of you had some kind of contact with the body?'

'Yes.' Rose looks at me. 'But why are you asking? It was obviously an accident.'

'Sorry. It's our job. It'd normally be a police officer, but there are none so you're stuck with us, I'm afraid.' I smile.

'What was he doing out here?' says Jake suddenly. 'He must have passed quite close to the lighthouse to get here so why didn't he just take shelter there. He just needed to follow the concentrated beam from the lighthouse. Those things have like a million candle power.'

'That's true,' says Ash, 'the trouble is you've no idea what the terrain is like between you and the lighthouse so it's really no help. That's why we tell people to stay inside, including those of us that know the island inside out.'

'It makes no sense,' says Rose. 'Forrest knew the rules. I can only think that one of the animals got out. He went looking for it and it led him here. He loved his animals.'

'I'm guessing you want to go down into the ravine and take a closer look,' says Ash.

'Yes, I'd like you to show Jake exactly where you found Forrest's body.'

'Sure,' says Ash. 'What are you going to do?'

50

The white sheet outlines the contours of Forrest's body, which has been laid out on the kitchen table at Lookout Cottage.

'We couldn't leave him uncovered. I hope that's okay,' says Rose, who insisted on accompanying me as some kind of penance for not staying with Forrest in the ravine. She wipes her tears from the corner of her eyes with the back of her hand. 'You'd think as I nurse I'd be able to deal with this, wouldn't you?'

'It's different when it's someone you know.'

I open my case on the counter by the sink while Rose hovers in the doorway.

'I'm sorry we moved him.'

'That's okay.'

It's not, but I don't blame Rose. I blame Jocasta.

'We thought this was the best place for him. The cottage is really exposed so unless the heating is on, it's freezing. It's a bit away from the inn and the other buildings too,' she adds.

I ease my fingers into a pair of latex gloves.

'You did the right thing,' I say, telling her what she wants, needs to know.

'Poor Forrest. He was a nice lad.'

A nice lad who burnt a £50 note in front of a homeless man, but I've learnt that people can change and there's no reason Forrest wasn't one of them. Megan showed me that. She helped her friend Jay shake off the spectre of his childhood, a childhood infused with drug addiction that killed his mother and drove him into dealing.

'How well did you know him?'

'Quite well. When the atmosphere at Grannus House got a bit too full-on, he'd escape to the pub.'

I loop my camera strap over my head. 'Full-on?'

'You've seen what Jocasta can be like. It's one thing to care about the environment, it's another to treat it as a war and everyone the enemy. It can get a little intense over there.'

'I thought she'd stopped all the activism.'

'She has, but Kieran and Ben's plans seemed to ignite something in her, but Forrest and Dove just wanted a quiet life.'

'Does Forrest's family know yet?'

'Not yet,' she says, biting her lip. 'I was going to phone them after I brought you here. His poor, poor mum.'

'You know her?'

'I only met her once. She brought Forrest to the island. They seemed really close, but the poor lad was just broken. We never knew why. People come here to forget their past, not relive it. You learn not to pry. Jocasta didn't either. She says there's nothing to be gained dwelling on the past. She was the one that put him back together. She was like a second mum to him. So . . . what are you going to do to him?'

I slot the close-up lens onto the front of my camera.

'Not too much. I'm not a pathologist either. I'll photograph him and then I'll remove his clothes for testing.'

'Testing?'

'DNA, fibres, that kind of thing. Then I'll photograph any injuries on his body and I'll also take some samples.'

'Samples?'

Rose is horrified at this violation of Forrest's body. I understand that. There's no dignity in a violent death. I can barely bring myself to tell her, but there's no way around it.

'I'll keep it to a minimum, but I'll scrape under his finger-nails and comb his hair and take some swabs.'

She shudders. 'Do you have to?'

'It's just a process that we have to go through, Rose. Just in case.'

'Just in case what?' She frowns.

'It wasn't an accident.'

51

Most postmortems I attend, I don't even know the victim's name. It's better that way. It's why I avoid the news. It colours in a person's life, gives them substance, makes them real. This job is a whole lot easier when it doesn't feel real.

But I knew Forrest. He was the young man who taunted a vulnerable man, who, disowned by his family, escaped to Liars Island where he reconciled his past and refashioned himself into an individual he could be proud of. He was the young man who fell in love with Dove, who fretted about her in prison. But mostly, he reminds me of Megan's friend, Jay. He didn't make it either.

Sitting on the bench outside Lookout Cottage, staring across the Bristol Channel, its waters blackened by the lingering storm clouds, I take out my phone. I want to tell Megan that I'm thinking of Jay and he'll never be forgotten, but the signal is too weak to make a call. At that moment, I feel even farther away from her. I don't even know if Julian has given her her phone back or if they've sorted their differences. I tap out a text telling her I'm missing her and can't wait to see her soon and press send. My phone buzzes and at first I think it's Megan responding at the kind of speed that only teenagers seem to possess when it suits them, but it's not Megan. It's Howard. Again. I'm guessing he's still on a mission to demonstrate Dad didn't take his own life, excusing his role in his death, but you can't find proof where there is none and wishful thinking doesn't equal evidence. I delete it without bothering to read it and slide my phone back into my jeans pocket just as Ash appears around the corner of the cottage.

'Rose asked me to check you were okay and walk you back to Jenny's Cottage. She couldn't face coming out here again, not with Forrest . . .' he glances at the cottage '. . . you know, and to be honest, no one should be walking around the island on their own. The winds are still too high.'

'Is Rose okay?'

'Not really.' He sits down next to me on the bench. 'She's called the police.'

'His poor family. His mum'll be devastated.'

'What about you?' asks Ash. 'Are you okay?'

'I will be.'

'I thought you guys were used to this kind of thing.'

'You never get used to it.'

Sensing I'm in no hurry to move, Ash allows the silence to close around us.

'Rose said you think there's a possibility Forrest's death wasn't an accident.'

'I don't think anything. The evidence, if there is any, does that for me.'

'I can't imagine anyone wanting to hurt Forrest.'

'Someone hurt Kieran.'

'Someone? Don't you mean Dove?'

Good. Rose has kept her promise. She hasn't told him that Bagshaw confessed to Kieran's murder too.

'Yes, of course.'

'At least we found Forrest.' He looks at me. 'Rose told me what happened to your dad. It takes courage to return to a place that holds such heartache for you.'

'It was a long time ago.'

Ash shudders. 'This island has claimed more than its fair share of victims, including Forrest.'

'So you think it was an accident?'

'What else could it be? The real mystery is what the hell was he doing wandering around the island at all hours. We all know the drill, Ally. A storm hits, we all stay inside even if that means not being able to get the animals to a safer place. It's island living 101.' He shakes his head. 'First Kieran, now Forrest. Two deaths in a fortnight. It's going to take us a long time to get over this. Most of us came here to escape stuff. This is our haven. Or it was.'

'At least you have Rose.'

'That's true. God knows where I'd be without her. She's helped me through so much.' He looks at me. 'I've got a past.'

'Haven't we all? And I'm sure you're a great support to Rose.'

'I like to think so. She's a long way from that person who divorced her husband. He was a complete shit to her. I'm sure she told you that when they found out she couldn't have children, he went off with her best friend and got her pregnant.'

'That's really rough.'

'She was devastated. She's always wanted to be a mum.'

'Yes. Even as a child, she loved looking after the little ones while their parents sat in the pub.'

'That's Rose.' He smiles.

'But it sounds like she'll be a parent after all. She told me you and her are planning to adopt.'

Ash rolls his eyes with mock exasperation.

'I told her not to say anything until it was confirmed, but yes it's true. A young lad. We're just waiting to hear if we've been successful.'

'Good luck.' It's then that I remember Rose's CSI report and Jake saying that her threats to kill her husband would be enough to prevent her adopting a child.

'Ash, I don't know how to say this, but I think there's something you should know.'

'What's that?'

'When Rose broke up with her husband she attacked him with a cricket bat.'

'Yes, she told me. Do you blame her?'

'No, I don't.'

'Her ex dropped the charges.'

'Yes, but threats to kill is a serious offence, serious enough to stop her adopting a child. I'm sorry.'

'Don't worry.' He smiles. 'The agency knows all about Rose's past. We haven't kept anything from them. Plus, technically, we're fostering. The rules are slightly different.'

'Sorry, my bad,' I say, relieved to be wrong. 'I shouldn't have mentioned it.'

'No, it's fine. The agency knows people have had complicated lives and, like I said, I've been no saint.' He looks at me before deciding he can trust me. 'I've a history of addiction

309

and a sideline in supplying. It's not something I'm proud of, but it's over now.'

'So you're clean?'

'Two years now. I don't go near the stuff. I've got this place to thank for that. I never thought I'd see the day I called a soggy bit of land in the Channel home.' He laughs.

I smile, but my thoughts are elsewhere. If Ash is sober and no longer supplying, why was he acting so suspiciously the first day I met him? What has he got locked up in that barn? And if Ash isn't dealing, where did Forrest get his drugs from?

ASH

Yianni: Run, my friend. The Niki has been raided. Someone tipped off the police. They found the cargo and they have your name. A friend of mine will be in touch. Do as he says. He'll get you off the island. Go now. There is no time to lose. You have more to worry about than just the police. You must disappear for good or they will find you. These people want their goods back and they have contacts everywhere. I will take care of everything here. I will keep her safe and make sure they don't find out about her. You have my word. But you can never come back. They will kill you.

Ash never intended for any of this to happen. Crewing yachts for the rich was an easy way to bring in a bit of dope for personal use. No one ever checked – a few hundred euros slipped into the palms of the customs officers saw to that. Besides, it was harmless enough. No big deal. The police weren't interested. He was small beer. It meant he could make things easier for Hana. She'd suffered so much.

That was before someone higher up the food chain found out about his little operation and he was offered the chance to make more money. Grass was one thing, but there was more money to be had in class As. He didn't say anything to Hana even when she told him she thought someone was selling heroin to the migrants or when they had their first overdose. He told himself he was doing it for them. A necessary evil.

He planned to get out, once he had enough money to set themselves up, but it didn't stop there. There were greater profits to be had in people trafficking and there were thou-

sands on Lesvos who were desperate. No price was too high.
No risk too great.

He drew the line at trading in humans, but they wouldn't
listen and that's when he made his biggest mistake; he threatened to go to the police. It was an empty threat. He was in
way too deep, but he couldn't be trusted anymore and that
meant only one thing. They'd make it look like an accident or
suicide to dodge any awkward questions. The drugs planted
on The Niki were all part of an elaborate plan that would end
in his killing.

He didn't even have time to say goodbye. A friend's fishing boat got him to Italy where he lived on the streets. That's
when he started on the harder stuff. Life was easier when it
was a blur. Then he remembered his friend Rose, a nurse who
worked in one of the camps, talking about an island where
she grew up, a tiny place in the Bristol Channel that no one
had ever heard of, much less cared about.

Not holding out much hope, he messaged her asking for
work. She replied instantly – the island's Trust needed a general maintenance man, if he was interested. Two days later
he arrived on Liars Island. It was a cold, damp place but it
would do for now until he could find a way back to Greece,
back to Hana. But someone must have told her the truth
about him because she didn't even open his messages. His old
life was over for good.

He tried to break his habit. No one knew except Dove.
It takes one druggie to know another. He didn't have much
choice but to let her get high with him. A dangerous one, that
one, into everything. She'd come out with all sorts when she

was off her face, but he wasn't interested and once she met Forrest, she too lost interest.

He tried to be careful, seeking out remote spots on the island, but he was wrong. When Kieran found him propped up against a dry stonewall, he didn't say anything. He didn't have to. Pupils dilated, spaced out, it was obvious what Ash had been up to, and it was obvious it was more than dope. Would he tell Hilton?

There was a time when he wouldn't have cared, but now he did. Things had changed. He and Rose were going to be a family. He'd even grown to like the island. But if Kieran told Hilton that his bar manager and general maintenance man was an addict, that would be the end of everything. He couldn't let that happen.

But he belonged here now. This is his home. He couldn't leave Liars Island. Not now . . . Not ever.

52

Jake is already back when I return from Lookout Cottage via the church where I've locked the samples away with the other exhibits. Standing by the kitchen table, I have the impression he's been waiting for me, and he has news.

'How was it?' he asks.

'Pretty grim. I didn't find anything, but I'm not a pathologist. I take it you didn't find anything at the ravine either.'

'A few shoe prints. I took what I could, but we already know all four of them were at the scene so they're not much use.'

'Fair enough.'

'But . . .' Jake smiles. 'I did find this.' He eases a small black box from his pocket.

'What is it?'

'It's a birdcam. There was one just before the ravine. I almost tripped over it when Ash and Rose showed me where Forrest died.'

I take it from him, turning it over.

'Norm mentioned this in the first briefing, but it was nowhere near the watersports centre so the investigation discounted it. Do you know how to view the footage?'

'I certainly do.' He grins. 'Soph's parents have one. They live out in the sticks. They've got foxes living at the bottom of the garden. It's motion-censored. It's just a case of taking the SD card out and putting it into the laptop. I wasn't sure I was allowed to do it so I waited for you.'

I give him back the birdcam. 'Go for it.'

Jake slides the little black card out of its compartment and slots it into the laptop. He downloads the footage and sets it on play. It's set off a couple of times by wandering cattle, their eyes shining like diamonds into the camera, but the third time it's triggered by a human and they're wearing a red coat.

'That's Forrest,' says Jake, pointing to the figure on the screen striding away from the camera. 'He looks like a man on a mission.'

I check the timestamp.

'It says 10.15pm. Jocasta says she saw him last at 9pm.'

'How far is it from Grannus House?'

'About half a kilometre.'

'Even in a storm it wouldn't take that long to get there so if he left the house at 9pm, what the hell was he doing wandering around the island for over an hour?'

'Oh God. Really? Poor kid,' says Harriet, when I deliver the terrible news that Forrest has been found dead in a ravine and his corpse is under a sheet on a table in the kitchen of one of the cottages. Then after a respectful pause, she adds, 'What's your gut feeling about it?'

'Honestly, I don't have one,' I reply, scanning the black skies overhead. 'Obviously, as an unexplained death we did the usual. Jake examined the ravine while I photographed Forrest's body at Lookout Cottage.'

'Did Jake find anything at the scene?'

'He did his best, but they'd already removed Forrest's body by the time we got there. The scene had been trampled all over. It was next to useless, apart from the birdcam, a hundred metres or so from the ravine.'

'Birdcam?'

'Yes, it caught Forrest walking towards the ridge at around 10.15pm. Jocasta last saw him at 9pm.'

'So he'd been out in the storm for over an hour? It sounds like he died quite soon after he left Grannus House then. Were there any injuries on his body?'

'Nothing obvious, but I'm not an expert. I did what I could in terms of photographing and taking swabs and samples and I bagged his clothing.'

'We might get some decent DNA then?'

'Only all four of them held his body at one point so the forensics on this aren't going to help us much.'

'Was that deliberate, do you think?'

'I don't think so. Rose tried to revive him, Ben and Ash put him on a stretcher and Jocasta hugged him. That feels like instinctive behaviour to me.'

'Whose idea was it to move him?'

'Jocasta. The others wanted to leave him until I got there.'

'She's the one who's trying to stop the extension of the watersports centre, right?'

'Yes, but she and Ben seemed to have made peace. He led the search and rescue party for Forrest.'

'Is there anything about this that says it could be something other than an accident? What about suicide?'

'It could be. I've dealt with other deaths where someone has gone for a long walk on a freezing day. It doesn't take long for hypothermia to set in then you're in all sorts of trouble.'

'And Forrest's behaviour sounds erratic. You said he was distraught over Dove and he'd had some kind of a run-in with Ben.'

'That's true, but he seemed to have calmed down by the time Ash did the storm briefing, and when I asked him about it, Jocasta intervened before I could get anything out of him.'

'Jocasta? Her name seems to be cropping up a lot.'

'Yes, but she wouldn't hurt him. She's like a mother to them all.'

'From what you've told me so far, we can't discount anything.'

'Theoretically, she could have followed him to the ridge and pushed him off the edge, but she would have been picked up by the birdcam.'

'Not if she knew it was there.'

'Why lure Forrest that far from Grannus House?'

'Deflection.'

'But she could easily have been blown off into the ravine and besides, she loves Forrest like he was her own.'

'In my experience, love or some skewed form of it is enough. But what about Ben Dawson? Where was he when all this was going on?'

'He didn't leave the watersports centre all night.'

'How do you know that?'

'He had to dig his way out to get to the inn this morning. There'd been a landslip on the track down to the watersports centre.'

'A landslip? That's a new one on me, but okay. So what about Ash and Rose?'

'They had the opportunity if they were prepared to brave the storm, but I'm not sure what their motive would have been.'

'Okay, we'll keep an open mind. There's nothing more we can do until we get Forrest's body back to the mainland for a full PM so just leave him where he is. We're trying to get you off the island asap.'

'Any news on that?'

'No, the weather conditions have grounded the helicopter and the seas are still too rough to send a boat. You're stuck for a little while longer, I'm afraid. We tracked the owners of those glasses you found at Hidden Cove, by the way. They were bought from a branch of Specsavers in Brighton twenty years ago by an elderly lady who passed away two years ago. As far as her surviving relatives are aware she never visited North Devon.'

'So they were washed up in the storm then?'

'Probably. Those frames haven't been on sale for at least ten years either, but nice try, Ally. So, one of the theories we're working on at the moment is that Dove lured Kieran to Hidden Cove to confront him over his threat to tell Forrest they'd slept together. When he gets there he finds her and Bagshaw waiting for him. They hit him over the head and Bagshaw paddles his body back to Devil's Cauldron to give himself time to get back to the vestry before Kieran's body is found.'

'Sounds about right, I guess. Why would Bagshaw help Dove though?'

'I don't know.' Harriet sighs.

'Maybe she's his secret daughter or something.'

'For God's sake, Ally. As if,' she snaps.

'Sorry.' The phone goes silent. 'You okay, Harriet?'

'It's just this case. It's as frustrating as hell and I'm getting a lot of heat from the top floor. They're not interested in theories, they want collars, and I'm no nearer charging Dove or Bagshaw with Kieran's murder than I was a week ago. And we checked. Dove isn't Bagshaw's daughter.'

'What did Harriet say about Forrest?'

'Nothing much. The feeling is Forrest's death is most likely to be accidental. The only person he appeared to have beef with was Ben and he was blocked in by a landslide all night. So it's just a case of waiting for the authorities to arrive and transport him to the mortuary for a full PM. Besides, she's got bigger problems on her plate. I get the impression the investigation is rapidly going south.'

'But there's the exhibits still locked in the church?'

'Which she's still no nearer getting her hands on. No one's coming for them or us, Jake. Not until the weather improves. Besides, I'm not sure they change anything. Finding Kieran's blood on Bagshaw's jacket, that just confirms Bagshaw's version of events, and the blood we found at Hidden Cove isn't enough to prove Kieran died there. The glasses don't belong to anyone on the island and the forensics from Hilton's Land Rover and Forrest's death aren't related to Kieran's murder.'

'And she now knows that Dove and Bagshaw lied about meeting each other.'

'Being in the pub at the same time for a few minutes doesn't really constitute meeting each other and it certainly isn't long enough to cook up murdering a person in such a way they both get off scot-free.'

'So what happens now?'

'Dove and Bagshaw are currently released under further investigation, where technically they can remain for years, but it doesn't mean anyone's still doing any investigating.'

'What do you mean?'

'It's all about budgets. The money is always found for murders as you'd imagine, but it's finite. If it's not going anywhere, the team will be quietly scaled back until they'll only respond to new information. Officially, the case will remain open. Unofficially it just joins the great unsolved.'

'Hilton Deveney doesn't strike me as the kind of guy to give up.'

'He can scream and shout as much as he wants. It won't make any difference. Police budgets bend for no one.'

'So is that it?'

'Yes. Unless they can drive a wedge in Dove or Bagshaw's stories soon or new evidence turns up, no one will go down for Kieran's murder.'

Jake looks over my shoulder. 'Look out, here's trouble.'

I twist around as Jocasta strides into the pub. When she sees Jake and me she approaches our table. She seems smaller than I remember, diminished. She's taken Forrest's death hard.

'Did . . . did . . . you . . . ?'

I know what she's asking.

'I was very quick, very gentle. I treated him with dignity, Jocasta.'

'Where is he now?'

'He's still at the cottage. Under lock and key.'

'Can I see him?'

'No, I'm sorry, you can't,' I reply, bracing myself for an argument.

'I understand.' She nods. 'And I'm sorry about earlier. I think it was the shock and now I need to speak to his poor family, tell them what a wonderful young man their son was.'

'I'm sure they'll appreciate it,' I say.

'I still can't believe it. I said goodnight to him and I was sure he was heading to bed. The next thing I woke up to the sound of the door slamming.'

'A door slamming? You didn't mention that before.'

'I assumed it was Forrest going to bed.'

'So it was an internal door. It wasn't the front door then?'

'Now I come to think of it, it could have been, I suppose.'

'What time was this?'

'Ten. I checked my bedside clock. If only I'd got up, gone after him. He'd be here now.'

'If only': such an overused phrase in my line of work.

'You couldn't have known what was going to happen.'

'Thank you, and thank you for taking good care of him. I should make that phone call now.'

Rose lifts the bar up for her and she disappears into the hallway to call Forrest's parents.

'So, it didn't take Forrest over an hour to get to the ravine then. That makes more sense. Another?' says Jake, holding up his empty pint glass.

'No, I'm good, thanks.'

Jake goes to the bar for a refill, but my mind is elsewhere.

If Jocasta is right, it took Forrest fifteen minutes to reach the birdcam and then another couple to reach the ridge above the ravine. Perfectly doable in broad daylight, but at night, in a howling gale, that's fast. So fast, Forrest might even have had to jog there. Like Jake said, he looked like a man on a mission. That's not the behaviour of someone who's lost and disorientated, that's the behaviour of someone who knows exactly where they're going and wants to get there quickly. And there's only one reason why someone would do that. Forrest had arranged to meet someone.

53

The wind has whipped itself into a frenzy by the time Jake and I return to Jenny's Cottage. It's late and Jake, four pints deep, takes himself off to bed, leaving me at the kitchen table, mulling over enough questions to keep sleep beyond my reach.

Did Forrest really risk going out in storm force winds to meet someone last night? But why? Why not wait until daylight? And if he did meet someone, was that person responsible for his death? But who would want Forrest dead? Besides possibly Ben Dawson. Is it someone from his past? His behaviour publicly humiliated a homeless man and almost destroyed his father's career but neither of them is on the island. And where does Kieran's murder fit in all this? Two killings in two weeks is too much of a coincidence – they must be linked. This all starts with Dove and Bagshaw and their confessions. We've missed something, but what?

The CSI examination reports Harriet sent pop up on my laptop screen. Jake and I spent the evening poring over them. Was that only twenty-four hours ago? So much has happened since then. Another young man has died.

I ponder them for a few moments. We've already gone through them with a fine-tooth comb and found nothing.

Maybe I'll check them again. *Slack sank the ship.* Dad would be proud of me. Pity I can't say the same of him.

I start with the break-in at the Bidecombe church. It was a bog-standard burglary, just like so many I've attended over the years. Nothing unusual. Scuff marks on the drainpipe where the assailant – Cal Meeth – scaled the building. Footmarks on the roof where he pulled the lead away. Glass recovered, mostly from the ground beneath the window, where he broke into the vestry. No shoe marks this time. Like I said. Nothing unusual.

I click out of the report and move on to Dove's sister's case. This one wasn't mine. It took place in the West Midlands ten years ago. The CSI was called Matt Birch. I've met a few CSIs from around the country at various conferences, but I don't know him.

Like all CSI reports, there's a series of ticks and hurriedly drawn diagrams outlining the evidence that's been recovered and submitted with a few notes to remind the CSI of any pertinent details. In this case, Matt noted there were two fatalities and a female survivor – Dove or Stacy as she would have been called then. There's no tickbox for the horror or sadness Matt himself might have felt, or carried with him since.

Two lives obliterated in an instant. It's the kind of tragedy that ripples through a small community for years. I linger on the list of evidence. All of it was submitted to the laboratory for forensic examination except the interior tapings. The amount of forensics gathered at a scene is always greater than the amount submitted for analysis. The skill is working out what's relevant and what's not, given budget limitations. That isn't unusual. Unusual. That word keeps cropping up.

There's nothing unusual about any of these reports, but there's something that's not quite right either. There must be a connection. I sense the answer is there, in black and white, I just can't see it.

I spend the next few minutes flicking between Dove's and Bagshaw's crime scene reports, but all I see are differences. Two different areas of the country. Two different CSIs. Two different victims. Two different crimes. Two different perpetrators: one a petty thief, the other a drunk driver. There is no way they could be linked. Then I remember my conversation with Jake in Bagshaw's spotless vestry when we couldn't find anything of any note: nothing can be as significant as something.

And then I see it.

54

I've barely slept, veering from convinced I'm on to something to appalled I could suggest something that barely qualifies as supposition, let alone evidence. It's easily done. In the desperate pursuit of a result, the mind gives credence to undeserving notions. Is that what's happening here? Am I seeing things that aren't there? In the end, I decided I have nothing to lose.

I check my watch. It's 8am. Harriet should be in by now. I dial her number, pressing myself against the church wall to avoid the rain thrashing the grasslands. She picks up.

'I think I found the link between Dove and Bagshaw in the files you sent me,' I say, not giving her time to speak, in case I change my mind.

'Okay, what have you got?'

'I looked again at the crime scene examination report on the fatal crash that killed Dove's sister, Freya?'

'And?'

'Dove was only fifteen at the time, right?'

'Yes, that's correct. Her sister had gone to collect her from a party at a friend's house and stayed for a few hours before driving Dove home. From what I remember, they rounded a corner on the wrong side of the road, swerved to miss an oncoming car and drove into a wall. The other car flipped over. Freya and the driver of the other car died instantly. Dove walked away with cuts and bruises. Freya was something like three times over the limit. It was a crash waiting to happen.'

'Looking at the crime scene report, the tapings from the front seats were never submitted to the lab for testing.'

'Tapings?'

'For fibres.'

'Is it normal to do that?'

'Not really. I've only done it a couple of times where there's some doubt over who was actually driving.'

There's a pause at the other end of the phone.

'So what you're saying is that whoever attended the scene of the collision had reason to think that Freya might not have been the driver?'

'Yes. The report says both girls were thrown clear of the car. It would be a natural assumption that Freya was driving, given Dove's age, but it looks to me that the crash investigator was suspicious enough to direct the CSI to take some seat tapings, but they were then never sent to the lab.'

'Why wasn't it followed up?'

'It could be any number of reasons. Maybe a witness confirmed it was Freya.'

'There were no witnesses.'

'Budgets then, or maybe Dove's age meant they never seriously considered there was any other driver but her sister, Freya. The family had already lost one daughter.'

'Supposing it's true and Dove was driving that night, that makes her responsible for the death of her sister and the other driver. But how does that relate to the break-in at Bagshaw's church hundreds of miles away, years later?'

'I'm a bit surer of this one. Probably because it's mine.'

'Go on.'

'It wasn't just lead that got stolen from the church roof that night. Cal took the silverware too. Now the reason Cal stole the lead is because he had a buyer. He didn't deal in religious artefacts. That wasn't his bag at all.'

'He's a tea leaf, do you really think he'd hesitate to swipe anything shiny?'

'Yes, I do. His MO was to shin up the drainpipe, rip the lead off the roof, chuck it onto the back of a truck and get the hell out of there. There's something else too. Something more conclusive.'

'Oh?'

'I didn't see it the first time round, but the more I look at it the more convinced I am that the vestry window was broken from the inside.'

'You're not actually admitting you made a mistake, are you?' Harriet laughs.

'Yep. I missed it at the time. I was just starting out and was still very inexperienced although that's no excuse.'

'The important thing is, you're telling me it was an inside job.'

'Yes. I think Bagshaw offloaded the artefacts himself and then made a false insurance claim.'

'Double bubble. Smart. But why would Cal Meeth take the fall for the vicar?'

'The Bidecombe church break-in was a TIC. Cal got done for another burglary and admitted quite a few others including this one, probably because detectives told him he'd get a reduced sentence if he helped the police with their clear-up rate.'

'Can't believe they still fall for that shit, but why would Bagshaw burgle himself?'

'Didn't you say that one of the reasons his marriage broke down was over money.'

'Among other things. Anyway, the bottom line is Bagshaw potentially stole from his own church and Dove potentially killed her sister? It's a stretch, Ally.'

'I know.'

'But it's also not beyond the realms of possibility. Let's say you're right on both counts, what has any of this to do with the murder of Kieran Deveney?'

I take a moment to think it through. Harriet's only going to give me one shot at this.

'Firstly, it means both Bagshaw and Dove had a secret that was big enough to destroy them. What if someone discovered what they'd done and decided to use it against them by forcing them to confess to killing Kieran?'

'You mean blackmail?'

'Yes.'

The line goes silent. She's running with it.

'There's only one possible reason a person would do that,' she says, finally. 'And that's because they're the real killer.'

55

When I return from speaking to Harriet, Jake is already up, making himself breakfast.

'Oh,' he says, momentarily startled by my appearance at the back door. 'I didn't know you'd gone out. I'm making a cuppa, do you want one?'

'Thanks.' I watch him drop a tea bag into a mug.

'Everything okay?' Jake hands me the mug.

'Yes. I went to check in with Harriet.'

'Any news?'

I haven't told him I suspect Forrest met someone on the night of his death or that I believe Dove and Bagshaw are being blackmailed into confessing a crime they didn't commit by someone on the island. Is it negligent not to warn a colleague they could be sharing three square miles of land with a murderer? But it's still all conjecture and Jake has been on edge ever since we arrived. The last thing I need is a CSI who can't keep their shit together.

'It's not looking good for today, but they're expecting the storm to blow itself out so they're hoping to send a boat out to us tomorrow.'

'Not soon enough for me. This place is doing my head in.'

'I know what you mean, but we'll be out of here soon.'

There's a loud rap on the back door. Through the glass in the kitchen door, Rose is smiling at us. I beckon for her to come in.

'Not disturbing anything, am I?'

'Not at all. We were just talking about how we're looking forward to getting home.'

'Yes, of course. The weather eases tomorrow so hopefully it won't be long now. Anyway, I've come to let you know that Ben, Ash and I are going over to Grannus House. We're leaving in the next few minutes while there's a break in the weather, and we're planning to stay the night with Jocasta.'

'So we'll be on our own here?' says Jake.

'Yes, but the internal phone is back up so if you need anything, you can just call us and help yourself to anything in the pub, but once that wind gets up, you should stay in the cottage for your own safety. If you get into any real trouble, there are flares at the pub and the centre, obviously. They're kept in the cellar. The three of us will be back early tomorrow morning.'

'How is Jocasta?'

'She's okay. She spoke to Forrest's mum. I think that was quite hard. She feels so guilty.'

'Why?'

'First Amber, now Forrest. She seems to think it's her fault.'

'She shouldn't,' says Jake. 'It was an accident.'

Rose catches my eye. I nod.

'It looks that way and I'm sure Jocasta will be glad of the company.'

'That's not the only reason we're going. She wants to hold a special service for him tonight to prepare him for his journey.'

'His journey? You do understand Forrest's body can't be moved from the cottage, don't you? A postmortem still needs to be carried out to find the cause of death.'

'Yes, she understands that, but she'd still like to hold a Wiccan ceremony for him.'

'Wiccan?' asks Jake.

'Yes, the Wiccans believe in the afterlife, a place where the soul goes on to rest forever. It's called Summerland.'

'Sounds nicer than here!' He grimaces.

'I'm afraid we won't be able to come,' I say.

'Sorry.' Rose's cheeks colour. 'I wasn't coming here to invite you two. I just wanted to let you know that there won't be anyone around. Jocasta specifically requested that you don't attend.'

'I understand.'

'Thanks. I'll see you tomorrow then.'

Jake waits for her to leave. 'Reckon we dodged a bullet there. I'd rather stay here and sit it out until we're rescued.'

'Me too.'

'There's probably a pack of cards around somewhere to help us while away the hours.'

As I watch him rummaging through a kitchen drawer, my mind wanders back to my conversation with Harriet. Just before she rang off, she told me that Jake and I should lock ourselves in the cottage until we're rescued, just as a precaution. It's a great plan with just one flaw – we don't have a key.

My back flat against the barn wall, I wait until I hear three voices telling me that Rose, Ash and Ben have set off for Grannus House. Stepping from behind the building I watch them disappear over the horizon. I could have asked Rose or Ash for the key to Jenny's Cottage, but right now I've no idea who can be trusted.

I also waited until Jake left to call Sophie to tell her we weren't getting off the island today before slipping out the back door.

The pub is eerily silent, reminding me of my first day on the island. The key to Jenny's Cottage is helpfully labelled and waiting for me on a rack in the hallway, alongside the keys for every property on the island. Unhooking it, I slide it into my pocket. I'm about to leave when I stop myself.

The last time I stood here, Rose was horrified to catch me going through a box of clothes she'd bought for their longed-for foster child. When I met Ash here on that first day, he also made it obvious he didn't want me to go upstairs. They're hiding something. I glance back through the doorway to the bar and the window beyond to the track that leads to Grannus House, but Ash, Rose and Ben are long gone.

I take the stairs two at a time arriving at the top of the landing in front of a door. Turning the handle, it swings open on to a bare-walled bedroom furnished with a double bed and single chest of drawers, a phone charger resting on it. A creased grey duvet covers the bed, at the base of which is a jumble of clothes. My foot nudges the pile to reveal jeans and T-shirts that I recognise as belonging to Ash. Crumpled boxers spring out of the top drawer. The lower drawers contain more men's shirts and jumpers. I feel around the back of the drawer and even lift the mattress – you'd be amazed what people still stash under there – but there's nothing. Besides I don't even know what I'm looking for so I leave the room as I found it, closing the door behind me.

There are several other rooms along the corridor, but I opt for the one at the end, the one I saw a light on my first night on the island. As soon as I step inside, my nostrils are assaulted by the smell of potpourri, a bowl of which competes for space with the make-up on the dressing table. Next to it is an unmade double bed – only one side of it has been slept in. In the wardrobe, I find a rack of Rose's clothes.

It's then that I realise Ash isn't sleeping here. When I saw the two lights that night, I thought they'd had a row, but there is nothing of Ash in this room. He's never slept here. Have they split up? If they have, they're doing a fine job hiding it and if they're no longer together, why are they still going ahead with the fostering?

Opening the drawer to Rose's ornate dressing table, I rummage through an array of Alice bands and scrunchies, my fingers feeling their way towards the back of the drawer. There's a tiny ridge where the smooth base becomes more resistant. I slide a nail underneath it. Pinching it between a thumb and forefinger, I ease out a large brown envelope.

It's already open so I slide the sheath of papers out and flick through them. It takes me a few moments to figure out it's Rose's decree nisi from her first husband, Rob Lullcott, the man who left her but only after first impregnating her best friend. Poor Rose. But she turned her life around. She came home and she's about to achieve her dream to become a mum to a young boy who desperately needs one, whatever is going on between her and Ash.

I continue to sift through the document out of curiosity more than anything and it's then that I realise that this isn't a decree nisi. These are the divorce papers that Rob Lullcott served on Rose. I turn to the last page. The sight of it catches me off guard. There should be a signature on it, but it's just a blank page. Rose never signed it. She's still married to her first husband. But that's not the only thing Rose Griffiths has lied about.

ROSE

Dear Mrs Griffiths,

We are delighted to inform you that you and your husband Ash have been chosen to take on the lease of The Barbary Inn.

The field was particularly strong with over three hundred applicants. However, the committee felt that, growing up on Liars Island, you offered a unique perspective and as a young, newly married couple the two of you would bring energy and dynamism to the Inn and the island as a whole. What swung the committee's decision was your and your husband's commitment to raising a family on the island, the first couple to do so in several decades, creating a stable and sustainable environment on Liars Island. We look forward to hearing your happy news in due course . . .

Rose couldn't remember a time when she didn't want to be a mum, it was as natural to her as breathing. She'd always had terrible monthly cramps but whenever she sought help, doctors told her some women just suffered heavier, more painful periods than others. She had her first miscarriage within a year of getting married. She and Rob were devastated, of course, all that hope evaporating in a moment, but they built themselves up, stayed positive. After the fifth miscarriage, she saw a specialist and that's when she discovered she had stage 4 endometriosis, the severest the doctor had ever seen. She would have to have her womb removed. She ignored his advice at first. A hysterectomy would be the end of who she was, who she had always been. There would be no way back.

She'd never hold her own child. This way, she could tell herself there was still hope, miracles do happen, but the pain worsened and Rob said her condition impacted his life too. A hysterectomy was their chance at a normal, healthy future together. Once it was over, they could explore surrogacy, even adoption, he said. He promised her she'd be a mother. So she agreed.

Those months after the operation were the worst. When she wasn't raging at the unfairness of it all, she mourned the life that should have been hers. But that was better than the emptiness she felt, her worth bound up in her womanhood, she didn't know who she was or how she was going to carry on, but she knew she didn't want to be this person. It was only Rob's promise that kept her going. Until he changed his mind.

He said he hadn't really understood the implications of surrogacy and that he couldn't go through with it. Or adoption. Instead, they would carve out a new childless life for themselves. That's what marriage was all about. For better. For worse.

She didn't even know he'd been cheating on her until he told her he was leaving. He'd been seeing her best friend behind her back. He hadn't intended for any of it to happen, he told her, but she'd become so morose and difficult to live with that he found comfort elsewhere. So, in a way it was her fault. And then she found out his girlfriend was pregnant.

When she confronted him, he told her it was her choice to have the hysterectomy. It was then that something came over her and she wanted to hurt him as he had hurt her. She grabbed the nearest thing, a cricket bat, and told him she was going to kill him. He fought her off, but the police were called and now she was looking at a prison sentence. By then she didn't care.

Rob's girlfriend persuaded him to drop the charges as long as she stayed away from them both. It wasn't a difficult decision to leave. Everyone knew what she'd done. She'd never be able to hold her head up this side of Exeter. Moving from country to country, talking to people who knew nothing of her past helped her suppress the pain.

She found herself working in a camp, treating young children. For a time she hoped the strength she drew from their need for her would be enough, but it wasn't. They would always be a reminder of what could have been. She stayed as long as she could.

Her parents begged her to come home to Liars Island. She was nervous about returning to North Devon in case her ex found out so she took a taxi straight to Bidecombe Quay and walked onto the boat, hoping no one would recognise her.

As soon as she stepped onto the jetty at Liars Island, that same sense of safeness she took for granted as a child settled over her. She was home for good. It lasted until her parents told her they were retiring. She knew the island's Trust wouldn't let her take the lease on alone and she'd have to leave. Panicking, she was about to ask Jocasta if she'd take her in when Ash contacted her out of the blue. He didn't say why, but he had to leave Greece and had nowhere to go.

She invited him to the island, on one condition: they pretend to get married. He agreed, mocking up a fake Vegas marriage certificate on a computer. Having never seen one before, the island's board of trustees never queried it. Things seemed to be working out just as they had planned. No one noticed they kept separate rooms at the inn and when Ash asked for a favour in return, it felt like it was meant to be.

Then it all went wrong. She was going to check on Lookout Cottage a month back when she ran into Kieran. She hadn't had much to do with him. He seemed a nice enough guy, a bit flirtatious, maybe, but that was it. Dove had told her that he had a habit of appearing when she was out walking, but he was nothing she couldn't handle. She could tell that he wanted to speak to her, which wasn't unusual. His father Hilton probably wanted something fixed at the house he commandeered as his own when he was on the island.

'Everything okay?' she asked.

'Yeah, all good . . . Something really weird happened when I was on the mainland yesterday.'

'Oh?' she said, unsure of why he was telling her this.

'Yes, you know we're planning to extend the watersports centre.'

'Yes.'

'I went to have a chat with the guys at Lullcott Construction.' She tensed on hearing her ex-husband's family name. 'I mentioned I lived on Liars Island and the guy, Rob, told me that he was married to the daughter of the people who managed the pub. It took me a moment to realise he meant you. So I put him right and told him you ran the pub with Ash. Do you know what he said to me?'

'No.' Her voice was barely louder than a whisper.

'He said, "That's strange, because last time I checked, she was still married to me. Next time you see her, can you tell her to sign the fucking divorce papers?"'

It was true. She'd ignored all his attempts to get her to sign them. They were still in a drawer in her bedroom, a reminder she was still screwing his life up like he had screwed hers. She didn't know what to say so Kieran said it for her.

'So you're either a bigamist or you and Ash faked your wedding. Why would you do that?'

'No . . . Rob's lying,' she stammered before turning and stumbling away as fast as she could but she had convinced no one, least of all Kieran. Her conversation with him ate her up. She couldn't get it out of her mind. Does he know about the couples clause? Would he tell Hilton? If he did, she'd be kicked out.

But she belonged here now. This is her home. She couldn't leave Liars Island. Not now . . . Not ever.

56

'Wow. So Rose is a bigamist then? Who'd have thought it?'

When I returned from the inn, I found Jake waiting for me at the kitchen table, after his call to Sophie.

'Yes, unless she and Ash aren't really married,' I say, blowing the steam from the mug of tea he handed me. 'She told me that they'd gone to Vegas and got married in one of those drive-through wedding chapels. Are they legal in the UK?'

'Yeah, definitely. Sophie's sister did that. It was wild. The fallout was nuclear. Her parents haven't really forgiven her. So why didn't Rose sign the divorce papers? You'd think she'd want to get shot of her first husband as soon as possible.'

'I don't know, payback for all the pain he'd caused her, maybe.'

'She'd already threatened to kill him with a cricket bat! You'd think that'd be enough.'

'And she destroyed his car. She's not the Rose I knew growing up, that's for sure. That Rose would do anything to avoid conflict.'

'Maybe it's different when your husband gets your best mate up the duff. Rose was desperate to be a mother, right, but couldn't get pregnant? I reckon that's the sort of thing that can make you do irrational things.'

'But she must have shown her licence to the board of trustees when she took over the pub.'

'I've seen Soph's sister's marriage licence. It wouldn't be difficult to forge, but why would the trustees need to see her marriage licence?'

'There's this ridiculous clause in the contract for the inn. It's been there forever. I remember Rose's parents joking about it. They could never split up because they'd lose the pub. I'm surprised it's never been taken out.'

'So what does it say?'

'Basically, only married couples can take on the licence. The idea behind it was that couples, preferably with children, would bring greater stability to the island. They didn't want the place turning into Magaluf.'

'No chance of that,' says Jake, grimacing at the thick dark clouds through the kitchen window.

'Well, it looks like Rose is married. Just not to Ash.'

Jake shakes his head with disappointment. 'It's like everyone on the island is hiding a dirty little secret, even Rose. Thank God we're out of here tomorrow. I have got one question though.'

'Go on.'

'What were you doing at The Barbary Inn in the first place?'

The one question I was hoping he wouldn't ask.

'Stupid fucking thing.' I stomp around the church, phone held aloft in pursuit of a signal as the wind tries to whip it out of my hand. A single bar appears.

'Finally.' I press Harriet's number.

'Ally, thank God you called. I've been trying to get hold of you. I even called the pub, no one's picking up.'

As if on cue my phone buzzes with Harriet's missed calls.

'Er yeah, there's no one there,' I say, disconcerted by the concern in Harriet's voice. 'They've all gone to Grannus House to hold a Wiccan service for Forrest. We weren't invited. What's the problem?'

'They better not be putting Forrest's body on a raft and setting fire to it or whatever.'

'I think that's the Vikings. So what's this all about?'

There's a pause at the end of the line.

'Your blackmail theory? We're running with it.'

'What?'

'Yes. We think there's a third person involved who is blackmailing Dove and Bagshaw to disguise the fact they killed Kieran and we think they're . . . still on the island.'

I look across the battered grasslands towards the north of the island where Grannus House perches on a cliff. They're all there – Jocasta, Ben, Ash, Rose. And one of them is a killer.

'Okay,' I say, banishing the thought I'm sharing a scrap of land with a potential double murderer. 'I'm guessing you've found enough proof then.'

'Yes, we think so. We spoke to the lead investigator who dealt with the crash that killed Dove's sisters.'

'And?'

'You were right. The lead guy did have strong suspicions Dove was driving that night.'

'So why didn't they submit the forensics?'

'The SIO blocked it.'

'What? Why?'

'He didn't know. He queried it, but got waved away.'

'Okay, do they still have the samples?'

'Yes, we're getting them sent off for testing, but that could take some time, but it doesn't matter so much anyway.'

'Oh?' I ask, conscious of all the times an SIO has grumbled at me over the length of time it takes to get forensic results back.

'Dove admitted it.'

'What? She admitted to driving the car that night?'

'Yep,' says Harriet. 'We got her in last night, barely got started on her and she just crumbled. Her brief couldn't shut her up. I guess she's been carrying that weight around for a long time. So good work on that, Ally.'

'Did she say anything else?'

'Only that she's never told anyone, which was strange because we hadn't got round to asking her that. She just volunteered the information and in my experience murder suspects don't volunteer anything.'

'You think she's lying.'

'Yes, which brings us to who on the island potentially knows her secret.'

'And?'

There's a pause, but not the pathologist Alex kind that leads to some big reveal.

'It's open season,' Harriet sighs. 'Dove has lived on the island for a few years, first at The Barbary Inn and then at Grannus House. It's an incredibly close-knit community. It's entirely possible that she's confided in quite a few people. She's very close to Jocasta.'

'Yes, Jocasta sees herself as a proxy parent. Okay, so what about Bagshaw? Who knew his secret that he broke into his own church?'

'We've had him back in too. Not surprisingly, Bagshaw denies stealing the artefacts. In fact, he was appalled by the very suggestion.'

'But you've spoken to Cal?'

'Ah, yes, the lovely Cal Meeth. It turns out being implicated in a murder inquiry is the best cure for the sudden-onset amnesia that afflicted him at our previous meeting. He told us all sorts.'

It sounds like Harriet finally wiped the smile of that toerag's smug face.

'Such as?' I ask.

'Exactly what you told me. He only nicked the lead. He took the fall for the rest of it because he thought he might get his sentence reduced.'

'How does Bagshaw figure in all this?'

'Prison records show the Reverend Bagshaw visited Cal Meeth in prison when he was on remand. It wasn't to give him absolution, that's for sure.'

'Hush money?'

'Yes. Half the insurance. He agreed to admit to stealing the silverware if the police spoke to him about it. It meant he had a tidy sum waiting for him when he got out. So what we now know, and can prove, is that Bagshaw and Dove both had secrets they didn't want getting out.'

'You say that a few people could have known about Dove, but who could have known about Bagshaw? He'd only been on the island a few weeks.'

'You're not going to like this. Cal Meeth came over on the boat with Bagshaw. He recognised him instantly.'

'Oh my God. Yes, he did. He brought the headlight over for Hilton's Land Rover.'

'Well, he thought the whole thing was hilarious, the idea that the vicar he'd taken the rap for all those years ago was on the boat about to take up a brand-new position at the church on Liars Island.'

'Go on,' I say, sensing where this is leading.

'It seems like he just couldn't contain himself. The little gobshite told everyone he met. Cal's job is to unload supplies and drop them off at various points including the Bara Watersports Centre, but also Hilton Deveney's place, The Barbary Inn and Grannus House.'

'Fuck. They all knew.'

'We have to assume that's the case.'

'So where does that leave us?'

'With the $64,000 question: which one of them wanted or needed Kieran dead?'

'And do you have any idea who that is?'

'Kieran told Ben he wanted out of the business.' She doesn't give me a straight answer because she doesn't have one.

'Why?'

'He got a phone call from someone who knew Ben's family. She saw an article in a magazine about the watersports centre and recognised Ben. She told him about the cheques. Kieran didn't know his friend had tried to embezzle his grandmother. It turns out he wasn't very happy about it.'

'But Kieran was no saint himself, judging by what happened at uni.'

'Yes, he might have been using it as an excuse to get out of the partnership. It seems he was quite jealous of Ben's relationship with Hilton. Anyway, he told Forrest he wanted to leave. Forrest told his mother who then told Kieran's mother.'

'How come this didn't come out in the police interviews after Kieran's murder?'

'She was abroad,' says Harriet. 'Detectives spoke to her, but she was distraught as you can imagine. She couldn't think of any reason anyone would hurt her son, including Ben.'

'And she couldn't have known how much the centre meant to Ben.'

'No, probably not, but if Kieran wanted out, Ben may have assumed Hilton would withdraw his investment and that would mean the end of the watersports centre.'

'In fact, Hilton has made him director.'

'Yes, but Ben couldn't have known that at the time. Plus it isn't as simple as that. We did some more digging. Ben tried to steal from his nan to prop up his business, but it wasn't enough to keep it afloat so he declared bankruptcy.'

'So?'

'So he's barred from being a director of a business, any business. Hilton might turn a blind eye to a few cheques but not bankruptcy. Ben would have been kicked out of the company.'

'And off the island. So is that what Forrest was referring to in the pub when he told Ben he knew all about him?'

'We're not sure,' says Harriet. 'Forrest's father's own business went bankrupt. His new ventures are all in his wife's name. If Kieran told Forrest Ben was a bankrupt, Forrest might have known this meant Ben couldn't be a director.'

Harriet gives me a few moments to process the implications of this.

'So Ben killed Kieran and Forrest?'

'I wish it was that easy, but we can't discount Ash Griffiths either.'

'Ash?'

'He's using and possibly supplying drugs.'

'He told me his addiction issues were in the past.'

'The CCTV at Bidecombe says different. It shows him meeting a known dealer. Kieran used to kayak to the mainland with him sometimes. It's possible Kieran knew Ash was dealing. Maybe he threatened to tell Hilton. I'm fairly certain Hilton would take a dim view of his pub landlord taking drugs and, if there's one thing worth killing over, it's drugs. I learnt that a long time ago,' says Harriet with a certain weariness.

'Only Ash wasn't even on the island when Kieran was killed.'

'Which is the only thing that lets him off the hook at the moment.'

'At the moment?'

'He's still in the frame, as is Jocasta.'

'Jocasta? You're kidding. I mean she's a bit of a dragon, but I'm not sure she'd stoop to murder.'

'Well, that dizzy spell you saw her have? We checked out her medical history. She has a slow-growing brain tumour and, according to her ex-husband, it's terminal. We asked Hilton why he leased Grannus House to her given there's no medical facilities on the island. He had no idea about her condition. Apparently, because there's no doctor on the island, everyone has to sign a medical disclaimer. In other words, Jocasta would never have been allowed to rent Grannus House if Hilton had known the truth about her.'

'That might explain why Jocasta keeps seeing her daughter, Amber. She died here years ago.'

'Her ex seems to think she returned to Liars Island to be near their daughter as she sees her days out.'

'She told me it's the reason why she runs the retreat. She's trying to make up for not being able to save her own child. So did Kieran know about her condition?' I ask.

'We're really not sure, but if he did, we believe Jocasta would go to extreme lengths to stay on the island. You'll be pleased to hear that at least your friend Rose appears to be in the clear.'

'I wouldn't be so sure there.'

'Oh?'

'She never divorced her first husband. She and Ash either faked their marriage or she's a bigamist. Either way, she lied on her application for the licence to The Barbary Inn. If Hilton found out, she'd definitely be chucked off the island too, and this place is her whole life.'

Harriet lets out a long sigh.

'In that case, Ally, in answer to your question, it could be any one of them.'

Or all of them.

57

'What the fuck do you mean one or all of them could have killed Kieran?'

Jake is pacing the kitchen floor, staring at me in horror. I couldn't keep information about Dove and Bagshaw to myself any longer, so I told him what I knew.

'Ben, Ash, Rose, Jocasta, all of them potentially knew about Dove's and Bagshaw's past. Any one of them could have blackmailed them into confessing to protect themselves. They all have a motive and the means.'

'That's what you have been talking to Harriet about all this time?'

'No, only the last couple of times. I'm sorry I should have told you earlier. I didn't want to freak you out.'

'Well, I'm freaking out now. One of those fuckers is a killer,' he says, pointing out of the kitchen window. 'I don't know how you can be so calm about it.'

'Because we don't know for sure.'

'Okay, but I don't get it. Was the whole thing a set-up and they're all in it together? Right down to getting all the other people who live at Grannus House out of the way long enough for the rest of them to bump off Kieran?'

'Theoretically, I guess.'

'But how . . . why would they all agree to do that?'

'I don't know that either. What we do know is that Kieran was a threat to all of them, one way or another. If he told Hilton what he knew about them, they'd be thrown off their beloved island.'

'It's just an island.' He shrugs. 'There's plenty of others. Nicer ones too.'

'It's their home, Jake.'

'But killing someone to stay in this hellhole still feels like an overreaction.'

'Maybe there's another reason we don't know about.'

'Like what?'

'I've no idea. Look, none of this is confirmed. It's all just conjecture at the moment.'

'Yeah, well one thing I've learnt in this job is that hunches have a funny way of becoming fact. So what does the CSI rule-book have to say about finding yourself on an island of killers?'

'It says we shouldn't panic.'

'I'm not panicking.' He looks at me. 'Okay, I might be panicking a bit, but can you blame me?'

'No, but let's take a step back and think about this logically. The only thing we know for certain is that Kieran knew Ben was bankrupt because Kieran told Forrest who told his mother. The rest is supposition. So far there's no evidence that Kieran knew about Ash's drug habit, Jocasta's cancer, or Rose's non-divorce, but it doesn't matter anyway.'

'Why's that?'

'Because none of them know what we know. We just have to keep it that way until help arrives.'

'That's not difficult. There's no way I'm leaving the cottage until I hear the sound of helicopter rotary blades. God knows who's out there.'

'But there's no one within three miles of us. They're all up at Grannus House for this service for Forrest, remember?'

'Well, I'm not taking any chances.'

'Jake, you do know that we walk among thieves and murderers on the mainland too?'

'That's different. You can get away from them there. I mean from what you're saying every one of them could be a killer.'

'You're letting your imagination run away with you. We're safe, Jake, we even have the key to Jenny's Cottage.'

'Since when have we had the key?'

'Since this morning.'

'You told me you'd gone over there to get some bread and then decided to have a snoop around.'

'I didn't want to worry you. Even if this blackmail theory is right, Kieran's real killer doesn't know that we suspect anyone other than Dove and Bagshaw. How can they? Think about it. All they've seen us do is examine the vestry. They don't know we examined the other properties, or that we found the scene at Hidden Cove or that we suspect Kieran's kayak was used to paddle his body back to Seal Bay.'

Jake nods. 'Yeah, yeah, that's true.'

'Besides, we're CSIs. Half the time people don't even know what we do. No one cares about us. Believe me, Jake, nothing is going to happen to us here.'

'Okay, thanks. I feel a lot better for that. Anything else I should know?'

He says this jokingly. If only it was a joke.

'Sorry. Yes. There is.' I take a breath. 'The footage from the birdcam shows that it took Forrest fifteen minutes to cover a mile in a storm. That's fast. He wasn't lost. I think he met someone on the night of his death.'

'You mean he was murdered too?'

'Potentially. Two deaths on a small island like this is a hell of a coincidence. Chances are Forrest knew something about Kieran's murder and it cost him his life too.'

'Fucking hell, Ally. So Ben killed Forrest as well? And you didn't think to tell me?'

'Sorry.' I thought I was protecting Jake, but maybe I was wrong. Is this what Jim Dixon meant when he said I wasn't a team player? 'I just wanted to be sure.'

'And?' says Jake.

'Ben could have killed Kieran and Forrest because they both knew he was bankrupt, but I can't work out how Ben met Forrest on the ridge the night Forrest died.'

'What do you mean?'

'They didn't speak to each other during Ash's storm briefing and I followed Forrest out of the pub so he couldn't have spoken to Ben then. After that, he and Jocasta returned to Grannus House. Ben had no way of contacting Forrest. The mobile phone signal is patchy. The watersports centre doesn't have a landline.'

'What about the internal phone lines?'

'They're not connected to each other. They only route to The Barbary Inn, so whoever arranged to meet Forrest made the call from the inn. Ben was also cut off by a landslip.'

'But . . . but we know that Ash couldn't have killed Kieran. He was in Bidecombe the morning Kieran died and Jocasta loved him like a son which only leaves . . .' Jake looks at me as if to apologise. 'Rose.'

58

Jake appears in the doorway of the living room waving half a bottle of whiskey and two glasses at me.

'I found this in a cupboard. Thought it might make the time go quicker.'

Sitting down on the sofa, he sloshes the brown liquid into the tumbler and hands it to me.

I knock the glass back. I don't even like whiskey, but sharing a tiny island with one or more killers can have that effect on you. I try to extinguish the burning sensation at the back of my throat with a gasp.

'Christ, that's strong. Sorry about not telling you sooner about Forrest.'

'That's okay. So how do you think Kieran found out that Rose was lying about her marriage to Ash?'

'Apparently Kieran had already met building suppliers about the extension. The Lullcotts are the biggest firm in the area and they would definitely know the Deveneys. Maybe Kieran got talking to Rob Lullcott and he told him he was still married to Rose.'

'What about Forrest?'

'When he left the pub, he said he was going to phone Dove.

My guess is Dove fell apart, telling him everything, including the fact Rose was blackmailing her and Bagshaw into confessing to Kieran's murder. You saw the state Forrest was in. I think he was about to blow the lid on the whole thing.'

'So Rose arranged to meet Forrest when she made the safety call and then killed him to stop him going to the police.'

Just hearing this said out loud sounds absurd. Rose? My sweet childhood friend? How can that be possible?

'She just seems so . . . gentle,' says Jake, as if reading my thoughts.

'Yes, but she out of all of them has the greatest attachment to Liars Island. She grew up here. It's the only place she's ever been truly happy. Everything is going right for her. She'd taken over the inn from her parents and she's finally about to become a parent herself, but she stood to lose everything if Kieran told Hilton her marriage was fake.'

'She could easily have waited for Ash to leave and then met Kieran at Hidden Cove, but how did she kayak his body back to Devil's Cauldron?'

'It would be hard, but not impossible. The currents wouldn't bother her. She knows this island better than anyone.'

'It all makes sense,' he says, taking another swig of whiskey. 'Thanks for earlier, by the way. I feel much better. I thought about what you said. You're right. Whether it's Ben, or Rose, Jocasta or even Ash, somehow, we're perfectly safe. There's no reason for any of them to suspect we know anything.'

'They're all at Grannus House and no one in their right mind is going to be out on a night like this. It looks like the storm will blow itself out overnight. By the time any of them return, we'll probably be gone.'

'Can't wait. When I get back, I've decided to ask Sophie to marry me.'

'That's fantastic, Jake. Good luck. I hope she says yes.'

'Me too. I wouldn't blame her if she turned me down though. I've been an idiot, messing her around. I don't know why I've waited so long. She's always been the one for me. It's times like these that you realise what's important in life.' He looks at me. 'Yeah, yeah, I know, we're safe, but you know what I mean. Funny, it took being stuck on an island with four potential killers to see what's important.'

'That's one way of looking at it, I guess.'

'Maybe when you get back home, you and the barista guy can sort something as well.'

It's then that I remember Liam never called me back. I guess he didn't find anything.

'That ship has sailed.'

Jake pours me another whiskey. 'You sure about that?'

'Yeah, why?'

'Whenever you talk about him, you always have a smile on your face.' He grins.

'No, I don't. He's just a friend.'

'Whatever you say,' he says, relishing my discomfort. 'I bet you're keen to see your daughter too. Did she and her dad sort things out?'

I shake my head. 'I don't know. The last time I spoke to her she was pretty miserable. She wanted to come home, but I told her to suck it up. I haven't been able to get hold of her since. Not after her dad confiscated her phone.'

'So you don't know what's going on?'

'No, other than she's hating it. I feel really bad about it. The holiday was my idea. I thought it'd do her good to get out of Bidecombe, away from Seven Hills after what happened to Jay.'

'The lad that died in the fire?'

'They were best friends. She was devastated. I thought getting to know her biological father and his family would be a good distraction for her, and Julian, her dad, insisted he was more than capable of looking after her, but you can't just tell a teenager what to do and expect them to do it. I've no idea what's going on, but I'm pretty certain none of it is good and there's nothing I can do about it.' Jake's mildly stunned expression tells me I have, as Megan would say, gone off on one. 'Sorry. I'm just worried about her, that's all.'

'Can't the lady who runs Seven Hills help out? She's a friend of yours, isn't she?'

'Penny? She's a lot more than that. She gave us a home when we had nowhere to go.'

'So call her.'

'I've kind of burnt my bridges there. We had a big row about Megan. I told her Megan and I didn't need her anymore which was a pretty shit thing to say.' I swirl my drink, too embarrassed to look Jake in the eye. 'Penny is Megan's second mum. She's always been there for her and for me. Christ, I'd probably be dead if it weren't for her.'

Jake doesn't say anything. When I look up, he's frowning at me.

'If Penny hadn't found Megan and me in the park that Boxing Day, we'd have had to return to my ex who'd already beaten seven bells out of me,' I explain. 'She saved us. She put us both back together.'

'I can't imagine anyone pushing you around,' says Jake, 'let alone hit you. You never really talk about your past.'

'I guess that's what happens when you're holed up on an island with four would-be killers. It concentrates the mind. Either that or it's all this whiskey you keep plying me with.' I smile.

Jake smiles back. 'You should phone Penny.'

'I doubt she'd even pick up.'

'I wouldn't worry about that.' He finishes his whiskey, letting out a satisfied gasp. 'My experience of mums, whether they're first, second or even third, is that they're pretty difficult to get rid of.'

59

I'm wrong. Penny answers immediately.

Whiskey glass in hand, Jake locked the cottage door behind me and watched me like an anxious parent trudge up to the church, determined to make things right with my friend. Fighting the biting wind coralling me towards the island's edges, I wedged myself into a corner of the building and dialled her number.

'Ally? Are you all right? Where are you?'

No judgement, no recriminations, no cold shoulder, just concern. That's how it's always been. I just couldn't see it.

'Pen,' I say, clearing the sudden constriction in my throat. 'You've every right to put the phone down on me, but I kind of need your . . . help.'

'Of course,' she says without hesitation. 'What is it?'

'I'm on Liars Island.'

'Liars Island? That explains why there's no lights on in your cabin. I popped up last night to have a chat about . . . some stuff. I thought you'd gone away without telling me. Megan isn't picking up either. I was worried about you.'

'I'm sorry, I should have told you. It was only meant to be a day but a storm came in and now we're stranded.'

'Okay, so what do you need me to do?'

'I can't get hold of Megan. Or Julian. They had a fight and he confiscated her phone and I'm worried things have got out of hand. I should have gone to get her as soon as I knew things weren't working out.' The words tumble out of me. 'I thought it was the right thing to do, getting her away from Bidecombe for a while, letting her spend time getting to know her dad, but it's all gone wrong.'

'Ally, stop. You didn't know how this was going to turn out.'

'But I should have listened to you and now I'm stuck on this fucking island and there's nothing I can do about it.'

'Yes, there is. You can leave it to me. I'll go and collect her now.'

'You would do that?'

'Of course.'

'I don't deserve you, Penny.'

'You're right. You bloody don't.'

'Thank you and I'm so sorry for all the things I said to you. Seven Hills is yours, not mine. It's none of my business if you're selling it. I'm just grateful you let us live there for as long as you did. You've always been there for me and Megan.'

'Don't worry about that now. Look, Will and I can leave right away. I'll keep trying Megan's mobile to let her know we're coming. I'll call you as soon as we have her.'

'Thank you. Before you go, you said you came up to the cabin because you wanted to talk to me about something. What was it?'

There's a pause but I can't detect if it's Penny or poor reception.

'Let's get Megan home first,' she says.

I lean back against the church wall. Thank God for Penny. Just knowing she's gone to fetch Megan has lifted my mood. Megan will be back at Seven Hills tonight and I'll be home tomorrow. Jake and I just have to sit it out for one more night and then we're off this fucking island for good. Christ, by the end of it, there's nothing we won't know about each other's lives. Smiling at the thought, I ram my phone into my back jeans pocket, but hang back waiting for a lull in the wind. There's a loud bang. Assuming it's a lightning strike, I smack my back against the church wall, but the sky remains dark. It comes again – a short sharp crack, almost like a gunshot, but it's not coming from the heavens, it's coming from inside the church.

I slip down the side of the building to the front where I discover the heavy oak door is wide open. Surely the wind couldn't have forced it. I slide through the gap into the church into a pitch-black nave. My iPhone light throws a watery circle of light on the back two pews while the altar remains shrouded in darkness. They're empty.

I make my way down the aisle, softening my footsteps so I can listen out for sounds that I'm not alone. I think I hear breathing and stop dead, straining to confirm this until I realise it's the wind reduced to a soft moan by the dense church walls. There's no one here so I turn to leave. Jake will be wondering where I am.

A sudden gust of wind rushes me and there's another loud bang. I swing round, directing my phone torch towards the back of the church. It lands on the cupboard in the corner of the nave where we've stored the exhibits. In the gloom, I can just make out a door swinging on its hinges.

'Fuck.'

The cupboard is empty.

'That's it then,' Jake throws his hands in the air. 'We're dead.'

'I wouldn't go that far,' I say.

He sits back on the sofa in a cloud of whiskey fumes. 'So when do you think it happened?'

'I don't know. I haven't checked the cupboard since I put the samples from Forrest's PM there.'

'Why would anyone steal exhibits?'

'I guess they think we've got something that could incriminate them.'

'Which means the person who broke into the cupboard is the real killer.'

'Maybe or maybe there's another reason, but let's work through this logically before we jump to any conclusions. Firstly, whoever did this found Bagshaw's bloodied jacket implicating Bagshaw in Kieran's murder. If they're the killer, they'd know that anyway.'

'How do you mean?'

'They're blackmailing Bagshaw, they probably planted the jacket in the first place. So no giveaways there.'

'Okay.' Jake nods, allowing himself to be talked down. 'What else is there? What about the drinks can we found at Hilton's house?'

'I'm as certain as I can be that the dabs on it don't belong to anyone on the island or Hilton Deveney. I checked them against the elims Harriet sent me.'

'So whoever broke in would just discard the can as irrelevant anyway. What about the samples from Forrest's body?'

'That's difficult to say. Ash, Rose, Jocasta, Ben – they knew I'd examined him so the fact I took samples is no surprise. We won't know what they contain until they're properly analysed, but even if there is DNA, they all touched the body, remember? I doubt the samples from Forrest's PM are going to worry them.'

'What about the glasses from Hidden Cove? Even though they belonged to an old lady from Swindon, the thief would know we've discovered the cave.'

'That's true.'

'Same with the fingerprints on the kayak. They'd know we suspect Kieran took the kayak out the morning he died and then there's the blood samples from the cave.' Jake looks at me. 'It doesn't take a mastermind to work out we think Kieran was killed there.'

'Yeah, that is problematic. I still think the reason Kieran's body was taken back to Devil's Cauldron was to deflect our attention from looking elsewhere for the murder scene. Whoever did this didn't want us to know about Hidden Cove.'

'At least we can assume the blood we took from the cave wall is Kieran's and he was attacked there. Otherwise why go to the trouble of stealing the exhibits?' says Jake.

'*Could* be Kieran's. We don't have it anymore. They took it.'

'We still have photographic evidence showing the blood in situ.'

'That's not enough. The dark stains in the photos could be anything. Without the blood samples, we can't prove anything.'

'But once we get off the island, Harriet can send another team in there to collect more samples.'

'In the meantime, there's nothing to stop the killer going back and scrubbing the walls down with bleach. It's what I would do if I was them.'

Jake looks at me and sighs. 'You want to go back to Hidden Cove, don't you?'

60

Within minutes of leaving Jenny's Cottage, the downpour started up again, as if it had been lying in wait for us, and quickly found its way under our navy CSI jackets as we traipsed to Hidden Cove in sodden silence, any conversation cancelled by our discomfort.

The only other sound beyond the rain pelting my hood like a thousand tiny arrows, is the wild seas thrashing the stony beach just metres away. The tide is coming in fast. It won't be long before the bay is submerged under water.

Jake emerges from the cave, patting his pocket. 'I got it.'

'What was the scene like?'

'Exactly as we left it. I don't think anyone has been in.'

'Good. Let's get back to the cottage.'

We scramble back up the side of the hill, the wet grass slipping underfoot, the weight of our cases threatening to unbalance us and hurl us back into the ravine. Grabbing the wet rocks to steady ourselves, we reach the top and pause to catch our breath behind a large boulder. Jake flashes his torch at the darkness, glinting off the horizontal rain.

'No wonder we're drenched. Look at it,' he says, with undisguised disgust.

A phone buzzes, making us both jump.

'It's not mine,' Jake says.

'We must be in one of the few areas of reception.'

I take my phone out and answer without checking the screen.

'I've got the results,' he says in a businesslike voice.

It takes me a moment to register who it is, long enough to rouse his concern.

'Ally? Are you okay?' The gentleness in Liam's voice catches the back of my throat.

'Yes, I think so. It's . . . it's just good to hear your voice.'

'Oh. Right. Okay. Well, I have some news for you.'

'News?' I say, still confused by the nature of the call.

'Yes, remember the photos you sent.'

'Yes,' I say, suddenly recalling our previous conversation.

'It's a match.'

'Are you sure?'

'Keith's ninety-nine per cent certain. There are apparently some very distinctive marks that make it conclusive.'

'How can that even be possible?'

'I don't know, but it is. Is that good or bad?'

'I don't know. I really wasn't expecting this.'

'Ally, are you sure you're all right? You sound a bit distant.'

'I'm fine,' I say, trying to pull myself together. 'It's this island. It just gets to you after a while.'

'What do you mean?'

I can't ignore it any longer. I've been holding on to this since just after we arrived first because I wanted to get the job done and get the hell out of the place and then because I didn't want to stoke Jake's fears, but this is Liam and I can't pretend anymore.

'Liam, there's something really fucking weird going on here. I don't understand it. None of it makes any sense. Everyone's lying and . . . people are dying. First Kieran and now Forrest.'

'There's been another murder? How come when you've already got two killers in custody.'

'Forrest's death could have been an accident, we don't know, but we think Dove and Bagshaw are being blackmailed.'

'By who?'

'We don't know that either but whoever it is we think they killed Kieran and even Forrest. It's . . . it's just all so fucked up and now someone's stolen all the exhibits.'

'So the real killer could still be on the island?'

'Maybe,' I say, trying to ignore the horror in Liam's voice.

'Are they on to you?'

'Ally.' Jake taps me on the shoulder. 'I think someone's coming.' He points into the distance. Through the rain-drenched darkness, I can just make out a pinprick of light.

'Jake, switch off your torch. Liam, I've got to go.'

'What's going on?'

'I don't know.'

'Okay, but one more thing before you go. The image you sent over wasn't good enough so Keith went on to the Facebook page to see if he could find a better version which he did, but he also found something else out too.'

'Go on.'

'She died. Three weeks ago.'

'Are you sure?'

'Positive. It's genuine. I checked.'

The line goes dead before I have time to tell him that's impossible.

61

'It has to be a torch,' whispers Jake.

Neither of us have moved since I got cut off from Liam. Standing in the darkness, soaked to the skin, we fix our eyes on the tiny yellow dot on the horizon.

'It's definitely moving so I can't see what else it could be.'

'Who do you think it is?' he asks.

'It could be any of them and there could be any number of innocent reasons why they decided to leave Grannus House.'

'Really? I can't think of a single one,' he says drily.

A rustling sound reaches me. Jake is patting his jacket.

'Shit,' he says.

'What is it?'

'I can't find my phone. I must have dropped it at Hidden Cove.'

'We don't have time to go back for it now.'

'So what do we do?'

'We go back to Jenny's Cottage and barricade ourselves in until we're rescued. We can take it in turns to keep watch.'

'What about them?' It's too dark to see Jake's face, but I'm assuming he means the figure making their way along the track.

'It could all be completely harmless.' I don't believe that any more than Jake does. Rose was clear. Everyone is at Grannus House all night. 'But I think we'll let them go first.'

Concealed by a rocky outcrop, lashed by the wind and rain swirling, we watch the swaying light draw level with us. Whoever is carrying it is too far away for us to identify them so we wait until they recede into the distance before returning to the main track.

Nearing The Barbary Inn, I dip behind one of the out-buildings, motioning for Jake to follow me. Peering around the corner, I spot the figure pass under the pale safety light above the entrance to the pub. Before they slip back into the shadows I think I catch sight of a huge overcoat similar to Jocasta's, but I can't be certain.

'What's happening?' asks Jake.

'I'm not sure, but they're not going into the pub. They appear to be making their way to the church. No, wait, they've stopped. Outside the back door of the cottage.'

'Our cottage?' says Jake, coming alongside me.

'Yes, but they won't be able to get in. We locked it.'

But I'm wrong. The door opens and the figure disappears inside. A few seconds later there's a glow in the kitchen. Whoever it is hasn't attempted to rouse us before entering the property.

'Oh God,' says Jake. 'They didn't knock. They just let themselves in. There's nothing harmless about that, Ally. They're onto us. We can't go back to the cottage.'

He's looking at me for answers, but I don't have any. Think, Ally. Think.

'You've got the samples from Hidden Cove in your pocket, right?'

'Yes.'

'Then we'll leave our cases here, they'll just slow us down.' I stack Jake's case on mine, close to the wall.

'Where are we going?'

Ignoring his question because he won't like the answer, I point my iPhone torch towards a stretch of rough ground leading away from the buildings.

'This way.'

After a good few minutes when I pray Jake doesn't ask me what the plan is because I still don't have one, we reach the stretch of the steep woodland that hems the track before it doglegs down to Seal Bay.

'Almost there,' I say, but my artificial cheerfulness is punished with a grunt.

I take another step and my foot slides away from me. As I go down, I snatch a branch in my peripheral vision. The gnarly bark slices my hand as it slips through it until I finally find purchase and I'm able to right myself.

'Shit. Be careful, Jake, it's really slippery.'

'Gotcha.' A voice behind me replies.

Heart pounding, I take a moment to compose myself, taking my time to test the mossy ground underfoot until I'm confident it will hold me. Leaning into the hillside, I sidestep my way down the hill. I'm almost there when the ground gives way completely. This time there's nothing to save me and I'm thrown forwards and slammed into a tree trunk. Winded, pain shoots through my shoulder. By the time I muster my breath to warn Jake, it's too late. In the darkness, I hear the thrashing of undergrowth and the snapping of branches: Jake has fallen too.

'Jake?' I call out, groping the ground for my iPhone, its torchlight still on.

'Here,' he shouts back. 'But I think I'm hurt.'

Thank God, he's alive.

'Okay, I'm coming. Keep talking.' My phone swoops across the dark, dense woodland. 'I'll find you.'

'I don't know what to say.'

'Say anything.'

There's a pause and then I hear strains of a song.

'Ten green bottles hanging on the wall . . .'

'That'll do.'

Following Jake's less than dulcet tones, I find him some twenty metres further down the hillside, near the track, lying on his back, covered in twigs and moss.

'It's my ankle. I think I twisted it.'

'Do you think you can stand? It's not far from here.'

He holds a hand out for me to take. He's much taller than me, but his slight build means he's surprisingly easy to pull up. Once upright, he lowers his injured foot and immediately cries out in pain.

'It might be easier if you slide the rest of the way down the hill on your backside. It's not far.'

I go on ahead, picking out the clearest route for Jake who, leg raised in front of him, uses his knuckles to propel himself along the ground. Finally, we come out about halfway down the track, just before the bend leading to Seal Bay.

'I'll help you from here.'

Jake drapes a long arm around me, dwarfing my small

frame, pressing my wet clothes against my skin. A shiver passes between us. Our progress is tortuous, every hop accompanied by a gasp of agony.

When we round the final corner, the light above the entrance to the watersports centre shines like a beacon. Not far now.

'I need to rest,' says Jake, breathlessly.

Lowering him against a sloping bank, I step back and scan the terrain. The cliffs rising up behind us are barely distinguishable from the inky black sky.

'I think the rain is finally easing.'

'That's something, I suppose. Who do you think it was in Jenny's Cottage?'

I'm not listening. There's a light on top of the hill. And it's moving towards us. I was hoping when they'd found Jenny's Cottage empty, they'd assume we'd taken refuge in one of the other properties. I assumed wrong.

62

A satisfying hiss fills the air, followed by the pungent aroma of propane and butane, just what I hoped.

We'd passed the wooden shed nestled in the hillside just below the last bend down to Seal Bay a couple of times since we arrived, but I remember from when I was a girl that it stored the island's gas supply. To my relief, it wasn't locked and, when I opened it, a dozen gas cylinders stood to attention in the light of my iPhone.

I thought Jake would be resistant to my suggestion, but he agreed it was the only option to ensure our safety.

'We don't know who's chasing us or why and to be honest, Ally, I don't want to hang around to find out.'

He also said he'd back me to the hilt in any disciplinary so I told him to go on and wait for me at the watersports centre.

The second cylinder is as wheezy as its stablemate and I decide two will be enough. I race down the hill to the watersports centre where Jake is resting against the wall, but I don't have time to stop so I give him the thumbs-up before disappearing inside the building.

A padlocked chest in the corner of the reception area is the most likely place I'll find it so I grab the set of keys hanging up behind the counter and sift out the smallest one first, but my numbed and wet fingers fumble it and it drops to the floor.

'Fuck.' On my hands and knees, under the light of my phone, I scramble around for the key.

'Ally!' shouts Jake from outside the centre, his voice tight with fear. 'Someone's definitely coming down the track.'

'I'm coming.' My hand lands on metal. I thrust the key into the padlock. It clicks apart and I rip it off and yank open the chest where I immediately spot an orange barrel. Grabbing the flare gun and cartridges, I rush outside.

'Hurry,' says Jake.

Pushing the barrel of the gun away from the hammer, I slide the cartridge into the cavity and snap it shut. Then I press the button on the side and pull back the hammer.

'Cover your ears.'

Fear and cold fight me for a steady hold on the gun as I point it into the darkness, but I don't need to hit the bullseye. It just has to be close enough. I pull the trigger, drawing the hammer back, before releasing it to strike the detonating cap.

There's a loud bang and the gun releases a purple-tinged ball of light that catapults up the track. A second later, a deafening explosion followed by a flash that lights up the entire side of the island, forces Jake and I to recoil. By the time I look again, the few remaining flames attached to what's left of the shed burn themselves out, leaving behind an eerie silence.

'It hasn't worked,' says Jake. 'The track is still intact.'

Just as the words leave his mouth, the hillside emits a low growl like I've awoken some slumbering monster. It's too dark and we're too far away to see anything, but I know I'm listening to the earth fracturing. The air fills with the thunder of boulders hurled down the hill like pebbles as the land shifts. There's a crack and then another and another: trees snapped in half like twigs. It lasts less than thirty seconds, long enough for the entire track to be obliterated.

'I take it back,' says Jake. He looks at the flare gun in my hand. 'How d'you know how to use one of those things?'

'My dad.'

'He sounds like a bit of a legend, your old man. Now the road's blocked, there's no way down to the centre. We're safe,' says Jake.

I help him hop the final few metres inside the centre. If I don't voice my fears then maybe, just maybe, they won't be realised.

The building shudders under a fresh onslaught of wind and rain. Jake is perched on a chair in the reception area, his foot resting on a stack of kayaking books in front of him.

'I found these in lost property in the back along with a first-aid box.' I hand him a sweater and tracksuit bottoms. 'Not sure if they're your size, but it's better than nothing.' I've already changed into pink joggers and a hoodie, while pointedly ignoring the age fourteen to sixteen tag.

'Thanks,' says Jake, immediately peeling off his coat. While he dresses, I position myself by the window, but there's nothing out there but the weather.

'Right, let's see if we can patch you up a bit, otherwise Sophie's going to think you've been in the wars.'

'She wouldn't be too far wrong, would she?'

'Hold this.' I pass Jake my iPhone torch so I can roll up his trouser leg. His ankle has swollen to twice its size. 'Looks nasty. I'll put a bandage on and there's some paracetamol for the pain. It might make you feel a little more comfortable.'

'When do you think we'll be rescued?'

'Harriet wasn't sure. It depends on the weather.'

'Can't come soon enough for me.'

'Me neither, but get some rest. I'll take the first watch. Just a precaution,' I add hastily.

Jake makes himself comfortable under a throw and drifts off to sleep. As the minutes pass, my eyes also grow heavy. The wind eases until I only have silence for company and, in the stillness, my aching body reminds me I've tested it beyond its limits. I've patched up my hand from the medicine cabinet, but my head throbs and pain sears my left shoulder where I collided with the tree. I get up to stretch out, pacing the room to keep myself alert.

Flicking my iPhone torch over the walls in search of a distraction, it lands on the tide chart that caught my eye when I visited Ben before the storm. For all its chaos and volatility, the sea's rhythms are remarkably predictable. Next to it is a map tracking the currents around the island. I had the same one on my bedroom wall at home, fascinated how the island's currents bucked the behaviour of those in the Bristol Channel. The final poster shows the effects of the phases of the moon on the tides. Spring, neap, low, high and the rest: Dad taught me them all. He lived by these charts. He would say they were all he needed to keep us safe at sea.

'You'll need to know these things, Ally, if you're to become Bidecombe's harbourmaster. They might save your life one day.'

But I never became the harbourmaster and he didn't need his knowledge to keep him alive because it wasn't the sea he needed to fear. It was himself. He just didn't know it.

I amble over to the counter in search of something else to fill my mind. A rummage produces a pair of binoculars. Through the window, I scan the magnified darkness, just as a precaution. To my dismay, I land on a light in the distance, a light that shouldn't be there and my fear hardens into reality.

63

It takes Jake so long to respond to my not-so-gentle prodding that I worry his injuries extend beyond a broken ankle.

'What? What's happening?' he says, stirring awake. 'You're covered in sand.'

'They're coming along the deer path.'

He sits up. 'What?'

'It'll be heavy going and, with luck, hopefully the storm will have felled some trees which will slow them down, but they'll still be here long before first light so we have to move now.'

'But where?'

'Devil's Cauldron. I've already taken a double kayak down there. Hence the sand.'

'We can't go out into the water. You told me it wasn't safe. We'll drown.'

'We're not going out in it. It's just a precaution. We won't even leave the beach. When they find the centre empty and a kayak missing, hopefully they'll think we've launched from Seal Bay and escaped the island.'

Jake's wounded leg dangles over the edge of the kayak, resting on the cold sand, and his breathing has become laboured.

Inevitably, the rain has returned in the form of a drizzle, but still enough to compound our misery as we perch on the kayak, stranded on the sand.

The kayak rocks precariously and I wonder if the wind is getting up again before realising it isn't the weather. It's Jake, shivering violently.

'Jake? You okay?'

He doesn't respond. Surely he can't be asleep.

'Jake!'

The sharpness in my voice jolts him back to consciousness. He doesn't know where he is and immediately tries to get up before gasping with pain and collapsing back into the kayak. I jab my paddle into the sand to stop us tipping.

'Woah. Take it easy. You're in a kayak, remember? Help is on its way, but you have to stay awake.'

'Yeah, yeah. Sure, Sophie, sure.'

'I'm not Sophie. I'm Ally. Your colleague.'

'No, right, yes, of course not. Sorry.'

'That's okay.'

'What time is it? I need to get back. It's mine and Soph's anniversary.'

He tries to get up again, but he's weak and it only takes a gentle hand on his shoulder to stop him.

'What are you doing? I've got to go. Where's Harriet?'

He's delirious. There's no point in reasoning with him.

'She'll be here any minute. While we're waiting, why don't you tell me about your first proper date with Sophie?'

'Cool. Okay, but you're gonna laugh. It was a disaster.'

'Try me.'

'We went beach litter picking.'

'Blimey, Jake. How the hell did you ever get a girlfriend?'

'Yeah. I know. I forgot I'd promised my mate that I'd help with a beach clean-up and I didn't want to let him down or cancel my date with Sophie so I said I was taking her to my favourite beach.'

'What did she say when you got there and you handed her a black bin bag?'

'Well, that's the funny thing. She'd also signed up to do the beach clean, but she'd cancelled it so she could go out with me instead.'

'What did she say when she found out?'

'She laughed. We both did.'

'And did you spend the afternoon picking litter?'

'Maybe half an hour before we snuck off to the pub. I knew straight away I'd met my soulmate and that if she felt the same way about me then I'd never let her go.'

It's 4am. Jake and I are still alone at Devil's Cauldron. Hell's Gate conceals our presence but also blocks my view so I have no idea where our pursuer is.

The persistent drizzle has worked its way through my clothing and once again I'm frozen to the core. Conversation between Jake and me ran out some time ago. His mutterings became incoherent and I'm worried his delirium is linked to something more serious than a busted ankle. There is nothing I can do other than listen out for his breathing and when it becomes too laboured prod him awake, but I'm exhausted too and the effort becomes too great.

I wrap my arms tightly around my body trying to stop what warmth I have seeping away, but every shudder to kick-start some heat is futile. The pain in my shoulder has been usurped by another, a numbness spreading to my arms and legs as it invades my body. I know what's coming. Of course, I do. My dad told me. Many times. 'It's the cold that kills you first, Squid.' Is that what happened to him? After he leapt from *The Aloysia*? The shock of the cold followed by a gradual warming lulling you to sleep, guiding you to the end. Oh, Dad. Is that what's happening to me now? Is my core temperature plummeting below thirty-five degrees leaving me just a few minutes for any final thoughts?

I close my eyes. In the distance, I hear the lap of water against the shore: rhythmic, soothing, almost lyrical. I'll be there soon. Not long now. My mind turns to the never. Never will I know the woman Megan is on her way to becoming. Never will I tell Penny that Will is the best thing that ever happened to her. Never will I apologise to Bernadette for reacting angrily for keeping the truth about Dad's death from me and never will I tell Liam that I want to be with him. But never is just another word for regret and I can't leave it like this.

Shaking myself from my torpor, my trembling fingers dig around my jacket pocket for my phone. It takes all my effort not to drop it. There's no signal and just a tiny amount of battery life left, but I have to believe I can do this. Summoning what little energy I have, I tap the letters out, slowly, deliberately and press send. When it's done, I'm spent. I lean against the backrest and close my eyes again.

Strange: I am no longer shivering. I don't even feel cold anymore. Quite the reverse. A warmth has soothed my frozen limbs. Maybe the temperature has risen, I don't know, but I feel relaxed and calm. Maybe I can get some sleep and then

I'll be ready for when we're rescued. Yes, that's what I'll do. I'll sleep.

A voice whispers in my ear.

'Wake up, Ally!'

My eyes spring open and there he is standing in front of me. It can't be. It's not possible.

'Dad?'

'You must stay awake, love.'

'What are you doing here?'

'I came to see how my little girl is doing.'

'Not good, not good at all. I can't see a way out of this and I'm . . . scared.'

'Don't give up, Ally. You'll think of something.'

'No, I won't. I can't. I'm too tired. I just want to sleep.'

'I know, but you have to stay awake.'

'Honestly, Dad, I can't. I really can't. I want it all to end. I want to be with you.'

'No, you don't. Think of Megan. You can't leave her. It's too soon. She's not ready.'

'Megan? How do you know Megan?'

'She's beautiful, Ally.'

'Yes, she is. She's the only good thing in my life. I just couldn't see it, and I let terrible things happen to her. I wish I'd been a better mother.'

'Don't talk like that. You're a wonderful mum.'

'But it's true. And now I'm going to leave her too. Like you left me. I tried. I really did and I'm just so sorry.'

'You've nothing to be sorry for.'

'Yes, I have and so have you, Dad. I'm so angry with you. How could you do that to us?'

'I know, love, and I wish it could have been different. I really do, but I had no choice.'

'Yes, you did. You had me. Wasn't I enough of a choice for you?'

'Of course you were.'

'So tell me why then?'

'You know why.'

'No, I don't. Not really.'

'I never left you, Ally. I've always been here, by your side, guiding you. In all things. You just didn't see it.'

'I don't understand.'

'Slack sank the ship, remember?'

'Remember what? I don't get it.'

'Yes, you do. Check, check, and then check again. Just the way I taught you.'

'I did. I checked everything.'

'Then you missed it because the answer is right in front of you.'

'Right in front of me? What you do you mean? Wait. Oh God, of course. Now, I see it. Bara Watersports Centre.'

'I knew you would. You're my daughter.'

It explains everything. How could I have missed it? I know who killed Kieran.

64

I open my eyes to a cloudless sky awash with oranges and pinks and relief diffuses through me. It's dawn. We made it, but my respite is interrupted when the kayak lurches to one side. Putting my hand down to stop us tipping, it's immediately immersed in water which can mean only one thing: the tide is upon us.

'Jake.' I nudge my colleague. His body slumps back against mine. A dead weight. He's out cold. I give his shoulders a firm shake, but he rolls to one side, threatening to capsize us until I grab his torso and centre us. Finally, he stirs.

'What? Where am I?' Shivers convulse his body.

'Devil's Cauldron, but we're safe. It's daylight. They don't know we're here otherwise they'd have found us by now. Help is on the way.'

'Devil's what?' he says, trying to twist around to face me.

'Try to stay still. You just have to hold on a little bit longer. They'll be here very soon.' I turn my head to scan the horizon beyond the bay for signs of a rescue boat. Jesus, they must be on their way by now. They know the score. Bagshaw and Dove are innocent. The real killer is still on the island. They always have been. 'We'll have you back to Sophie in no time.'

Jake doesn't reply. He's already slipped back into what-ever state his body has deemed his best chance of survival. I fold my arms around his wiry frame – whatever body heat I have is his.

The incoming tide tugs at the kayak's mooring. It isn't strong enough to carry us out, but it won't be long. Being swept out to sea via Devil's Cauldron is definitely not my plan A. Or plan B. But it won't come to that. It's just a matter of time now. A waiting game.

Closing my eyes, I lean against Jake's damp jacket, and fast forward to a better place. Megan will be waiting for me at the cabin. Penny will have collected her by now. Now the storm has passed, the fine weather will reassert itself, and maybe the two of us can go surfing at Morte Sands. We haven't done that in a long time. I'll buy her one of Liam's famed Mocochinos from the Coffee Shack. Perhaps Penny and even Bernadette will come too although I can't remem-ber the last time Bernadette went to the beach. It's not really her thing, but she might make an exception and then we'll all be together again.

'You don't honestly think you're going to escape in that, do you?'

I look up with a start.

'Stay back. The coastguard is on their way. They'll be here any minute.' I say.

'No, they're not.' Ash smiles. 'You don't look surprised to see me. I must admit I almost didn't bother to check Devil's Cauldron. Lucky I did.'

'Stay where you are.' I lift the kayak paddle. 'Don't make this any worse than it is.'

'What?' he says, offended. 'You think I've come to hurt you?'

'Haven't you?'

'No, of course not . . . I've come to give myself up.'

'You expect me to believe that you've spent half the night trying to find us just to confess?'

'Yes, I killed Kieran. There you go, I said it.'

'You weren't even on the island when he was murdered.'

But he was. I know that now.

'I'm guessing you already worked out how I managed that little trick. For the record, I also killed Forrest.'

'Why are you telling me this? Why not just wait for the police to arrive?'

'Because you're Rose's friend and I want you to know the truth. Ask me anything, like I said, I'm here to give myself up. I'm tired of secrets.'

'Okay.' Rescue can't be far away. If I can keep Ash talking maybe Jake and I can get out of this alive. 'How did you come up with the idea of forcing Dove and Bagshaw to confess to a crime they didn't commit?'

'I might have dropped out of a law career, but I still knew enough to know that if the police couldn't prove a link between them, neither of them could be charged with murder. They'd both get off and so would I.'

'How did you find out about Dove?'

'She told me herself not long after she arrived here. She was in a real state. She'd get off her face on drugs.'

'Supplied by you.'

'Yeah, sorry, I lied about being clean. Anyway, one night she just came out with it. She didn't even remember telling me. As for Bagshaw, Cal shot his mouth off to anyone who would listen about the vicar he'd sailed from the mainland with, who'd stolen from his church and claimed on his insurance. So when I needed to . . . deal with Kieran, I knew their secrets were big enough to destroy them, especially if the police found out.'

'So what went wrong?'

'Dove. She called Grannus House yesterday, wanting to talk to Forrest. Jocasta told her he was dead. She fell apart. He was her life. I knew then she had nothing to lose and that she'd tell the police everything. It was just a matter of time. I thought I'd get in before she did.'

'So why did you kill Kieran?'

'Rose and I lied about our relationship. We're not married. Rose never divorced her husband. Kieran found out and was threatening to tell Hilton.'

'Why would Kieran care?'

'He didn't, but he was constantly trying to prove himself to his dad. I think he thought telling Hilton would earn him brownie points, not that Hilton gave a shit about him. He made it pretty obvious Ben was the son he'd rather have had. Sad really, but Kieran would get us kicked off the island. I couldn't let that happen to Rose. This is her home so . . . I killed him.'

'What-what about Forrest?'

'That was an accident. As you saw he was in a right state about Dove and although I told her not to, she couldn't help herself. She told him it was all a set-up and she'd be out soon. He just had to be patient, but he called me the night of the storm and told me he was going to tell you everything in the morning. I persuaded him to meet me, hoping to get him to change his mind, but we got into a fight and I pushed him. The fall killed him.'

'So how did you get Kieran to meet you in the cave that morning?'

'I didn't. He told me the night before he'd planned to kayak there. He asked if I wanted to go with him. I told him I'd already planned to go to Bidecombe.'

'But when he got to the cave the next morning you were waiting for him?'

'I did try to reason with him, honest. What difference did it make to him if Rose and I were married or not? But I couldn't compete with the chance for him to get into daddy's good books. As he was walking away from me, I picked up the nearest rock and hit him over the head. He dropped like a stone. He wasn't dead then but I knew he didn't have long.'

'Why take his body back to Devil's Cauldron? It was day-light. Someone could have seen you.'

'I wanted him to be found. I didn't want his family to go through years of not knowing what happened to him. I knew that would at least give his family closure.'

'How very noble of you.'

'I did it for Rose.'

'So she's in on this too?'

'God no,' he says, ignoring the waves lapping his ankles. 'This is all on me. You have to believe me, Ally. Rose has no idea about any of this. I swear to you. Keep her out of this. That's why I'm telling you all this. I'm trying to protect Rose. She's innocent.'

He steps towards me and I raise the paddle once more.

'I told you not to come any closer.'

He frowns at me, confused by my actions.

'But I'm not going to hurt you. I'm giving myself up. I'm confessing. I killed Kieran because he was going to tell Hilton that Rose and I lied about our marriage and then I killed Forrest because he was going to tell you I'd set up Dove and Bagshaw.' He spreads his hands out. 'So you see I was never going to hurt you.'

I'm almost convinced. Almost.

'Nice try. Only it's bullshit.'

Ash frowns. 'What?'

'You heard me. People only confess when they've been backed into a corner and they've no way out. There's no way you could have known we were on to you.'

'I told you, Dove's a wreck. I can't trust her to stay quiet. She's probably already told the police the truth by now. By telling you everything now, at least I keep Rose out of it.'

Ash's sudden readiness to confess to murder after formulating such an elaborate set-up to deflect attention from himself doesn't add up.

'No, I don't buy any of it. You might have killed Kieran and Forrest, but the reason – or motive – is total crap. Sure, you and Rose faked your marriage and you knew Bagshaw's and Dove's secrets and used them to blackmail them both, but you didn't kill Kieran and Forrest because they threatened to go public.'

'What the hell are you talking about?'

'It's same reason you took Kieran's body from Hidden Cove to Devil's Cauldron. It had nothing to do with his family getting closure. You needed Kieran's body to be discovered quickly because you knew Hilton Deveney wouldn't have given up until his son was found and you couldn't risk the police combing the caves.'

'Why would I care about the police searching a few old tunnels?'

'What was it that you were looking for when you broke into the cupboard in the church? Was it the glasses? They belonged to your ex-girlfriend, Hana, didn't they?'

'Hana?' He frowns. 'How . . . ?'

'There was no sign of any corrosion. Those glasses were dropped recently. Then when my SIO said the style was at least twenty years old, I remembered where I'd seen them before. Hana was wearing similar glasses in the photo above the bar so I got them compared. I must admit I wasn't expecting them to be a perfect match.'

I've read about forensic optometrists but I've never used one before. When I saw the glasses in the cave, I figured it was worth a go. Incredibly, Liam was able to track one down.

'Hana is dead,' he says, bitterly. That's the part I don't understand, the part that isn't adding up.

'So how and why did Hana's glasses end up here?'

'She gave them to me before she passed away. I went to see her a couple of months ago when I did my last yacht delivery. I wanted to say goodbye. She didn't have much but what she did have she gave me. The glasses were among her belongings. I hid them in the cave because I didn't want Rose to know I visited my ex.'

I look at him for a moment. He's not bothered that I know

about Hana's glasses which means there must be something else in that cupboard, something he is bothered by.

'So if it's not the glasses, what is it? It can't be the fingerprints on Kieran's kayak. If they're yours, and I'm assuming they are, you'd easily be able to explain them away. It's not Bagshaw's jacket because you planted it under his sink in the first place. The samples from Forrest's PM are unlikely to tell us much. That just leaves . . . the drinks can we found at Hilton's place.' Ash's demeanour shifts. It's barely perceptible, but it's enough. 'I'm right, aren't I? You knew those prints didn't belong to Forrest. In fact, they don't belong to anyone from the island including Hilton. I checked against everyone's elimination prints. I assumed they belonged to whoever packed it in the factory, but why would that concern you?'

'It doesn't.'

We hold each other in a stare as I try to work out what the hell is going on, sifting the important from the irrelevant: why Ash moved Kieran's body, how he escaped from Liars island, why he faked his marriage to Rose, why he has Hana's glasses, why he's so bothered about the can, Forrest's death, his CSI report, all of it, until the answer is in reach.

'Well, that explains the rabbits,' I say, my mind seeking out more evidence to shore up my theory. 'It's been bugging me ever since I saw it.'

'Saw what? What are you talking about?'

'When Jake and I were out looking for Forrest, near Hidden Cove, the whole area was covered in rabbit droppings apart from a particular patch of grass. It reminded me of my mother's lawn.'

'Your mother?'

'Her neighbour's tom cat keeps relieving himself on her lawn causing all these yellow patches, just like the one near Hidden Cove, but there are no cats on the island. The only predator rabbits have are humans, and the smell of human urine is more than enough to frighten them off, particularly male.'

'Are you suggesting I spend my days pissing all over the island, scaring the rabbits?'

'No, I'm suggesting that the person that you've been hiding on the island does.'

'Hiding?' He laughs. 'You really are fucking mental.'

'You're right. It sounds crazy, but it's the only thing that explains moving Kieran's body, the dabs on the can, Hana's glasses.'

'Hana isn't on the island. I told you she died of a brain tumour. About three weeks ago.'

The only reason I believe him is because Liam told me the same thing, but if it isn't Hana, then who is it? Who would Ash be prepared to kill to protect? There is only one explanation that would drive him to murder. I should know.

'Christ, it's a kid, isn't it?'

It all makes sense now. That's what Liam was about to tell me when he got cut off. Hana had a child. It's then that I remember the doll found near Kieran's body with the parts of the body written on its limbs, like it was being used to teach someone English. The investigation team dismissed it as irrelevant because it was a kid's toy, but the ink was faded which means it wasn't permanent. Just like the tag on which Dad wrote *Perfidious*, *The Aloysia*'s original name. The sea water would dissolve it in time. If the writing was still visible on the doll, that means only one thing – it hadn't been in the water long. Ash's child must have dropped it at Hidden Cove.

'Jesus, Ash, what the hell have you done?'

'Nothing. You're making this shit up.'

'That's why you sailed to Greece to do a yacht delivery a couple of months back. It wasn't just to say goodbye to Hana. It was to collect someone, someone very dear to you? Hana's kid. Your kid?'

'No. I don't have a kid.'

But my mind is too busy joining the dots.

'Hold on, is this the same child Rose told me about, the child you're meant to be fostering through an agency? Was that just a cover story? Wow, that's clever, bring them to Liars Island. No customs, no coastguard, no border patrol. One last run to make some money to renovate the pub and bring back a stowaway or two.'

'This is fucking hilarious. You're making it sound like I'm some kind of trafficker.'

'People do bad things for good reasons, Ash. Christ knows, I'm not judging you, but two innocent men are dead and I can't ignore that.'

'That's what I've been trying to tell you. They're dead because I killed them. Jocasta is right about you lot. You just manipulate the evidence to fit your version of the truth. But it's all lies.'

'Then you won't mind me relaying what I've just told you to my colleagues when they get here.'

'What? Now, wait a minute. You've got it all wrong.' He takes a few paces toward me. His expression has switched from faux outrage to a killer running out of options which makes him dangerous. One arm secured around Jake, I stab the sand with the paddle and push the kayak's stern into the water, only the bow is keeping us anchored to dry land. It's as far as I dare to go. I just hope it's enough. 'That isn't necessary, Ally, let's be reasonable about this.'

'Then you need to tell me exactly what's going on.'

'Okay. His name's Amir. Hana is, was, his mum. He's not my kid, but he may as well be. When Hana and I got together, I raised him for seven years until our relationship ended suddenly.'

'Because the police were on to your drug smuggling activities and you had to leave Greece quickly?'

He's surprised I know about his past.

'The police, and others, but yes, I had to get out. When Hana found out, she refused to have anything to do with me. I didn't even know she was ill until she wrote to me. She was terrified for Amir. You don't know what it's like in these camps. Kids go missing all the time. So I told her Rose and I would raise him on Liars Island. Rose leapt at the chance. Hana knew Rose from her time in the camp. She knew she'd be a great mum to Amir so she agreed. Our plan was to hide Amir while we pretended to go through the fostering process and then eventually Amir would "arrive" on the island.'

'Does Rose also know that you killed Kieran and Forrest?'

'No, I promise you. I'm not lying about that. She has no idea. She just wants to be a mum to Amir. She's waited a long time.'

'So you smuggled a young boy into the country?'

'I had no choice. No, there's no legal route for him. I've checked and checked. They won't let them in. He's not bio-logically mine.'

'Can't he claim asylum?'

'Maybe, but it takes years to process applications and he could still be turned down. God knows where he might end up. I can't risk that. I promised Hana I'd take care of him. Liars Island is the best place for him.'

'But you'll be in prison.'

He shrugs like it's nothing. 'I've done a lot of bad stuff in my life, caused a lot of hurt. It kind of feels like I should pay for it. Just keep Amir out of it. Please.'

'You know I can't do that. The authorities have the right to know about him.'

'No, they don't. I've made my choice. You need to make yours. Can you live with yourself knowing you condemned an innocent boy to a life of fear and uncertainty?'

'That's not fair.'

'Tell that to my son.'

Ash comes towards us again. I dig the paddle into the sand, pushing us into the shallows. The kayak's bow still clings to land, but the tugging on our stern tells me the rip is on to us.

'Don't do this, Ash. You know what will happen to us if we go any further.'

'You give me no choice.'

'Stop, baba! Stop!'

A teenage boy appears at the entrance to Hell's Gates and jumps down from the rocks. Waving his arms, he stumbles across the sand towards us. He's wearing a red coat. I can't see the insignia from here, but I'm guessing it's Manchester

United, his favourite football team. This is who Jake and I saw when we arrived that first day to examine the vestry. This is who was watching us when we went to the watersports centre. That's why Forrest didn't know us. It wasn't him.

Ash swivels round. 'Go back, Amir. I've got this.'

'Baba, come back. Please. I'm sorry. I'm sorry.'

'You've nothing to apologise for, son.'

'God forgive me for what I've done.'

Even from here, I can see his cheeks sheen with tears.

Ash walks towards him, his hands crossing each other in a cutting motion. 'Stop, Amir. Stop talking.'

But the boy is too distraught to understand what he's saying.

'I promise, Daddy, I-I didn't mean to do it. I didn't.'

Ash glances back at me, hoping I haven't heard. I wish I hadn't because I can't ignore the terrible truth.

'Oh my God.' I look between them both. 'It was Amir.'

65

'Wait, it's not what you think.' Ash pats the air as if to calm the situation. 'It was an accident, Ally. I swear. He's just a kid. He panicked. Please let me explain.'

I'm too shocked that the young boy shivering on the beach is a stone-cold killer to tell Ash that no amount of words will reprieve Amir. He killed Kieran. That's an irrevocable fact. It's now just a matter of the degree.

'Kieran spotted Amir on the shore at Hidden Cove when he was kayaking and followed him into the cave. Amir got scared. If you knew the things this kid has seen, you'd understand why.'

'What . . . what happened?'

'He thought Kieran was going to hurt him. He tried to escape but the cave was a dead end so he climbed the wall just to get away.' That explains the dry patch of wall where the rock had sheared off. 'That's when he lost his glasses. He has the same prescription as his mum. Kieran tried to follow him, lost his footing and fell, hitting his head on the way down.'

'Oh God.'

'Amir came and got me immediately and I kayaked him

back to Devil's Cauldron. I knew Kieran would be dead by the time he was found.'

'I'm sorry, Baba.'

'Hush now, son. It's not your fault.' Ash turns to me. 'Ally, please, let him go. He's been through enough.'

'I can't do that. You have to come clean. Tell the police what really happened. Amir will be taken care of.'

'We both know that's not true. It'll destroy Rose. All she ever wanted to be was a mum.'

I remember how Rose's eyes lit up when she told me she was about to become a mother. Her only real dream in life had finally come true. But a man is dead and his killer is standing right in front of me.

'There's no other way.'

'Yes, there is. You know there is. His father and siblings were murdered and now his mother has gone. He's got no one. Amir deserves a chance in life. Rose can give that to him. She can be a second mother to him. No one needs to know.'

'This is madness. You won't get away with it. He'll be found out eventually.'

'He won't.'

'But you'll be convicted of a crime you didn't commit.'

'But I did kill Forrest. That's on me.'

'You're asking me to put my job on the line for you.'

'No, all I'm asking is you forget you ever met Amir, let him grow up safely and in peace, for the first time in his life.'

'I'm sorry. I really am, but I can't do that.'

'You're a mum. Wouldn't you do anything to protect your kid?'

'This . . . this isn't about me.'

'But it's the right thing to do.'

Arms stretched wide, appealing to me to forget I ever set eyes on Amir, Ash makes a move towards us. My paddle pushes the sand away, launching us into the water. I take us out as far as I dare, beyond Ash's reach, but I can feel my paddle battling the current beneath the surface. It wants us.

'Come back to the shore, Ally. This is suicide, I'm not going to harm you.'

'I don't believe you.'

'You've got to understand. I can't let them take Amir.'

'So you're going to get rid of us as well, are you?'

'You made your choice.'

He wades into the water, his conciliatory air vanishing like sand on an offshore wind. This is the real Ash, the Ash I met on the stairs the first day we arrived. The Ash who blackmailed two innocent people and put them through the hell of a police murder investigation. The Ash who murdered another man and is more than capable of murdering two CSIs.

'We're one of theirs, Ash,' I say, battling the current. 'They'll come after you and I guarantee you they won't give up until they see you sent down and they'll find Amir and it will have been all for nothing.'

Shaking his head, he takes another step closer towards us, ignoring his knees buckling. The rip has him in its sights too.

'Your bodies will never be recovered. Just like your dad's. Oh, I'm sure the police will have their suspicions, but they won't be able to prove anything and they can't charge everyone on the island.'

'Let's talk about this.'

'There's nothing to talk about. Not anymore,' he says still coming towards us. You've made yourself very clear.'

The water is now up to Ash's waist and the sway of his body tells me he's already caught in a powerful undertow. We're not the only ones in danger. Pacing the water's edge, Amir senses it too.

'Baba, come back!'

Ash ignores him. The water is lapping his chest, but if he turns back now, he can still make it to shore.

'Listen to your boy, Ash. Go back now.'

He shakes his head, but it's too late anyway. The unseen current lifts him off his feet. He lets it take him, believing he can control its power. Within seconds, he gains on us. If he reaches the kayak, he'll tip us and we'll all be swept into the whirlpools. He's prepared to sacrifice us all to save Amir. We'll have to take our chances with the rip and hope that I can paddle us out of the bay to safer waters. I lift the paddle and the kayak twists around and heads straight for the circling waters.

Beyond the rocks, the sea is empty. No one is coming to rescue us, but there's something else. Out in the Atlantic. I'm mesmerised by the sight of the horizon which appears to be rising up and moving steadily towards us. The chart in the watersports centre predicted its arrival, but I've never seen one before. I can't quite believe what I'm witnessing until I feel the kayak lifting us up, taking us clear of the whirlpools and I realise there's nothing imaginary about this. It's a huge wall of water and it's coming straight for us.

'Oh God,' I gasp.

This is how Ash got off the island, but he was ready for

it. He knew how to ride it. I don't have the first idea. All I can do is clip my life jacket to Jake's, wrap the rope attached to the stern around my waist, securing us both to the kayak, and hope for the best. But what about Ash? He's five metres away, and still heading in our direction. He hasn't seen it. Christ, he stands less of a chance than we do. I drive the paddle through the water, taking us back towards Ash where I hold the paddle out to him.

'Ash, take it!'

He stops and frowns.

'Behind me!' I shout. 'Look behind me.'

Still frowning, his gaze shifts upwards and his eyes flare with terror at the sight of the enormous white-tipped wave surging towards us. He digs his arms into the water, propelling himself towards us. I lean over as far as I dare without tipping the kayak, but just as Ash's hand reaches for the paddle the swell swallows him. He goes under, resurfacing seconds later, spluttering and gulping for air, but he's now several metres away. He won't reach us in time. In desperation, I launch the paddle at him. He needs it more than we do. It's his only hope. It lands close to him, but as he swims towards it, the wave heaves once more and I lose sight of him for good.

There's nothing more I can do. Gripping Jake's lifeless body as tightly as I can, I brace myself for what's coming. The black wall of water rushes towards us, pushing us higher and higher, tilting the bow until the kayak is almost vertical and I find myself staring into the abyss.

66

Liam is leaning over the edge of *The Aloysia*, his hand extended towards me, but the boat isn't real and neither is he. I'm hallucinating.

'For Christ's sake, Ally, just give me your hand.'

Do people blaspheme in hallucinations? Come to think of it, should I be able to feel the seaspray on my cheeks, or salt in my mouth? Unsure of the answer to either of these questions, I extend a trembling, tentative hand and, to my surprise, it's immediately seized in Liam's warm grip and he lifts me onto the deck of *The Aloysia*. But something is wrong. Someone is missing.

'Where is he? Where's Jake? He was with me. Oh my God.'

'It's okay. It's okay,' Liam says, soothingly. 'Howard has him below deck. You insisted we take him first.'

'Did I?'

'Yes, and he's going to be fine, but you need to get out of these wet clothes.'

I nod, but my body shudders uncontrollably and even if I could steady my fingers, they're too numbed to pinch the zip on my coat.

'I can't.'

Liam hesitates for a moment.

'Then I'm going to have to do it for you.'

In one movement, he unzips my jacket, dropping it down to the ground for me to step out of before yanking my sweater over my head and wrapping a thick wool blanket over my bare shoulders. Folding me in his arms, he presses himself against me, transferring his body heat while vigorously rubbing my back.

'Thank you,' I say as the shivers subside and the feeling begins to return.

He pauses, holds me for a little while longer and then releases me.

'That should do you.'

He grabs a Thermos and pours me a mug of tea, closing his hands over mine and guiding it to my mouth. I close my eyes as the hot liquid thaws my insides. When I open them, Liam is looking at me, his head to one side.

'You okay?'

'I will be.'

'What were you even doing out here on a kayak?'

'We had to get off Liars Island. We weren't safe.'

'But you're so far from shore. I've seen you bodyboarding.' He laughs. 'How the hell did you manage to get so far out?'

'We had a little help. I'll explain later,' I say, waving away his frown.

'Well, whatever it was, sounds like it saved your life.'

'I guess it did, but I don't understand. What are you doing here?'

He hesitates before his smile resumes.

'You sounded scared on the phone. I figured you might

need some help and the only person I could find in the harbour with a boat willing to take me out was Howard.'

'Oh so it wasn't because—' I stop myself just in time.

'Because of what?'

'Nothing.'

'It doesn't sound nothing. What is it?'

'I . . . I thought it was because you got my text.'

He gets his phone out. 'You texted me?'

I lay my hand on his arm. 'Save it for later.'

'It's okay. I'll check now.'

'Is Tanya okay with you going out to sea in the tail end of a storm?' I say, trying to change the subject as Liam scrolls through his screen.

'I don't know. I didn't ask her. We're not together anymore.'

'Sorry to hear that.'

'It wasn't serious.' He looks up at me. 'Sorry, I don't think I got it.'

'Oh.'

I'm surprised at how disappointed I am.

'What did it say?'

Maybe Liam wasn't meant to receive it.

'Nothing much.'

'Good to see you, Squid.'

Howard emerges from below deck in a yellow oilskin coat. He folds me in his arms and hugs me hard, just like Dad used to. I don't resist.

'We thought we'd lost you, for a moment.' He looks to the sky. 'Can't help thinking we had a little extra help with the search.'

'Thank you. I think this is the part where I tell you I owe you my life.'

'I'm only here because your boyfriend threatened me with all sorts if I didn't take him out.' He laughs.

'Er . . . we're not together.'

'He's not my . . .'

'Whatever,' says Howard, brushing aside our protests. 'It was the least I could do. I'm sorry for everything. Truly, I am.'

'I know.'

'I loved your dad. If I'd known he was going to do something silly, I'd have got on the boat that day with you and I'd have stopped him.'

'I know.'

'If I could go back and change that day, I would.'

'Actually, Howard, there's something I need to ask you about that day.'

67

An aroma of strong coffee stirs me awake. I check my bedside clock; it's late afternoon. I've slept for sixteen hours
which means it's been two days since Liam and Howard rescued Jake and me as we drifted off the coast of Liars Island.
Doctors kept Jake in for what turned out to be a broken
ankle and severe hypothermia, but I was discharged yesterday morning.

Megan was waiting for me at the cabin when I got back.
Penny, true to her word, picked her up from Julian's holiday
home. He's since said sorry for his heavy-handedness, but he
isn't the only one who needed to apologise. I shouldn't have
sent her. It was too much too soon for Megan. I know that
now. Thankfully, father and daughter still want to be in each
other's lives so we've agreed to take things more slowly.

Seeing her again was all I needed to wipe away the previous forty-eight hours, and for once I enjoyed her ranting
about all the perceived injustices she'd suffered at the hands
of Julian's parenting, but by midnight even I was done.

Slipping on my dressing gown, I shuffle into the cabin's
open-plan kitchen-living room where Megan is sitting at the
breakfast bar shovelling cereal into her mouth. Relief that I

survived Liars Island to see my daughter again has yet to fully ebb and I give her a hug.

'Mum,' she says, wrestling free. 'Watch my Shreddies.'

'Just saying thank you for the coffee, that's all.'

Her mouth full again, she acknowledges my gratitude with a wave of her spoon.

'So what are you up to today?' I ask.

'More to the point, what are you up to?'

'What do you mean?' But I know exactly what she means. I still haven't seen Penny since I returned from Liars Island.

'I haven't had time.'

'You haven't got anything on now.'

'I know, but—'

'Mum. Do it. You and Penny not talking to each other is just too weird.'

'You're right.'

Changing into a pair of jeans and jumper, I take the path down to the reception at the entrance to Seven Hills Lodges. A squirrel scoots up the trunk of one of the pines punctuating the holiday park. Its branches splay, splintering a sun that sits boldly in the sky as if it has always been there. There's not a cloud in sight. The storm has passed for now. God, I'm going to miss this place when Penny sells it.

Penny is sitting at her computer in reception. When she sees me in the doorway, she steps out from behind the counter and embraces me. It's then that I know everything will be good between us, but I still have some making up to do.

'I'm sorry I didn't come up to the cabin. I didn't want to disturb you and Megan.'

'You've nothing to apologise for, Pen. I wanted to thank you for going to fetch her.'

'It was nothing. She was fine, just grumpy about her phone.'

That's Penny all over, always trying to make me feel better about my parenting.

'You were right though. I shouldn't have let her go on holiday with Julian. I just couldn't admit I was wrong. I should have listened to you. You don't even have kids and you're better at raising Megan than I am.'

'That's not true, Ally. I'm just an extra pair of hands, that's all. It's no big deal.' She smiles. 'And in any case, you'd do the same for me.'

'What do you mean?' It's then that I remember Lottie telling me Penny had a hospital appointment the day I found the estate agent wandering around Seven Hills. 'Is this to do with your hospital visit?'

'You know about that?'

'Not really. Is . . . is everything okay?'

'Yes,' she smiles. 'It was just routine, but it is connected to my decision to sell Seven Hills.'

'I don't understand if you're not ill.'

'Running this place and helping Will out on the farm is just too much for me and it's only going to get worse.'

'I can help out,' I say, still uncertain about what she's trying to say.

'You'll be back on Major Investigations soon and Megan will be heading to college and uni. Things are changing, Ally, but it's not that.'

'Then what is it?'

'I'm struggling to cope.' Her cheeks suddenly reddened. 'Because . . . well . . . I'm going to have a baby.'

'Oh my God, Penny.' I throw my arms around her. 'That's amazing. Why didn't you tell me?'

'It was a bit of a shock, if I'm honest. It took me a little while to get used to, but Will is made up and now I've got my head around it, so am I.'

'You'll be an incredible mother.'

'Will I?' she says, biting her lip.

'Yes. You will. You've had enough practice with Megan, for God's sake. Does Megan know?'

'Yes. She's decided it's a girl and she'll be the little sister she never had.'

'That's so cute.'

'Ally, I'm so sorry it means selling Seven Hills.'

'Forget it. Megan and I will be just fine.'

'Will has a cottage on his farm that's available for rent. We'd love it if you took it.'

'Megan will never forgive me if I move her to the back of beyond. Don't worry about us, Pen.'

'Promise you won't go far. I'm not sure I can do this without you.'

'Are you serious? You're a natural. Look at what you've done for Megan.'

'It's easy when it's not your child, I'm guessing it's a whole different ball game when it is. The truth is, Ally, I need you.'

'Good, because Megan and I need you.'

It's early evening when I amble back up the path to the cabin, Penny and I having exhausted the subject of her impending motherhood, for the time being. I'm so excited for her and I'm determined to be there for her and her child as she has been there for me and mine. It takes a village.

I open the cabin door just as Megan barrels past me.

'See ya.'

'Where are you off to?'

'I thought I'd put some flowers on Jay's grave.'

'You didn't say anything.'

'Just decided.'

'It's a little late.'

'It's only seven, Mum,' she says, skipping down the steps. 'I won't be long.'

'Hang on. I'll come too. Just let me grab a coat.'

'No,' she says, finally stopping.

'What's going on, Megan?'

'Nothing. I just arranged to meet Helena there, that's all. You'll just . . .'

'Cramp your style?'

'If that's an old person's way of saying "get in the way" then yes.'

'Okay. Be back by eight.'

'Will do. Have fun.' She grins.

'What do you—?'

But she's already tearing down the path towards the main entrance, waving at Penny through the reception window as she passes by. She seems to have recovered from her disastrous holiday with Julian. Even the shadow cast by Jay's death appears to be lifting. For the first time in a long while, I'm certain Megan is going to be fine.

I go back inside the cabin that suddenly feels too quiet, too empty. Slumping down onto the sofa, I turn on the television to fill the void when there's a knock on the door. Maybe it's Penny, come for more babytalk.

'Come in!' I call.

I spring to my feet at the sight of Liam's head around the door. He waves a bottle of wine at me.

'Fancy a drink? Megan mentioned she was out tonight and that you might like some company.'

So, that's what this is all about, Megan setting me up with Liam. If only it were that simple.

'Sure. Take a seat.'

I grab a bottle opener and glasses from the kitchen and join Liam on the sofa. He pours our drinks and holds his glass up.

'So what are we celebrating?' I ask.

'How about me helping to save your life.' He smiles. 'Howard helped obviously, but it was mainly me.'

'I'm pretty sure I've already thanked you countless times, but credit where credit is due.' I tap his glass with mine. 'Thank you for saving my life.'

We sip our wine in silence, searching for niceties to exchange. Liam wins.

'Megan looks well. I just passed her on my way here.'

'Yes. She's none the worse for wear after the horrific ordeal of her holiday with Julian. Her words, not mine.'

'How are things between her and her dad?'

'They need a bit of space, but she still wants him in her life which is good.'

'Speaking of Howard,' Were we? 'I noticed *The Aloysia* is still in the harbour.'

And so it continues: the dance of discussing everything but us.

'I asked him to stay a little longer. Did you know Penny's expecting a baby?'

'Really?' Liam's face lights up. 'That's great. Will's a good guy. They'll make great parents.'

'It means she's selling Seven Hills.'

'That's a shame. It's been your home for a long time.'

'It has, but we all have to move on, don't we?'

He looks at me. 'Yes, I suppose we do.'

Oh God. This is excruciating. I can't avoid the subject any longer.

'You know, Liam, for what it's worth. I am really sorry about what happened between me and that other guy.'

'It's okay.'

'No, it's not. I spent months telling you I couldn't go out with you because I needed to be there for Megan only to jump straight into bed with someone else.'

'Seriously, Ally, you don't have to explain yourself to me.'

'But I want to. I don't know why I did it, but weirdly, I think I might have found the answer on *The Aloysia*.'

'Your dad's boat?'

'Yes, when Howard sailed her back into Bidecombe. It stirred up a lot of memories. It was the first time that I've ever really thought about Dad and how he left me. He promised me he'd always be there for me, but he wasn't and if you can't count on your dad, who can you count on? When Julian came along, he confirmed what I knew all along. The men in my life – the ones I care about – leave. I just hadn't really made the connection until now. It's what

I've come to expect and it . . . it makes it difficult to . . . commit.'

'Yeah.' He nods. 'That's pretty much what Penny said.'

'Oh my God.' I tap him playfully on the arm. 'I can't believe you've been talking to Penny.'

'Sorry,' he says, sheepishly. 'I just wanted to try and understand. One minute you seem to really like me and then as soon as I get close, you pull away.'

'Now you know why.'

'Yes, but I was kind of hoping that what I've shown you over this last year is that I'm not going anywhere.'

'I know you've always been there for me. Christ, you saved my life.'

'Finally' – he raises his eyes to the ceiling – 'she notices.'

'I'm sorry it's taken me so long.' But my smile fades as I seek out the right words. 'The problem is, Liam, I don't think I can change. I tried, but I honestly think it's too late for me. I just hate the idea of making myself vulnerable. I can't bring myself to be that person, but I know that's what I have to do if a relationship with you is to succeed.'

'But you already have made yourself vulnerable.'

'Have I? When?'

He pauses, grappling with his thoughts. 'I wasn't sure whether to say anything, but I think you should know that I lied.'

'Lied? About what?'

'On the boat. I lied . . . I got your text.'

His words echo in my head.

'You got my text?'

'I didn't say anything on *The Aloysia* because I wanted to

make sure you were okay and it didn't seem to be the right time to talk about this, but yes, I got it.'

I nod, my calmness masking a mind frantically trying to work out the ramifications of the words I'd typed, words that I assumed would be my last on earth. Words I can't take back. Words Liam read.

'You-you know I sent that text because I thought I was going to die,' I say, furiously backpedalling.

'Yes, I know.'

'I-I had so little battery left that I-I had to send the same message to everyone.'

'Everyone?'

'Well, you know, people that matter to me: Penny, Megan, Bernadette and . . .'

'And me?'

Everything is moving too fast, but I can't deny it.

'And you.'

'Did you mean it though? That's really all I need to know.'

All? But it's everything. I don't know if I'm ready for everything. If I'll ever be ready.

'I only had enough juice to type a few words.'

Liam nods, trying to make sense of what I'm saying.

'So you didn't mean it? What you're saying is that if you'd had more battery life left then you'd have texted me something different?'

His eyes fixed on mine, he waits for a response, but he knows a 'no comment' when he sees one. His shoulders sag with disappointment, but disappointment is preferable to heartbreak further down the line. Or so I tell myself.

'I think I should go.'

He gets up and leaves in silence, closing the front door behind him. Self-congratulation ripples through me – the chaos of emotional commitment cleverly averted at the eleventh hour – but victory is fleeting and a sadness settles over me. Penny is right. I almost certainly have abandonment issues. First dad. Then Julian. But Liam isn't either of them and it's unfair to punish him for the behaviour of others. It's time for me to move on.

He's already halfway down the path when I call after him from my veranda. For a moment I think he's going to ignore me but then he stops and turns.

'What is it?' he calls back.

When I don't answer, he retraces his steps. There's still time to back out, to make up some lame reason why I shouted after him. He takes the steps in one bound and now he's standing in front of me. I don't say anything and neither does he. My heart is pounding. There is no going back and I have no idea what the future holds with Liam, but I know what it looks like without him.

'The text I sent you.'

'What about it?'

Gripping the rail, I take a steadying breath and look Liam straight in the eye.

'I meant it.'

68

Swiping my card against the reader, I step through the door to the Major Investigations Unit after it clicks open. I take a deep breath and push it wide to let myself in.

Harriet holds her briefings in the conference room above the canteen which means I haven't been inside the MIU building since I left over a year ago after people quietly made it known that they didn't work with police grasses. I packed the photo of Megan and me at Morte Sands and tried to hold my head up high under the accusatory gaze of those that had held on to their jobs. I could have stuck it out, but anyone who works in policing will tell you, if people want you out they'll find a way so I took the offer to return to my original patch – North Devon where I've been ever since. Today, there are no resentful glances, just people with too much on and too little time. Another day. Another case. It never ends.

DS Henry Whiteley greets me, his dark suit as sharp as the points on his slicked-back hair.

'Harriet's waiting for you,' he says, smiling.

He leads me through the huge open-plan office. As I pass DC Norman Grundig and DC Juliette Hollis they pause their conversation. Norm picks up a receiver and holds it out to me.

'The SAS called. They want you back.' He laughs. Clearly, news that I blew up the shed on Liars Island and then attempted to escape by kayak has reached MIU.

'Ignore him,' says Juliette. 'It's just Norm's way of saying it's good to have you on the team.'

'It's good to be back.'

There was a time when I never thought I'd say that.

Harriet gets up as I enter her office and smiles. Dressed in a beige trouser suit, offset by her matching blood-red lips and nails, she still looks like she'd be more at home in the board-room than a police station but looks can be deceiving.

'Really good to see you, Ally.'

'Thanks.'

'How's Jake getting on?'

'He's home now, but his ankle will take a few weeks to heal.'

'I hope he's got someone to look after him.'

'He has.' I smile. It seems there's nothing like a near-death experience for your loved one to realise they still love you and want to be with you. Sophie hasn't left Jake's side since we were rescued from Liars Island five days ago. Jake is planning on buying an engagement ring just as soon as he's up and about.

'That's good. And what about you?'

'I'm good. Any sign of Ash?'

'No. They've called off the search.'

'So, Liars Island has claimed another soul.'

'Looks like it, but it means no one will stand trial for Kieran's murder and we'll never know what really happened to Forrest. I said this would be about drugs, didn't I? We found Ash's stash in a barn near the inn, like you said. We think he was dealing in Bidecombe but as you can imagine none of the druggies are saying anything. But we suspect Kieran found this out and was planning to tell Hilton. Ash killed him to cover up his operations and then blackmailed Dove and Bagshaw into pretending they'd murdered him.'

'Did you find out why Bagshaw made a false insurance claim?'

'We certainly did. He has a terrible gambling habit. That's why the church sent him to Liars Island. They hoped to keep him out of trouble.'

'And where does Rose figure in all of this?'

'We interviewed her and the feeling is she had absolutely no idea what he was up to.'

'And Forrest?'

'The PM results show he broke his neck in the fall. I don't know if that'll help Forrest's family with closure or not. At the moment, they seem more concerned that the papers don't get hold of his real identity.'

'What about the rest of them?'

'Hilton now knows that Ben was declared bankrupt when he was nineteen. It's down to him what he does about it. Ben can't be a company director, but he can still work there. The place is proving to be a goldmine. From what I know of Hilton Deveney, I suspect profit will win out over the personal. Apparently, Jocasta told Hilton about her illness and he told her she can stay at Grannus House for as long as her health allows her.'

'Will Rose be charged with bigamy?'

'No, her marriage certificate was faked but Hilton has told her she can keep the inn.'

'Really? Doesn't sound like him.'

'It's purely practical. Who'd want to work on an island where people get murdered? He's drawing up another licensee contract with the family clause removed, which just leaves Bagshaw and Dove.'

'I take it you're charging them with wasting police time.'

'Too right I am, but the most they're looking at is six months. I can't see either of them getting a custodial sentence. The jails are full enough as it is. Makes my blood boil though. All that time and money wasted.'

'And . . . er . . . what about the gas shed I blew up?'

Harriet looks at me.

'That did take a little explaining to Hilton, but as long as the force picks up the tab, he isn't going to pursue it. Just don't do it again. Anyway, I do have some better news for you which is why I asked you to come to the office.'

'Oh?'

'We have an official date for your return to MI. Three weeks today. It's all been signed off. I don't know what was going on in HR. I never did get to the bottom of it, but it's all sorted. Not only that, I want you back as my CSM.'

'Crime scene manager? What about Jim?'

'He's put his papers in.'

'Retiring?'

'Yes. He says he's been ready to go for a while. I think he's pretty sore that he didn't spot that Kieran wasn't killed at Devil's Cauldron.'

'It was pure luck. My dad was obsessed with everything to do with the sea including Liars Island.'

'Luck or not, it means we have a vacancy. So what do you say?'

'I accept, of course.'

'Great. Now I need standard-grade CSI. Any thoughts?'

'As a matter of fact, I do.'

'He doesn't look like he knows his arse from his elbow but if you rate Jake, then that's good enough for me.'

'Thanks.' I get up to leave, but Harriet stays seated.

'Speaking of Jake, there was one more thing.'

'Go on.'

'He told the police officer who interviewed him that he thought there was someone else on the beach, not just Ash.'

I frown. 'Oh? Like who?'

'That was the weird thing. He thought he saw a young lad.' My breath catches in my throat. Shit. Jake saw Amir. He must have drifted back to consciousness at some point when we were on the kayak. 'Obviously there are no children living on the island. I wondered if he was just delirious, but the detective said he was really insistent about this. He said he was of Middle Eastern descent.'

'Middle Eastern?' I repeat her words as I picture the image of the terrified boy pacing the water's edge pleading for his father to come back.

'I know, right? It doesn't make any sense to me either but I said I'd check with you.'

So, the police didn't find Amir. Just like Ash said. No surprises there, Rose will have hidden him beyond reach. When the island slips off the front page and once again returns to a shimmering shadow in the Channel, Amir will be welcomed by Rose as if it is his first day in his new home and she will raise Hana's boy as her own.

I hadn't planned to keep quiet about Amir after I was rescued, but as I lay in hospital, my delirium spirited me back to Devil's Cauldron where Dr Cassius appeared by my side to tell me an orca pup's only hope of survival was if another matriarch adopted him. Dr Cassius melded into Jocasta telling me that if you were born to be a mum, that's what you were regardless of whether you had or could have children. Next, I heard my own voice telling Penny she'll always be Megan's second mum and, finally, I saw Rose, standing in the hallway at the back of the bar in The Barbary Inn, her eyes alive at the thought of fostering a child, fulfilling the only dream she ever had: to be a mum. So, by the time the detectives appeared by my bedside, I decided that if they didn't ask, I wouldn't tell them, knowing I was the only one aware of Amir's existence. But I was wrong. Jake knows.

'So was there anyone else with you and Ash at Devil's Cauldron?'

What I'm about to do is illegal, but I crossed that line a long time ago when I learnt that what is right and what is the law are not always the same thing. I look my SIO square in the eye.

'No. There was no one else on the beach.'

69

Bernadette stiffens with disapproval at the sight of Howard Trevelyan standing on her doorstep. The feeling is mutual. He took a lot of convincing, but I need them both to hear what I have to say.

She turns her glare on me. 'What's he doing here?'

'I invited him.'

'He's not coming in.'

'In that case, we'll do this on the doorstep.'

She throws an anxious glance at the house over the road.

'And give Eileen Mason something to gossip about? I don't think so, but you better be quick. I've got book club in half an hour.'

Leaving the front door wide open, she disappears inside the house. Howard looks at me.

'Don't take it personally,' I say, touching his arm. 'She's like that with everyone.'

He follows me into the kitchen where Bernadette is waiting for us, arms folded.

'Well?' she says, refusing to acknowledge Howard's presence.

'I went to Liars Island.'

'Why would you want to go there?'

'It was for work. I didn't have much choice, but while I was there I discovered something, but firstly I need to say sorry for accusing you of withholding information from the coroner just to protect yourself. I know now that you did it to protect me too. You knew that losing my dad was one thing, but discovering he deliberately left us would have been too much for me and you were right.' She frowns. She's not familiar with contrite Ally. 'It would have changed how I thought about Dad, which would have been a terrible mistake.'

'A mistake? What are you talking about?'

'There's something I need to tell you about Dad, about something that happened to me when I was on Liars Island.'

Bernadette looks at Howard who shrugs.

'I've no idea what's going on either.'

That Howard is privy to no more information than she is appears to placate her and she turns her attention back to me.

'I'm listening.'

'Actually, it begins with an orca called Maisie that got washed ashore at Morte Sands a few weeks back. The oceanographer told me she had drowned, likely caught in fishing nets.'

'Yes, I heard about that.'

'Well, it got me thinking. That and Howard insisting that Dad would never have taken his own life. I began to wonder if maybe that's what happened that day on *The Aloysia*. Maybe a dolphin or an orca got caught in someone's fishing nets and Dad got into the water to free the animal. The sea was very calm that day. There was no danger, as far as he knew, and he'd done it before.'

'So why did he take his life jacket off?' asks Howard.

'He had to, otherwise he wouldn't have been able to dive down deep enough to untangle it.'

Howard nods.

'That would explain the dent in the propellor blade. I never could work out how it got there.'

'This is nonsense, Aloysia. I thought you were all about the science. This is the stuff of fairy tales. I'm surprised at you.'

'Is it though?' says Howard. 'I mean Davy had a great love and respect for all marine life.'

'Don't talk to me about Davy,' Bernadette snaps back.

'Anyway,' I interject. 'Yes, you're right, Bernadette. It does sound far-fetched but when I attended Maisie at Morte Sands, Dr Cassius told me orcas have been tracked for decades so I contacted someone working on the programme. I asked them if there were orcas or any large sea animals in the vicinity of *The Aloysia* that day. It took a while, but they got back to me. They had data showing a basking shark had remained static for an extended period of time close to where Dad was potting for crabs.'

'Close?'

'They can't be exact but yes, it was nearby. Basking sharks have to surface to breathe so the team believe the most likely reason the animal stopped for that length of time was because it tangled up in a net.'

'That still doesn't explain why Davy didn't just climb back into the boat afterwards,' says Howard. 'You said yourself the sea was like a millpond that day.'

'That's the bit I couldn't work out. There was another

problem too. Although *The Aloysia*'s radar showed her near the site of where the animal appeared to stop swimming, she was found several miles away.'

'But her engine was switched off, she would have been pretty much becalmed,' says Howard.

'On a normal day, yes, but this wasn't a normal day. I just didn't know it until I came across the tide charts in the water-sports centre on the island. That's when I worked it out.'

'Worked what out?'

'The day Dad went missing, there was a tidal bore. A big one.'

Bernadette frowns. 'A tidal what?'

But Howard knows exactly what I'm talking about.

'It's where a large amount of water is funnelled into a smaller area. The Bristol Channel has one. It's like a mini tsunami wave that starts out in the Atlantic Ocean and as the land narrows it gets larger and faster. It happens around 160 times a year.'

'Howard's right. Dad told me about them years ago, the first time he ever took me out on *The Aloysia*, but I'd forgotten about them until I saw the chart in the centre. I checked back. There was a bore the day Dad went out. If he was in the water when it came, he wouldn't have had time to get back into the boat. It would have swept them both away.'

'No, no, that's not possible,' says Bernadette, shaking her head. 'I don't need to tell you your father knew the seas better than Neptune. He'd have known all about this tidal bore you're telling me about. He checked those tide charts religiously. What was the phrase he used to use?'

'Slack sank the ship? You're right, normally he would

have. You know what he was like. He double checked everything.'

'Yes, I remember.' Bernadette allows herself a rare smile.
'Slack sank the ship. That was one of his favourites.'

'But that day, Dad didn't check.'

'Why not?'

The colour drains from Howard's craggy features.

'Because I checked them.'

Bernadette throws him a withering look. 'I might have
known you'd have something to do with it.'

'Hold on, Bernie, I know what you think of me, that I'm
feckless and unreliable.'

'That's not the half of it,' says Bernadette.

'But I'm a sailor too and I don't take risks, not where the
sea is concerned. I remember going into Davy's office and
reading through those charts properly.'

'Yes, you did, Howard. I remember too, but Dad kept
information about tidal bores in a drawer because although
they were quite frequent, they're not usually a problem until
they get much farther up the Bristol Channel towards the
River Severn estuary. *The Aloysia* would have been able to
ride it out as she always did.'

'*But if* he'd known about it, he wouldn't have left the
boat,' says Bernadette.

'Not necessarily. This one was much larger than predicted.
Even if Dad had looked at the charts, he couldn't have known
how big it was going to be. I think you and I both know he
still would have gone into the water to save whatever was
tangled in those nets. I think Dad's death was an unavoidable
accident. Just like the coroner said.'

Howard takes my hand in his, tears filling the creases under his eyes. 'Thank you.'

But Bernadette is less easy to persuade. 'So why did Davy drop you at Liars Island that day? Why didn't he just let you stay with him on *The Aloysia*?'

'Howard thinks he was worried that he might run into the smugglers.'

'That's true, Bernie. I told Davy they wouldn't try anything on, but I guess he didn't want to take the risk with his girl on board.'

Bernadette stares at Howard, her expression unreadable. Eventually, she turns to me.

'Dad would never have left us on purpose.'

Lowering herself onto a kitchen chair, Bernadette looks down at her wedding ring.

'No. He wouldn't have done.'

She twists her wedding ring until a smile radiates across her face. A tear rolls down her cheek. She's finally allowed herself to unlock all those cherished memories of her husband, to remember the man she married. Her hero, and mine. For the second time I sense Dad's presence. He taught me well.

The mood is broken by Howard, shifting awkwardly.

'I'll get going then.'

'I'll drop you off at Bidecombe Harbour. Howard's leaving today, Bernadette.'

But she isn't listening.

'Yes, time to set sail, Bernie. I'll take good care of *The Aloysia*. I promise.' He waits for her to respond, but she's slipped into another realm.

'I'll wait for you in the car,' he says to me, in little more than a whisper.

Not wishing to break whatever spell Bernadette's memories have cast over her, I leave quietly.

Bernadette's voice reaches me in the hall.

'Aloysia, I want you to be completely honest with me . . . Do you really believe that it was . . . an accident that killed your father?'

I look back at her, her cheeks flooded with twenty years of tears. Embarrassed, she tries to rub them away.

'The unusually large bore that day, the basking shark in trouble in the vicinity, Dad's love of marine life, his life jacket on the deck. Evidence is evidence.' I smile. 'And it's good enough for me.'

'Thank you,' she says. 'By the way.'

'Yes?'

'I-I love you too.'

Mum got the text.

AMIR AND HANA

'It's time, habibi. Ash is waiting. Noula will take you. She's made some food for you and bought you Fanta, your favourite, for the journey.'

'I don't want to leave you, Mama.'

'I know Amir, but you have to go. Now, take my glasses. You may as well have them now.'

'I want you to come too.'

'I can't. You must go alone, and you must go now. Ash can't wait much longer. It's too dangerous.'

'But—'

'You must be brave, habibi. Ash will be there with you. He'll look after you.'

'Ash is a bad man.'

'That was before. He's not a bad man anymore. He wants to help. He loves you, Amir. He has a new home waiting for you. With Rose. You remember Rose?'

'Yes, but my home is here with you.'

'Not anymore. Sometimes we don't get to choose our home, it chooses us. Haven't I always told you that?'

'Don't make me go, Mama.'

'Save your tears, habibi. You know I can't protect you anymore and you can't stay here alone. It isn't safe.'

'But I belong here . . . with you.'

'And soon you will belong somewhere else. Liars Island will be your home for good.'

Under the cover of darkness, Noula drove me to a remote beach where a dinghy was waiting for me. In it was Mama's friend, Ash. I hadn't seen him since he left suddenly without saying goodbye. He was much more than a friend but I couldn't bring myself to call him Baba, at first, and I didn't know any other way to describe the man who'd treated me like his own son since I was five. I met him when he came to the camp to see Rose. They both came from England.

I liked Ash. We had lots to talk about. We both supported Manchester United. Ash had even seen the Reds play, including my favourite, Marcus Rashford. He'd come to the camp and play football with us kids while he waited for Rose to finish work. Mama liked him too. She'd smile and laugh when he was around and she began to look at him like she looked at Baba. Then she started saying she needed to leave the camp, go for a walk, to clear her mind, but really she was meeting Ash.

I followed her once and saw her kiss Ash. When I told her, she begged for my forgiveness for bringing shame on our family, but there was no family. It was just me and her. Baba and my sisters were gone. I wanted her to be happy again. After that the three of us would go for walks and Mama even went in goal when Ash and I practised our tackling. We were like a real family.

Then Ash disappeared. Mama told me he'd got caught up in bad stuff and we were better off without him, but I could tell she missed him. I did too. Ash wrote to her, but she never wrote back. Then she got ill and everything changed.

Rose was waiting for me on the beach. I hadn't seen her in years either, but she hugged me hard like Mama used to before she grew too weak. She told me that she couldn't replace her, she wouldn't even try, but she'd be the next best thing and she'd love me like her own. For the first time since I left Greece, I felt everything would work out.

Mama was right. The island had trees and beaches, but I only saw them through windows. Ash told me I couldn't go out in case someone saw me. He kept moving me from place to place. Sometimes I slept in a house as big as a castle, sometimes a horrible damp cave. It was boring being on my own all day. The only thing I had was a doll that had belonged to my little sister. Mama had written the names of body parts in English to help me learn, but I lost it moving around all the time.

One day, I decided to explore on my own. There were lots of houses, but no one was living in them. It was so strange, but one house with people in it had a vegetable garden and I was hungry so I helped myself to some carrots. Another time

I saw a lady sitting on a large stone. I thought she'd seen me because she called out to me but I hid behind a rock. She seemed to know my name, but when she shouted it out again I realised she was saying Amber, not Amir.

I got back to the castle I was staying in to find Ash waiting for me. He was really angry. He shook my shoulders, telling me I mustn't go out. It was too soon. They had to be very careful. They had to do things slowly because if anyone found me, they'd throw me in prison. After that, I didn't go out, but I thought it would be safe to play on the beach in front of the cave because I couldn't be seen from the hilltop, but I was wrong.

It wasn't until the last minute that I saw a man on a kayak paddling towards the shore. I ran back inside the cave hoping he hadn't seen me, but I was too late and he followed me into the cave.

When he found me, he laughed and shook his head.

'Dad will definitely want to know about you.'

I didn't understand what he was talking about, but I was terrified. Was this the man Ash told me about? The man who would send me to jail. He asked me who I was, where I was from, why I was there. He was scaring me. I'd met men like him before, asking angry question after angry question like I'd done something really bad.

I wanted to get away, but the cave was a dead end so I started to climb the cave wall so he couldn't reach me. My glasses, the only thing I had of Mama's, caught the rock and fell to the ground, but I couldn't go back for them. I hoped the man would give up, but he started climbing too. He grabbed my foot, but I managed to kick myself free. That must have been when he lost his balance because I heard a scraping sound followed by a loud thud.

I didn't dare look down until I reached the top of the cave wall and that was when I saw the man had fallen. I got down to help him. He was bleeding from his head, but he was still alive. I needed to find Ash. He would know what to do. As I raced across the fields to the inn, the man's last words to me played over and over in my mind until I finally understood them.

'You can't stay here. This isn't your home.'

But he was wrong. Mama told me . . . this is my home now. I belong here. I can't leave Liars Island. Not now. Not ever.

Acknowledgements

It takes a village to do many things including write a novel and I'm extremely lucky to have a fantastic group of people behind, alongside and often in front of me. Firstly, thank you to my agent, Lucy Morris at Curtis Brown, for seeing something in my story about a female CSI from North Devon and for being my unwavering champion, and latterly to Rosie Pierce, a constant and reassuring presence in the world of publishing. Equally, I could not ask for a better team at HQ Stories including the brilliant Cicely Aspinall, Seema Mitra and Sarah Lundy – thank you for your kindness, your humour and your industrial scale patience. Character names are a blind spot for me so I'd like to thank Rose, Ben and Scott for lending me theirs this time around. Suggestions for my next book are very welcome. A special mention also to the magical island of Lundy, just off the North Devon coast, the inspiration for Liars Island. If you're ever in these parts, it's well worth your time. I'd also like to extend a special thank you to the people and organisations of North Devon who have given me so much support since I began my publishing journey, in particular the brilliant Poppy, Eleanor and Rheannah at Barnstaple

Waterstones – the future of book selling is in safe hands! But also the Instow Book Club, the Appledore Book Festival, Mortehoe Museum and the wonderful Women's Institutes including Barnstaple, Mortehoe, Instow and Yelland, Ilfracombe and Georgeham. I've been bowled over by your warmth, your curiosity and, of course, your cakes. You've helped keep imposter syndrome at bay more than you can know and I am grateful to each and every one of you. I'm also very lucky to have the support of my family and friends. Seeing my novels on a shop bookshelf or being read in a far flung corner of the world still thrills me because I never thought it would happen – thank you Gin, Graeme, Jo, Laura, Steph, Bruce, Alistair, Philippa and Isabelle for your photos. Thank you also to Mick for all the police-isms. Every police team should have a Mick. Thank you also to Frank, Rosie, Joseph and Alice who will always be my favourite story of all. And, finally, to Richard, for so long the only member of the village. Thank you.

If you were hooked by Ally Dymond's latest shocking case, find out where the story began in *Breakneck Point*

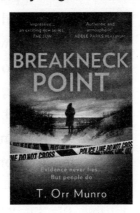

'Packed with authenticity' *Mail Online*

Evidence never lies . . . But people do.

CSI Ally Dymond's commitment to justice has cost her a place on the major investigations team. After exposing corruption in the ranks, she's stuck working petty crimes on the sleepy North Devon coast.

Then the body of nineteen-year-old Janie Warren turns up in the seaside town of Bidecombe, and Ally's expert skills are suddenly back in demand.

But when the evidence she discovers contradicts the lead detective's theory, nobody wants to listen to the CSI who landed their colleagues in prison.

Time is running out to catch a killer no one is looking for – no one except Ally. What she doesn't know is that he's watching, from her side of the crime scene tape, waiting for the moment to strike.

Out now in paperback, ebook and audio.

ONE PLACE. MANY STORIES

Don't miss *Slaughterhouse Farm*, the second in the gripping, heart-pounding CSI Ally Dymond series.

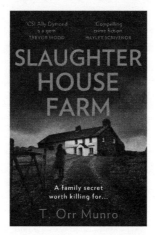

'Compelling crime fiction with a beating heart of authenticity'
Hayley Scrivenor, author of *Dirt Town*

A family secret worth killing for . . .

In the dead of night, 72-year-old Miriam Narracott is found wandering on Exmoor, holding a knife and covered in blood. Inside the family farmhouse lies the body of her adult son, Gabe.

CSI Ally Dymond is on compassionate leave, but when approached by the new DI, recently arrived from London and eager to have Ally's keen eye and local knowledge on the case, she finds herself being drawn back in.

With their only suspect Miriam unwilling – or unable – to talk, the team must dig into the family's history to uncover a motive. Instead they find evidence that Gabe was involved with a criminal network, suggesting a completely different chain of events. But if Miriam isn't the killer – then who is?

Out now in paperback, ebook and audio.

ONE PLACE. MANY STORIES

ONE PLACE. MANY STORIES

Bold, innovative and empowering publishing.

FOLLOW US ON:

@HQStories